EVERY BEND IN THE RIVER

EMERSON FORD

Storm
PUBLISHING

To request permissions, contact the publisher at rights@stormpublishing.co

Ebook ISBN: 978-1-80508-910-0
Paperback ISBN: 978-1-80508-911-7

Cover design: Sarah Whittaker
Cover images: Shutterstock

Published by Storm Publishing.
For further information, visit:
www.stormpublishing.co

ALSO BY EMERSON FORD

What the Silent Say

To my children. Thank you for our many happy days together adventuring through forests and fields.

AUGUST 7, 1749

Dear Mama,

You always said I'd be the death of you. How did you know?

I am in the Slough of Despond and can only cry and cry.

Charlotte and Pearl won't want me as their mother. Bordroyne, Tom, and Edward will grow wilder without you to civilize them. Phil will do what he wants, for no one can tell him what to do.

I am but thirteen. I only know how to track and fish and follow Phil. The corncake I made for dinner went down our throats like buckeye burs. Charlotte cried that I killed her too.

I promise to leave Phil to his adventures and learn to be a lady. If you but stay and teach me, I can be like you.

Your sorrowing daughter,

Rosanna

ONE
ROSANNA

Earlier that day

I dragged the sodden dove-gray linen skirt over the washtub's edge, catching the end before it dusted the ground. Gathering it together, I twisted the water from its length until my arms shook.

Mama stood at the boiling kettle, stirring Father's shirts with a paddle.

The cicadas' song swelled, a vexing echo of the buzz in my head. I wiped the sweat on my upper lip with my shoulder. How could one be expected to scrub and beat and wring all day in this heat?

Phil's spirited shouts floated from the forest.

I should be with him. I would be, if Mama hadn't bid me stay when Phil ran off with John to the river.

John, a boy from a nearby farm, tolerated me only because wherever Phil was, I was also. He always gave me such a scowl, I would've scratched his eyes out if he weren't twice my size. But I couldn't hate John all the way. His visits had dwindled since his brother left home and their father required more help. I pitied John for his loss of freedom. It was a terrible thing indeed to be forced to toil the whole day long without diversion.

My arms drooped. The skirt brushed the dirt.

Mama took the cloth from my listless hands. "Like this." She raised it behind her head and slapped it on the smooth, flat rock sticking out of the grass. She swung again, her strong arms making arcs against the cornflower-blue sky. The cotton landed with a satisfying *thwack* on the boulder.

She handed it back.

My hands didn't dip as they did before with the weight of it.

"Try again." Mama stood, hands on hips, watching me.

I swung the cloth behind me with all my might so I could sling-shot it onto the rock like she did. The momentum threw me back, and I fell on my bum.

Mama snorted, a most unladylike sound for such a refined woman.

I couldn't look at her for shame.

My arms might be strong, but I wasn't tall and sturdy like her. She once said Phil had taken my share when she'd carried us inside her. It would be just like Phil to find a way to pester me, even before he was born. Though we were twins, he was large and loud. I was small, but to Phil's credit, not once had he excluded me from his fun.

I gripped the stiffened linen under my bodice and pulled. "I hate this wretched thing."

Mama herded me back to the washtub. "Do not hate except the Devil and thy sin," she said, as her own mother had taught her.

Dear Mama. Beautiful and serene, wise and patient. Why couldn't I be more like her?

A quick *swish-swish* came through the tall grass behind me.

"Hullo, little mouse." Phil snatched my cap, sending my riotous curls cascading down my back.

He knew I hated it when he called me that. I swiped at the scrap of white linen he dangled above me but missed.

He only grinned. "I've come back for another bucket. We've filled the other with fish already."

I yanked the cap out of his hands and quickly stuffed my hair into it.

Mama clucked. "You must do it right. Come here, child." She sat me on the washing rock and gathered my hair in her hands. "Take out your primer and read where we left off this morning."

Shooting a glare at Phil, I pulled the book from my pocket and traced my finger along a line of words, pretending to read.

Phil loped toward the barn. Boots, our plow horse, whinnied from her pen as he passed by. Even she wanted to join him.

"Read aloud," Mama said.

I sagged further into my seat of stone. "'Our weak-ness-es and in-in—'"

"Inabilities."

"'Inabilities break not the bonds of our... of our duties.'"

"So many knots." Mama pulled her fingers through my hair, yanking at a stubborn tangle until it broke free. "You would have beautiful hair if you would only tame it."

Phil didn't have to worry about his hair. It was smooth and straight, shiny and black as a raven's wing. Why couldn't I have been given his hair, and he, mine?

"I know you would rather be with Philemon, but would you be happy knowing work waited on your return?"

Yes, I would. It was a wonder she couldn't tell. I peeked at her.

The sparkle in her eyes belied her words. "Tush. I cannot blame you, but we must all do things we do not like. Do I enjoy plucking feathers or weeding fields? No, but I do it just the same." Finished with my hair, she stood and brushed off her skirts. "I will fetch us drink and porridge. Mind the fires."

"Yes, Mama."

Pail in hand, Phil reappeared and put his arm about my shoulders. "I'll take you fishing tomorrow."

I shrugged his arm away. "I want to go today."

"You can't leave Mama." He turned away and high-stepped through the knee-high grass toward the river.

"Phil, wait!" I followed, pumping my legs as hard as I could. It had always been thus, me following him like on the day we were born—him first, me second. Philemon and Rosanna. Phil and Rosie. Always together but with him in the lead. Did living nine more minutes give such an advantage?

"Catch some jumpers for fishing first," he called behind him.

Grasshoppers? I narrowed my eyes. He knew I hated the nasty things. He was trying to keep me home, but he would soon find out how stubborn I could be.

I glanced at the farmhouse where Mama prepared our meal. I looked again at Phil. With every passing second, he drew farther and farther away from me.

Two feet away and swaying on a long blade of grass sat a fat grasshopper. On impulse, I leaped and cupped my hands around it.

Something wet and warm shot onto my skin, seeping through the cracks of my fingers. I retched. Jumper tobacco, brown and slimy. The little goblin scratched its spiked legs on my palms, but I locked my elbows. I would get my grasshoppers and be with Phil.

One by one, I dropped the bedeviled creatures into my apron. Mad as hornets, they beat their wings against the walls of their linen prison. With the sack clutched in my fist, I ran, my stomach revolting with every step.

I arrived at the river and scrambled down the steep ledge, using the roots and rocks jutting from the black soil as steps.

Phil and John leaped to their feet, fishing lines still in hand.

"Got 'em?" Phil asked.

I lifted my wriggling sack, dotted with brown spots. The grasshoppers hadn't taken kindly to the journey. They would like even less what we did with them next.

Phil grinned, a glimmer of pride in his eyes. He trudged through the boggy river marsh and held out his hands, receiving my loathsome burden.

"John said you couldn't do it."

My earlier pity for John losing his liberty vanished in an instant. "Then he doesn't know very much."

John glared. "Keep quiet, mop stick."

My hand went to my curls. They'd fallen out of my cap in my tussle with the grasshoppers—grasshoppers *he* would use to catch his fish. I marched past him and, with a little tap of my hip, sent him bum-first into the mud.

He let out a cry of outrage.

"*Keep quiet, mop stick,*" I said, echoing his earlier words.

He stood and swiped at his rear. "Pox-faced witch!"

With a garbled cry, I lunged toward him and boxed his ears.

He yelped, pulling my wrists to my side. I kicked him in the shanks with my thick-soled shoes.

"Get her off me!" he yelled.

Phil came over and wrapped his arms around my waist and pulled me away from John, my arms still swinging wildly.

John touched his ear with his fingers and sucked in a breath. "She cut me!"

Phil dropped me on the bank without warning. I hit the ground with such force that it knocked the wind out of me.

"You two make my head ache." Phil tossed a stick into my lap. It was a willow branch, tied at the end with one of Boots' long tail hairs and a hook. "Fish, if you haven't chased them away with your hollering."

I settled on a large boulder close to the water, the one Phil called the Dragon for its pointed bits of stone that resembled teeth.

"Here." Phil handed me a wriggling grasshopper.

John watched me with not a little glee. He didn't think I would do it. I snatched the insect from Phil's hand and pierced the brute with the hook. John turned his attention back to his line without a word.

We sat there for hours, the three of us, pulling out fish after fish, the grasshoppers having done the trick.

Shadows changed.

The sun shot arrows of light through the trees on the other side of the river. I had a passel of fish almost as fat as their buckets were full.

John stood and brushed off the seat of his pants. "I must go help Father. I can show you the abandoned Indian camp I found."

Phil jumped to his feet. "Let's go, Rosie."

A feeling came over me worse than what I felt when the grasshopper spit on my hands. I didn't want to go home. I didn't want to remember that I left Mama to toil over the washtubs alone. I didn't want to see her face when I came back. I tugged Phil's shirt. "A little while longer, please."

"I can't leave you here."

"One quick swim in the river."

Phil looked at John, who waited with arms folded, then back at me. "Don't you want to see the Indian camp?"

"I'll catch up with you on the way."

John huffed. "Come, Phil. I have to go."

Phil picked up the buckets, his eyes reluctant. "I'll leave the rifle with you. Be quick about it. Father will skin me alive if I come home without you."

Once the boys disappeared, I climbed atop the Dragon and removed my shoes then stripped to my shift. I hadn't lied—I really did want to swim. I jumped into the river and flipped to my back, hooking my foot under a jutting root so the river wouldn't carry me away. I sighed loudly. Oh, blessed coolness. I could forget about all else in this water.

My ears bobbed above and below the surface, bringing me from muffled burbling to birdsong and rustling leaves and back again. My hair fanned about me like water snakes, swirling in the icy currents.

The sound of a horse's pounding hooves broke my idle daydream.

"Rosanna!"

Mama.

I sucked in a breath and went under. But she would still be able to see me through the water.

I threw myself against the flow. Grabbing a fallen tree limb, I left the water in one great, sucking pull and stood in the mud once again, soggy and trembling, my hair a tangled, sticky mess.

I untied the line of fish from the tree and pulled them from the water. "Coming!" I held them aloft and ran toward the cliff, like Moses with his serpent held high. If she could but see my bounty of fish, I might be saved.

At the edge of the cliff, Boots' head came into sight. Then Mama, riding bareback atop our horse, her eyes and face afire. My body trembled. I'd never seen her like this, not even when Father had mistakenly plowed through her garden and destroyed her month-old seedlings.

Mama's chest heaved. "Get up here."

"But, Mama, look!" I lifted the fish higher. "I've enough for a week's meals."

"You left work unfinished and me to finish it."

My tongue felt thick and woolen in my mouth. Why couldn't I say sorry?

"I've allowed you too much independence." She regarded me, her cheeks flushed, her eyes pooling with something I couldn't name.

"I should've stayed. I know I should've, but Phil—"

"I've failed you, Rosanna." Mama turned her head away. She was governing her emotions, just as she taught me to do when my own feelings grew too big or too strong. She liked to compare me to flick weed, whose seed pods exploded with the slightest touch.

"I'll do the wash and carry water for your garden every day. And I'll clean Boots' stall."

"Yes, you will. And more." Boots shifted and backed away. A rock tumbled down the short cliff. Mama goaded him forward with her heels. "Enough. Put on your clothes and come."

I scrambled to the place where I'd left my clothes in a crumpled heap. Wriggling my stays over my sopping shift, I donned my bodice and then my skirts. I lifted my threadbare skirts and tied them into one large knot at my thigh, baring my legs for all of creation.

Mama inhaled sharply. "For shame!"

"Who's going to see me out here? Besides, I can't both carry the fish and climb with skirts." If she let me wear pants like I asked, she wouldn't have to see my knees.

"Then leave the fish."

"But Mama! *All* of them?"

"Better to discard the fish than your modesty."

I dropped my catch in the river. Gripping the roots lining the wall of wet earth, I put my foot on a stone and grabbed an overhanging tree limb. Just as soon as I pulled myself up, it cracked in two, landing me back on the riverbank.

Boots startled at the crack. He took a few steps back, sending a shower of debris on my head.

I tried the stone ledge again, but the wet soil gave way. Rocks tumbled again to the river. Getting up the embankment wouldn't be as easy as coming down. I'd have to take the path by the river, which had a gentler slope. "I'll go the long way," I called, already heading toward the easier trail.

"Do not walk away from me."

I swallowed my exasperation. "It's too wet."

Boots' hooves slipped.

The cliff's edge sheared away.

Mama pitched forward, her eyes wide with fright.

Limbs frozen, I could only watch in horror as Boots' front legs collapsed.

The sudden downward movement ripped the reins from Mama's hands.

She flew over our horse's head, arms flailing, and landed on the dragon-toothed boulder.

TWO
ROSANNA

I screamed, a strangled, inhuman sound.

Mama crumpled on the rock. Her head hung over the side, her straw hat askew and a waterfall of her shining black hair cascading over her face.

I ran to her and brushed her hair aside with shaking fingers. "God, oh God, don't let her be dead!"

I put my finger under her nose. A second passed, then another. My own chest burned for want of air.

A long moment passed.

The crimson faded from her cheeks, replaced by a ghostly white.

Any hope I had of her surviving splintered into agony.

I wailed and threw myself to her bosom. "Please don't die! Please, please don't die." I clung to her like the skirt had clung to the washtub, but even with all my crying, never once did Mama's eyelids open.

I shivered in my damp clothes though I swam in the Devil's lake of fire. I had killed my own mother.

Someone nudged my shoulder.

Boots! "Oh, Boots." I wrapped my arms around her and stroked her hairy muzzle. She didn't seem any worse for the accident. I sagged against her and wet her nose with my tears. I was no longer alone.

My keening must have carried across the glen, for the sound of Phil's and Father's yells and pounding footfalls reached the riverbed.

Father appeared above me, his chest heaving. I knew the moment he saw her, for he nearly jumped off the ledge in his haste. He scrambled down the bank and dropped to his knees. Gently cupping her cheek, he touched her lips. His desperate gaze pierced mine next. "What happened?"

Phil hastened down and put his arm around me. I could only moan and shake my head slowly from side to side.

Father ran a light hand over Mama's hair. "Why is she here?" he asked, his voice hoarse, more to himself than to me.

Heaven help me when he discovered the truth. It was my fault. I'd made her ride to the river without taking time to saddle Boots.

He put his fingers to the side of her neck. "She lives, just."

A black veil fell across my vision. She was still alive?

"Phil, turn away," Father commanded.

With shaking hands, he flung Mama's skirts back.

I gasped. Her legs were angled in ways they shouldn't be, with a cracked bone jutting from one of them. My knees gave way. I fell to the ground with a thud.

"Has she woken at all?" Father did not wait for my answer and peeled off his shirt. "Philemon, fetch the doctor. We'll meet you at home."

"Aye, Father." Phil sprinted to Boots, climbed the ridge with her, and galloped away.

Father strode toward a slender aspen tree and, with his hand ax, notched it on one side and then the other. He gave it a swift push, and *crack*, the tree separated from its bottom and fell. "Drag this to her."

I forced myself to my feet and did as he bade while he felled another tree. Soon, both saplings lay beside her. He retrieved his shirt from the ground and tied each sleeve to a pole. "Your skirts."

I made short work of removing them.

Ripping the ends, he tied them to the branches and with the gentlest of movements set Mama on top of the makeshift carrier. He pulled me to his eye level. "You must be strong. Lift the end, and don't jostle her. I'll carry the bulk of the load."

So I was to be at her legs, where most of the damage had been done. Father lifted his side, and I lifted mine, biting back a cry of pain from the rough bark gouging my palms. I drew upon whatever strength I had left and stumbled forward, keeping my eyes ahead and not on Mama's mangled legs, twisted and bare in front of me.

An age passed as we made our way through the forest and fields. Father was silent. I choked back tears and made quiet pleas to God for help. We were within sight of our home when Father barked out, "Bordroyne! Tom! Edward! Relieve your sister."

My brothers tumbled out of the house. Their eyes widened.

Edward was the first to reach me, and as soon as he grabbed my end of the carrier, I fell to the ground, my limbs burning and twitching.

Father and Edward carried the cot to the house. Only a moment later, Philemon tore through the fields on Boots, with the doctor on his own horse.

How had Phil found the doctor so quickly?

The rotund doctor slid off his horse and staggered toward the house on unsteady legs. His greasy hair fell from its binding and lay in strings across his forehead and down his sweaty neck. His hair was flat except for a bird's nest at the back of his head. It looked worse than my hair ever did. "Take me—" He let out a belch. "Take me to the miss-sus."

Bordroyne snickered.

The doctor set a severe look upon my brother. "At once, boy."

"Please, Bordroyne," I begged. The doctor might be drunk, but he was the only person for miles and miles who could help. We couldn't afford to offend him.

Father stepped out of the house. "Do what you can, man. Phil, the horses."

The doctor followed Father inside. I sidled up to Phil, who led the horses to the watering barrel. "Where did you find him?"

"Mrs. Watson was having her baby."

That explained the swiftness of the doctor's arrival. The Watsons' farm neighbored ours. "But how did you know he was there?"

"I saw the doctor's horse and heard the Watsons' mother squallin' all the way from the road. I came upon them just as her baby was born."

I shuddered. Why any woman chose to have a baby was beyond my understanding. I'd been present for Pearl's birth, and there was nothing on this earth good enough to make me want to put a baby inside of me. When I'd asked Mama how Pearl had come to be, she'd only said, "Love. 'Tis the way of husbands with their wives."

I would never let a man love me.

"Will Mama live, Phil?"

"I pray to God she will. Come, let's help Father."

We ran to the house together and entered.

The doctor spoke too loudly for indoors. If Mama had been awake, he'd have been chastised and redirected outside to continue his conversation.

"I can set the other leg, but this one? Nothing for it but to lop it off. Here." With his hand, he sliced through the air, landing on her upper thigh, showing us exactly where she'd lose her leg. "A pity to lose such a fine leg." He slapped Mama's thigh soundly as if he assessed horseflesh. "Well, what was once such."

Father leaped at the doctor with a ferocious growl. He grasped the man's shirt in his fist and threw him away from Mama. "Don't touch my wife! Better yet..." He grabbed the doctor once again and marched him to the door. I scrambled out of his way. Father threw him out and took the doctor to a barrel of water, dangling him by the scruff above it.

"How much drink do you have in you?" He pushed the doctor's head into the water and after a long moment pulled it out again. The man sputtered and choked. "A pint?" He dunked him again and, just as quickly, yanked him out. "A barrelful?" He drew the doctor up so they were nose to nose. "Are you sober yet, man?" he asked through gritted teeth.

"Your wife will die if I don't attend to her," the man said in a wheedling voice.

Phil turned desperate eyes to the pathetic, sopping man trapped in our father's grip. "Father, there's no one else."

Father dropped the doctor, who fell in a heap in the dirt. Closing his eyes, Father rubbed his temples. "Go," he commanded the doctor. "Do what you can."

The man struggled to his feet. He straightened his dripping waistcoat and swiped his hair back from his head. His mouth worked as if to protest his treatment, but he mashed his lips together and marched into the house instead, with Father following behind.

"We need your help, Rosanna," Father called.

Me? My stomach clenched. If he knew what I'd done, he wouldn't let me anywhere near her. But though I'd defied Mama, I'd never defy Father, so into the house I went.

"It's good she still sleeps," the doctor muttered. "Take hold of her arms."

I peeked at Mama, lying on the bed, and allowed myself a proper look at her legs. A cold sweat broke out on my forehead and down my neck. "I cannot." I looked at Father. "I cannot!" I tore out the door and ran as fast as I could away from the house, into the trees, their spindly arms catching the tangles of my wild black hair.

THREE

ROSANNA

Some time later, Phil found me, tucked away inside the sanctuary of a willow tree. His hand parted the curtain of hanging branches. "Father wants you with the little ones. They're scared."

I was scared. I sat back against the tree. "Why not you?"

"You're the oldest girl. Besides, I am to snare rabbits."

I sighed and let my head fall against the trunk behind me. "Is Father angry with me?"

That Phil didn't reply straight away was answer enough.

"What will we do if Mama doesn't—" My voice caught.

"You must have faith, Ro."

"Do you?"

"Aye. I must. It's too awful otherwise."

I folded my legs to my chest and rested my forehead on my knees. "What did the doctor do with her leg?"

Phil's face darkened. "I buried it next to Little Sister."

I was glad our dead baby sister wouldn't be alone anymore, even if it was just a part of Mama to keep her company.

"Where's my plucky Ro gone to?" Phil lifted my hair and glanced beneath. "Is she hiding underneath this nest?"

"How can you joke when Mama... when she..."

Phil pulled me to my feet. "Don't make me hitch you to Boots and drag you home."

I sighed as loud and long as I could so he'd know just how much I hated going. I ducked under the branches and followed him all the way back to our home in waning dusk. Not even a full day had passed since she'd fallen at the river.

We parted at the house, he to the barn and me to our threshold.

The doctor's horse was gone.

As soon as I arrived, Bordroyne plopped a screaming Pearl in my arms. "She needs changin'."

My sweaty, woebegone sister arched her back away from me, but I clamped my arms around her. It was then that I noticed the smell. Gracious, but I would give Bordroyne a good knocking when all this was over for handing her over to me in this state.

"Shh, little one." I jiggled her up and down. "Let's get you clean." I glanced around for Father. Where was he? I peeked over to the corner of the cabin. A cloth had been tacked to the roof, creating a curtain on one side of Mama's bed, hiding her from prying eyes. Perhaps he was in there at Mama's side.

I set Pearl on her back and took off her wrappings. Her cries grew more strident. I brought her to my chest and crooned the song I'd hummed earlier at the washtub. "There came three men out of the west, their victory for to try..." Pearl stopped crying and stared into my eyes. Heartened, I continued, "And they did take a solemn oath, poor Barleycorn should die." I bounced her in my arms with every word.

"You can't sing that to her!" Bordroyne yelled.

Pearl burst into tears again. Drat my brother.

"Why not?"

"You're singin' 'bout killin' a man. And drinkin'!"

"So? It's working, isn't it?"

"I'm younger than you, and even I know better than that."

I turned my back to him, pretending his words hadn't stuck a barb in my heart. Bordroyne was right. Killing songs weren't for babies, and drinking songs, even less.

My stomach growled.

Oh. Was that why Pearl was upset?

I set her in a patch of sunshine on the dirt floor next to Charlotte, who played with her rag doll. I dipped a tin cup in the pail of milk and handed it to my baby sister. "Here you go."

She greedily gulped it without stopping to take a breath.

Poor little flower. I *was* terrible at this.

Father stepped into the house and set his rifle upon the mantel. "Make corncakes for supper, Rosanna," he said.

He must not have caught any game. "Yes, Father."

Without looking at me, he walked past and tied back the curtain. He sat hunched over, propped by one fist, and stared at Mama.

I'd watched Mama make corncakes my whole life. It should be easy enough. Putting a handful of corn in the grinding stone, I worked the corn to the size of pebbles, then sand. When it looked just right, I mixed it with milk and poured it into a hot skillet. The sweet scent of simmering corn and cream filled the cabin. After adding a dash of salt, I stirred the lumps until they disappeared.

A few minutes passed. Bubbles formed on the surface. Wrapping my apron around the skillet's handle, I lifted the pan from the fire and jerked it forward, but the cake didn't flip.

The acrid smell of smoke reached my nose.

Sweat trickled down my spine. I'd forgotten to spread bacon grease on the skillet before pouring the batter in. I scraped a knife between the pan, and the cake gave way in crumbly bits.

"I'm hungry, Rosie," Isaac whined.

"Just a moment."

I mixed milk with the charred remains, hoping it might blunt the taste.

Pearl banged her empty tin cup on our hearth. I scooped a spoonful of burnt corncake into it then placed it on the window ledge to cool. She flapped her arms and hit the ground, her wails now deafening screams.

I grabbed the trenchers and plopped a mound of runny cake on each one. "Here!" I said, none too gently, to my three brothers. "Eat." *And be grateful, you brats.*

I took a trencher to Father and set it on the floor beside him. "Father?"

He smoked at his pipe, staring into nothing.

"Are you angry with me?"

The shadows moved across his face as he turned away.

"I—I didn't..." But what could I say that could change what I did?

Without looking at me, he grabbed my arm and squeezed it.

My throat tightened. I put my hand on top of his, but he pulled away and returned his attention to Mama.

Swallowing my hurt, I left him and settled Charlotte at my feet with her own bowl of food, then pulled Pearl onto my lap and began to feed her bits.

Charlotte gagged and scraped at her tongue with her dimpled fingers, spitting the cake onto the ground. The look she set upon my face was one of grievous injury. "You're killin' me, Arse!"

Rose, I wanted to scream. My name is *Rose*. I had long given up trying to get her to pronounce *Rosanna*. She could be forgiven for not saying my name right, but why must she refer to me as a hind end?

Bordroyne gagged a mouthful onto the floor. Edward and Isaac joined him in declaring the food fit only for pigs.

"Hush," Father called from his corner. He was brushing Mama's hair and pulling it back from her face, tucking one of her treasured pearl combs on each side of her head. She was so very still. So very white.

I set Pearl down and ran out the door for the second time that day, little caring what they'd eat if not my cakes. Let them starve.

Throwing myself in a pile of hay in the barn, I sobbed.

They *would* starve if I had to take Mama's place. With her gone, everything was wrong. *I* was all wrong.

I fumbled for the primer in my pocket and flipped to an empty page. I could write to Mama, even if she would never read it.

In the moon's light, I scratched out a letter to her as neatly as I could, making my loops and lines just as she'd taught me.

From now on, I would be good and gentle. A lady like her.

It was easier being me, but that didn't mean easier was right.

The next thing I knew, Father jostled me awake to morning light streaming into my little sanctuary. "Come."

I bolted upright. "Is she... does she live?"

But already, he was gone.

I ran to the house, drawing to a halt in the doorway.

Mama leaned from the side of the bed, vomiting into a basin with Father holding her hair. She turned her head and glanced at me. Her skin was waxy and gray, like a drum's skin pulled too tight. She laid her sweaty head back upon the pillow. "Rosanna," her voice scratched.

I couldn't move.

"Bring her water," Father commanded.

I faltered to the pitcher and filled a cup, trying not to look at the empty space under the blanket where her leg should be. "Are you thirsty?"

She nodded, and I lifted her head with my free hand and trickled water into her dry lips.

She swallowed and laid her head down. "I hear you nearly killed the others with dinner."

My heart caught. Her words were halting, as if each came with the cost of great pain. "Oh, Mama." Tears streamed down my cheeks.

Father bolted upright and hurried outside as if I'd offended him.

She grasped my hand. "I am well."

I ripped my hand away. "You are *not*. I prayed and prayed, but it didn't matter!"

"*Rosanna!*"

The shock in her voice shut my mouth in a trice. Perhaps it wasn't wise to invite God's wrath further.

"I live," she said.

"Only just. You wouldn't have lost your leg if I'd done what you asked. What if you get a fever? You could die!"

Her face flinched as if she'd been hit by a wave of agony. She gathered the blanket in her fists. "The fault is mine."

"How can you say that?"

"My anger forced Boots to the cliff's edge."

"But if I'd stayed home, if I hadn't chased after Phil—"

She grabbed my hand again. This time I hadn't the heart to take it away. "I watched you go and did nothing. I gave in, first to you and then to my anger. But the sun grew hotter, and so did my temper."

She had never had the heart to separate me from Phil. But even that was too generous to me. I took advantage of it as often as I could, as I had yesterday.

Charlotte ran into the room clutching her silky chicken, Mrs. Syllabub, who squawked and screeched at being handled so.

Mama winced and brought a hand to her temple.

Charlotte clomped over to the bed, her too-big second hand shoes slipping off her heels with every step. "Bubbie wants to sleep with you." The little sprite lifted her chicken and shoved it on the bed beside Mama.

Mama closed her eyes, her chest rising and falling in rapid breaths.

I pulled Charlotte away, but Mama stayed me with a lifted hand. She gave a glimmer of a smile to her next-to-youngest child. "I don't have grubs in my bed, sweetling. How will Mrs. Syllabub eat?"

Charlotte considered with her mouth scrunched to the side. Her eyes lit. "I can get them."

"Take your chicken to her pen. I'll visit with her another time," Mama said.

Charlotte's bottom lip trembled. I grabbed the chicken from

the bed and plopped it back into her chubby arms. "You must do as Mama says."

My little sister's eyes filled with tears. "You made Bubbie sad."

"Is Charlotte sad too?" Mama asked.

She gave a jerky nod.

"Come. I'll give both you and Mrs. Syllabub a kiss, then off you go."

I lifted both Charlotte and her pet for the kiss and shooed them out the door with a gentle pat on my sister's bum.

"See?" Mama fell back on her pillow, her breathing labored. "If you will be my hands and feet, we'll do quite nicely, the two of us."

I stood, desperate for escape so she wouldn't see me cry.

"Wait."

"What is it, Mama?"

She swallowed forcefully. "I'm glad for the accident."

I drew back. "I'll never be glad for it. Never!"

"I see now that I've let you become a hoyden, and great is my shame for it." Beads of sweat dotted her ashen brow. "You'll bridle your wildness. You'll learn to sit and read and write and govern your emotions." Her chest rose and fell quickly. "I've earned your obedience, have I not?"

The smell of blood and sick pressed against me. My stomach, empty, convulsed. I'd already promised I'd change in my letter to Mama, but now that it was upon me, how would I bear it? My mind raced through the days as they would stretch before me, misery upon misery. Being inside when I wanted out. Wearing shoes and keeping my person tidy, just as Mama always wanted. Becoming better at reading and writing and keeping control of my tongue. Worst of all, I wouldn't be free to be with Phil like I had before.

With a wail, I threw myself over Mama's chest. "I don't know if I can ever be a lady!"

"Take heart, my girl." She ran her fingers over my curls. "There'll be good from this yet."

FOUR

CALLUM

July 1749

Fire. Hot, scalding fire.

A man sobs, begging for his children. My sharpened staff, lodged in his belly.

Flames lick my skin, then my chains of rope and rags.

Down, down I fall into a pit of smoke and ash. The bloodied man calls to me, his plea an echo in the dark.

A meaty hand clamped my shoulder.

I shot up, chest heaving, my face wet. I gulped the rancid, stale air. Would I never be free of that day? How it haunted me, even in my dreams.

"Wheesht, lad. Dinnae fash yerself." The man beside me cracked his hardtack in two. He felt for my hand in the pitch black of the prisoners' hold and handed me half.

I was too hungry and weak to argue. I clutched the biscuit to my chest and closed my eyes. There was no man crying for his children. Just the creaking of rope and sails, coughing, moaning, and water dripping from the wooden planks above our heads. The slimy cold crept through my thin breeches. I was in the ship taking me from England. Had it been weeks? With so few trips above deck, it hadn't been easy to track the passage of days.

From one prison to another. I should have gone from the battlefield straight to the scaffold, if not for the jailor who'd taken pity on me. He hid me in his jail for three years—or forgot me, rather—until a disease swept through the cells, killing him and half the prisoners. Why my life had been preserved, I couldn't say.

The trapdoor above swung open, flooding the rotting bowels of the ship with light.

I winced and shut my eyes tight.

"Up top," one of the ship's crew called. "And be sharp about it."

We'd arrived in the port at Virginia. My new home. America.

My teeth clattered uncontrollably.

"'Tis time." The man who'd given me his biscuit held out his hand and pulled me to my feet. "*Dia is Muire dhuit.*"

God be with you. Was God with me? I couldn't say.

The man buttoned his vest and smoothed his hair.

By habit, my hand felt for the small bundle in my pocket, filled with the only memories I had left of home. Relief flooded me. It was still there.

I ascended the ladder on trembling legs and tripped into the fresh air and blue sky.

They shoved us into lines. Sailors sheared our heads, clumps of hair and vermin falling to the deck. They doused us with buckets of water. It beaded on our skin's black filth and rolled off our shirts and breeches.

They shuffled us down the gangway, our ankles connected by circlets of iron.

We were halfway down when the men ahead of me swayed and stumbled as if someone had knocked them off balance. The chains at my own feet pulled, threatening to yank me over. I gripped the ropes of the walkway tight. The fibers scraped my hands like needles.

A prisoner toppled over the side and dangled, headfirst. The men nearest him held on, their arms shaking, desperate not to be pitched into the water along with their fellow convict.

"Heave!" the men shouted.

We pulled. The hanging man thrashed for something solid to hold on to, the whites of his eyes ablaze. At last, he was dragged onto the planks.

It was quiet, except for our gasping breaths and the man's sobbing.

I stepped onto solid land.

I was met with shouts, raucous laughter, hammering, horses' hooves clomping by. Some accents sounded familiar, others not. The captain's man directed us into a line in front of the ship.

My ears seized upon a Scottish brogue filtering through the mass. It came from a man outfitted in the finest of breeches and a shimmering waistcoat. He stopped in front of us.

A kinsman who might sympathize with my troubles. For the barest of moments, hope flared.

The man eyed us, then held a cut of fine linen to his nose and went on his way.

I glanced at my rags and dirty skin. I wouldn't have wanted me either.

The captain commanded us to remove our shirts.

I lifted my damp, grimy shirt over my head and gripped it tightly in my hands. Who knew when I would get another? I fought the urge to put it back on. The grooves between my ribs and my hairless, scrawny chest would surely keep me from any master's interest. Then what? Would I be shoved back into the hull? I swallowed a wave of nausea. Anything would be better than that.

Moments later, my friend who had shared his biscuit was chosen and taken away.

A bearded man as dark as polished wood and large as a standing stone walked down our line and stopped in front of me. His eyes filled with what looked like pity.

"How old?" he asked.

The captain lifted my arm and slapped my scrawny bicep.

"Not a day younger than sixteen. Old enough to not need much minding, not too young to pull his weight."

An outright lie. Anyone could see I wasn't more than fourteen.

"You will look better with meat in you, boy," the swarthy man said in an accent strange to my ears. He turned to the captain. "This one."

"That'll be seventeen pounds sterling."

The captain's man gave a sputtering cough—surprised, no doubt, by the absurd price for an unskilled, half-starved boy.

To my shock, the large man signed the papers without protest and handed over the money.

Satisfaction gleamed in the captain's eyes, and his man slipped the knotted ropes off my wrists.

"This one's sticks and bones, he is. Won't survive the Seasoning," he said.

The captain shot him a scalding look. "Who's to say? If Smythe will have him, the boy will be better off than most."

My heart hammered harder. Who was Smythe?

The dark man pointed at me. "You. Come with me." He walked away, not looking back to see if I followed.

Yet again, I was at the mercy of strangers, just as I had been since the day I'd been captured.

I stepped forward and collapsed.

My new master retraced his steps and pulled me to my feet. "You will be fine, boy." With his arm bracing me, he led me to a stable. "I am Bembe, from Jamaica." The man pulled a sliver of wood from his pocket and set it between his teeth. The beads upon his wrist caught my eye. They were unlike anything I'd seen before, shiny and brightly colored.

The stable hand brought forward a wagon, pulled by two matched draught horses and filled with sacks and barrels. Bembe sprang into the seat in one smooth movement, like a selkie leaping from the water.

I stepped on the iron-rimmed wheel and pulled myself

upward. My shoe slipped, and my weakened limbs sent me to the ground in a heap.

Bembe stared straight ahead, as if he hadn't noticed.

I wiped my palms and tried once more. This time, I kept my balance and settled beside Bembe, folding my lanky frame into the seat.

He made a clicking sound with his cheek and slapped the reins on the horses' backs. "What is your name?"

"Callum."

He nodded once. "Call-oom."

We didn't speak until nightfall when we stopped and set camp. He had me fetch kindling for a fire, and he set off through the woods. A short time later, he came back bearing a fat rabbit in his fist.

Greed, powerful and swift, swept through me.

Bembe placed it on a spit and roasted it.

My mouth watered, thinking of the way my belly would feel once warm food filled it. Even in prison, there'd only been moldy bread and cold porridge. The last bit of meat I'd had was at the meal I shared with Da before he'd strapped his broadsword and shield to his horse and left for Culloden. I'd taken the pike I'd made from a branch of alder and followed, creeping in the gorse and bracken over the empty and lonely moor.

Had I known what would happen, I'd have never left.

Bembe handed over the rabbit. I set upon it like a ravenous wolf. He sat and watched me eat the whole thing before I realized what I'd done.

I shrank back. "I—I'll catch another."

Bembe took the toothpick from his teeth and pointed it at me. "You are not fit for anything but sitting." He tossed me a leather pouch.

I undid the leather ties and opened the bag. Inside were stems with bunches of deep purple fruit. I recoiled from the rotten odor.

"Eat."

I hesitated.

He smiled widely. "Chokecherries smell like feet, but the taste, it's not so bad."

I put one in my mouth. It tasted of unripe blaeberries. I would've spit it out had Bembe not been watching me. I forced myself to swallow. "Bembe?"

"Yes?"

"Are ye Smythe?"

He shook his head. "He is the one who owns you now."

"Is he a good master?"

"When you see his horses, then you will know."

Horses? What could I know by way of horses?

Bembe stood. "I will get more rabbits." His eyes sparkled. "This time, you save one for me."

He left, and I leaned into a bed of moss and leaves and stared at the slivers of night sky through the treetops. Everything was strange in this new country, the air as hot and thick as cock-a-leekie soup, its berries nothing like the bush-ripened fruit I would make myself sick over every summer back home in Scotland. The birdsong here echoed in a thick mass of green so unlike the barren, craggy mountains of home. This land was so full of woodland, the colonists would be rich if trees were crops.

The rabbit had gone a long way in soothing my dread of Bembe. But what of Smythe? Would he be kind, like his overseer?

Bembe returned, and with another rabbit in my belly, I started nodding off. Bembe handed me a blanket and settled himself under a tree opposite mine, turning his back. He trusted me not to run, then.

How could I? I didn't know this land or what dangers awaited me outside of Bembe's keeping. I had no weapon, no money, no food. I was safer staying near this sizeable stranger than I was anywhere else.

Minutes passed. I waited and was soon rewarded with the sounds of Bembe's snoring. I pulled the balled bundle of tartan from my pocket. Peeling back the sides revealed a small mound of *smeeshin*, the ground tobacco Da kept in his ram's horn. I brought it to my nose. It still smelled like him, a little. Memories flooded of him and me, sitting around a small fire, the night damp with mist on our last night together. He'd fed a pinch to the fire and winked. *Lang may yer lum reek*, he'd said. Long may your chimney smoke. The powder sparked in the flames and was gone, leaving behind a sweet scent.

'Tis not Hogmanay, Da, I'd said.

I ken, ye clot-heid. Here's a wee nip fair me. He sniffed a pinch. *And here's a wee nip for ye, my wee heartie.* His little heart. He held out the powder to me. I eyed him, suspicious he'd clamp the mull on my fingers. He didn't, though. He laughed when I gave the powder a hard sniff and coughed and sputtered.

Tears filled my eyes. I blinked them away. Da's face disappeared, along with the flames. Even if I returned to Scotland, I'd never see him again.

I dug *Màthair*'s thin wedding band out of the tobacco and closed my fist around it. I could no longer hold back. Stuffing the blanket in my mouth, I gave myself over to wracking sobs.

Three days later, we arrived at the plantation.

Bembe released the horses from the wagon and handed me the reins. "Take them to the stables." He gestured to a large wooden structure not far from the road.

I took the lines and walked the horses through the building's cavernous opening. A fellow servant led them away.

The stables were light and airy. It didn't smell of wet hay and dung.

Bembe said I would know once I saw the horses.

I stood in a shaft of light pouring in from the open doors and wandered the aisle, looking for something that might tell me what I should know.

In a stall closest to me, a sleek horse, black as night, turned his head and stared.

The rolling of a creaking wheel sounded behind me then stopped. I glanced over my shoulder.

There, holding the handles of a cart, stood an older gentleman in rolled shirtsleeves and dirt-dusted breeches, his white hair cropped short. He stared like the horse had.

It was as if they waited for me to do something, but what?

"I... I'm new here."

Still, the man didn't move.

"Bembe brought me. To work."

The man's face twisted as if he'd tasted soured milk. "Did he?"

The horse nudged my back, and I stumbled a little closer to the man.

His gruff voice cut through the silence. "He's taken a shine to you." He left his cart and hobbled toward me and the horse.

"He's beautiful," I said.

"His name is Obsidian."

I ran the back of my fingers down the horse's muzzle and over his coarse mane. "Ob-sid-ian?"

"Obsidian. It's black glass, formed by lava."

I didn't want to appear a simpleton and ask what lava was. "Oh."

His mouth hitched. "Lava is melted rock that comes from volcanoes. When it cools, it becomes rock again, hard and shiny." He took a muckrake and pushed the bits of straw into a pile.

I stepped on a stool and leaned over the door, reaching further into the stall to stroke the horse's flanks. "He looks like he could fly."

The man stopped raking and stared at me, propping his hands and chin on the end of the muckrake. "Do you know much of horses, then?"

"Aye." With *Màthair* dead and Da preoccupied with our clan teetering on the edge of war, I would ride our horse as far and for as long as I wanted.

Obsidian pawed at the ground.

"He wants tae run," I said.

"Take him out, then. He hasn't had a good working in a long while." The man returned to raking with rough quickness. "Not too far. Just along the tree line and back."

My mouth dropped. This creature was the finest piece of horseflesh I'd ever seen. "Me, sir?"

He stopped and glowered at me, his silvery eyebrows clapped together in thunderclouds above his eyes. "Yes, you. Is there anyone else in here?"

"Will the master mind?"

The old man's eyes glinted. "Mind? No, I don't think he will."

FIVE
CALLUM

Obsidian ran as fast as the wind that whipped in and out of the sea caves near my home. Riding him, I was back in Scotland, feeling its wildness again.

The horse understood slack reins as permission, just as I'd intended, and we flew past the boundary the old man had given, along rushing waters and into open fields, until we found ourselves hemmed in by a narrow glen. Greenbriar stabbed my skin, leaving bloody trails running down my legs.

I backed Obsidian out of the brambles and leaped to the ground. Running my hand over his dark flesh, I found a nick in his hind leg. My stomach dropped. How could I have hurt such a creature?

I rode toward Mr. Smythe's house, sick with dread and shame. Why had I listened to the old man and ridden Obsidian? Any lord who stewarded his holdings well wouldn't allow an untested servant—a criminal at that—to ride his finest horse, and he would have been right to do so. I'd hurt Obsidian in my longing to feel at home in this strange new land.

The main house was built on a small rise. The setting sun traced the house with shafts of light. Red bricks and gleaming windows—finer than anything I'd seen in my life.

In the distance, Bembe climbed the steps to the front door and entered. Dare I follow him? He hadn't told me where to go after stabling the horses, and he hadn't given me permission to go for the ride. Fear coursed through my middle. Would I be whipped for hurting Obsidian?

I let Obsidian drink, then wiped him down and tended to his wound. I trudged to the house. After knocking bits of hay and mud from my shoes, I entered a side door and closed it softly behind me.

There were no servants running to do their master's bidding. A clock sounded the seconds in slow, muted clicks. To my left was a room filled with bulky, sheeted lumps resembling ghostly animals.

Voices drifted from a room close by, words first in Bembe's thick accent, answered by a thunderous reply.

I turned my steps into a slow, sliding gait and drew nearer. The wood planks creaked under my shoes in the long corridor.

"We don't need the help, Bembe," came the voice from the man I didn't know. "Send him back."

My heart gave a painful knock against my ribs. They were talking of me.

"I could not leave him on the docks. You see how he looks."

"Bah!"

"That is what you say when you know I am right."

"How kind of you to remind me."

A moment of silence passed.

"You know more than anyone what you ask," the man said.

"You trust me to take care of everything. Why not this?"

The man sighed. His chair squeaked like he'd reclined against its back. "What do you know of our new arrival?"

"I know the captain lied when he said the boy is sixteen."

"And?"

"He cried the first night. And the other nights too."

Heat rushed to my face. How could they talk of my deepest griefs so lightly?

"What is it you suggest I do with him?"

"That is for you to say."

"Until I decide whether to keep him or not—"

Bembe gave a loud, disapproving grunt.

"—until *then*, put him on a cot in the old servants' quarters."

"But they are empty."

"And?"

"He will be alone."

A chair scraped against the floor. Steps plodded toward me. I jerked my ear away from the door.

The door swung open. There stood the old man from the barn, now in wig and shiny silk finery. "You will hear much better without a door between us."

I was stunned silent. The master of this grand place was the same man shoveling horse dung earlier this day?

Bembe's opaque eyes gave no hint that anything was amiss.

"Well?" The older man motioned me into the room.

I obeyed slowly.

He returned to his seat at his desk. "I suppose you want to know what you'll do now that you are here." He stared at me as if he expected me to supply the answer. "Do you have any useful skills?"

"I—I can cut peat and... and..."

"And ride like the devil? I saw you, tearing out of the barn."

My legs trembled in earnest then.

Mr. Smythe swiveled to face Bembe. "So, he cuts peat. Just what we need on a horse-breeding farm." There was the tiniest twitch to the side of his mouth when he turned back to me. "Do you read?"

"Aye."

"Write?"

"Fine enaw."

He pulled out a sheet of paper. "Let's see it, then."

I bent over his desk and took the quill from the inkpot. I wrote my name—*Callum Stewart*—with a little flourish at the end.

He peered at the page. "Your definition of *fine* is tenuous." He stood and tucked his hands behind his back. "You will tend to my horses in the morning. Then, Master Callum Stewart, you will go to school."

I blinked. Was it the way of things to send servants to school in the colonies? I glanced again at Bembe. A look of what could only be called satisfaction marked his features.

"*And* after school, you will take Obsidian for a ride. I'm far too busy to do it myself. Now, off with you. Bembe, show him to his room."

"His room?" Bembe asked.

"I am not a complete blackguard."

Bembe crossed his massive arms and smiled as if he were a cat that got the cream. "Which room?"

Mr. Smythe set a mocking glance upon his foreman. "You know the one."

After my chores, Bembe rode with me to school two days later, he on his horse and me on Obsidian. "Just this time. Tomorrow, you go alone," he said.

I sat tall in the saddle, for a moment pretending to be a grand gentleman on the finest horse in history. Then I sagged, thinking of what was ahead. Why couldn't I work in the barn or on the fields like a normal servant? Going to school would be worse than cleaning a pig's stall. At least, I felt it might. I'd never been to school before.

We carried on in silence except for the crunching of dried pine needles beneath our horses' hooves. I hadn't told Mr. Smythe that the only schooling I'd received was at *Màthair*'s knee. The books Smythe had given me were the first I'd held in my hands.

"Scared?" Bembe asked.

"Good as a pup at its mither's teat," I said, making myself sound as brave as I could.

Bembe laughed heartily. "You will be fine, boy."

Why had he asked me my name if he never used it? "Bembe, how did ye come to be at Mr. Smythe's? Were ye bound to him?"

He nodded. "He let me stay when my time was over. I was glad to stay."

We arrived at a clearing where a small one-story structure stood on the property of a larger home. Without a word, Bembe left. I was alone in a new land and new life, about to meet other boys my age.

I eyed the schoolhouse and then myself. My clothes, given to me just that morning, had been made for a much stouter man. I cinched the waist of my breeches, but there was nothing I could do about the waistcoat. It hung on me like a turtle's shell.

I led Obsidian to a pen filled with grazing horses, then took a fortifying breath and pushed open the door.

Boys, young to old and already sitting at their desks, turned to look at me.

I gave them a tentative smile.

A plump boy in fine clothes snickered.

"Ah. Master Stewart," the schoolmaster said. "Mr. Smythe mentioned your joining us. Have a seat." He pointed to the empty space beside the boy who'd laughed at me. "Master Grenville? Show him where we are in *Metamorphoses*."

I sat on the bench. My stiff waistcoat lifted above my shoulders, my skinny arms too small for the arm holes. I pulled the linen vest and tucked it beneath my bum, ignoring the tittering behind me.

My bench mate shoved his book closer to me. His name, *Master Frederick Grenville*, was written in a heavy hand at the top of the page, along with the sketch of a busty mermaid.

"You've hog bristles for hair," he whispered hotly.

My hand went self-consciously to my hair. He'd told no lie. The ship's shears had been dull, and the man sawed at my hair to cut it. I'd seen my cropped hair for the first time yesterday in the mirror hanging above my washbowl. The mirror was now hidden in my garderobe so I wouldn't have to see myself again. At least, not until my hair grew.

"Master Stewart? Begin where I leave off. 'As the father, he of

Saturn, saw these things from his highest citadel.' *Quae pater ut summa vidit Saturnius arce...*" He stared at me, eyebrows raised.

The lines of my palms beaded with sweat. I raced over the words with my finger, trying to find anything resembling the words he'd read aloud, but I could barely decipher English, let alone Latin. "...hack parr-tee... po-tent-ess... ca... ca-ell-ic... ic..."

The schoolmaster's eyes closed. "Stop!" He pinched the bridge of his nose. "Stop. That's quite enough."

The tittering turned to snorts of laughter.

The man looked over his spectacles at his students. "Master Baldwin? You may continue where I left off."

My portly bench mate slid his book away, eyeing me with contempt. "Hog hair *and* hog brains."

And ye have the breath of a dead badger.

By the end of the school day, I was no better at reading or writing, but I was a master at counting the cracks in the ceiling and the walls.

I waited until everyone poured out of the schoolhouse, then I picked up my dinner pail and walked out alone.

Just as I put my foot into one of Obsidian's stirrups, someone pulled my shirt at the neck, tightening it like a noose. I twisted against it but couldn't escape.

My assailant yanked me to the ground.

The blue sky and its clouds swirled above me. A cool trickle of blood dripped from my ear to my neck to the back of my ugly waistcoat.

The boy who'd been forced to share a bench with me stood above me, smirking. "Does Mr. Smythe know you stole his horse?"

I struggled to my knees. Gripping Obsidian's saddle, I rested my forehead upon it and concentrated on the scent of oiled leather. I couldn't blame this Master Grenville for thinking Obsidian stolen. I would have thought it, too, if I were him.

He grabbed my shoulder and whipped me around to face him.

I braced myself for only a second before Frederick's fist landed square in my middle.

His hit was no more powerful than the swat of a horse's tail. I laughed. "'At's all ye got?"

Frederick took a step forward, fists raised. "Want another one, then?"

I met his menacing stance with one of my own. "Go 'heid, ye tubby coo."

"Speak so people can understand, you dirty Scot."

I spoke slowly, as if he were simpleminded. "I said, ye're a big, fat, tubby *coo*."

"I heard you Scots go 'round, arses to the wind, passing water where you stand, like animals. Go back to Scotland. We don't want you here."

A familiar fire shot through my arm, curling my hand into a fist. I took a menacing step forward.

He flinched.

It was the smallest of movements—another less experienced with fear might not have caught it, but it turned my fist to ice.

In Frederick's place stood the man from Culloden. The one I still saw in my dreams.

My hand dropped to my side.

The alarm in Frederick's eyes turned to mockery. "That's right. You're too much of a scrag to make this a fair fight, anyway."

My body trembled with suppressed anger.

"I'm telling my father about Smythe's horse." Without another word, he strutted toward a group of boys who'd been watching us. They laughed over my clothes, my hair, the way I spoke.

I pulled myself into the saddle. I'd been right about school. It would have been better to clean pig dung.

Bembe met me at the stables and studied my face and clothes. "What did you do?"

"I didnae do anything! It was that Freddie Grenville."

Bembe swore an oath. "Did you hit him back?"

I tightened my jaw and said not a word.

Bembe sighed. "Now that boy will never leave you alone." He took the reins and handed Obsidian to a stable hand. "Come." He settled his large hand on my shoulder and guided me toward the house.

I tried to tug my shoulder from his grasp, but it was no use. It was as if a mountain had been laid on my shoulder.

Bembe guided me into the house and through the empty rooms until I stood before Smythe's desk.

The older man glanced up from a letter. His hard gaze went from me to his foreman. "What have we here?"

I could not control my quaking. My anger melted into fear. Was it to be a beating, then? Would he cast me off? Send me away without food or money?

"It was young Grenville," Bembe said. "Who can blame him? Look at the boy."

They both turned to stare at me. I shrank into my turtle shell.

Smythe clamped his lips into a firm line. "That family is a menace." He pushed away from his chair and came to stand in front of me.

I retreated until my back bumped into his desk.

He looked me up and down with a critical eye. "I should have known there would be trouble."

"I—I never meant to cause ye trouble, sir."

"Young Master Callum, I believe I owe you an apology."

My jaw went slack. What punishment was so bad he needed to apologize before it was even done? "I dinnae ken what ye mean, sir."

"I didn't prepare you well before sending you into a pit of vipers." He picked up a bell sitting on his desk and rang it. "I believe the best way to attack something is head on, do you agree?"

A round-cheeked woman bustled in.

"Are you finished with them, Mrs. Heaney?" Smythe asked.

"Yes, sir."

"Good. Bring them in."

She hurried to do his bidding.

He set his attention back on me. "Now, as to your... situation. Your hair will grow, and, in time, your brogue will soften."

My brogue? Why did the way I talk need to change? And what did that have to do with what happened today? Perhaps the way *he* talked was wrong. I crossed my arms over my chest, bunching my overlarge waistcoat. "What if I dinnae want my hair to grow?"

He waggled his finger at me. "Head on, remember? Now, as for your clothes, Mrs. Heaney has taken in some of mine to fit you. They'll do until new ones can be made. How did you get on with Latin?"

Now it was my turn to flush. "I... cannae say."

"Just as I thought." He returned to his desk and sat, his fingers steepled together. "You'll still take Obsidian on his ride after school, but then you'll come to me for lessons. You have some catching up to do. I will not let those boys think I keep simpletons for servants." His eyes glinted at me in unspoken challenge. "You aren't a simpleton, are you?"

So this was to be my punishment. Latin at school and another dose when I returned? *Devil language.* I thrilled a little, thinking a word Da would've boxed my ears for saying. *Devil, devil, devil,* I repeated for good measure.

"Well? Out with it. I can tell you have something to say."

"What's the point o' me going to school, anyway? I dinnae need it to work."

"And I didn't need another servant when Bembe bought you, but here we are. As to that Frederick Grenville..." He jabbed his quill at me. "Avoid the little brute as much as you can. I'll send a note to the schoolmaster informing him that if he desires to maintain his position, he must keep a better eye on his pupils."

I didn't know much of the world, but I knew enough to know a master didn't usually take such interest in his servants. Hadn't Bembe told him I'd come from a prison? That I'd done something terrible enough to be cast across the ocean and placed into servitude? "Why are ye doin' all this? I'm a nobody."

"Bembe doesn't seem to think so." He gave a pointed glance at his overseer. "As I've learned over the years, he's rarely wrong."

Bembe scoffed. "What time am I wrong?"

"Yes, well, let's see if this boy becomes your first." He turned back to me. "One more thing. If you believe Frederick a demon, his father is the devil himself. You are never to trust either of them, do you understand? Mr. Grenville whips his horses and servants alike, and he won't think twice to whip you if he finds you trespassing on his land. Bembe will ride out with you and mark the boundaries of my land so you won't mistake his portion for ours."

I swayed a little.

Smythe turned to Bembe. "I'm afraid I've shocked the poor lad. Take him to the kitchen for a bite and have a bath drawn for him."

Mrs. Heaney entered, carrying a bundle of clothing.

"Ah, here we are. Callum, take these, and I'll see you tonight for your lessons."

I reached woodenly for the bundle and followed Bembe out the door.

"He didnae ask what the fight was about," I said to Bembe as we climbed the stairs.

"You better fight back next time, boy."

SIX

ROSANNA

Against the doctor's prediction, Mama lived, though with little of her former strength. With one leg gone and the other badly set by the doctor, she only left our home when Father carried her outside for brief respites. But even that pained her too much.

Over the next months, she directed my reformation from her bed. From sunup till sundown, my time was not my own, and I submitted to it. I would never go against her wishes again.

When I wasn't helping the younger children with their learning, I was applying myself to my own. Yesterday, I'd taught myself to make a pottage of chestnuts. Today, I would truss and roast a chicken. *The Lady's Companion* made it sound simple enough. I would go to the butchering shed and return before Mama woke. I smiled, imagining the look of pride on her face when she found me preparing a meal of chicken without her direction.

Knowing how difficult it was to get blood stains out of cloth now that I'd taken over the washing, I lifted Father's leather butchering apron from its hook and put it on. The heavy layer would also shield me from the biting December wind.

One hand to a hitching post, Charlotte swung in circles, round and round. "Where you goin', Arse?"

Two of her teeth had fallen out, and now her *Arse* sounded like *Arth*. I bit back a smile. She didn't like to be laughed at.

"I'm starting our meal." I put on the apron and tied it behind me. My shoulders sagged from the weight of it, and the bottom scraped against the top of my shoes. I lifted the ax from its hook and left Charlotte behind, kicking up the apron as I walked. "See if Father needs help feeding the animals."

I set more wood under the kettle in the shed and held my hand over the water. It was hot enough to scald the chicken.

An unlucky chicken walked by the butchering shed, pecking at the ground. The poor thing didn't know death was at her door. Not allowing myself time to change my mind, I scooped it up under one arm and twisted its neck as Father had taught me.

An ear-piercing shriek sounded behind me.

I startled and dropped the chicken. Charlotte must've followed me. Thank goodness I hadn't chosen Mrs. Syllabub. "Hush. How do you think we get our food?" Surely she'd seen Father carry in headless chickens, day after day, for our evening meals. "You are a farmer's daughter, and one day you will be a farmer's wife. You'll have to kill your own chickens if you'll want to eat."

Her scream of rage filled the shed. "No, I *won't!*"

My back and my face grew slick with sweat. How did Mama remain so calm when Charlotte had her tantrums? I liked killing chickens no more than she, but what choice did I have? We must eat. As she sobbed behind me, I beheaded the chicken with one swift chop of the ax and, holding it by the feet, dunked it in the steaming water. Once, twice. I tugged a feather, and it slipped out easily. It was ready for plucking.

I carried it out of the shed with a sobbing Charlotte following close behind.

When we came inside our cabin, she was a disheveled, hiccupping mess. Mama woke. She took one look at Charlotte and then another at me wearing a bloody apron and holding a headless chicken.

She sucked in her cheeks as if trying not to laugh and sent

Pearl to her mat for her nap. Then she turned her attention to me. "If I'd known you were going to butcher a chicken on your own, I'd have told you that Charlotte thinks the chickens we eat grow headless and already plucked on a special bush in the butchering shed." Her mouth tipped. "Or used to think, rather."

My mouth dropped. It was too far-fetched to be believed. "But surely she's been in the shed and has noticed there was no bush."

Mama folded her hands primly on her lap. "Your father told her that the bush was only visible to him as he was the one who planted it."

"But that's a lie." I could hardly fathom it. My God-fearing mother, a liar. Did I know her at all? "Has there been anything you've lied to *me* about?"

"It's not lying. She is just not ready to know the truth. It's the same for you. You must trust that if I haven't told you everything, it's because you are not ready. You're a tender heart, as is Charlotte."

My pride flared. "I'm not weak and childish."

She patted the bed beside her. "Come. I want to talk with you."

I lowered myself to the bed gingerly so I wouldn't disturb her comfort. "What is it?"

"You are miserable."

I picked at my dress. Phil had asked me to go with him into town after he did his chores, but I'd turned him down. It had boiled me to say no, but such was my lot and my penance. I wasn't allowed to follow the whims of my heart any longer.

But even if I did feel free to do what I liked, Father wouldn't have let me. He'd taken up Mama's cause of reform even more strongly. He thought putting an end to my hunting and fishing and running through the woods would gentle my spirit. But he didn't know that every time he handed his rifle to Bordroyne instead of me, my discontent only grew. I'd submitted to the goal of changing, but wanting to do something and having it forced upon you were two different things. "I am as well as I deserve."

She furrowed her eyebrows.

I touched her forearm. "What is it? Are you in pain?"

"Rosanna, I won't have you be a whipping boy to your mistakes. Pitying yourself is unbecoming in a lady."

I sagged on my stool. "*Everything* I do is unbecoming to a lady, no matter *what* I do."

"Giving up already? That's not the Rosanna I know."

A sudden urge to fight for myself rose from the muck of self-pity. "I must have *some* fun, Mama. I can't go from everything to nothing at once."

She cupped my face and ran her calloused thumb across my cheek. "Come now, I wouldn't have you tortured. I only ask that you try to see the good in this."

"I'm trying. I promise I am. But sometimes I can't make myself *feel* what I know I ought."

"Feelings are mulish sometimes, aren't they? Especially when they are wrapped in our nature." She leaned back upon her pillow. "Do you remember Samson, Mr. Smythe's stallion? You used to love petting him when we came across him in town."

I nodded. He was beautiful, with a glossy coat and a shimmering black mane that rippled as he trotted.

"Did Mr. Smythe let you ride him when you asked?"

I winced a little, remembering my impertinence. "No, he never did." There was some hope in my reformation if I could see my childish behavior back then and be embarrassed by it. "I don't see why Mr. Smythe didn't agree to it. Samson liked me. He would've never thrown me or kicked me in the head."

"Is Mr. Smythe miserly or cruel?"

"Of course not."

"The first time Mr. Smythe brought Samson into town, it was madness. He pulled the reins with all his might to control the wild beast. 'Have a care!' he called, waving his arm, warning us from his path." She laughed of a sudden, her eyes alight with mirth. "Poor man."

Her laughter was infectious. Soon, we both laughed, her from the memory but me from the pure joy of seeing her happy again. "So he denied me because he was afraid Samson would hurt me?"

"Just because Mr. Smythe had Samson well in hand when you knew him doesn't mean the horse was no longer that untamed creature I witnessed long ago. Under his owner's instruction, Samson learned it would go easier on him to allow himself to be held in check. But even after all that training, if Mr. Smythe ever let go of the reins, what do you think would've happened?"

"Samson would become wild again."

"Surely he would have."

"So I am to be tamed. Like a horse."

"Is that so bad?"

"I like my horses wild."

"So do I." She placed a tender kiss on my forehead and then peered into my eyes until I returned her smile. "A spirited horse is coveted among breeders. Mr. Smythe wouldn't extinguish the fire that made Samson so valuable to him. You must only harness your passion, managing it so it won't be managing you."

"But I feel as if I am being broken."

Her mouth twitched. "I suppose you are right. It's unreasonable to expect you to adjust to the harness so quickly."

I found myself nodding eagerly as she spoke. Here was sense. Here was hope.

"Suppose I let you have a day with Phil..."

I grasped her hand hard, forgetting to be careful. "Oh! I'll never complain again! I'll do whatever you ask, even if it's to memorize an entire psalm every day for a month!"

"A month? Well, you are serious, aren't you? Only repay me by letting me see a little of the old Rosanna again. A *little*, mind?"

I bounced my head. "Only the veriest little."

"Only one more thing..." She fingered one of my sleeves. "You have grown, daughter."

I tucked my hands under my bum to hide my sleeves. "Aye. I'm to Phil's shoulder now." My dress had faded from red to a muted rose, and the cuffs, once snowy white, were frayed and dingy and were now well above my wrists. The skirt had singe marks, too, left when I'd accidentally dragged the hem through our smoldering kitchen fire. If Phil hadn't been there to put it out with his hands, I'd have gone up in flames like a witch at a stake. There had been no point in cutting out the singed area and mending it. My dress no longer fit. Several seams stretched enough to reveal glimpses of my shift beneath my bodice, and the bottom was inching up my shanks. Why did women wear dresses when breeches would be more practical?

She pulled a pouch from inside her dress and undid the drawstring. Turning it over, she dumped two coins in my hand. "When you are in town, get cloth enough for a new dress. And oranges, one for each of you. Christmas is within the week."

"But I can't leave. What if Charlotte or Pearl need help? Or the boys get into trouble?"

"Father will be here to help."

"But—"

"Go on, now," Father said in his gruff tenor. He stood behind me, closing the door. "I think I can keep my children alive for one day."

"You planned for this?" I asked, wide-eyed. Mama had already decided before our conversation to give me freedom for a day. And Father had agreed to it.

She turned her cheek upward for a kiss. "Do as your father says."

I leaped to my feet and raced to the door.

"Wait," she cried out. "Your hair."

Unrestrained by a cap and pins, it tumbled over my shoulders in a tangled mass.

She held out her comb without a word.

I yanked it through the knots until my hair was soft and rippling like Boots' mane. It was no crown of glory, but it was fine enough for me. Gathering my tresses into a knot, I stabbed four pins into it and plunked my cap on my head.

"Goodbye, Mama! Thank you, Father!" I threw my wrap around my shoulders and raced out the door, pumping my legs as hard and fast as I could. The cold air whipped past my cheeks, stinging them like nettles. I laughed at the pain. It made me feel alive for the first time in months.

SEVEN

ROSANNA

By the barn, Philemon leaned over a trough, splashing his face with water.

I sneaked behind him and, with a quick push, toppled him into the trough.

He came up sputtering. "You little cr—" He cut off mid-sentence, staring. "Ro?"

"Did you think I was John Barleycorn?"

He wiped his face upon his sleeve and grinned. "What are you doing here?"

"I'm to go with you to town to get some things at Mr. Edwards'. Just you and me. Do you think he has a pineapple?" Ever since Freddie Grenville had bragged of tasting one, I couldn't get it out of my mind. He'd said it tasted like all the fruits put together, but tart.

"We couldn't buy it if he did."

I gave him a sly look. "Mama gave me money for a dress."

"Hush. I'm a boy, and even I know you should throw the one you have into the fire."

"I was just jesting." Truth be known, the thought of wearing something new and beautiful excited me.

"So." He put his wet arm about my shoulders. "Shall we sing

along the way? *Some said kill him, some said drown, some to hang him high...*" he belted out.

The song I sang to Pearl to calm her, the one Bordroyne had chastised me for. A lady wouldn't sing songs about barley beer turning men into asses, but Mama could have no real objection, seeing as Phil had been the one to teach it to me.

I pulled away and curtseyed low. "*For as many as follow Barleycorn, shall surely beggars die,*" I finished.

"*Then with a plough they ploughed him up, and thus they did devise, to bury him quick within the earth and swore he should not rise,*" we sang together, my arm tucked in his as we made our way down the flattened grass path toward town.

I inhaled a hearty lungful of the cool air and mist, my face upturned toward the sun streaming through the leaf-bare branches. Inside my chest, prickles of happiness budded where there had been only gloom for too long.

"I must tell you something, and you mustn't laugh," Phil said of a sudden.

"I can't promise that. You always make me laugh."

"Do I? I've forgotten, for you've been nothing but serious of late." His lip curled in disgust. "I miss the old Rosanna."

I rested my head on his shoulder, not so long that he shoved it off. I missed the old Rosanna too. "What is it you wish to tell me?"

"I think John's sweet on you."

"*John?*" A laugh sputtered out of me. "He is not. He hates me."

"He asked after you the last time we went fishing."

"Well, *I* hate *him.*"

"*Do not hate except the Devil and thy—*"

I slapped my hand over his mouth. It was fine hearing it from Mama, but not from him. "He's a blockhead."

He pulled my hand away. "He's not. He works hard on his family's farm and has plans for his own." Philemon glanced sideways at me. "He thinks you're brave to take on the care of Mama and our home."

John *had* come to our door two months ago carrying a basket of dried meat and blackberries. He told me he was sorry for what had happened to Mama and that he would build her a table to put by her bedside. Then he'd walked away without asking for Philemon. I avoided the blackberries for fear of poison, and I would've thrown out the dried meat if the boys hadn't found it first.

What if I'd been wrong about him and I'd thrown out perfectly good berries?

"He must be playing a trick on me. When I find out what it is, I'll give him the beating he deserves."

"You shouldn't hit boys, just as they shouldn't hit you. Hasn't Mama taught you that yet in your lady lessons?"

I punched him hard in the arm. "She said nothing about hitting brothers."

We came into a familiar glen, where two wooden huts made of sticks and long strips of bark awaited us.

I used to spend many happy hours here imagining being one of Bunyan's Shining Ones guarding Christian on his journey. Other times, I was a troll who exacted extravagant gifts like wagonsful of sugared berries from the deer and bears who trespassed upon my kingdom. The hut was my fortress, and in it, I was the queen.

But today, as I stepped inside the quiet of the long-abandoned space, my mind didn't imagine those things as easily as it once had. The abandoned moss beds for squirrels and acorn-hat teacups—it was as if I'd intruded on a little girl's play. Had a few months brought so much change?

"Come, Ro. We can't linger."

We traveled a little while longer and came into town.

Phil walked me to the shop's doorstep. "I'll see Mr. Peters about his wool and then come back to find you. You'll be fine without me?"

"As fine as you."

He chuckled. "I daresay that's true." His eyes strayed behind me. A strange look fell over his face. He straightened his waistcoat and licked his fingers, sweeping back a strand of hair.

I gave him a disgusted look and shoved an elbow into his ribs.

"Stop acting like a popinjay. You're fine enough for anyone, least of all Mr. Peters."

"Hello, Philemon. Rosanna."

There stood Charity Taylor, the most beautiful girl in the county—a lady, even at fourteen years. No wonder Phil acted the fool, but I couldn't blame him. I myself felt all elbows and knees around her, though for different reasons than Phil.

It was one thing to want to be gentle and good but another to see it come so naturally to someone else—to know that no matter how hard I tried, I could never, ever be *that*. She was light and graceful, golden haired and soft-spoken. I didn't fault her for it. How could I blame the Creator for giving Charity an extra measure of what he'd denied me? It was no business of mine what he did with his gifts.

Phil smiled unsteadily. "Hello, Charity." His voice was high-pitched, his cheeks a splotchy pink. He cleared his throat.

I snared a laugh between my teeth. I didn't laugh at dear Charity. That would be reserved for my dolt of a brother on our way home. The only way I could enjoy this more was if John were here. He'd outpace Phil's mooncalf wooing by a mile. If Phil was half in love with her, John was full in love, as far as I could tell.

"Hello, Charity," I said, tucking one hand primly in the other. "Are you making preparations for Christmas?"

"I came for ribbon at Mr. Edwards', but he hasn't the right kind."

What made ribbon right or wrong, and could I learn to tell the difference? "I am to get oranges," I blurted out. "I've had one each year since I was eight."

My face heated. *I am to get oranges*, I'd said, like a good little child proud of being trusted with a task for the first time.

Phil wrinkled his nose at me. Now he would have something to make fun of me for on our way home.

But Charity only nodded sweetly. "Oranges are my favorite part of Christmas. Why, I count the days to my next orange as soon as the last is eaten!"

No one would believe that she had only one orange a year, not with her father's plantation rivaling Grenville's, but it was kind of her to try and ease my discomfort. "I must go." I fished behind me with my hand for the doorknob. "I hope you find your ribbon!" With one push, I was inside the store.

A portly man with jiggling cheeks popped up from behind a table. "Miss Rosanna! You've grown since the last time I saw you. And so pretty too. Almost as pretty as your dear mother." His jowls drooped. "Sad business, that."

"Do you have any oranges?"

"That I do." He bustled over to a small pyramid of the fruit and stacked nine in my basket. "One for each of you. Now, where's your brother? It's never been where I see one of you without the other."

"He's seeing Mr. Peters about some wool for Mama's pallet." Before I could lose courage, I blurted out my next question. "Do you have a pineapple I might look at?"

"A pineapple?" Mr. Edwards laughed. "If I did, I wouldn't be a shopkeeper. I would be hosting kings and queens for dinner."

"Oh." How would I ever see a pineapple if Mr. Edwards didn't sell them? "Freddie Grenville bragged of tasting one."

"He didn't get it from me. I wonder if he truly had one at all." He gave me a knowing look.

Freddie was known as a liar. It would be just like him to have bragged about something he never did.

A knock sounded at the door. A harried woman entered, holding a crying baby in one arm and an empty basket hooked around the other. Mr. Edwards went outside to speak with her, closing the door behind him.

Muffled, raised voices drifted from the back of the large room. Two boys were having a heated discussion about... hog brains?

I crept nearer to them and hid behind a cabinet filled with rolled pieces of printed cotton and spools of thread.

"If you didn't tell the schoolmaster about our fight, who did?" The snarling thick voice could only belong to one person:

Frederick Grenville. His father owned the largest parcel of land in the area, while Frederick owned the loyalty of every easily led boy in the county. Was it because he was rich, or was it because he was a bully that so many fell to his sway?

"Leave me be, ye mumper," said a voice in a heavy accent.

"Oh, mumper, is it? And from you, a dirty Scot!"

I smiled a little at the outrage in Frederick's voice. Only Philemon ever dared speak to him like that. If this Scottish boy were anything like my brother, Frederick was about to be delivered a comeuppance. I craned my neck around the side of the cabinet to see the boy facing off with Frederick.

His hair was the color of the sun as it began to set. It was cropped strangely, as if it had grown out after a scythe had been used to cut it. It wasn't long enough to be tied back and hung in his face. His clothes were neat, however, and his shoes smooth and well-made.

"Aye. Ye're a mumper and a puff guts," he said.

A thrill threaded through me at the boy's bravery. He was David, thin and scraggly, facing Frederick, a well-fed and brutish Goliath.

Two of Frederick's friends surrounded the boys, ready to defend their leader. "Give Callum a go, Freddie," one of them said.

Frederick shoved Callum's chest. "*You*'re the mumper."

Callum's eyes darkened. Hands fisted at his sides, he stepped forward.

"Well?" Frederick asked. "Are you going to let me trounce you like the last time?"

Callum's tight face looked like it held back a tempest of rage.

"What're you waiting for?" I stepped out from my hiding place. "Knock him down!"

His gaze flew to mine. His eyes flickered with surprise.

"Don't let him get away with it," I said a little louder, tossing Frederick a little sauce with my glare.

Frederick pointed a finger at me. "Shut your mouth, rag-a-ninny." He eyed me from neckline to hem. It took everything I had not to hide the burn mark with my hands. "I don't take orders from girls who get their clothes from the scrap barrel."

"Leave her be," Callum commanded Freddie. He turned his attention toward me again. "Go on, miss," he whispered. "I dinnae want ye to get hurt."

"Just give him one good knock," I said aloud, staring right at Frederick.

Frederick's face turned redder than I'd ever seen it. "You wait until you're alone, Rosanna Waters." He stared at me through slitted eyes like he could see through my dress to my shift. "You'll learn not to mess with me."

Heat swept down my body to my very toes. I crossed my chest with my arms. Boys shouldn't be staring at girls' chests. The look on his face made me sick to my stomach.

With a ferocious growl, the red-haired boy charged and knocked Frederick down. He drew back his arm. "It's time ye get what's comin' to ye!"

For one glorious tick of a clock's pendulum, Frederick blanched, perhaps for the first time in his life.

"Hit him!" I yelled.

Callum landed his blow.

Frederick's head hit the floor with a *crack*.

My new Scottish friend swung his thin arms, boxing Frederick's temples, bloodying his hands.

The two bystanders grappled Callum off Frederick and stretched his arms to the side. Frederick staggered to his feet.

There was no way Callum would come out on top with three boys against one.

"Mr. Edwards!" I screamed. "Mr. Edwards, come quick!"

Frederick grabbed a pouch that had fallen from the boy's pocket and dangled it between two fingers. "Ho! What's this?"

Callum thrashed about, but the others held him fast. "Give it back!"

"If you want it back, give me Obsidian."

"He's not mine tae give."

"Fine. Let me race him to the river and back, and I'll leave you with only one purple eye."

"Never!"

"Have it your way." Frederick threw the tartan bag to one of his friends. He didn't even bother to undo the simple knot but ripped open the fabric and dumped its contents on the ground. A cloud of dark flakes fluttered down, along with a flash of yellow.

With a strangled cry, Callum wrenched himself away from the boys and swept the flakes into a pile with his bleeding hands.

Frederick swiped his foot across the mound, mixing it with the dust and dirt on the wooden planks. A gold ring, the flash of yellow I'd seen, rolled across the wooden slats past my shoe. I quickly bent and stuffed it in my apron pocket.

Callum's face was a mottled red. "Ye had no call doin' that!" Tears glittered in his eyes.

Frederick and one of his friends pushed him back to the floor while the other grabbed a few tufts of Callum's hair and slammed his head against the boards.

"No!" I rushed forward, but a hand upon my shoulder stayed me.

Philemon pushed me behind him. "Step aside, Ro." He stalked forward, rolling up his sleeves as he went. "What's the trouble?"

At the sight of Philemon, one of Frederick's friends scrambled away.

"This has nothing to do with you," Frederick said, panting.

"I didn't ask you." He turned to Callum. "Are you alright?"

Frederick's chest heaved. "I said, this has nothing to do with you."

Philemon shrugged and planted his fist in Frederick's face before I could blink.

Frederick's head flew back, spraying blood on the bolts of cloth to his side. He yowled like a cat who'd gotten his tail caught in the thresher's teeth and bent over double.

Frederick's remaining friend backed away, his hands lifted.

Philemon motioned toward the outside of Mr. Edwards' store with his chin. "Off you go."

Frederick spat out a dark curse. "I'll tell my father. You'll be put in jail, and this dirty slave will have no one to do his fighting for him."

Mr. Edwards bustled up at last, red-cheeked and sweaty. "Leave, Master Grenville. I'll have no trouble in my shop."

Frederick held a crooked wrist under his nose, stemming the flow of blood. "See if I come back."

Mr. Edwards rolled his eyes and guided a sniping Frederick and his friends out the door. "I'd much prefer you didn't."

I turned to Philemon and grinned. "Well done, brother."

Philemon held a hand out to Callum and pulled him to his feet. "I'm Philemon. This little imp is my sister, Rosanna."

"I'm not little," I protested. Next to Philemon, anyone would be considered small.

"She didn't deny being an imp." Philemon patted my head like I was a baby.

I ducked away from his touch.

"What's your name?" Philemon asked the boy.

"Callum." The boy eyed Phil a little resentfully. "I might've had them if I'd had a wee bit more time."

"Aye, you would have. But I never say no to a good fight."

"They're scared of Phil," I said, a touch of pride in my voice. With only a moment's thought, I held my orange out to him. "I'm sorry I pushed you into fighting Freddie."

He glanced from the fruit to my face.

"It's an orange. The sweet is on the inside." I cut into the rind with my fingernail and peeled a sliver back, revealing a white-laced mound beneath. The glorious, bright scent made my mouth water. "See?" I took his hand and placed the orange in his palm. "It's yours for defending me."

His features reddened. "I need no prize for that."

"Why not? I've had an orange every Christmas. I don't mind giving mine up for one year."

Philemon slapped him on the back. "Take it, or she'll vex you until you do."

Callum closed his fingers around the fruit. "'Tis kind of ye, lass."

"*Rosanna*."

"Rosanna," he repeated, giving me a tentative smile.

"I've not seen you before," I said.

"I'm bound to Mr. Smythe."

"And your parents?"

"Dead."

That explained why his hair looked the way it did. My heart ached for the poor boy. First he loses his parents, and then he must be a servant for a stranger. "Why does Frederick hate you?"

Philemon shook his head at me. "Don't be nosy. Freddie dislikes everyone."

"But Frederick *hates* him."

"He wants my horse," Callum said.

Philemon scoffed. "He always wants what others have."

"He seems too angry for only wanting a horse," I said.

A little of the spark I'd first seen in Callum's eyes returned. "It's because I leave him in my dust with my horse every chance I get."

Philemon and I exchanged grins. Any boy who wasn't afraid to annoy Frederick was a friend of ours.

Callum looked again at the black flecks on the floor. For a moment he was quiet. "Thank ye for stepping in."

"Do you fish?" Philemon asked.

"Aye."

"If Smythe gives you leave tomorrow, will you meet me by the river just before the falls?"

I smiled encouragingly. "Philemon knows where to catch the fattest fish."

Callum twisted the torn pouch in his hands. "I will try."

"Well, goodbye, then." It was time I returned to Mama. "God be with ye."

"And with ye."

Philemon and I threaded our way back through Mr. Edwards' displays, but almost at the door, I remembered the ring.

When I turned around, Callum was standing there still, orange in hand, watching us.

I dug the ring out of my pocket and ran back to him. "It fell out of your sack." Even his smallest fingers were too large for the circle of gold. Had he stolen it? I held the ring closer to him. "Go on. It's yours, isn't it?"

Quick as the flick of a snake's tongue, he grabbed it and put it in his pocket. "I thank ye, miss."

"*Rosanna*."

He dipped his head and smiled. This time, his smile reached his eyes. "Rosanna."

EIGHT

CALLUM

I brushed Obsidian's coat with long, slow strokes over his flank while Mr. Smythe, occupied at the horse's hooves, worked with me in silent harmony.

I welcomed the quiet. It gave me time to think over the events of the morning. The boy, Philemon, had jumped to my defense though we'd never met, and then there was his sister. I shook my head and smiled. The bright-eyed magpie. She was small. Not small in pluck, though.

She'd hid *Màthair*'s ring from Frederick and returned it to me. She couldn't have known how precious a thing it was, my last piece of home.

It dangled now on a length of twine, safe against my chest. I wouldn't risk losing it again.

I had made two friends. But the knowledge couldn't dislodge the stone in my gut. I'd broken a promise to my father in fighting Frederick.

"How goes it at school now?" came Smythe's muffled voice from below the horse's haunches. "How do the boys treat you?"

My hand stilled. "Fine en—"

"Not *fine enaw*. Say, 'It went very well, thank you.'"

I opened my mouth to protest then closed it again. What

choice did I have but to do as he said? He was my master, and I was his servant. "It went verra weel, thank ye," I said woodenly.

"Hmm. We'll continue to work on that. Your clothes are dirty. You've had a tussle, haven't you?"

"Some boys dinnae like that I have Obsidian."

"Some boys, some boys," he muttered. He straightened and peered into my eyes. "Frederick, you mean."

"Smythe!" A man's strident tone traveled to us from outside the stables.

Smythe shoved me behind him. "Speak of the very Devil," he muttered. "Grenville."

My heart jumped.

Smythe stepped forward. Surely he wasn't going to greet Frederick's father in his current state. He appeared much the same as he had the day I'd met him, except this time, there was dirt on his breeches from where he'd rested Obsidian's hooves to clean them.

The doors swung open and clattered against the stable walls. "Smythe! I would have a word with you."

"I'm not at my leisure for callers, least of all you."

I shivered. Smythe's voice had turned to ice. I'd never heard Smythe sound so like the man I'd imagined him to be when I first saw him in his wig and silks.

Grenville stalked toward my master and eyed him from head to foot. "I never knew you for a shabbaroon. Fallen in with the pigs, have we?"

"What is it you've come for? I've pigs to attend to, as you say."

Grenville pointed a meaty finger in my direction, lace sleeves dripping from his wrist. "That servant of yours planted his fist in my son's face."

Dread made my knees weak. This wouldn't be the first time I had been caught out for trouble with Frederick. Would Smythe send me away?

"He did, did he?"

"It will take days before my son's fit to be seen."

"If my boy did as you say, it was only in his own defense. I have it on good authority that your son, without provocation, has laid his hands on Master Stewart, not once, but *twice*."

"Ho! Next you'll say your boy did nothing to deserve it. Your boy's a hellion. An uncivilized savage who'll murder you in your sleep. Get rid of him, Smythe. For your own sake and for the safety of everyone around you."

"You're the one who should worry, with a son like yours."

"Send him away or I'll—"

"I'm keeping the boy, and that's that. Teach your little whelp—for that's what he is, a sniveling whelp—that if he hits my—" He faltered for a moment and lowered his voice to a deadly calm. "If he hits Callum again, there'll be hell to pay."

The steel in Smythe's voice must have communicated his absolute intention to do as he said, for Grenville blinked and stepped back. The coward. He placed his hands behind his back and rocked on his toes. "Now, now, calm down. There's no need to come to blows." He gave a strained laugh. "Why, I've never seen you so red in the face. You're almost purple!"

"Do you have anything else to say before I throw you out?"

"Ah, well. As a matter of fact, I do. That horse of yours. Obsidian. I'm looking for the right kind of mount for Frederick. I'll give you double what he's worth."

My breathing hitched. Without forethought, I bunched Smythe's sleeve in my hand, pleading with him silently.

"He's not for sale," my master answered.

"Name your price."

"I wouldn't take less than all you own."

"How can you let one animal come between old friends?"

I rolled my eyes at the whine in Grenville's voice. I was fourteen years old and more of a man than he was.

"Friends? Nonsense. You and I have never been friends."

Grenville straightened his waistcoat. "I shall remember that the next time you need something."

Smythe stalked toward Grenville, leaving me behind. "I'm afraid I shall just have to take that risk." The backs of Grenville's knees bumped into the feeding trough behind him. "But since we are *friends*, you won't mind hearing a little advice."

"I wouldn't take advice from you if I were dying from the lack of it!"

"When a man says no, he's to be taken at his word. And when a son is a peevish brat, you don't give in to his every whim, or he will become a plague to all who know him. Neither do you debase yourself to please him. You tell him to go to Hades if he should ever needle you again for my horse."

Grenville was close to toppling into the feed. "How dare you presume to tell me how to raise my son!"

The two old fellows were close to blows.

I reached over the wall and pushed the latch to open Obsidian's stall door. A slap to Obsidian's hindquarters sent him crashing into the aisle.

Their shouts of surprise rang through the barn. A scuffle ensued as the two men subdued the stallion together.

Grenville's enormous gut heaved from the effort. His wig was lopsided, his coat soaked with sweat in the armpits. "This won't be the last you hear from me!"

"Yes, yes." Smythe ushered Grenville out, and the stable was filled with quiet once again.

Smythe came back and peered over the stall at me. "I know what you did."

"I dinnae want to be the cause of any more fights."

"You weren't the cause of the last two."

"Freddie's da thinks so."

Smythe settled Obsidian in his stall and called me into the middle of the stable. "Come. Sit."

I joined him on a bench.

"How do you find it here?"

I twisted my mouth to the side and stayed quiet.

"You will adjust soon enough."

A bird took flight from a beam and out of the stable, its flapping wings echoing in the rafters.

Smythe wiped at the dirt on his breeches, quiet for a long while. "I knew a young boy once. He was tall and had red hair just like you." He glanced at me. "His name was Harry. He was my son."

His son?

Then it came to me. The bedroom I slept in, the one that had been covered in sheets, had been the boy's. But where was he? If Smythe had a son, he hadn't visited in years.

"Seeing you in my stables that first time... I knew it wasn't Harry standing there, but you are so very much like—" He broke off, swallowing, a click sounding in his throat. "You reminded me of him."

I glanced at my new shoes, the ones that Smythe had given me, along with all my genteel clothes. He'd given me a finely furnished room and let me ride Obsidian. I'd stunk like shiprot when I'd arrived on his doorstep. A prisoner. A murderer. I was nothing like his son. "Dinnae ye care what I did? Before I came?"

Smythe eyed me. "Do you know, I never once wondered. You don't look capable of hurting even a beetle."

I scoffed. If only he knew.

"Alright, then. Tell me. What is it you've done?"

Now that it came to it, my stomach dropped like a stone. If I told him, he would know who I was for certain and might make me leave. I didn't want to leave. Even with Frederick and everything being strange and hard, Mr. Smythe's home was a rock in the middle of a choppy sea. This farm, with Obsidian and Bembe and even Mr. Smythe himself, were all I had, and I couldn't bear thinking of letting go.

He nudged his shoulder against mine. "Out with it. I promise I won't be angry."

I halfway believed him. For all his gruff, he'd defended me against Grenville. He might take pity on me now.

"I kilt a man," I blurted before I could think better of it.

I pressed my hands against my eyes, remembering.

Da lay in the brush, blood rattling in his throat.

The dragoon lifted his sword to finish him.

I raised my pike, hidden in the grass, and sank it into the man's belly. Felt the solidness of his flesh surrounding the pointed end.

The man's wide-eyed gaze flew to mine. The entire front of his uniform darkened around the wound. He fell back into the flowering gorse. *Help... me.*

I covered Da with my body. *No!*

The soldier pulled, but his hands only slid up the bloody stick. *Please*, he cried. *I've a daughter, just born. I'll not hurt you.*

Why hadn't I helped him?

Smythe remained quiet for a moment. "Well, that is serious indeed."

I trembled. He knew now, and no matter what happened, I didn't have to feel guilty for taking the privileges once afforded to a better young man than me.

He tapped my knee with one finger. "You have your story, and I have mine. We are not the things that happen to us."

I looked up at him in shock. This wasn't pity. This was mercy even greater than I gave myself. "But it didnae *happen* to me—I did it—*me*, and I cannae undo it."

"No, we cannot do that." Smythe stared into the rafters, seemingly lost in thought. For a moment, there was nothing but the sound of horses grinding their hay between their teeth and doves cooing in the trees outside the barn. "But what a sad thing it would be if our past was all we had to look forward to."

"But what if there is something bad in me that I cannae get out?"

"You asking the question tells me that isn't the case."

"A man is dead because of me." I squeezed my eyes shut to the flashing image of the man's stricken face. "I cannae change what I've done." I held up my hands and studied them. I still saw the blood, still felt that shuddering realization that I'd ended another's life.

"You were young. Surely, you had cause. What had the man done just before it happened?"

"He had stabbed my father. He was going to finish him. But the man... he begged me to help him. He had a bairn—" My vision blurred.

"Look at me, lad." Smythe spoke with a low, urgent voice.

My eyes flickered to his and to my lap again.

"You couldn't have helped that more that I can help going bald. I can see it now, you bravely standing up to the man who killed your father. Tell me, was there another person Frederick threatened today?"

I forgot about my tears and met his gaze. "Aye. A girl. Frederick said he would—" Heat rose to my cheeks. I wasn't sure I should repeat it. "I was so angry I couldnae keep from knocking him down."

"Ah ha! See?" He elbowed me, a spark of humor in his eyes. "Why, that pompous sprig would still be terrorizing her if you hadn't beat him soundly. What a state that boy must be in! Do you know, I would pay a pound to see it."

"But Da made me promise not to fight. Just before he died."

They were the last words he'd spoken. *Ye must run before they catch ye,* he said, fisting my tartan in his hand. *Swear tae me... swear ye'll never raise a hand against another soul. You run instead of fight. Hie away and hide. If they take ye, keep yer mouth shut and stay alive. Swear it!*

I had gone against my promise to my father and fought back against Frederick. Da's dying charge, and I had failed in keeping it. I'd stayed when I should have run. I'd fought when I should have pocketed my fists.

"I do not blame him. What would you do if you were close to death and your young son would soon be without you? It was his only hope of keeping you safe."

"But I dinnae want to go against my word!"

"I'm afraid you must."

My mouth dropped open. "It would dishonor him."

"It's not murder when another's life is on the line. It is selfless. It is brave. It cannot be wrong to defend the defenseless. It is why you protected your father. It is why you protected the girl. I, for one, am glad for it."

"But—"

"No, I won't hear it. You mustn't give up this part of you, promise or no." He poked me in the chest with a stubbed finger. "I forbid it. There's some purpose in you being fashioned this way, and I am anxious to see it come about."

"Why do ye care? I am just yer servant."

He opened his mouth to speak then closed it. "Well, I suppose I would like it if you were to feel at home here. To be happy, as I'd hoped Harry would be."

Though I wanted to stay, Virginia was not home. "I dinnae think I will ever be happy again."

"I have my regrets too. The older you get, the more you collect. It's better to come to terms with them early on." Smythe glanced at me. "Is there anything you can find to like about being here?"

"I like Obsidian."

Something about my answer must have pleased him, for his face relaxed into a smile. "Harry spent more time in here, with Samson—Obsidian's sire—than anywhere else. I suppose that's why I muck about in this place." His gaze traveled the beams and open space of the stables. "It is my chapel and the place where I feel closest to him." He abruptly stood and brushed the dirt off his hands, avoiding my eyes. "It's only that it makes me happy to have young life about the house again and to see Samson's son used by a boy who appreciates him. That is all." He gave me a stiff smile and turned to go. "I'll leave you to him."

After all he'd done for me—letting me sleep in his son's room, defending me to Grenville, helping me to understand myself better —I couldn't let him go with such a sad look on his face. "Will I still have tae do my Latin, then?" I blurted out.

He stopped and glanced back at me, a look of confusion on his face. "Your... Latin?"

This was my chance to start over. A chance to forget all that came before. "There was no Latin in Scotland. If I'm tae feel at home here..."

He looked down his nose at me. "You scamp. You'll do your Latin *and* Greek. And if you think you can forget about your Euclid, you're sorely mistaken. There'll be time enough for that if I've anything to say about it." Without another word, he walked toward the stable doors.

"I'll do Latin, so long as I ride Obsidian before and after," I called after him.

He stopped and turned around again, a sparkle in his eyes. "I know it will be a hardship to ride him, as much as it is to study Latin and Greek. So you will continue your rides, for his sake?"

A lightness came into my heart I hadn't felt for many months. "Aye. For Obsidian's sake."

NINE

ROSANNA

September 1751

With my apron gathered in my hands, I pulled the baking kettle off the trivet and lifted the lid. Steam—not smoke—billowed from the pot, stinging my cheeks. The tendrils of vapor carried the scent of sugared apples and unburnt crust.

I almost dropped the dish and danced around the table.

I had done it.

After all my tribulations, after all my brothers' mockery, I'd made four perfect tarts, bubbling and buttery golden.

I'd spent all morning working with the stiff flour paste and thinly sliced apples, burning the dough then starting all over again. No matter what I did, the juice spilled from the small confections, turning their bottoms into coal. I threw each failed attempt at the hogs, but the animals only sniffed the charred lumps and left them uneaten.

But these—no one would be unimpressed with these. Not even Philemon.

I pinched a piece of crust and popped it in my mouth.

The buttery sweet taste of sticky apples and baked dough went together like a hymn of praise and jubilation. Warmth spread from my chest to my toes. It had taken two years under Mama's tutelage to do it, but I hadn't given up.

Heaven be thanked, I'd finally become more lady than hoyden.

I wrapped the tarts carefully in linen, said goodbye to Mama, and set out toward the river to meet Phil, John, and Callum. She'd given me leave for a day of freedom. A happy whistle sprang to my lips. Wouldn't the boys be surprised at what I brought them!

An almost overwhelming urge to frolic down the path and leap like a deer came over me, but I forced it away. I wouldn't do anything to risk the tarts not arriving whole.

Halfway to the river, I skidded to a stop and whistled a chickadee's call.

An answering whistle filled the empty spaces of my forest trail.

"Where are you?" I yelled.

"Callum will fetch you," Philemon hollered back, his voice faint in the lush greenery.

Callum had better hurry. I was determined to catch as many fish as them, no matter how much earlier they'd gotten started. I settled in a dip of land to the side of the trail, soft with moss and soil, and sat back on my elbows. I drank deep the scent of moldering leaves and mushroom-frilled rotting stumps. I would build a home here if I were free. I would fill my cabin with wildflowers and honeycomb and let vines cover it with green.

"Hullo, Magpie!"

Callum's voice came from the rushes. He emerged, his breeches wet to his thighs.

I jumped to my feet, waving so heartily Mama would have chided me had she seen it. But wasn't it good that I had a friend? And he called me *Magpie*. From anyone else, it would've seemed a rebuke, but from Callum's mouth, it was the highest praise. He once told me that magpies were the smartest of all the creatures, and the most beautiful, too, with their shining black and purplish-blue feathers.

Callum smiled, his face ruddy with good health, his eyes light and happy. He hardly resembled the wretched boy we'd come across at Mr. Edwards' store two years before. "Have you waited long?" he asked.

"No. Have you caught many fish?"

"Not a one."

"Is the new place so bad, then?"

"Phil and John have had no trouble." He gave me a shy smile. "I was waiting for you."

My eyes widened. Even my own brother wouldn't have waited, and I wouldn't have blamed him. "But why?"

"So you might have a fair start with one of us."

Warmth spread through my chest, just as it did whenever he was near. Was there any boy as nice as Callum?

He nodded toward the bundle. "Are these the tarts your brother was telling me about?"

The warmth died. Phil was not one to hand out compliments. "What did he say, exactly?"

"Only that ye made some."

"*Only* that?"

He shrugged uncomfortably. "Phil says lots of things."

Anger kindled, destroying the last bits of my happiness. I knew by the look on Callum's face that Phil had mocked my efforts. How could Phil be so disloyal? To me, the only twin he would ever have? It was one thing to tease, another to do it behind my back. He knew how much I struggled with my duties.

Mama had told me it was the way of boys his age to be thoughtless. But no matter. He would get his comeuppance right here in these tarts.

Callum lifted my hand and held me steady through the marshy wetland to a line of cattails. He parted them and held them to the side for me to walk through.

The river was peaceful here.

The sun was just so that it sparkled off the water, with midges flashing in the golden light.

Philemon sat on a flat finger of crushed rock jutting into the shallows. He grinned. "The fish are hungry today. I've caught eight."

John nodded at me. "Hello, Rosanna."

I picked up my fishing line, nodding to John but ignoring Phil.

"Are you ready?" Callum asked. "One, two, three!"

We tossed our lines in the river and settled onto the riverbank.

The stillness in this part of the river suited me. I used to love the rapids, but I had my fill of loudness and chaos at home with my siblings.

My anger ebbed in the quiet. Phil was Phil. He would say anything for a laugh, even if I were the target. Even if it was about my tarts, which he would soon enjoy.

Water lapped on the shore and trickled over a messy line of stick and bark. On the other side of the river were willow trees gnawed at the base, felled by beavers building their dams. I'd always loved the industrious creatures. If I stayed still, they might appear, and I could watch their unceasing labor.

Exactly as I'd hoped, a mother beaver pushed her kit into the water a few minutes later. The baby floundered a little before righting itself. The older beaver came to its side and guided its clumsy attempts at swimming. "I wish I was a beaver. Wouldn't it be interesting to live in a home beneath the water?"

"Why ever would you want to do that?" John exclaimed.

"Why shouldn't she?" Callum asked.

"Because... because it's a childish thing to do!" John said. "She's almost sixteen. Girls are married younger than she."

My hackles raised at the way he said *she*, as if I wasn't worthy of being referred to by name.

"You have no spirit, John Farrow!" I said.

"No spirit!" Phil turned to John. "Recite that poem we found in that book. The one you said reminded you of her."

When had they started reading poetry?

"Don't be mean, Phil," John said.

John was telling *Phil* not to be mean? Now I had to hear it. "What does it say?"

Phil waggled his eyebrows. *"If hairs be wires, black wires grow on her head."*

My jaw dropped. "Wires!"

Phil doubled over in laughter. *"And in some perfumes is there more delight than in the breath that from my mistress reeks."*

"I was only jesting, Rosanna," John said, in the most regretful voice I'd heard him utter.

I grabbed a handful of worms to put down both their shirts.

John swerved away from reach. "How about the poem Callum liked? It was worse."

Callum sucked in a breath. "Please don't."

Worms forgotten, I turned my full attention on Callum. Why was his face so white?

Phil jumped to his feet and climbed atop a rock. *"Come live with me and be my love, and we will all the pleasures prove."* His voice boomed across the water.

John and Phil bent double, laughing riotously.

I couldn't laugh. Not when my heart stirred so.

Come live with me and be my love.

Imagine someone loving you so much he wanted you to live with him and be loved by him forever.

Callum jumped up and pushed Phil from the rock, falling with him in the water. Soon they were laughing and splashing each other. They came out of the water soaked but grinning.

Boys ended their fights so easily. Perhaps if it were acceptable for girls to tussle, I'd be rid of my frustrations more easily.

Callum flopped on the riverbank, his skin glistening with beads of water. "I once wished to be a selkie, Rosanna."

I laughed. "What?" Seals in water, people on land, selkies moved between two worlds when they chose.

"One time, I swam as far as I could into the sea hoping to catch one." He picked up a stone and threw it across the river. "Wanting to be a selkie is not so different than wanting to be a beaver, I should think." A smile spread across his face.

He was trying to make me feel better about earlier. Grinning, I leaned over and gave him a big hug. When I pulled away, his face was almost as red as his hair.

"The both of you are addled," John said.

Phil grunted his assent. "I'm hungry. Where are the tarts, Rosie? Or was the last batch thrown to the hogs as well?"

I stifled a grin. His shock would be all the greater for not anticipating what was to come, and so would my enjoyment in proving him wrong. I opened the linen bundle, handing a still-warm tart to Phil and Callum, then John, though he didn't deserve it.

Phil raised it to his nose and sniffed. "It smells nice enough." He took a small nibble. His eyebrows rose. "Blow me over, these are as good as Mother's!"

My insides danced a high-legged jig. Such high praise, and from Phil. "They are?"

"Better, even." He jutted a thumb at Callum. "He said they'd be good."

I gaped. "You did?"

Callum's cheeks turned a ruddy hue. "You don't like to give up on things."

My insides uncurled like a fern in the sun. He was so sure of me that he went against Philemon to defend me. "Thank you," I whispered.

Callum grinned and winked at me.

My heart caught in my chest for one heady moment. He had such nice, white teeth. Most of the other boys' teeth were stained with tobacco. "Did you really want to be a selkie?"

"Aye. To be both human and seal, to live on both land and in sea? I could be with my family in the day and swim the darkness of the waves at night."

It was the first time he'd ever said anything of his home. I scooted to the river's edge and stuck my feet in the water lapping the sandbar. "What's Scotland like?"

"It's different than here."

"How?"

He eyed the tall, marshy grass and towering pines beyond the river. "The hills there are bare. The wind blows in from the sea and skelps over the hills till they're nothing but scrub an' stone." He looked in the distance as if he were back in his homeland noting every blade of grass, every bend and wind of the hills. "Everything drips with *haar*, and I'm cold, even in summer."

"What is *haar*?"

"A mist as thick as stew."

I shivered, imagining him in such a wild, wind-whipped place. "Do you want to go back?"

He gave me a smile that barely touched his eyes and shrugged. "How's your mother?"

"Father built her a chair with a long seat she can rest her leg upon. She will sit outside at times." I pulled my knees to my chest and rested my chin upon them. "Her half-leg plagues her. It itches, and she can't reach to scratch it without pain." I shuddered, remembering the taut skin turning purple when she leaned forward to scratch it.

"I'd rather put up with Freddie than with that."

I tilted my head and studied him. There was something in the way he'd said it that comforted me more than anything else I'd heard on the matter of my mother. He didn't recoil or brush off the hardest part of my life with honeyed words. He listened to me, no matter how uncomfortable the details must make him feel. I wanted to be a friend like that to him. "Callum, do you miss your—"

"Shhh. You'll scare the fish away," John said, eyeing the two of us.

I turned my chin back to my forearms, but I could feel Callum studying me, long after I'd looked away.

One week later, I stuck my paddle in a kettle of boiling, cloudy water and gave the clothes a vigorous swirl. My arms were stronger than they'd been two years ago when Mama first made me do laundry. Now, I could go for long minutes before I had to take a break.

"Arse! Callum is here."

My heart tumbled, much as it had when Callum had winked at me a few days before. I pretended disinterest and continued stirring the clothes. "Oh? Did you tell him Phil is away?"

"He asked for *you*." Charlotte tugged my skirt and pulled me toward the house.

I brought my hand to my wind-mussed hair and attempted to smooth it.

He stood at our barn, watching us approach.

"Hello, Callum." It was the first time I'd seen him since the tarts—since he'd waited for me to start fishing and defended me to Phil and John. He had always been kind to me. Why, then, did this time feel so different?

His gaze traveled to my hair.

"My cap fell off."

"Why does a girl wear one at all? Don't you like the sun and air on your head?"

"Of course, but 'a lady with wandering or indisposed hair shall not be thought as comely or fair.'" I dropped into an exaggerated curtsey.

Callum laughed heartily. "Where did you hear such blether?"

"It isn't *blether*. I'm to learn to become a lady, and Mama's books are teaching me how."

"You shouldn't hide hair as bonnie as yours, Magpie."

My mouth went dry. No one called me *or* my hair pretty. Except for Mama, but she called me pretty even when my face had its monthly spots, so she was not to be trusted in this matter.

Charlotte, who'd been dancing and twirling about holding my hand, stopped and stared at Callum. "Why don't *you* wear a cap? Your hair isn't bonnie."

"Charlotte!" I jerked her hand. Callum's hair was long enough to be tied back, though some of it came into his eyes and he had to brush it away. "You shouldn't tell a person something like that."

Charlotte's chin trembled. "But his hair is red."

Callum and I exchanged confused glances.

He bent and looked her in the eye. The smile on his face was gentle. "Do you know what *bonnie* means, lass?"

She didn't shrink back from him but put her finger in her mouth and twisted from side to side, letting her skirts swing this way and that. "Black?"

"It means *beautiful*. Like your sister and her hair." A burning thrill raced through my heart. He gave one of her curls a gentle pull. "Like you."

She tilted her head to look at me. "Arse, my hair is bonnie too."

Callum's mouth trembled with a suppressed grin. "Why do you call your sister such things?"

He'd make no inroads there. My nickname had stuck like corn-cake in an ungreased pan. "Did you come for Phil?"

He stood and pulled from his back pocket a long, carved stick with two curved prongs at the end. "This is for your mother."

"What is it?"

"A scratching stick. For her leg."

"You remembered?" It had only been one comment in passing telling him about Mama's trouble with her stump.

He smiled shyly at me. "Aye."

I took his hand and tugged him forward. "Then you must give it to her yourself."

Philemon's voice carried across the field. "Hullo!"

Callum dropped his hand from mine. "There's your brother now. And John."

Sure enough, the two materialized through the trees, trudging through the tall grass toward us. Philemon raised his hand in greeting. "We came to get rope—the storms last night felled a tree, and it blocks our path. You can help, Callum. And then we will go hunting."

"Can I go?" Charlotte asked.

"You must stay with Rosanna," John said, ruffling her hair.

Charlotte burst into tears.

Ignoring her, I gently took the stick from Callum's hand. "Thank you for making this."

John narrowed his eyes at Callum and me. But what reason had he to be disturbed? He now had more help to move the tree, and then he would run after deer in the woods, feeling the earth beneath his feet. He was free to go, while I would stay, laboring over our sopping, foul laundry.

"Come, John, Callum," Philemon said.

"Goodbye, Rosanna." Callum turned to go.

My hand reached toward him. I wanted him to stay, but what reason could I give that wouldn't make Phil and John look at me askance?

John lingered. "Rosanna?"

"Yes?"

"Would you like some of my rabbits if I catch any?"

I nodded, my throat too tight to speak.

He grinned. "Alright, then. Goodbye." He ran to catch up with the other two.

I tugged Charlotte's hand. "The washing waits."

She sniffed. "But I want to go with them."

"So do I, sweetling." Now it was she who had to be dragged to work at the kettles, and me who had to strong-arm the help.

I pulled, and Charlotte's reluctant feet plodded just a step behind me. It was good Mama was in the house and couldn't hear her whining. She'd have chastised us both—Charlotte for her rebellion and me for allowing it.

But I hadn't the heart to stop Charlotte. What could I say that would comfort her? That when she was older, she could do as she liked? Not even I had that hope.

TEN
ROSANNA

January 1754

My foot rocked the treadle of our spinning wheel, my fingers deftly adding puffs of wool to the string feeding the spindle. Mindless, numbing work. But it was work that must be done. My brothers made holes in their socks quicker than Mama and I could darn them.

More than four years had passed since the accident. I was a woman skilled in all manner of domestic duties and as educated as Mama could hope me to be, with penmanship as fine as hers and the Bible read front to back two-and-a-half times.

She slept peacefully just two feet away, likely lulled by the sound of the *ft-ft-ft* of the wheel spinning through the wobbling support arms.

In our small cabin, the air was close. The smell of bacon grease lingered, caught in my tight curls and coating the insides of my nostrils.

My limbs ached to move, to run barefoot over the frost-tipped blades of grass until I collapsed to the ground in burning, joyous exhaustion. It had been weeks since I'd had time for it. Mama had gotten sick, her lungs congested with fluid. I'd taken on new duties: thumping her back to loosen the phlegm and brewing horehound tea so she could breathe the steam.

I closed my eyes. My body swayed back and forth with the motion of the treadle.

I was on a rocking ship—no, I was a ship captain bringing molasses from the West Indies. There was a monkey perched on my shoulder and a sugar pouch tied at my waist, from which I took a nip. I had a beard to my belly and a glass eye, the old one having been pecked out by a bird.

"Rosanna."

I startled and swung around, one hand to my chest.

Philemon put a finger to his lips and jerked his head, directing me outside.

I stopped spinning and followed.

My body melted in a sigh and leaned against our cabin. The cold, clean mist chilled my cheeks and hands. I scraped my cap from my head and scrubbed my fingers over my scalp. "I would have gone mad if I'd stayed in there another moment."

Philemon dismissed my words with a disinterested grunt. "I need to tell you something." His jaw had a stubborn set, his eyes half-lidded as if he expected a challenge.

It had come.

The moment I'd been dreading for years. I knew it in my bones like I knew my brother. *Because* I knew my brother. He'd been restless for months. For a year, I'd caught him staring off toward the road leading away from our property more times than I could count.

"Governor Dinwiddie's drumming up a regiment to protect Virginia's claim to the Ohio Valley. Those who join will be rewarded with a parcel of land once it's all settled."

The Ohio Valley? The French and their native allies had been trying to drive English traders out and were building forts to claim it for France alone. Why would a country build forts if they didn't expect a fight? And if Dinwiddie was sending a regiment, that's exactly what he was asking too. My heart pounded so hard my head grew fuzzy and my fingers numb. It was as if I were back at the cliff watching Mama go over, powerless to stop it. "What has that to do with you?"

"I've joined up, Rosie. I'm eighteen. It's a way to get land and a farm of my own."

"But what about Mama and Father? And the little ones? You can't leave me to do it on my own." I said that as if he spent much of his time helping me.

"They're not so little anymore. Besides, they have you. I'm sixes and sevens with them, anyway. Father has all the help he needs with the boys. I want to be *doing*, Rosie."

A flash of anger swept away my grief. I wanted to be doing too. "When?"

He hesitated. "Tomorrow."

"Tomorrow!"

"It's not as if I *want* to leave."

Oh yes, he did. "But how will I be happy if you are gone?"

He turned his eyes to pleading. "This is my chance, Rosanna."

Rosanna, as if I weren't his Rosie anymore. He was distancing himself already.

I tore away from him and ran through the plowed field all the way to the road. I rounded the bend and caught sight of Callum, walking straight toward me. Of course. He always seemed to come around after Philemon riled me. I wouldn't be surprised if Philemon had prepared him ahead of time to coax me out of my dark humor.

I stopped in front of him, my chest heaving gulps of air. "Did you know?"

His gaze flitted away from mine. "Aye."

"Are you going with him?"

"The law would be after me if I did."

I'd almost forgotten about his indentureship with all the time he spent with Phil and me. Smythe was a generous master. I sighed and plunked myself on a large rock by the side of the road. "*Would* you go with him? If you could, that is."

He joined me on the rock, settling back on his hands. "I don't want to be a soldier."

"What *would* you do, then? Once your indentureship is over and if you could choose anything you like."

The silence between us stretched until even the birds seemed to stop their song and listen.

I turned and gave him a questioning look. "Callum?"

He eyed the field across from us. "There are things I'd like to do, but I haven't the means to do them. I don't know if I'll ever have the means."

How well I understood that.

"What would *you* do if you could do anything you wished?" he asked.

"Anything?" I thought back to my earlier imaginings. "Captain a ship across the ocean to places I've never seen. Wear breeches and bring back a year's worth of fruit for Mama to eat."

He tore his gaze from the field and stared at me, his mouth open and eyes wide. "Truly?"

I laughed and swatted his arm. "Imagine me, commanding a crew of men two heads taller. I can't even command my siblings."

His eyes twinkled. "Och, don't ye doubt it, lassie. Yer sailors would never think of crossing ye."

I returned his grin, feeling warm all over at the return of his thick brogue. I didn't really want to be a captain, but that he believed I *could* was enough.

"What an adventure that would be, captaining a ship," he said, looking off into the distance again.

"I wouldn't mind a *little* adventure before I die." Would he laugh at what I said next? I eyed him carefully. "I want to do something good. Something that matters."

He gently bumped his shoulder against mine. "You take good care of your mother and brothers and sisters. Isn't that worthwhile?"

"There's nothing special in that."

"How about being nice to me when I was new here? It was special to me."

"You're the nicest boy I know, even nicer than Phil. It's not hard to be kind to you."

I leaned against his shoulder, savoring the feel of his solidness. I could always count on him to be there for me. A strange thought came to me then, that the Callum I knew was going away too. Mr. Smythe had done his best to train away Callum's brogue. It had left only a lilt, only discernible with certain words. I loved it when he slipped back into it. It reminded me of when we were younger.

He'd grown taller, too, but instead of the beanpole he'd resembled four years before, he had become a man, his chest filling his waistcoat without much space to spare. His forearms were knotted with muscles and covered with wiry hair, shimmering in the sun like golden wheat. I had the strangest urge to smooth it with my hand. The boy I'd known was becoming someone altogether different, and it made me inexplicably sad.

Everything was changing.

Callum was different.

Phil would leave me.

And we would never be close again, not like now.

"You will always be close to him, you know, even if he goes away for a little while."

Did he always know what I was thinking?

"At least *you* will not leave me." On impulse, I took his hand and squeezed it. "I won't feel so abandoned with you by my side. Another brother, more faithful than my twin," I said, placing my head upon his shoulder.

He slipped his hand from mine and stood abruptly.

I rose and tickled my fingers at his hard middle in an attempt to wipe that cloudy look from his face. "What's wrong?"

Quicker than the flick of a frog's tongue, he grabbed my hand with his own and held it away from him, his face a mask.

Warmth rushed to my cheeks. "What?"

"You shouldn't touch me like that."

Cheeks flaming, I yanked my hand away. "Like what?"

"It's not for me to teach you."

"You can't know much more than me. I'm your age."

His lips became a thin line. He looked at me, then, eyes simmering. "I'm almost a man. You're almost a woman."

"What has that to do with anything?"

He scrubbed a hand through his hair. "You can't know what it's like, not being able to... to never—" He cut himself off, tensing his jaw.

I barely breathed. I'd always depended on Callum to be placid and wise when I was not, quiet and gentle when I was in a passion. I'd never seen him like this before.

"Callum, I'm sorry. I understand what it's like, to have your future decided for you. But think—you have less than three years left of your servitude. You can do what you like then."

"How? I have no land, no money, no future but hired work for the rest of my days." His look was of pure fire that I felt deep in my belly. "I could bear all that if I were content to be alone."

My heart caught in my chest. "What do you mean?"

"Rosanna! Callum!" My brother's voice carried up the road.

Drat that Philemon. I kept my eyes on Callum. In my urgency, I grabbed his forearm. "Go on."

He stared at my hand, his face so like it had been when his bundle had been ripped open and its contents scattered across Mr. Edwards' floor.

Philemon came upon us, a grin on his face. "There you are. I thought I might have to chase you all the way to England."

I pulled my hand away and folded my arms in front of me. "Well? You found me. What is it you want?"

Philemon jerked a thumb at me and glanced at Callum. "There's no talking sense to her when she's mad. Why even try?"

I'd put slugs in his gruel tonight. "I'm going back home."

"Don't be angry with me, Ro."

"I'm not *angry*." With a strangled cry, I threw my arms around him and squeezed as hard as I could. "Is there nothing I can do to make you stay?" I whispered into his ear.

"What would you want me to say if you were me?"

I closed my eyes from the pain of it. "That if you have the chance to live as you like, you should take it."

"Thank you," he whispered back and stepped away. "Now, I have more news I would have told you if you hadn't run away," Philemon said. "Of Frederick."

"He's not joining the regiment, is he?" I asked.

"And have to do a day's work?" Philemon shook his head. "Not likely. He's been sent away."

This was news indeed. "Sent away? Where?"

"Nobody knows. He was caught..." Philemon lowered his voice. "He... was insincere with Charity."

Callum blanched. "How do you know this?"

"Everyone in town knows of it. She has been sent away until the scandal dies down."

I glanced between the boys. "But insincere? He's insincere with everyone."

"Rosie, he dallied with her as Shechem with Dinah," Philemon said.

"*Oh*," I breathed out. Mama had forgotten about that story when she'd given the Bible to me to read in full. When I'd asked her why Shechem was in trouble for lying down with Dinah and what was so bad about *lying down* with someone, she gave me an answer that made me wish I was young enough to be lied to, just as she'd lied to Charlotte about chickens growing on bushes.

A man would have to be the cruelest blackguard in the world to harm Charity. She was gentle as a doe, a delicate and soft-spoken creature I secretly envied. When Mama talked with me of what it meant to be a lady, I knew it had been Charity she pictured, Charity she used as her aim. I was sure the girl was as ladylike in her thoughts and feelings as she was in her dress and manners. She was agreeable and quiet, with never an ill word to anyone, kind and even-tempered, even to those who were cruel.

A sickening thought came to me. Perhaps that was how Frederick had been able to take advantage of her. Perhaps it was better in this one instance that Charity should take after *me*. If Frederick had attempted with me what he did with Charity, I would have kicked him between his legs and gouged his eyes out with my thumbs.

"He's lucky he wasn't put in the stocks. Or worse," Philemon said. He was quiet for another moment, studying me with a worried look in his eyes. "I feel better leaving with John and Callum to look after you while I'm gone."

"I don't need looking after. Frederick's gone."

He crossed his arms. "You would do well to marry John, you know."

"Marry John?" I burst out laughing and glanced at Callum, wrinkling my nose as if I smelled a rotted egg.

He appeared just as sickened by the thought as I was.

"I am the last person John would think of for a wife."

"You don't know him as I do."

"We've been at loggerheads our whole lives. Why would I want to marry someone who doesn't like me? Besides, I can't marry. Mama needs me." I didn't *want* to marry. I would have babies, which I'd already sworn never to do, and would carry the weight of their upbringing when I couldn't even raise my siblings well.

"Father and Mother won't always be around, and then what will you do? I can't say where I'll be. John can take care of you."

I raised my hands in frustration. "Callum, what say you of my addlepated brother's idea?"

Callum was quiet, his eyes serious and sad.

"What is it?"

"Everything is changing."

Philemon draped his arms around our shoulders and tugged us close. "Don't worry. I will write you both, and when I come home, it will be just as before."

I was too sick-hearted to respond.

He gave us a jiggle. "It won't take long for the regiment to settle things. You'll see."

I wouldn't hold him to his promise. If the regiment settled things, the Ohio Valley would come firmly under Virginia's control, and if that happened, Phil would get his piece of land and leave me for good.

ELEVEN
CALLUM

I sat on a stool in the kitchen, stuffing the last bit of bread and raspberry jam in my mouth and washing it down with a cup of fresh milk. It had been one month since Philemon had left, and though I missed my friend, I consoled myself with the bits of news I heard from Rosanna. Today, Bembe and I were to rebuild a wood chimney at the servants' quarters, lining it with clay—the servants' quarters Mr. Smythe had threatened to keep me in on my first day. I smiled a little. How I'd shivered and shook at Smythe's gruffness. If only I'd known then what I knew now. I wish I could go back to the young boy in the stables and tell him that, one day, that mean old man would become a friend.

Bembe poked his head into the room. "You ready, boy?"

I brushed the crumbs off my lap and stood. "Mrs. Heaney has our pails ready," I said, bending to pull a pant leg that had been caught around my calf. "I got her to give us two tarts each."

We walked together down a path dappled with shadows cast by the morning sunshine. I breathed deeply of the crisp air, savoring the scent of dew-soaked cedar and leaves turning to soil under melting ice. When had this land begun to fit like broken-in leather breeches?

Soon, we were slinging clay and singing the old Scottish song

I'd taught him, the one my mother used to sing while she worked. It wasn't really something a man sang, but it made me happy to think of her, singing and smiling, healthy and strong.

When it was done, I walked back to the main house, parting with Bembe at his cabin.

I wouldn't mind living in the servants' quarters if they were like Bembe's home. His house was well-made and filled with all the comforts a man could want—he had two fireplaces, one for cooking and a smaller one in his sitting room with a painted fireboard, quarter-sawn pine floorboards, a stuffed chair with a stool, and a bed covered with an indigo-printed cotton quilt. A painting hung over the mantel of a ship floating in a placid Jamaican bay. The man who'd brought it to him, a friend of Bembe's, had shown great curiosity in me, but I'd been too shy and slipped away after his arrival.

I entered the main house. Just as I put my foot on the first step, an angry voice drifted from the direction of Smythe's study. Grenville's, if I wasn't mistaken.

My master had always been able to keep Grenville in check, but Smythe had been tired of late and unsteady on his feet, a shadow of the man of action I'd first met. The thought of him facing Grenville alone drove me toward the study. The length and muscle I'd gained over the past few years might be a welcome addition to the effort. I put my hand on the knob and peeked into the cracked doorway.

Smythe leaned over his desk, his fingers spread upon its surface, his face a bright red. "The matter is closed. The horse is meant for Callum. Those papers I have just signed"—Smythe pointed to a neat stack of documents—"will make him my heir and the inheritor of all I have."

My hearing blunted. The corridor spun. I almost forgot to breathe. Me, his heir? I wasn't even a distant nephew. I was a former prisoner. His indentured servant.

Grenville's mouth flopped like that of a beached fish. "You've lost your senses!" His outrage echoed in the high-ceilinged room.

"You have been on a campaign to buy my land to expand your holdings for years. Years!" Smythe exclaimed. "What's worse, you have used my childless state—the loss of my son—to manipulate me into handing it over to you, piece by piece, horse by horse. No longer, I tell you."

"So you'll hand it over to a... a convicted criminal instead? Have you gone mad?"

"Oh, I'm quite sane, I assure you. But you won't have to worry about my handing property to a criminal. I'll be giving it to my son."

The bread and jam settled like a cannonball in my stomach. I was going to be sick.

"What are you on about? Your son is dead."

"Callum will become my heir *and* my son... by virtue of adoption."

I staggered back from the door. I would be Smythe's heir, his son in all ways except blood?

I had become fond of Smythe. We had worked together to ease my way here. He'd cajoled me into memorizing Latin declensions and Greek aphorisms, though Euclid had been a lost cause. Smythe met me every day after school, no matter how trying the previous day's lessons had been.

When I could concentrate no longer, he walked with me on the old Indian paths deep in the forest. *A young man cannot be expected to be still* all *the time,* he said. The vigor of action oiled my tongue. I talked of school, and after some months of our walks, I opened up to him about my strife with Frederick. I never spoke of my previous home, except to tell him of my first horse and my rides through the wet Scottish sand by the sea caves.

Smythe had many things to say in return—of how a man should treat others and what it meant to be a friend. He was honest, brutally so, forcing me to press on when I wished to sit and wallow. On the occasions that I indulged in self-pity and reported ill treatment, he would tell me that any man who chose to stay in the mire others have tossed him into has only to blame himself. And so I pulled myself out, because I respected him.

We'd grown comfortable with one another, but to be this great man's son...!

Grenville stormed out of the library. I flew into the room across the corridor and shut myself within. His steps pounded away and out of the house.

My door swung open in the next instant.

Smythe looked over his spectacles at me, a glimmer of amusement in his eyes. "Shall I install a secret passageway to my library with a listening hole?"

It was as if someone set a match to my insides, and I burned from the inside out. "That *would* make it easier."

"I should learn to shut my doors."

"How would I learn what was going on if you did?"

"Hmm. I take your meaning."

"Is what you said true, or were you only trying to get a rise out of him?"

"I had wished to discuss this with you beforehand, but that Grenville..." He shook his head. "He's maddening. I couldn't keep from making the point."

"So it isn't true?"

"Sit."

I obediently lowered myself into one of the chairs by the fire.

He sat in the one across from me and straightened his waistcoat. "Well, then." Smythe's gaze traveled to the mantelpiece behind me and then to the room's large paintings and the window cradled between them. "I love this house. I came to Virginia seeking something different than what I had in England. My father was a vicar, and everything was restricted and quiet. I wanted wildness. Savagery." He watched me carefully. "A place where I belonged."

I glanced away, uncomfortable.

"I arrived and made my fortune, as you see, and tempered my want for adventure in my old age." The fire cast shadows into the crags of his face and the darkness under his eyes. "Difficulties will do that to a man. The only regret is that when I'm gone, there is no one who will care for this land like I do. I don't want it parceled out to another who desires it only for what it gives to his own holdings. Or for the increased influence it will give him or his son."

I could see it—Frederick walking about this home and the stables like a grand prince. Not to mention what he'd do with Obsidian if he owned him. I'd seen enough lash marks on his own horse to be afraid of that.

Smythe leaned forward, his eyes gleaming. "I began to think, what if *you* were that person? You love the horses more than I do. Think—fortune enough for whatever else you want to do. A wife and family of your own, perhaps. What do you think of that?"

The blood rushed to my cheeks like it had when Rosanna's hand tickled my side. "I—I had hoped *one* day..." I had never allowed myself to even think of it, though I couldn't stop the fevered dreams that came in the night. Did I dare hope I could become the sort of man Rosanna would want to marry? I could have a family. With her. Philemon would be my brother. Charlotte and Pearl, my little sisters.

"Already someone in mind, is there?" Smythe asked, a jovial glint in his eyes.

I ground my mouth shut.

He sobered and patted my hand. "Don't mind my teasing. I'm just an old man who forgets sometimes what it is to be young. Wait here." He left the room and came back bearing a sheaf of papers. "In this stack is a signed document releasing you from your indentureship. And this—" Here he removed a lone sheet from the bottom of the stack. "This is the document making you my heir. It only awaits my signature, but I won't tie you to a fate you'll despise. As for what happens next, that is up to you, my boy."

I could hardly understand what he was saying. "Are you sending me away if I don't agree to the adoption?"

"Not at all! I've set aside money if you seek to find your own way. I give it to you with goodwill and my dearest hopes for success in your new life. But if you find that this home has been a place of peace, of solace, like it's been for me... if you think you might be happy here, I would very much like—" He paused for a moment and collected himself. "What I mean to say is, I know you already have a father. I don't presume to—if you might think of me as—" He broke off again with a self-deprecating laugh. "I've made quite a muddle of this, haven't I?" He looked at me again, his eyes shining with affection. "You're a dear boy, Callum, and I've so enjoyed our time together. I wish you to stay. For as long as you like."

His words seeped into my heart and sluiced through me like rain on parched ground. I was loved. I belonged, orphaned and torn from everything I'd ever known, but no longer. Perhaps everything Smythe had done for me over the past four years had been his attempt to show me just that. My feelings pushed their way into my heart, my throat, my eyes. If I didn't leave, I would embarrass us both. I surged to my feet. "I... It is that... May we finish this tomorrow?"

Smythe blinked. "Oh. Of course, my boy. Of course. There is no hurry."

And with that, I fled the room.

TWELVE
CALLUM

With each step I took, my conscience commanded that I return and tell Smythe all that he'd meant to me. Once settled in my room, I left it almost twice to go back to the study, but the thought of not having the words—the right words that would express my heart in full—kept me from leaving.

I lay on my bed, huddled in darkness and unable to sleep for hours.

Sometime in the night, Smythe's steps thumped on the stairs. His door closed softly, and it was then that I knew I'd lost my chance to tell him what I ought. Tomorrow, I decided. Tomorrow, I'd tell him that I'd accept his offer and that I was thankful for his kindness toward me. At the very least, that. I went over the words again and again in my head so I would remember them in the morning.

I drifted into fitful dreams at last.

Smythe and I roamed the trail following the river. The sun beat upon our backs and gleamed over the rolling water. He was quiet, waiting. But when I opened my mouth to speak, only my breath escaped. Then Da visited, his shirt gleaming white and soaked with blood. He leaned over me. *Run, lad!*

When I woke, tobacco smoke clung to the inside of my nostrils and wisps of gray peeped through the covered windowpanes.

The wood thrush began its warble. I would wait no longer.

I dressed carefully, for I wouldn't dishonor him by looking a sloven. From this day forward, I would prove myself worthy of Smythe taking me on as his own.

A short walk down the hall, and I stood at his door, hand raised to knock.

"Excuse me, young Stewart."

I jumped back. "Mrs. Heaney!"

Our housekeeper stood behind me with a silver tray in her hands, motioning to the door with her chin. "Open the door, dear heart. He's not come down for breakfast."

My stomach sank. Smythe was hiding away, embarrassed by my fumbling the night before. It was time I put an end to this misunderstanding. I leaned past Mrs. Heaney and opened the door.

The room was dark and still.

Mrs. Heaney clucked and retreated into the hallway. "Still sleeping," she whispered. "Poor man. His heart must be troubling him again."

Again? Something unspeakable prowled the edges of my mind.

"Come along. Let him rest," she said.

I pushed past her and stepped into the stale, thick air.

He lay under his covers, sleeping, just as Mrs. Heaney said.

"Mr. Smythe?" My voice echoed in the cavernous space.

The dark outline of his figure under the blanket didn't move.

I threw open the drapes at the window. Light flooded the room.

Mr. Smythe didn't flinch or thunder at me for disturbing him.

On shaking legs, I stepped closer to the bed.

Smythe stared up at me unseeing, his hands clasped over his stomach, gray, like they belonged to a marble statue.

"God have mercy!" Mrs. Heaney cried.

The room whirled. I gripped the curtains hanging from the bed frame.

Mr. Smythe, dead?

Dead, dead, the words clanged in my head.

I couldn't move or think or even cry.

My body broke out into a cold sweat.

A commotion sounded behind me—servants, drawn by Mrs. Heaney's cries. The room swelled with murmurs and keening.

I fled down the stairs and out the door, past the gravel front and straight to the stables. Obsidian watched me come to him, his bright, shining eyes seeing all.

Wrapping my arms around his neck, I gave in—violent, wracking sobs I'd stored since my first night in Virginia when I'd mourned the loss of my father and home. Obsidian stayed still and let me. He lowered his head even further until his cheek rested against mine. My faithful friend. He'd been the saving of me since the day we met.

I cried until all my tears were spent then sat in the corner of Obsidian's stall away from sight. I wasn't ready yet to return to the house. Once I did, my life would be unalterably, painfully changed.

Grooms came in, whispering of a visit from Grenville and Smythe's lawyer. Of items being taken from the house without so much as a by-your-leave.

I couldn't rouse myself to take charge of things. Mr. Smythe was dead—what did it matter if they took candlesticks and books?

Bembe called for me from the house.

Without any forethought, I jumped on Obsidian and urged him out of the stables and into the wilds, riding him until the path disappeared into thick underbrush at the base of tall, jagged cliffs.

The next morning came, but not even hunger could stir me from my shelter under a rocky overhang.

Bembe's deep voice pierced the quiet. "Where are you, boy?"

I couldn't unlock my throat to answer him.

He appeared, leading a horse through the tangled green. "I

could not find you." He tied his horse beside Obsidian and lowered himself beside me with a weary sigh.

I propped my elbows on my bent knees and rested my forehead on my fists.

Everything had come back—the rot, the dripping shadows, the black helplessness of the prison cell where I'd languished and where I'd spent the first days of my grief over losing Da. Now I mourned Smythe and the loss of that belonging I'd felt for one shining moment when he'd told me he wanted me as his son.

I'd prayed in the prison that I wouldn't be alone anymore. I hadn't realized how much those prayers had been answered in Smythe until it was too late to tell him.

His face, radiant with love and hope, stabbed at my thoughts, over and over. He'd gone to bed sadder than he would have if I'd only done what I ought. And I'd never, ever forgive myself for that.

I sighed and pressed my fists into my closed eyes.

What was left to me? I had Bembe and Philemon. Rosanna, too, though I was likely not the consolation to her that she was to me. A young buck's madness I'd not been able to shake myself of since she'd handed me *Màthair*'s ring.

"It was the heart," Bembe said. "He had trouble, but he did not want to worry you."

Of course he hadn't. On more than one occasion, he'd flinched after some exertion, his face squeezed in pain, but it had always been blamed on the sun, rich food, or too little sleep the night before. I hadn't thought to question it. A fool, I.

Knowing made it even worse. He'd sensed he wasn't long for this world. It would have given him comfort to know I would preserve his land and his legacy, but I'd denied him that.

Bembe shifted beside me and laid a hand as gentle as the brush of a swallow's wing upon my back. "What did I say to you the first day we met?"

I turned my head to the side and glanced at him.

"I said that when you see the horses, you will know."

"What is it I should know by looking at the horses, Bembe?"

"That he was a good man who did more for his animals than he needed to. Like he did for you."

It was true. I was taken aback at first by how nice and clean the stables were, but in time I understood that I should've been shocked only at someone living poorly on his plantation. It took one glimpse of Smythe's horses to see the measure of the man who oversaw it. "Then I was only a creature to be cared for? Allowed to stay because I reminded him of his dead son?"

"You heard us talk that first day. Remember?"

How could I forget my shock at finding out that the man who shoveled horse dung was the same man who had the power to decide my fate? "Aye."

"He did not want you."

I winced. Leave it to Bembe to wield his honesty like a sword. "I know."

"You do not know. He was scared."

"Because I was a criminal?"

Bembe scoffed. "I had never seen a more pitiful boy than you. He was not scared of you." Bembe paused, seeming uncertain for the first time since I'd known him. "He was scared of himself."

"Why?"

"The truth is, he loved his boy a little too much."

"How can a father love his son too much?" I would give anything to have a little of that love still.

"He gave his son anything he wanted. But in the end, Harry broke his father's heart."

Smythe's words of caution to Grenville in the stables came back to me, his warning against spoiling Frederick. There'd been anger in his words. How much of that had been reserved for himself?

"How did his son...?"

"Die?" Bembe gave a short grunt. "Smythe took Samson away. He wanted to make the boy listen, but it only made Harry angrier. He stole Samson back and broke both their necks in a race that night."

I swallowed, trying to rid myself of the lump in my throat. Smythe had died without knowing the love of a son. Believing it because I hadn't told him how I felt.

"You want to know why he wanted to send you back? Because he was scared to go wrong with another boy like he did with his son."

The words Smythe spoke to me the day Grenville had tried to convince him to send me away—*I want you to be happy, as I'd hoped Harry would be.* Hoped. I hadn't caught it at the time. But his son had never been happy, even with all Smythe had done. Surely, Smythe had sensed that *I* was happy.

I would never really know.

"After Harry died, Smythe shut himself away. He gave up everything but horses, but he was not happy, even with them." Bembe stroked his beard, the white hairs weaving through the black like curly willow branches. "I brought you to him because I thought to myself that you needed each other."

Bembe, who could cleave a boulder with one hammer's blow, looked on me with such tenderness that I could hold back no longer. I turned into the curve of his arm and let loose with my tears. Dear Bembe. So wise. So good. "You were right."

I could feel him smile against my hair. "Bembe is always right."

I wiped my sleeve across my eyes. "I'll take care of everything, just like he wished. I won't shame him."

Bembe studied me with sad, serious eyes. "Callum..."

I sat straight. He'd called me by name. "What? What is it?"

"Grenville has bought everything. The house. The animals. All of it is his."

"But the documents... on his desk..." My voice trailed off. Smythe had not signed them because I had fled from the room. The only one he had signed had been the one releasing me from my servitude. "Smythe had given me my freedom. He'd signed a paper saying so."

"There are no papers."

I blinked. I could hardly fathom such villainy.

"Why would the lawyer be loyal to you when Grenville would pay him more?"

The blackguard. The whole Grenville family was rotten to their roots. "But so fast!"

"Men move quick when they are greedy."

"What will happen to me?" If the papers were gone, I still had almost three years left of my indentureship.

"Your time belongs to Grenville now."

"We will run away, then. You and me."

He started shaking his head before I had even finished speaking. "It is not easy for me to go."

"But you are free. Why stay when you could go where you like?"

"I am old. Who would take me?"

"No one need take you at all! We can run away and find a way to survive."

"No."

"But—"

"No, boy. It is too late for me. But I am not afraid of Grenville."

I studied my horse grazing contentedly in the shimmering grass.

If I had Obsidian, it would be nothing to stay and suffer through Grenville's indignities.

But I didn't have him. He was Grenville's now and would be subject to Frederick's and his father's abuse. I could easily imagine Frederick taking particular delight in hurting Obsidian if only to get at me. "Obsidian and I will go."

"Grenville will hunt you."

It was true. If I ran away, the law had every right to find me and return me to him, along with a good lashing. And if I were caught, Obsidian would be lost to me for certain.

I risked my horse to Frederick's abuse if I stayed, I risked losing him if I went.

But if I left, there was at least a chance both of us might be free.

Where could we go that we wouldn't be found?

Philemon.

The thought came into my head as surely as if Bembe had spoken it aloud.

Philemon's last letter had said his regiment was to leave soon for the French territory near the Allegheny and Monongahela Rivers. When I'd asked Smythe why Virginia's regiment, raised to protect our own interests, would have cause to go into the Ohio Country, Smyth replied that they were more than likely on their way to the French-held Fort Duquesne. I could still catch them before they left if I hurried.

There was no war between France and Britain yet, but I'd seen regiments raised and the inevitable outcome. War was coming, and Philemon was headed straight toward it.

And now, so was I.

"Frederick will claim Obsidian soon." I strode toward our horses. "Will you fetch food and Mr. Smythe's rifle?"

Bembe squeezed my shoulder. "I will get all I can and bring it to you." He unwound the string of glass beads from his wrist. "Come." I stepped closer, and he wrapped the band on my own wrist and tied it tight. "So you do not forget old Bembe."

I clasped his forearm with my hand. "I don't need anything to remember you."

He put some coins in my fist and left.

I led Obsidian to water, and as he drank his fill, the seriousness of my plans began to sink in.

My father had made me promise to never raise my hand against another living soul, but a regiment wouldn't take a soldier if he didn't fight.

For Obsidian, for myself, I'd better make peace with breaking my vow before I reached the regiment.

THIRTEEN

ROSANNA

Mama's funeral took place on a gray and soggy Tuesday.

We huddled before the mound of fresh soil, drawing warmth from each other against the whistling February wind. Pearl reached toward me, so I scooped her up and tucked her head beneath my chin. Reading a liturgy from his tattered Book of Common Prayer, the priest committed my mother's soul to the Lord. His robes billowed in the gusts, revealing a set of spindly white legs.

Father had promised that once it could be paid for, a simple headstone bearing the name *Sarah Bordroyne Waters* would be added to the family plot. For now, Mama would lie in an unmarked grave, alone and enclosed in the sourwood trees next to her leg and Little Sister. Deer and bear would tread over her. Mushrooms would sprout from the spongy moss and dead columbine. They would be her only company while I would return home to our cabin with a cheery fire and the company of my family.

I tucked a limp curl behind one ear. Every part of me was wet. Even my stockings sagged from the weight of the damp. I wiggled my frozen toes, sloshing water in my toe boxes.

Pearl fussed, and I handed her off to Father.

The drizzle turned into fatter drops pelting the trees' quivering leaves, those stalwart enough to hold on through a dreary winter. I could almost hear the *plip* as the last leaves broke free and spiraled into rotting, waterlogged piles under a dome of bare branches.

Philemon and I had once used the sourwoods' long and pointy leaves as boats, sending unsuspecting beetles on river adventures. We chased them until they were sifted from the water by tree roots or beached on river rocks. Sometimes the current sucked them under.

Like the beetles, Philemon had set off on his adventure, but I couldn't chase him into Ohio territory. How long would it take before the letter reached him telling him that Mama was dead? He had left home just six weeks ago, but the regiment could be deep inside the frontier by now.

The priest turned the page. "'Where, O Death, is thy victory? Where, O Death, is thy sting?'"

I ground my teeth together. It was here, in this grove. Didn't he see it on our faces?

The priest paused and studied me. Did he see my rebellious thoughts?

"'Man that is born of a woman hath but a short time to live, and is full of misery,'" he continued. "'He cometh up, and is cut down, like a flower...'"

Cut down. The memories came like rifle shots. The crack of the branch, the debris falling from the cliff, the thud of her body on the rock. I couldn't stop my sharp intake of breath.

Father's hand went to my back. "Are you well?"

I dug my fingernails into my palms and nodded.

"'After they are delivered from the burden of the flesh, are in joy and felicity: We give thee hearty thanks, for that it hath pleased thee to deliver this our sister out of the miseries of this sinful world.'"

A few more words, and it was done. The priest and the mourners murmured their condolences and drifted away until we were alone.

I made no move to follow them.

Father shifted a sleeping Pearl in his arms and studied me, his face etched by sorrow. "Will you stay, then?"

"I'll be home in time to make our meal."

"Be quick about it. It'll be night soon."

"I just need a moment."

He disappeared into the trees with the solid lump of his daughter draped over his shoulder like a bag of feed.

A flash of something fierce swept through me, seeing Pearl cradled by Father. A yearning I never gave voice to.

I wish I was still small enough to be carried.

But as fast as my resentment came, it cooled.

I was eighteen. A woman. I couldn't choose to abandon my obligations, just as Father couldn't walk away from the farm and just as Mama hadn't been able to choose to walk again.

As far as it stretched in front of me, my life wouldn't be my own, especially now that Father was alone. It would continue to be given in service to my family, just as it had since the accident. But I would be without her, guiding me and helping me put to death my wild impulses.

I fell to my knees, sinking to the sodden soil at her graveside.

What will I do without you?

The only answer I received was from a lone woodpecker hammering at a sourwood. A darkening gray cast its pall on the trees and the headstones. The shadows between the branches thickened, and the circle of trees swallowed me in darkness.

I'd been away too long. Any bear that happened upon me would find me an easy meal, and I had only a shovel for protection.

A twig snapped in the distance.

Something wavered in the trees, black as the approaching night.

My breath caught in my throat. I stumbled over my skirts to my feet and swung the shovel in front of me. The bear wouldn't think me prey.

Obsidian broke through the tree line, then Callum, sitting tall in the saddle, pushing a branch out of his way.

My breath whooshed out of me. I dropped the shovel. "Callum!"

He leaped off his horse in one lithe movement.

I whacked my skirt to remove the dirt. "You shouldn't come upon a girl like that when she's alone!"

Holding the reins, he approached warily, as if I were the bear I'd thought him to be. "Are you well?"

I gave my skirt one last swat. "I thought I was about to be eaten."

"You shouldn't be alone without a rifle."

As if I'd take a rifle to my mother's funeral. "And you should have announced yourself before descending on me like a heathen spirit."

The hard lines around his mouth softened. "I'm sorry I couldn't be here. I came looking for you at your home. Then I saw them bearing the coffin."

I wrapped my wool shawl tighter around my shoulders.

He squatted to the ground and drew a cross upon the soil. He then held a palm to the rounded surface and uttered something in his foreign tongue.

My anger dissolved. The tears I'd been holding at bay throughout the funeral slipped freely down my face.

He removed his hand from her grave and stood. "Why are you here alone?"

"I needed more time."

"To say goodbye?"

I shrugged.

He put his hands upon my shoulders. His eyes were soft in the waning light. "Your heart will heal."

"How would you know?"

He stepped back, his eyes lanced with pain.

Burning acid lurched into my throat. I'd never spoken to him so sharply before, as if he were Bordroyne making fun of my cooking. "I'm sorry, Callum."

Callum stared into the sourwood trees. "'Tis alright. You're grieving."

"I've no excuse. It was—"

"Smythe is dead."

For a long moment, I stared at him. My words had been doubly cruel. In all the upheaval after Mama's death, the news hadn't reached us. She wouldn't be alone on her journey, then. "Oh, Callum."

"I came to tell you I'm leaving."

No. I faltered back a step. Blood pounded in my ears. "But *why?*"

"Grenville bought everything. My life's not my own, not unless I go."

"Father can help. I'm sure of it. He can—"

"No. If it were just me, I might stay, but I won't give up Obsidian to him."

At least he didn't leave me of his own accord. He did it to save Obsidian from the Grenvilles' cruelty. I gripped his forearm. "Stay and fight. Like you did with Frederick."

He gave me a sad smile. "You think I can fight against a man as powerful as Grenville? Even the law would stand against me. I'm alone in this, except for Philemon."

"You'll join the regiment, then?"

"As soon as I take my leave of you."

Take me with you. The words were unspoken, hovering on the edge of my lips. *Take me to Philemon and away from this mess.* But I couldn't leave any more than he could stay. "Will you ever come back?"

The woodpecker flapped his wings and flew away to his nest. The last drips fell from the trees onto my sodden shawl.

He shook his head. "Thank you for taking notice of me that day at Mr. Edwards'. For being my friend."

On impulse, I grabbed him in a fierce hug, the same as I'd given to Philemon before he left.

His arms stayed stiff at his side.

I only squeezed him tighter. "What will I do without you?"

His body softened. He wrapped his arm about my waist, tugging me closer. With his other hand, he cradled the back of my head, pulling it to his chest. "My bonnie lass," he whispered. "Ye dinnae need me."

I filled my lungs with the scent of him, leather and fire, wool and clean linen, memorizing it and the feel of his body close to mine.

"Surely, ye know," he whispered into my hair.

I shivered like a newborn calf. "Know?"

His hand slipped to my neck. His thumb brushed the hollow underneath my ear, gently, as if he handled a butterfly with a broken wing.

My heartbeat drummed the tension between us. I looped my arms around his neck, pulling myself closer to him than I had ever been. He couldn't leave. He wouldn't, not when it meant he'd leave me behind. On a pounding impulse, I pulled his head down and kissed him full on the mouth.

He froze. For a moment, it seemed he might reject me. Then he shuddered and crushed me to him, meeting me with a hunger of his own.

"Take me with you," I demanded before I could lose my nerve. "I can't bear life without you."

He stiffened and pulled away, chest heaving. "I shouldn't have... "

Bereft of his warmth, the chill settled back into my bones.

"Put me out of your mind, Rosanna. I'll not be returning."

And with that, he leaped onto Obsidian and disappeared through the mist and trees without a backward glance.

FOURTEEN
ROSANNA

March 1754

I yanked the heavy bedding across the floor. It reeked of all manner of sick. First Bordroyne had fallen prey to the stomach cramps, then Isaac and Edward. The girls and I had been spared, but who could tell how much longer it would be until we were knocked down as well?

"Rosanna," Bordroyne croaked from where he was splayed across the floor. He was doubled over and hugging a pail, his face as white as a full moon.

"What is it?" I asked none too gently, a little put out by what a demanding patient he was.

"I'm hot." He whimpered and implored me with doleful eyes. "Will you fan me, Rosanna?"

Mercy be to me, a poor sinner, but I almost laughed. There was a little satisfaction in seeing my wretch of a brother laid so low. Ever since I'd taken charge of the rearing of him after Mama died, he took special delight in stirring me to frustration. Perhaps it was because he now had fewer eyes on him that he felt free to do as he pleased. He would bring me to boiling and then laugh at my discomposure. I warned him that if no one else was laughing, then mayhap it wasn't funny, but he gave little care to that. Even last night, he'd banged his tin cup on the floor around the clock, having me fetch him water, straighten his blanket, move his tick mattress closer to the window, rub his feet. Well, no longer. "You're fourteen and almost a man. Are you so weak that you would have me fawn over you like a babe?"

"But I have the pox. I just know it. Isaac and I are dyin'!"

"You don't have the pox, and you won't die."

"When we die, you'll cry more than anyone for not believing me."

I swung around, hands on hips. "And what could I do if it were the pox? You'll die whether I fan you or not."

I ignored his answering wail and tugged the tick mattress once again. The contents of my stomach roiled at the stench of it.

I needed to breathe the fresh air, feel the sunshine beating on my head and the new spring grass tickling my feet. I'd be sent to Bedlam if I had to hear one more of my brothers' complaints.

They all took me for granted, every single one of them. Never once had I heard a thank-you for my troubles. They didn't know what it was like to stay home when Phil got to follow the river and see what lay beyond it. Provided that supper was on the table; their clothes woven, patched, and cleaned; the lard and tallow rendered; illnesses tended to; milk curdled and pressed into cheese, they gave me little notice. And I had no hope that it would change, not unless Father remarried. At least Charlotte could help, but the work didn't seem any lighter for it, for there was always more work to be done than time to do it.

My only satisfaction for working hard had been paying penance for the accident, but I didn't even have that with Mama dead. The whole point was that she might one day see my trying and say, "Oh, Rosanna, you're so refined. Your voice is as soft as dandelion fuzz. Your hair is shiny and neat. And, by my troth, your roast chicken is better than mine!" Now that she was gone, there was no point in trying.

I yanked the mattress closer to the door and dropped it to the ground, breathing hard.

My complaints were more vexing than Bordroyne's. Especially because I was old enough to know better how little grumbling changed things.

I ground a wandering weevil under my heel.

It wasn't Bordroyne or the sickness or not being appreciated.

I missed Callum.

Everything was dull, never-ending drudgery without him since he left a few weeks before, but I couldn't bear the thought of missing him forever. Something had to change, or I'd go mad with every day the same as it was before.

A knock sounded at the door. "Hello?"

"Just a moment." I blew my wayward curls out of my face.

"Here, let me help." Before I had time to protest, John came in and took the tick mattress from my hands, folded it in half, and threw it over his shoulder.

I cringed. Such a nasty chore, but the feeling faded with the sight of his wide shoulders bearing the load.

Mercy, but he was strong.

I thought back to when we were children. John had been all limbs with straight black hair, a perpetual sour look on his face directed at me. Now, he hardly resembled that boy, except for his hair. When had he become a man of looks? I couldn't deny he was handsome.

"Where do you want it?"

I pointed to the fence by the barn. He draped it over one of the poles and stood back. His hair was swept back and neatly tied, his neck covered with a cotton cloth. He wore his finest waistcoat, the one he wore to church. He took out a handkerchief, dunked it in the trough, and scrubbed at his shirt. "The same sickness went through our house last week," he said in a light voice.

"Ah," I said, as if I understood, but that still didn't explain his willingness to lug the disgusting mattress outside for me. And in his Sunday finery.

He tucked the cloth back into his pocket and pulled out something else. "I have something for you." In the middle of his calloused hand sat a thick gold and black ring engraved with letters.

I picked up the band and turned it around. A mourning ring. It had his mother's name engraved inside, and clasped between two shaped hands was a skull under scratched crystal.

"Your mother's?"

"Yes, well, Father's new wife didn't want him wearing it."

Understandable.

"I thought you might like it to remember your mother by."

His eyes were so hopeful, I didn't have the heart to tell him that mourning rings were made specific to the dead person. It wasn't the custom for another's ring to be used to mourn another. I slipped it on my middle finger anyway. "That's very kind of you, John."

He continued to look at me without saying anything.

I raised my eyebrows. "Thank you for helping with the bedding."

"I didn't mind."

Why did he continue to stare at me? "I'd better return to my brothers."

He squared his shoulders. "Rosanna, I'd like to speak with you about something."

I glanced back at the house, where Pearl slept and the boys were ragged from the illness, Bordroyne bent over a pail. "It isn't a good time."

"It won't take long."

"I suppose I can stay for a moment longer."

He put his hands behind his back and rocked forward on his feet.

His nervous posture was so unlike him. The longer the silence grew between us, the more my stomach twisted. "Well?"

He broke off a stem from the shrub of witch hazel next to him and shredded the curled petals until they lay in a pile at his feet.

He brushed his hands together and regarded me. "We're friends now, are we not?"

Like a bird of prey swooping in came the memory of him calling me *mop stick* and of me shoving him into the mud. I would've laughed out loud if it weren't for the earnest look on his face. "In a manner of speaking."

"You wish me well at the very least, then? I know I was rotten to you when we were younger, but I hope you can see that I've changed."

"I wish no one *ill*, John."

"I've decided to set out on my own. With the British paying a bounty to purchasers of colonial indigo, I'll grow that first, and once I have enough land, tobacco."

"Oh?" I tried to inject interest in my voice. He'd talked of his plans for a farm as long as I'd known him. "Do you already have land in mind?"

His dark eyes sparked with some secret meaning. "I do."

"And?"

"I will leave you to guess where the land is."

I knotted my hands on my hips so I wouldn't knock him over the fence. He shouldn't test our newfound friendship so soon. "You might have time to waste, but I have ill brothers to attend to."

I walked around him, but he jumped in front of me.

"It is near your farm. Quite near, in fact. Your father has sold me a piece of his own property. A small section, mind, but it's enough for my needs until I can expand. And it already has a small cabin."

Now that was news indeed. "But why would he sell off some of our land?" We weren't rich, but we were fed and clothed well enough to be considered respectable.

"The piece has been fallow for years. Mayhap it is a frustration to him, lying unused for so long."

It was true that after the accident Father spent time caring for Mama that he might've spent clearing and planting some of his unused land. "That's a fine thing for you, but you'll grow tired of being so near to us."

He stepped closer. "I'm very certain I will not."

My heart jumped for some reason, though he'd never given me cause to be afraid of him. I put a hand to his chest. "John, be plain."

"I want a farm of my own. And not just any farm, Rosanna. I want a farm to rival Grenville's." The gleam in his eyes was the same as Philemon's when he told me about joining the regiment. "Mark it now, I'll have the biggest plantation in Virginia, and you will help me do it. I want us to marry."

"*Marry?*" I stumbled back a step.

He engulfed my hands in his. They were rough and large, twice the size of my own. A man's hands. "When I got it into my head that I would have a farm, I knew I would need a worthy helpmeet."

"Wouldn't you like a wife you have hated less over the years?"

"You scared me a little when we were younger, I'll grant you. You were loud and frightened the fish off, and I never got the deer when you toted your father's rifle. A boy can only stand so much." His eyes twinkled with a hint of humility as if he, too, laughed at the boy he used to be. "But you're self-controlled now, and you work hard without complaint. Neither are you fanciful. A fine choice for a farmer's wife."

I almost laughed out loud. Me, not fanciful? What of my being a forest troll, a beaver, a one-eyed captain commanding a ship? And if he thought me self-controlled, he didn't know me at all. Didn't he know that I'd been forced to take over my mother's duties? If her fall hadn't happened, my mother would still be despairing of me ever becoming a lady. Perhaps I would have even run off after Phil when he left for the regiment. "Surely there's another woman who'd be a better fit."

"I would be honest with you. If we are to be married, we should begin with the truth. I approached Charity, but she has refused me." He watched me carefully, as if I would weep and moan at his honesty at choosing another first.

I felt nothing at his words. John had been calf-eyed over Charity since we were young. She would be the perfect complement to his well-built, masculine frame. But perhaps Charity didn't wish to get married after what she'd been through. John may not realize who her new baby brother was, but I had my suspicions.

"Why do you tell me this?"

"Building my plantation will be difficult at first," he continued. "She was right to refuse me. I need someone unafraid of hard work, not a fine lady like her. I need *you*."

The tender places in my heart curled in on each other, recoiling at his words.

"Think," John said. "You can have a home of your own. With children of your own, if God wills it. You could continue as you are in another home. Your *own* home. You'll be building your own future. Your own legacy. Don't you want something that's yours?"

The retort I was already building died on my lips. The only home I wanted was one with Callum in it, but what I wanted and what life allowed were two different things.

If he'd continued speaking of what I could do for him—if he had approached me on another day, one in which I hadn't taken stock of my life and despaired of it ever changing, his cause would have been lost. The building of my own home, *that* is where he should have started. Was this how I could keep from going mad with Callum gone?

"I'm not Charity, John. You claim that I'm practical and temperate, but I'm neither of those things. I may not swing my fists at you anymore, but I'm likely to chase after whatever idea comes in my head. I still get grass patches on my knees, my weaving's atrocious, and I'd rather sleep outside under the stars."

"Then I'll buy you an overlarge washing tub for your stained clothes, purchase our cloth from another woman more skilled than you, and build us a house without a roof."

A laugh burst from me despite the seriousness of our discussion. "You would not."

"I will, if that's what it takes to make you marry me."

The determined look in his eyes made me hesitate. *Did* he like me as Philemon hinted long ago? But how could John have asked Charity first if he truly cared for me? "What of taking care of my father? My brothers and sisters?"

"Your siblings are older now. Why, even Charlotte can manage most of it. You'll be near enough to help your father if he needs it, but your sister and brothers could shoulder most of your load. As for Pearl, we can take her with us."

Charlotte *could* handle most home duties. Even at almost ten years old, she had better management of our home than I did. She was far less distractible and better than me at sewing and cooking. That was all Father and the boys needed, really. And I could go over to my old home often and help with the harder tasks.

"If I am to even *think* about what you ask—"

He gave me a smug smile.

I held up my hand. "*If* I am to consider this, I've a few demands of my own."

His face flattened. "Demands?"

"I won't go into a marriage with someone who expects what I cannot give them. I want your understanding when I'm not what you'd hoped I'd be."

"Done."

As easy as that? I narrowed my eyes. "And I want freedom to run my days as I see fit. I won't neglect my duties, but neither will I wait to hear whether you like something before I do it."

He studied me carefully. "What is it you want to do, exactly?"

"I—I don't know." There was no Philemon to follow, no Callum at my side. "I want to know that I can do it if I discover it, though." At his hesitation, I rushed to add, "I'll never shame you, within reason, though there must be a little grace for my short-comings."

He thought for a long moment, tapping his finger upon his lips. "I promise to give you the freedom to do what you like, *within reason*, as long as you give me what I need in return."

"What more could you need besides a wife who'll work?"

His cheeks took on a rusty hue. "I can't have what I want without sons to work the land beside me."

My skin burned as all sorts of imaginings ran wild through my head. I knew a little more of the act now that I was older. Mama had been unable to avoid my questions with us living on a farm. But she'd been adamant that love was the seed from which the baby sprouted. Sudden pain gripped my heart. What I wouldn't give to have her wise counsel once again. "So you need me for... children?"

For the first moment since he'd shared his plan, he seemed uncertain. "Yes, children. And companionship." He slipped his hands from mine and began to pace. "I know it's strange to talk of marriage before we've talked of love, but you know I've always been of a practical mind."

"If there is no love between us, how will you have your sons?" Perhaps his mother hadn't told him how it worked before she died.

"In time it might... you might... I do care for you, Rosanna, and I won't force you to..." Here he waved his hands to indicate *something*, but I knew not what. Perspiration dotted his forehead. "Your mother had lots of children," he finished in a strangled voice.

"Yes," I said slowly, as if I spoke to a simpleton. "But you're not marrying her, are you?"

"Rosanna! You shouldn't talk so lightly of such things."

He couldn't say I hadn't warned him. My conscience was clean before God.

"It's not that I'm opposed to love." He took a step closer and tucked one of my stray hairs under my cap. "May I kiss you?"

I drew back, alarmed. "John!"

He laughed. "Am I as ugly as that?"

No, he wasn't ugly. I had never thought that. "You're teasing me."

He put his hands on my waist and pulled me forward. I staggered a step closer.

"I'll close my eyes," he said.

"If you can't abide my looks now, you best put an end to this. What will you feel when I age into a crone?"

He suppressed a smile. "It is only that I don't want to see you pull a face again." He closed his eyes and leaned forward.

All I could see was the boy he used to be, his scowling face and his crossed arms when he saw me join him and Philemon. I bit the inside of my cheek to keep from laughing.

His lips met mine.

All thoughts of laughing fled.

It was not unpleasant. It was only... different.

His lips were soft and warm. His hand traveled up my back, pressing me closer.

But all I could think of was being held by a friend and comforted in my grief. Of kissing Callum.

I pushed John away. I couldn't kiss John when I was thinking of another.

He wrinkled his forehead and stepped back. "What? What is it?"

I held a hand between us and steadied my breathing. "A moment. Please."

My insides swirled in a riotous mess. I couldn't think on that day at Mama's graveside without wincing. Why had I kissed Callum?

I'd only thought to be closer to him, to take all the comfort he would offer me. Pulling myself flush against him, chest to chest, my mouth to his, seemed the most natural thing in the world. But my traitorous impulses had once again led me astray. He'd broken our embrace, his face thunderous, and he'd left me drowning in grief and humiliation.

It was better to put him out of my head, to force myself to forget.

I took a tentative step forward. "I'm ready now."

"Are you sure?"

I nodded, and he took me into his arms again, placing his lips more softly on mine.

I squeezed my eyes shut and concentrated on what was taking place.

It wasn't terrible.

He angled my head and kissed me deeper.

It scared and thrilled me all at once.

I placed my palms on his chest and stumbled back.

John straightened his waistcoat and cleared his throat, a self-satisfied grin spreading across his face. "We'll be doing more of that just as soon as we are married." As if the matter were settled, he turned around and strode away, a jaunty whistle on his lips.

"I haven't given you my answer yet!" I called after him.

But he kept walking and whistling as if he hadn't heard me. The impudent skunk.

Had it been settled?

I would have more freedom than I had now and a greater chance of making my life what I wished.

The idea of having my own home, with things done to my own liking, appealed. And there'd be little risk of going through childbirth if I married a man I didn't love.

Guilt rose in me for even considering leaving Father, but John had promised I'd be free to care for both our homes when needed. And Pearl, still young at five, would come with us. John had left me with no reason to say no.

I'd been given a chance to do something else, if I would be brave enough to take it.

I let out a breathy laugh. Who would have thought it would come through the hands of someone who was once my greatest enemy?

Bordroyne's pitiful voice sounded behind me. "I'm sorry for the trouble I cause you."

I whirled around. He stood there, pale, his pitiful legs swathed in the folds of Father's shirt. "You're sorry?" He'd never apologized to me before. "And will you be back at it again once you are well?"

He broke down into hacking sobs and then heaved into the bucket he carried with him. "I miss Mama."

Tears pricked my eyes, but I held them back. It wouldn't help him to see how very weak I felt without her. "Oh, Bordroyne." I rushed to him and placed my hand upon his back. "So do I. So do I." I rubbed my hand in circles until his crying settled into shuddering hiccups.

He gave a long, wet sniff. "Why were you gone so long?"

My cheeks burned. I'd not talked with Father yet, but Bordroyne regarded me with such open, kindly interest, I could hardly rebuff him. Besides, I couldn't risk this newfound peace between us. "If I tell you, will you keep it a secret?"

He nodded solemnly.

"John wants to marry me."

His eyebrows drew together. "But you are... you."

I knew exactly what he meant. "I'll still come every day to care for all of you. And the cooking and cleaning will still get done."

"It's not that."

"What is it, then? Charlotte can do everything even better than I can."

"It will be different, is all. You are the closest thing to Mama, and if you aren't here..."

My voice dropped to a pleading note. "It's my only chance, Bordroyne."

He considered for a long moment.

Sighing heavily, he looked at me, his eyes brave. "You must say yes, Rosanna. You'll be happy in a home of your own." He nodded once. "And I'll help you with the chores here. But I won't do wash, for that's women's work."

FIFTEEN
CALLUM

It took me two weeks to travel to Williamsburg, keeping to little-traveled Indian trails so as not to be discovered. I had to force myself not to turn back and retrieve Rosanna. She'd always trusted me—depended on me to come to her defense. I'd left her behind when she had begged me to take her. It was impossible, but how could I call myself her friend and not find a way? Then I remembered my state and that I was in no position to take care of her. Would I take her to war? It was safer for her to stay. But still, she'd never forgive me. *I* wouldn't.

I came upon the regiment, with saddlebag emptied of oats and my stomach gnawing beneath my ribs. The regiment would never take me for the almost-adopted heir of a Virginian horse breeder with my appearance as it was. The best I could do was pass for decent, so I washed off the dirt and grime in a nearby stream and scrubbed my clothes, soaked with mud and sweat, with a bit of lye and a pinecone.

Night had fallen. Even so, the camp brimmed with soldiers like a stream with minnows. I jumped off Obsidian and led him by the reins inside its bounds.

"Hello."

I started at the sudden appearance of a tall boy in my path.

Obsidian tossed his head, whipping the reins out of my hold.

"Whoa." The boy held out his hands and cupped them along my horse's face. "You're alright, then." He carefully stroked Obsidian's cheek.

The boy was thin as a cattail, his face the puff, his body the stalk, and his hair as white as new-fallen snow. In the dark, I couldn't tell if his eyebrows and eyelashes followed suit.

"You've a fine horse. What's his name?" the boy asked.

His open, friendly face set my tension at ease. "Magpie." My heart twisted a little at the memory of Rosanna, her bright eyes, her hair tumbling about her shoulders.

"Magpie? *Him?*" A little of the respect he might've held for me owning such a horse died in his eyes. "You cannot call a horse like that *Magpie.*"

"What is your name?"

"Tileman Cruger. I'm soldiering with the regiment."

I held in a scoff. The boy was no older than Bordroyne. I could no more imagine him marching off to battle than me becoming king. "And what is your role?"

"I care for the horses, but they let me carry a rifle," he said with a hint of pride in his voice.

"How old are you?"

"Fourteen. Well, in ten months I will be."

I smothered a laugh. "Ten months? Well, that's not so far away. I didn't know they let soldiers fight so young as that."

He leaned close. "My father wishes for me to go to the West Indies and run ships of cargo, but what fun is there in that? No fun at all, so I've become a soldier instead."

I lowered my own voice. "And does your father know that you're here?"

He eyed me up and down. "You look like you have your own secrets, so you'll understand me keeping mine."

"Wisely said. Do you know of Philemon Waters?"

"Phil? Everyone knows Phil."

Of course they did. "Can you take me to him?"

He clicked at Obsidian, and without so much as a by-your-leave, took the reins and led us out of the shadows and toward the fire.

Even from a distance, I could pick Philemon's large frame and midnight hair from among the others. He hunched over his knees, poking at the fire with a stick.

Tileman stopped and turned to me. "Here he is. May I care for your horse?"

"That's kind of you, but no." I took the reins from his hand.

Tileman shrugged and loped into the darkness.

"Phil?"

Philemon turned around. The moment he saw me, he shot to his feet, his face white even in the firelight. "Callum!"

"Do you have anything to eat?"

Philemon blinked. "Sit." He nudged the man beside him, and the soldier obliged by vacating his space on the log. Of course there had been no argument. I didn't doubt Philemon had managed to muscle his way to the top of the heap, as far as his fellow soldiers were concerned.

After tossing Obsidian's reins over a low-hanging tree branch, I filled the space left by the soldier.

Philemon held out a piece of roasted venison.

Like a ravenous wolf, I bit off a large chunk, then another.

The weight of Phil's gaze was heavy on me.

"What?" I asked, my mouth still full.

"You know it's dead already."

I stuffed the rest in my mouth. "Is there any more?"

Philemon exchanged looks with the other soldiers. "How long has it been since you've eaten?"

"A day, or some such."

He made a disgusted sound and shoved a piece of rough bread in my hand. "Why were you not better prepared for your journey?"

I cast a glance at the other soldiers. "May we speak apart from the others?"

Phil's face grew serious. He led me out of the circle and faced me. "What is it?"

I hesitated. Did he know of his mother's death yet? I could hardly tell him of my own grief without addressing his. "Have you heard from home?"

His eyes glinted in the firelight. "Do you mean Mother dying?"

I knew first hand the pain of not being able to say goodbye. My throat ached with unspent tears for the both of us. "I'm sorry, Phil."

His hand went to the back of his neck. "I'd been preparing for it for years. When the letter arrived two days ago, I was relieved. I'm glad her pain is at an end." He braved a smile, which fell just as soon as he gave it. "Still, I miss her."

"Of course you do."

"But you didn't come all this way to tell me about her, did you? A letter would've done just as well."

"You'll hardly believe it, but Mr. Smythe died, and Grenville is to take over the farm. I had no other place to go."

He stared at me agape. "Are you bound to Grenville now?"

"I am."

"You did right in coming, then."

"Will you help me?"

"Of course." He glanced at Obsidian. "We're always in need of good horses. That will be in your favor."

"He is Magpie now."

"*Magpie*? After Rosanna?"

I ignored his penetrating gaze. Phil and I had never spoken of my infatuation with his sister. I'd made sure I never gave cause for him to guess it. As close as I was with the twins, he'd never abide by his sister being joined with a servant, as was right. How much less now? With running away, I'd become an outlaw. My connection with her was severed forever. "It's not only Obsidian's name I've changed. I'll go by John Bates now." In Virginia, there were more Johns and Bateses than fruit in a chokecherry cluster.

"John Bates? Such a boring name as that?" He squinted an eye at me. "No, you'll be Jack. Jack Barleycorn."

I rolled my eyes. "Away with ye."

"Drummond, then. No one would think you other than a Scot, anyway."

"Jack Drummond," I repeated. What did it matter what name I used? All that mattered was that Grenville couldn't find me.

A man's shadow fell over us. "Waters? Your turn to guard the stores."

Philemon glanced over his shoulder and jumped to his feet. He stood, chest out, feet together, chin high, and raised his hand to the side of his hat in a crisp salute. "Yes, Major Washington."

When I didn't join him, Philemon gave me a slight jerk upward with his chin.

I scrambled to my feet and imitated Philemon's ramrod-straight posture.

The man measured me with his ice-blue eyes. He couldn't be more than a few years older than Philemon and me, but he had an air about him that commanded respect.

"Did we pick up a straggler along the way?" he asked.

"This is my friend. He and his horse over there"—Philemon motioned with his chin toward Obsidian—"would like to join us."

The man glanced at the horse and then me, weighing me and my rumpled appearance on his no-doubt finely tuned scales of estimation. "I won't have horse thieves in our midst."

"He's no horse thief, sir. I can vouch for his worthiness."

A piece of ruddy hair fell across the man's forehead. "Name?"

"John—Jack Drummond, sir."

"Which is it? John or Jack?"

I whipped off my hat and held it in my hands. "Jack."

His gaze snagged on my wrist. "Those beads. Where did you get them? Did you steal those too?"

I steeled myself against the urge to cover the bracelet with my sleeve. Why should he care about Bembe's bracelet?

Washington grabbed my wrist and brought it close for his inspection. "My brother wore a band almost identical to this. I've never seen another like it." His piercing eyes settled upon me again. "Who gave them to you?"

I lowered my sleeve. "I knew little of him." It struck me then how much that was true. All I really knew was that Bembe was the best of men and had been the saving of me, along with Mr. Smythe and Obsidian. "I didn't know his name."

I lifted my chin. Telling a falsehood to protect someone I loved was surely justified.

He studied me for a long moment. "So, you feel like firing your rifle for king and country, do you?"

"Yes, sir."

"Not that we are setting out to do that, mind, but all the same, we must be ready. What skills do you bring?"

"My horse is fast, sir."

Washington took a step nearer to Obsidian and held out his hand to the horse's muzzle. Obsidian closed the distance and bumped the offered palm with his nose. The man murmured to the stallion and stroked his velvety flanks. "This horse and its saddle are not yours," he announced. "A man rich enough to own them wouldn't ask to be a part of my rag-tag regiment. I ask again, do I have a horse thief in my camp?"

Sweat sprang to the small of my back. Would he find out Obsidian rightfully belonged to Grenville and send him back? "Nay, sir."

"Why did you come here?"

"Because I'm not content to be under the thumb of another my whole life."

"The jailor's thumb or your father's?"

"I have neither."

Washington gave Obsidian's cheek one more rub. "At least you take better care of your horse than you do yourself. There's something to be said to that." He stepped back from my horse. "You will be a foot soldier and will have no need for him in battle. You agree to giving him up for the regiment's use?"

"As long as he is fed and cared for, and I am allowed to visit him."

Obsidian shook his mane and nodded, as if begging for the same.

Washington leaned close to my ear and lowered his voice. "I do not know who you are, but if you prove yourself worthy, I'll have no need of finding out, will I?"

I swallowed. "No, sir."

"I'm second-in-command to Colonel Fry. I can only allow you to stay until he joins us and decides your fate. A warning—he is like to be rid of you. I assume you know your way around a rifle."

"I've never seen a man shoot as he does, sir," Philemon said.

That was true for he had never seen me shoot at all.

"Be thankful Philemon speaks for you," Washington said. "His judgment hasn't failed me yet." I didn't miss his unspoken, *Do not let this instance be the first.* "Waters, take him to get his rations. If he's as good with his rifle as you say, we may have need of him."

"What are you doing?" I hissed under my breath as soon as Washington left.

"Saving your hide. If he'd dug any deeper, he'd have sent you back."

"But I don't know how to shoot."

"You can learn, and you must. I won't let you make a liar of me."

In April, we left for the Forks of the Ohio, where the Allegheny and Monongahela Rivers joined. We were to meet a small contingent of our force and build a fort, for the French would be at great disadvantage if we took root there. But when we arrived weeks later, we discovered our men gone and the French building the fort that we had planned.

Our force of one hundred and fifty men couldn't do anything against the French's one thousand, so we retreated over the

Allegheny Mountains, cutting a road through the dense forest for the rest of our regiment to travel when they came from Virginia.

It was slow, laborious work. We took turns dragging our one cannon over bridgeless streams and muddy, rocky paths in the rain. At night, we had no tents to protect us, save one for Washington.

It had been months since I joined the regiment. Swaying in Obsidian's saddle, I slapped the side of my neck and held my hand in front of me. In my palm lay a squashed mosquito in a dot of bright red blood. Governor Dinwiddie's decision to have the young Washington march through the Ohio Country as the weather warmed was madness. At least Washington let me ride Obsidian when we traveled.

A rider met us on the path, bearing a saddlebag full of correspondence, and we stopped our procession for him to pass out the letters. None of them bore my name, as expected, but Phil had the riches of two. He tore them open right away and walked away to his privacy behind a great oak. When he returned, his face was thoughtful.

"Have you had news from home?" I asked.

"Aye."

"And? All is well?" Was *she* well?

"Well enough."

"What's wrong?"

"Nothing."

I could bear it no longer. "How is Rosanna?" I pretended interest in testing Obsidian's cinch like his answer didn't matter. "What of her?"

"Callum..."

I straightened and looked at him.

Pity filled his eyes. "She's married."

The impact hit a second before the pain did. It was as if I'd been thrown from Obsidian. My lungs choked for air. Married? But of course. She needed rescue after her mother's death, and I hadn't given it to her. I'd forced her to find her help somewhere else.

"But—but what about your father?" My voice held the tinge of desperation, though I tried to hide it. Me, a runaway servant, pining for a woman I wasn't free to marry.

"She hasn't left him entirely. She and John live on our land."

John? Pictures came into my head unbidden. Of him smiling with her. Touching her. He wasn't right, not for her. She needed someone who loved her for who she was, not for who he wanted her to be. Who accepted and cherished every part of her. She needed *me.*

"Charlotte is old enough now to take on many of Rosanna's duties. Rosanna will still help. At least, until her own babies come."

I swallowed bile. I'd go mad if he said another word. "Babies?"

"Why, yes, that is what happens when a man and a woman—"

I held up my hand. "That's enough. I don't want to hear any more."

He tilted his head at me. "Does it bother you? Her marrying John?"

For so long I'd thought of her as mine. How would I ever untangle her from my thoughts? John was a good man. I had no reason to protest their marriage. He would take care of her, and she would be safe and provided for, which was more than I could do.

For only a moment, I allowed myself to remember. Sunlight crowning her capless head, her curls shining like polished river rock—black with hints of chestnut.

Obsidian whinnied, breaking the spell.

"She's a friend. That is all."

Philemon scoffed.

"I mean it. As much as Bembe is to me."

"How is the old man?"

I exhaled in relief at the change of subject. "I don't know. I haven't had the means to write him." Neither was it safe.

"I'll lend you my quill and paper, and you can enclose a letter to him in my response to Rosanna. She'll make sure he gets it."

Surely Bembe would know to burn it after receiving it, and I could trust Rosanna not to let it fall into the wrong hands. If it didn't reach her at all? It wouldn't be too difficult to word the letter in such a way that no one could be certain of its author.

I sat by the fire that night, twiddling with my mother's ring. The golden band was too precious to be risked to fraying twine and now hung from my neck on a chain I'd bought with the first coin Smythe gave me.

The circle glinted in the firelight.

So many times I'd dreamed of clasping Rosanna's hand to mine in betrothal and giving the ring to her as a pledge of my love and fidelity.

But it was already hers. The moment Rosanna held the ring toward me on the day we met, it had ceased to be *Màthair*'s.

Now that she was married, was it wrong of me to carry it still? To wear it against me, to feel it warm against my chest—a constant reminder of what I felt?

But even if I rid myself of this ring, I'd have to die to put an end to my feelings.

I took the quill from the inkpot and put it to a sheet of paper set upon my knee.

Dear Rosanna,

I hear that you and John have been wed. There will be just as many adventures for you in this new life as there might have been for a captain with a glass eye and a cargo hold full of fruit, for I believe you can make an adventure of anything.

Thank you for giving the letter to my friend. I beg that you would remind him to throw it into the fire after reading it.

I will think of you always, just as you were in that grove of trees the last night I saw you. I wish you peace in your new life and pray that God keeps you in his care always.

It read stale and wooden, a world apart from the last moments near her mother's grave—cold compared to what was in my heart, but what else could I do? Even if she were free, I couldn't give her more than this.

A letter to Bembe was trickier still, but in the end, I decided that it didn't matter overmuch if Grenville found the letter and deduced it was from me. What would he do? Ride into the disputed territory with all its natives and hostile French and look for me? The smooth-handed popinjay might send a man after me, but the Ohio Country was large. It wouldn't take much for an unimportant man such as me to disappear within it.

My dear friend,

I can now report that I and the companion I traveled with have been accepted and are settling into our new lives as well as can be expected. It is as good as could be hoped, given what I faced before. How strange to find that the danger I am in provides a measure of safety.

Write and tell me if you are well. Send any letters in care of the person I came to find. It may be months before your reply reaches me, but in that time, I will take comfort in thinking back on our happy times together.

Yours very affectionately,

Jack Drummond

The rider left in the morning carrying Phil's letter to Rosanna, with mine sealed inside. These would be my last words to her.

I slipped the ring back inside my shirt.

A relic of what had been. Of what still was, in my heart.

SIXTEEN
ROSANNA

I tucked my borrowed pearl combs in my hair, girding myself with her presence for what was to come.

A few minutes more, and I'd be a wife.

There'd been no reason to wait to marry John, not with the growing season upon us and John anxious to put his hand to the plow.

And his hands on me.

My heart tripped, remembering his fevered whispers the night before.

I didn't know what to do with this John. He didn't swoon and make eyes at me like he had with Charity, though I wouldn't have known what to do with that either. He smiled at things that used to frustrate him, gave me secret looks, and used any excuse to touch me, even when passing a trencher. I would give anything to go back to when we were children and tell him what a swain he would become—over me! I could hardly think on it without laughing.

Bordroyne entered the room. "Father said to fetch you."

I secured one of the combs more tightly. "What? No compliment for my efforts?"

"You look well enough. Come on."

Well enough. The first line of John's poem entered my head. *If hairs be wires, black wires grow on her head.*

Of all days to be reminded of that.

Then other words, spoken the same day as John's, flew past the barrier: a lance, swift and poisoned. *Come live with me and be my love.*

Love. What a day to be thinking of *that.*

With a movement near to desperation, I dragged Bordroyne against my side and hugged him tight. "I'll only be a short walk away. I'll be here every day. You might even grow tired of me."

"I'm tired of you now." He pulled away and pushed me out the door.

A protest died on my lips.

A gaggle of people stared at me—my sisters and brothers, Father, Mr. Farrow and his wife. John came from their midst and pulled me to stand before the priest, taking my hand in his.

Panic beat beneath my ribs. Now that it was upon me, I wasn't sure this was right at all. "John, wait."

He glanced at my hand. "You wear your mother's mourning ring? On our wedding day?"

I bit my tongue to keep from saying something I'd regret. "You gave it to me."

He rubbed his thumb over mine. "So I did."

The priest leafed through his Book of Common Prayer.

I tried again. "John—"

"Hush. Let's have this done so we can begin building something of our own."

My belly loosened. It was the way he said it—*our own.* Whatever came next, John offered me a piece of it. What belonged to me now other than Mama's pearl combs? Nothing but those and memories I would never escape if I stayed home. I could overlook him shushing me when he offered me an unmapped future, a future I would help shape.

So I bound my life to his, for better or worse and with God as my witness. We then made our way to John's cabin, leaving Pearl behind with Father for the night.

My combs lay on the table where John had placed them. My cap and dress, in a pile on the floor by their side. I was alone in a strange bed with an empty dip in the mattress beside me.

I buried my face in my pillow.

When would he return from his chores? I would die, seeing John again. Would he tease me? I could bear anything but that, especially after so awkward an endeavor the night before. Or would he turn into a lovesick idiot and expect the same from me? I would like that even less. I leaped from the bed and quickly dressed with shaking fingers. Just as I donned my shoes, the front door opened.

"I've finished plowing the back field." Without looking at me, he bent to remove his muddy boots and placed them against the wall.

At least he hadn't tracked mud through the house, as my brothers would have.

He sat at the table, not meeting my eyes. Did I imagine it, or was his neck redder than usual?

"I'll have it planted by the end of the day," he announced.

"Oh."

Finally, he looked at me. "Rosanna?"

My scalp and back prickled with sweat. If only he would say something to put me at ease. "Yes?"

"Is there porridge?"

He asked for breakfast as if nothing strange had occurred between us? "I've only just awoken."

"I can do with bread and cheese until you prepare it."

I placed the cheese and bread in front of him with a knife and a trencher.

His eyebrows curved upward.

"What?" I pushed a curl back from my flaming cheeks with my bent wrist. "Bread and cheese, as you asked."

"It's nothing." He picked up the knife, sawed a chunk of bread, then tossed the piece in his mouth.

In the silence, his chewing resounded like the sound of a cow chewing its cud.

I fled to the hearth and busied myself with breakfast preparations.

"I mean to retrieve Pearl after I eat," John said. "Do you want to come along?"

A long walk with him with nothing to do but talk? "I planned on going to Father's after my chores are done."

"Then I'll wait until you're ready."

I swallowed my frustration. "No need. I'll bring Pearl home with me."

He nodded and went back to chewing his bread and cheese.

"Arse!" Charlotte ran to me and threw her arms around me.

I laughed and pulled her tight. "You act as if I've been gone a fortnight."

We walked toward the house, arms at each other's waists. "You've grown since yesterday!"

Charlotte laid her head against my shoulder. "What's it like, being married?"

I hesitated before answering. "I have my own home to take care of, and that's nice. Now, I was thinking we could make candles."

She sighed, long and sonorous. "But we usually wait until it isn't hot."

"There's always a need for candles." And it would be a project that would keep me here for days.

Coward, a chiding brogue whispered in my ear.

I lifted my chin. Perhaps, but I wasn't ready to return home just yet.

We poured the rancid grease from the grease barrel into boiling kettles of water, skimming the dross from the surface, over and over again. All day, we skimmed. The sun beat on our backs. The trapped heat underneath my straw hat pushed sweat down my brow. I arched my back with a hand at my waist, stretching the cramp in my spine.

What was I doing?

I would go through all this just to avoid John? I *was* a coward.

I had made a decision, and it was time I got on with it.

"That's enough for today, Charlotte. Cover the kettles. I'll see you on the morrow."

I fetched Pearl, along with her things and the remains from dinner. I didn't mind my little sister's bright chatter. It made me think what a nice thing it would be to have it fill the spaces of silence between John and me until I could discover how to ease things between us.

When we entered, John was already at the hearth, turning over a cake in a pan. He twisted his head over his shoulder and glanced at me. "Hello, Pearl. Wife."

The same uncomfortable pit I'd had when I left returned.

I set Pearl's things down. "Hello, husband. I brought food for supper."

"I thought you might be tired after a long day, so I, well..." He rubbed the back of his neck. "No matter."

Pearl went to his side and turned her chatter toward him.

I used the opportunity to slip outside and milk our cow. Just as I was settled on the stool in the pen, our cabin's door creaked open.

John's heavy steps stopped behind me.

I forced myself to shift and face him. "Yes?"

He squared his shoulders. "Did you know?"

"Know what?"

"Of what... of the things that a husband and wife..."

"I grew up on a farm, John. Of course I knew."

He exhaled and nodded. "Good. Good. Well, I shall see you inside."

"Wait." I rose and came before him. "Is this something that happens often?"

His cheeks reddened. "It is a part of marriage, Rosanna."

I studied him closely for any hint of deception. I hadn't been aware of such goings on with my own parents, but granted, I slept more soundly than a hibernating bear, or so I'd been told.

"For what purpose?" I asked.

"I thought you said you knew."

"Of course. I was only making sure *you* knew." A partial lie. It was only that I didn't understand why the act would be done if there was no love and no hope of children. If the question had occurred to me earlier, I might've been able to ask Mama.

"I'm not a simpleton, Rosanna, despite what you might think."

The hurt in his eyes kept a check on my temptation to give too light an answer. "I've never thought that. Not even when we were children." He forgot that *he* was the one who used to call me an addlepate, but I wouldn't mention it, not now that we had to live with one another in a peaceable way.

"Well, good. I wouldn't like it if my wife couldn't respect me."

I nodded once, then returned to sit on the stool and went back to milking. "I didn't dislike what we did, John," I said in a small voice, half hoping he wouldn't hear it.

He stayed for a moment longer, then left.

SEVENTEEN
CALLUM

May 1754

The full moon hung above us, an orb wrapped in cottonwood down.

We left our encampment in the Great Meadows and marched a winding, muddy path. Tanacharison, a Seneca native otherwise known as the Half-King, led us in uneasy silence for hours, his warriors enclosing us from behind. He had been the one to report to Washington the existence of the French encampment miles away, and whatever he said must have worried Washington enough that we found ourselves traversing this treacherous black trail through the dead of night.

The soldiers behind me whispered that Tanacharison held a grudge against the French for boiling and eating his father—that he used his mighty warriors to gain back the power he'd lost among the other natives, and all to get back at the French. Yarns, more than likely. No Frenchman I knew would do such a thing. No man at all, for that matter.

Yet, here we were, marching after the French, led by Tanacharison. Did he use us too?

My chest tightened so I could hardly breathe.

All the cracks were there for a fissure between France and Britain. Both nations could feed and clothe a kingdom for centuries with the vast riches of resources in the Ohio Country. Neither would give it up willingly. One bullet, and the powder keg of war would be lit.

Morning light unveiled dips and rises in the land. The towering maples thinned, and the grouse began its drumming song.

We followed a rise, a rock ridge overlooking a glen, scattered with French soldiers dozing amongst the ferns and in bark lean-tos.

Tanacharison and his men quietly descended the slope, disappearing through the trees to the front of the camp.

Washington signaled some of us to stay on the stone rise and led the rest around the slumbering camp so the French would be surrounded on all sides.

We wouldn't be firing on sleeping men, would we?

Philemon raised his rifle.

I inched a shaking finger onto the trigger of my own rifle, sliding my other hand slowly up the lock plate, just as Phil taught me, and aimed my weapon.

My heart pounded so hard it might burst. So this was it. My promise to my father, broken. I wasn't running from a fight but straight into it. The Frenchmen below disappeared. I could only see the man with the spear in his stomach put there by me, and my father, his bloody hand gripping my arm, commanding me to run away.

A breeze kicked up, setting the leaves dancing. The wind carried the smell of iron and earth. Rain.

"Keep your flintlocks dry," Phil whispered.

My arms began to shake with the weight of my rifle. A lone, cold bead of sweat slipped down my temple and into the hollow of my ear. I didn't dare wipe it.

One of the Frenchmen below yawned and opened his eyes. He jerked upright, eyes wide. "*Aux armes!*" he shouted.

The half-dressed men scrambled for their weapons.

An otherworldly war cry sounded from the other side of the vale.

The hair on my arms and neck stood on end.

A shot rang out.

The glen erupted in fire, ours from the cliffs, theirs from below. A shot exploded from my rifle as if another man pulled the trigger.

A fog of gunpowder smoke swirled in a din of foreign commands, the sound of ax hitting flesh, cries of "*Pitié!*"

Mercy.

A blood-curdling scream from a young set of lungs pierced through the haze.

Tileman! He was several feet below me at the foot of the cliff. A Frenchman stood over the prostrate boy with a bloodied knife.

I wouldn't be able to load my weapon in time to save the boy.

Without another thought, I leaped off the short cliff, slamming into the Frenchman and crashing with him to the ground.

The impact knocked the breath from my lungs.

The man fumbled at his side for the knife.

I shot my knee to the side and pinned his arm, but still his fingers inched toward the blade. I cupped my hands around his neck and squeezed. He flailed beneath me, kicking and jerking from side to side. As soon as he went limp, I slipped my hands from his throat and jumped off him.

I ran to Tileman and fell on my knees before him, raking my gaze over his slight frame. Along his hairline and down his temple, his white hair had turned a ghastly bright pink from the blood dripping from a cut. "Are ye hurt?"

He only stared, pale and silent.

Had the back of his head cracked open, spilling his brains out? "*Are ye hurt, lad?*" I grasped his upper arm and hauled him to his feet.

Cries from the French filled the glen. "*Je me rends! Je me rends!*"

Surrender already?

Washington's hoarse yell carried out across the din: "Hold fire!"

The shots stuttered to a stop.

A large man, lying on his side, raised his arm and waved a leather pouch. "*Je porte des lettres de diplomatie!*" he called out. "*Je suis aux commandes, Enseigne Joseph Coulon de Villiers de Jumonville.*"

"Jumonville!" Washington shouted, climbing off his horse. "I accept your letters of diplomacy. Wait there."

Bleeding from a gash in his forehead, Jumonville grimaced and lowered his pouch to the ground. "*Paix,*" the pitiful man breathed out. "*Paix.*"

Peace.

Washington signaled another soldier to his side, and together they trekked through the dense grass.

Tanacharison, closer to the man than any of us, tossed the handle of his ax in his hand as if testing the weight of it, and within a few short strides, stood over the fallen man.

"Tanacharison!" Washington's voice boomed across the glen. "Leave him. We must see if what he says is true."

As if Washington's words had been the inconsequent buzzing of a gnat, Tanacharison raised his ax.

Jumonville lifted the pouch in his shaking, bloody hand. "I come in peace," he shouted in heavily accented English.

I took off at a dead run toward them, bounding over fern and tree stumps, my lungs burning, my heart pounding in my throat.

The Half-King yelled some indecipherable words, a mix of English and another tongue.

I strained forward, pumping my legs, branches slicing my limbs to ribbons.

Tanacharison swung his ax and sliced it into the man's forehead, splitting it in two.

Placing his foot on Jumonville's lifeless body, he pulled his ax free and bent to cup his hand inside the dead man's skull.

I skidded to a stop and clenched my eyes tight, unwilling to watch the rest.

With Jumonville dead, the battle came to an end.

Tanacharison and his men left. Fourteen French soldiers lay scalped or shot, their bodies twisted and scattered about the battleground and their commander, his skull cleaved in two.

Jumonville's brother, Captain Louis Coulon de Villiers, headed a French force in marching distance, and once he heard what had happened here, they would be in hot pursuit of us.

We hastened up the trail, away from the horrific scene, silent, uneasy.

Had the first shot been fired by us? The French?

Did it matter, with us trespassing their sanctuary, our rifles pointed at them? What would we have done if we had been in their position? If their purpose in being there was not to engage us in battle but present diplomatic papers, we had been in the wrong entirely.

My mouth burned with the taste of metal, blood, and death from Culloden. The pike buried deep in the dragoon's belly became the ax buried in Jumonville's crown. The Half-King's hands, my hands.

You cannot be other than you are made to be, promise or no, Smythe had said. *It is selfless. It is brave.*

There'd hardly been even a moment to consider what I was doing before I jumped into the fight. So easy, as if I was made for it.

This wasn't selfless. It was self-preservation.

By nightfall, we were back in the Great Meadows with our French captives.

Washington wasted no time preparing for Coulon's arrival. We built a circular stockage enclosing a small wooden cabin with a roof made of animal skins and birch bark to keep our gunpowder and food dry. We called it Fort Necessity.

Inside, the cabin reminded me a little of Rosanna's secret hut. I'd visited it once. She and I had huddled in the quiet, our heads almost touching the canopy of sticks and the air rich with damp earth. Waterfalls of light spilled between the cracks, unveiling the golden flecks in her dark eyes.

We went back to the road we had been cutting for Colonel Fry and our reinforcements before our interlude with the French soldiers. We cleared the creek beds of trees and brush, making natural entrenchments for battle, then created earthworks by building mounds of earth and breastworks, V-shaped logs stacked to the height of a man's chest.

For days, I hacked brush from the dry water ways winding around our fort, with Tileman beside me at every moment. Since I'd saved him at the glen, I hadn't been able to shake him.

"Jack?"

I threw a large branch of young mesquite out of the bed. "Yes, Tileman?"

"I've been thinking. Mayhap I don't want to be a soldier anymore."

"If I had a father with a ship for me to sail, I wouldn't be here."

"If I left, would you join me?" Tileman asked.

I smiled. "What would you have me do?"

"I could send back loads of rum, and you could sell it to the regiments."

I stopped and studied him. "Well, now. That's an idea." The plan wasn't half mad like most young boys' ideas were. "You might not need me when you're ready for such a venture."

"I'm ready to leave *now*. I've never been so hungry in all my life." With perfect timing, Tileman's stomach growled.

Poor boy.

Conditions had been deteriorating day by day.

We'd skipped many meals since we arrived, sometimes several

days in a row. Washington had even put a guard at the storehouse's door to keep us out of it.

We worked in grueling hot humidity without enough salt to replace what we lost in our sweat.

Our Indian allies had abandoned us.

One man deserted, then another.

We had no doubt they would find the French and fall upon them for mercy, exchanging food and water for information on our position. Soon, our enemy would know exactly where we were and how weak our position was.

I pulled out my last piece of dried venison and handed it to Tileman. It wasn't so long ago that I'd been a growing boy, surviving on scraps from a fellow prisoner who'd taken pity on me. "Take heart. There may be something in the traps today."

Tileman tore off a piece between his teeth. "They're *always* empty. Do you think if I caught a toad and held it over the fire, the poison would turn to smoke and I could eat it?"

Now *that* was the kind of half-mad idea I was used to hearing from him. "Don't let me catch you doing that."

Reinforcements arrived the next day—one hundred and fifty from our Virginia Regiment and one hundred of His Majesty's Independent Companies of South Carolina. We now matched almost half of the enemy's numbers. Not enough, but hadn't Gideon crushed a swarm of Midianites with only three hundred men?

Another sound joined the commotion—the lowing of fifty head of cattle.

I breathed out a prayer of thanks for the promise of a full belly to come.

A jovial mood infected the camp. The soldiers laughed and ribbed each other, their words swimming with rum and hope. We even went so far as to think we stood a chance against the coming enemy and the Indians who joined them.

With a full stomach, a man is likely to believe anything possible.

The men ate themselves sick that night, some retching and going back for more. I had my fill but couldn't muster the same abandon as the others, not with what happened to the French in their camp.

Washington stood apart from us, leaning against a tree and staring into the far distance. Even with the deprivations of the past few weeks, he still looked the part of a regimental officer, tidy and well kept, but his face was haggard, thin, grooved with heavy lines.

I picked up my trencher and carried it to where he stood. "Sir?"

He stirred and unlocked his tight face. "What is it, Drummond?"

I held out my trencher filled with a slab of meat layered with sinew. It was all that was left of the poor cow whose quarters had been the first upon the spit.

He turned his face away, staring into the trees. "You're uneasy about our run-in with the French."

I hesitated. How did he know?

He pushed off the tree and came to my side. "Colonel Fry is dead."

At least I wouldn't have to worry about the colonel deciding to be rid of me, as Washington had warned when we met.

"Fell off his horse. Just in time to hand off the regiment to me before the French come against us. The sly fox."

"You're in charge, then."

"I am." He met my gaze, challenge in his eyes. "What think you of that?"

Washington had prepared us well. He was a natural leader who inspired confidence, though he was only two years older than me. He was born to privilege, while I was a scrapper, a fugitive, a man without a home. Who was I to judge whether he was the right man to lead us?

But he had led us to that glen. If only I could be sure that the French had fired the first shot and that we'd acted in self-defense.

"I never intended... I didn't think—" Washington loosened his neckcloth and whipped it off. "Confound it. The battle had already started before I knew what had happened."

The tension in my shoulders dissolved. He was distressed by what happened. A lesser man would have defended himself so as not to lose face. His honest admittance to his uncertainty gave me leave to be open with mine.

"*Were* they on a diplomatic mission?"

"Perhaps. Their papers could have been a ruse. But they fired first—I'm sure of it."

I took hold of the line he tossed me. It would be easier to go forward believing that, with no other place for me but with the regiment.

I stuck out my hand. "I'll follow you, come what will."

Washington clasped my hand. "Thank you, Drummond." When I tried to pull away, he held fast. "The beads."

My senses sharpened as if preparing for battle. "What of them?"

"My brother wore the same in the last years of his life. The same pattern of repeating colors, the same Venetian glass bird in the middle with its hawk's beak. I thought it peculiar—no man in our circle wore such a thing, and Lawrence had always been careful about appearances. The beads must have meant something to him."

"I'm sorry, sir. I cannot say where they came from." I couldn't risk implicating Bembe as the abettor of a runaway indentured servant if Washington should ever find out who I was.

His face hardened. "No matter. I'll discover it whether you help me or not."

EIGHTEEN

CALLUM

Leaning against the pen's railing, I brushed my fingers along the velvety softness of Obsidian's nose. Had I saved him from one fate only to risk him to another? That I could die in the upcoming battle didn't matter so much as leaving Obsidian to someone else's care. Would they love him as I did? Would they read the spirit in his eyes and give him his lead? I rested my forehead on his cheek, girding myself with courage to leave him, perhaps for good.

"You'll be alright," I whispered. Away from the front lines, he'd be safe, awaiting whatever Frenchman would claim him as their own. Perhaps the commander. Obsidian was too beautiful to be used by anyone else.

He swished his tail and bent his head to the grass. I smiled a little. If only I could be as unconcerned.

I meandered to the breastworks, stepping over soldiers sleeping off their night of gluttony. Philemon stood at the furthest point, the appointed watchman for the night, with his rifle aimed across the meadow.

"I've come to keep you company," I said, leaning one shoulder against a pointed wooden slat.

He only grunted, a pained look on his face.

"Overeat, did you?"

"Better to leave this world on a full stomach."

"You expect them soon, then."

He jerked his chin toward the forest. "They're somewhere close. Wish they'd get on with it and reveal themselves."

Perhaps they would. Dark was descending. If the French wanted a surprise attack, it would be at night.

The downpour lightened. I took off my hat and wrung it in my hands. Rain had been falling off and on for days, filling the creek beds we'd worked so hard to clear.

"What'll you do when this business with the French is over?" Philemon asked.

"Haven't thought about it." All that mattered was surviving so I could keep Obsidian safe.

"What about going back home?"

"Not with Grenville's claim to me."

"Not to Virginia. Scotland."

Scotland? The circle of gold under my shirt burned against my skin. It was all I had left of my homeland. Nothing remained of Scotland, not my brogue, not even this ring, as it belonged to Rosanna. Return? To what? Obsidian was all I had, setting aside my thieving him from Grenville. It didn't matter where I went, as long as I had him.

"Let's see first if we survive the night," I said.

"You could get your own piece of the Ohio and follow me."

The clouds cleared. The moon overlooked the meadow, smoothing the grass in its light.

Philemon put a finger to his mouth and pointed in the distance. Quickly, he poured gunpowder down the muzzle and loaded his weapon with buckshot.

The wind-rippled grass took shape. It wasn't the storm moving the grass, but a line of three men on their hands and knees, draped with hog skin and grunting, as if to fool us into thinking boars had entered our perimeter.

They'd come.

Before I could finish loading my weapon, Philemon fired.

The sound of buckshot thudding into flesh, cries of alarm and pain, shattered the quiet.

A shout came from the trees: "*Nous sommes découverts!*" We are discovered!

The forest came alive. Horses cried, metal clanked. The moon receded behind a bank of clouds. A torch lit, then another. A chain of flickering lights threaded between the trees, each illuminating the faces of men who were after our blood.

"Awake!" yelled Philemon. "Awake!"

Half-dressed men leaped to their stations and scattered to the breastworks, the creek beds, the stockade, taking aim through the cracks in the upright slats of wood.

Philemon and I ran to the creek bed and lowered ourselves onto our bellies in the mud.

The French and their Indian allies stepped from the trees. The wind kicked up, lifting the flaps of their overcoats, and the clouds broke open. One by one, their torches fizzled in the heavy rain.

"Form ranks!" Washington called to his line of men in the open field.

A cannonball splintered the breastworks to my left. Soldiers' screams punctured the buzzing in my head.

I gulped a lungful of air.

Where was Tileman?

Rifle in hand, I scrambled from the trench.

"What are you doing?" Philemon yelled.

I ignored Philemon and ran away from the front line.

A streak of lightning cracked the sky, illuminating a flash of shining horseflesh and a shock of white hair belonging to a boy behind the stockade.

"Tileman!"

He started, the whites of his eyes flashing.

I grabbed his arm. "Quick, come with me."

"No!" He ripped away from my hold and locked his arms around Obsidian's neck. "They're scared."

Obsidian stared at me, almost as if he challenged me to take

Tileman from him. He had always had a soft spot for boys in trouble.

"He's going with you," I said, grabbing Tileman and throwing him on my horse's back. It had been the decision of a moment. I'd meant to bring him back with me, but now that the battle was upon us, I couldn't bear to take him closer to danger.

He steadied his seat and grabbed onto Obsidian's mane. "Where are we going?"

"Away from here." I quickly bridled the horse.

"But we're surrounded!"

I pulled the reins and led them carefully through the chaos.

"Fire!" Washington called in the distance. A crack of rifle fire exploded.

Obsidian reared, but to the boy's credit, he held on. I jumped onto the horse's back behind Tileman, taking control of the reins.

We made it to the stockade. I jumped off Obsidian and banged on the pikes with my fist. "Open!"

The gate opened. A man stuck his head out. "Go back to the lines!"

I stuck my foot in front of the gate before he could close it. "Take my horse and the boy, and I'll give you enough for a month of rum." Digging in my pocket, I retrieved what money I had left from what Bembe had given me. "Here."

"We don't have room," he said, looking from the coins to the horse and Tileman.

"Make room." I dropped the coins on the ground in front of him, and just as I suspected he would, he stooped and gathered them with his fat fingers. Before he could protest again, I pulled the gate wider and pushed my charges into the stockade. The men inside paid us no heed, as intent as they were on the fight. "Tileman, don't let them put you or Obsidian out, understand?"

He glared at the guard. "I won't."

"If the French break through, I'll come and find you."

He nodded his head once. "I'll take care of him. Don't worry."

"Good lad."

I ran in a crouch away from the stockade. A bullet hissed so close it stirred a rush of hot air past my neck. The creek beds loomed ahead, but no one was there.

From the breastworks, Phil caught sight of me and waved his hat in the air. "Over here!"

I joined him and stripped the rifle from my back.

A cannonball splintered the breastworks' wooden planks to our left. It missed a man by a hair's breadth. The next man would not be so lucky.

"We've had a time of it," Philemon said, his face streaked with rain and gunpowder. "With the rain, we're down to sniping."

That didn't bode well, not with them having the advantage in numbers.

We fought through the next hours without rest or drink. Men fell at our sides, one by one, leaving only a handful of soldiers in our trench.

Phil cursed. "Powder's wet. Give it over," he commanded, his hand outstretched to the soldier beside him.

The man tossed the screw that Phil would use to remove the lead ball and the wet charge behind it.

Phil held his rifle upright, then put the screw on the end of his ramrod and shoved it down the barrel, twisting the screw into the lead ball. "Devil take it!"

"What is it?"

"They're picking us off like we're caged animals." He pulled up the ramrod with the ball attached and dumped out the wet gunpowder. "Are we just going to wait here, getting shot, until we're all dead?" He tossed the ramrod to the ground and glared at me. "Well? Are we?"

An alarm clanged in my head. I'd seen that look in his eyes many times before. "We don't have much of a choice."

He turned toward the men still standing, scattered along the breastworks. "Let's meet them face to face. We're either dead in this muck or we go out there and die like men."

The soldiers exchanged uncertain looks.

I put my arm across Phil's chest and called to the men, "He's jesting!"

He threw off my hold, his face flushed.

I pushed Phil back against the wall and lowered my voice. "Sit, and stop being a hothead. You'll get yourself killed."

A man's voice carried across the clearing.

"*Voulez-vous parler?*"

Phil stopped struggling. The firing from the other side ceased. We peered across the meadow.

A man in a French uniform waved a white flag.

Again, it came. "*Voulez-vous parler?*"

The French wanted to negotiate.

Murmurs swept through our ranks. Perhaps we'd underestimated their losses.

Our translator left Washington's side and went out to meet the Frenchman. After a terse exchange, the two men walked toward the enemy.

An eerie quiet hung in the meadows.

"Wait here," I said to Philemon.

"Where are you going?" he called.

"To the stockade."

Philemon left the trench and followed me to the gate, entering with me.

Tileman, hale and hearty, sat on Obsidian, neither of whom bore a scratch. "I kept him safe, just as you asked." He jumped to the ground and handed the reins over.

I squeezed Tileman's shoulder. "I've need of you still. Can you hide him in the forest?" Who knew what terms the French would negotiate for themselves? It was possible they'd take all our animals for their own use or destroy them to hobble our retreat. Both had happened in other battles. With the break in fighting, Tileman and Obsidian might not get a better chance of escaping. "Can you do that?"

Tileman straightened his shoulders. "Aye."

Washington came within sight of the structure.

I lowered my voice and spoke urgently to Tileman. "If I don't meet you in the forest, head to Gist's Plantation. I'll find you there." A hollow promise, perhaps, but at least he and Obsidian would be safer at the settlement. "Now, go."

Tileman kicked his heels into Obsidian's flanks, and the two dashed from the gate.

Washington flung himself out of their path. "Cruger!" he yelled. "Get back here!"

But he'd not secured the boy's loyalty like I had, and Tileman only urged Obsidian faster.

Washington strode over to me, his hair unkempt and face streaked with sweat. "Your doing, I'd wager."

"What is, sir?"

His mouth tightened. "I'll deal with you later. Waters, help Drummond clear the storehouse. Negotiations will be settled there."

With the meager stores the regiment had left, it took little time to remove everything but a table and chairs.

After some time, the translator returned with two Frenchmen —a man of some authority, going by the stateliness of his uniform, and his guard.

Washington awaited them, already sitting at the table.

Several others stood behind him, and Phil and I squeezed into the dark shadows along the wall where we might not be noticed.

The French aide eyed the little storeroom as if measuring it for his commander's use as our translator read from the papers of capitulation.

The terms were surprisingly good.

We would be allowed to withdraw with the honors of war and have our personal effects remain with us. We would in turn give our swivel guns to them and the fortifications, of course, but he had not asked anything we weren't already prepared to give.

"Please tell the colonel that he has been most generous," Washington said. He lifted the quill in the inkpot and set the tip on the empty space at the end of the document.

The aide covered the paper with his hand, pushing Washington's hand out of the way.

Washington's eyes turned to steel, the only hint that he'd registered the disrespect.

"*Arrêtez*. A moment, please," the aide said in a thick accent. "Before you sign, there is one more thing Colonel Villiers asks. He says it will not be too much for you to grant when he has given you so much."

The silence went on for a beat longer. "No one can deny that he has been more than fair," Washington said.

"The sentinel who killed his scouts—my commander desires that you give him over so the man might be brought to justice."

Philemon tensed. He stealthily put his finger on the trigger and tipped his rifle at Washington.

What precisely did my friend think to do? Kill Washington, securing his own demise whether the French took him or not?

I shoved myself in front of him, forcing him against the wall.

To Washington's credit, he didn't give any indication that the very man the French colonel sought stood in this room. "That man fell in battle and is dead."

I did not draw a breath, nor did I lessen my hold on Philemon.

A thin, forced smile stretched across the aide's mouth. "A pity." He stared at Washington for a long moment, then removed his hand from the paper.

Washington bowed his head mockingly at the man and swept the quill across the paper.

The aide tucked the paper in his coat and put his hat on. "I will have the colonel sign on my return."

The man and his guard withdrew from the hut.

Washington stood. "Not a word," he said to all of us, then strode out of the hut.

I waited until the others filed out of the storehouse before letting go of Philemon.

Philemon jerked away from me, his chest heaving. "If Washington had answered *Phil Waters*, he would not have spoken again."

No doubt. It had been exactly why I'd pushed myself in front of him.

Mr. Smythe had deemed me a defender of the defenseless, but by *defenseless*, he couldn't have meant hot-headed friends and regimental commanders.

NINETEEN
ROSANNA

December 1754

The brick at my feet had long since cooled. Our bed, a block of ice.

My abdomen, full with babe, tightened into a stone lying heavy on my spine.

Christmas had come and gone. A new year waited only for the passing of a few days. Frost hung heavy in the air and crept along my toes and into my knees and thighs. Even lying on his side with his back toward me, John took up most of the bed, a hot, burning lump of flesh. Yet, I dared not touch him. He worked himself ragged and needed every bit of sleep available to him. Every morning, he fed the animals under the twinkling of the night's last stars. In the quiet, he readied the plow and hauled water from the well for the day's use. By the time I usually woke and brought him a cup of steaming coffee, he'd been hard at work for hours.

I'd be no use to him without sleep. My toes stretched toward his calves and closer to his warmth.

An irritated groan came from his side of the bed.

I pulled my feet away.

He fished with his leg behind him and hooked my knees, tucking them into the angle of his own. "Be still," he mumbled.

Every rigid muscle in my body thawed into blessed softness. With my large stomach between us, he couldn't have meant for it to be a romantic gesture. Still, I had the impulse to reach toward him and kiss his neck, just to see what he would do. The only time we touched was at night, and our touches were nothing so full of feeling as that.

Not that I wouldn't have minded it. Though I'd been closer to him in body than I'd been with anyone else, I was lonelier than ever.

Mama had lied. As it turned out, one could have children without love.

I blushed now, remembering my ignorance.

John had taught me in full what Mama had meant the night we were married. The way between a man and a woman was as unladylike an undertaking as I could imagine. But it was the closest thing to the wildness I craved.

Beyond that, John had been true to his word and had let me run my life as I saw fit, though I'd determined not to take advantage.

Like any good wife, I prepared his breakfast and cleaned his clothes, and as for caring for Father and the boys, Charlotte had taken over my duties without any trouble at all. She'd adjusted quickly to running things, freeing me to hunt and fill our smokehouse with meat, to go for my forest walks, to take Pearl to visit Phil's and my abandoned huts. Pearl took up the abandoned acorn cups and bark trenchers, while I picked off squirrel intruders with my slingshot and kept my loaded rifle on my lap in case a bear should cross our haven's boundary.

John and I fit well together. I made my days my own, and so did he, planting and tending to his fields. He pleased me, and I seemed to please him, especially now that I was carrying his child.

I eased my hands between us, soaking in the heat seeping from my husband's back.

Close to morning, my eyes grew heavy at last.

. . .

It seemed only a minute passed before I awoke. My heart pulsed with sudden anxiety, my skin prickled as if I'd woken from a nightmare.

What reason had I to fear? The sun's first light streamed through the cracks between the logs in our little cabin, and I was wrapped in our quilt in our warm bed.

Then my belly cramped so hard I grabbed for John's arm, but the side of his bed was cold and abandoned.

As I sat up, a gush of water flowed onto the bed.

My breath quickened.

It was too early.

The truth of what was about to happen hit me with the force of a squall.

"Pearl!" I called to my sister, who was playing quietly by the hearth. "Get John. The baby's coming."

She dropped her doll and tore out the door in the direction of the barn. "Brother John!" she screamed. "Come quick!"

I paced, three steps forward and then three steps in the other direction. It wasn't *too* early. John and I had been married eight months. Charlotte had been born before her time, and she was the healthiest of all us Waters children.

But I was so small, and the babe so big.

Another cramp hit, so strong it folded me over. I held the stacked-log wall with one hand so I wouldn't topple over.

John broke across the threshold a few moments later, short of breath. "Are you well?"

"The babe is coming."

He whooped and threw his hat into the air. "How long?"

I caught my tongue in my teeth so I wouldn't lash out at him for yelling. "I'm as learned as you are in these matters." Another cramp overtook me, and I moaned, an animal who couldn't escape the trap.

He bent and swept his hat off the ground. I caught him taking a peek outside the door. "It's just that the fence is only half up. Do you think I might have time to finish?"

"A pox on you! A pox on all your kin and your horse too!"

"But, Rosanna, you're my kin. You can't wish for a pox upon yourself." He grinned, clearly proud of himself for his joke.

All I could see was that mocking, knows-everything boy at the river.

My next groan came out as nearly a scream of rage.

"Shhh." He came beside me and put his arm about my shoulder. "It's nothing that hasn't been done before. Cows give birth. Sheep. Dogs. Rabbits..." He patted my shoulder with plodding awkwardness.

I smiled, sickly sweet. "And cats?"

Sweat dripped down his temple. "Yes, cats. And they give birth quietly too." He gave me a look of mild censure.

"I'll try to keep silent, then, so as not to bother you!" I poured all my fury into that last word. "Or would you like to try in my stead?"

Father crashed through our door, a wild look in his eyes. "I came as soon as Pearl told me."

Shame washed over me. Had he heard us squabbling like children?

"Are you well, child?"

At the gentleness in his voice, some piece inside of me broke.

Loud sobs I didn't recognize as my own wracked my body and filled our little cabin.

"John, go and fetch the midwife," Father said quietly. "I'll stay and keep watch."

Without another word, John turned and left.

I stood half bent, holding on to the wall, shuddering with sobs like a child.

Father set Mama's rocking chair beside me, the one he'd given to me the day I'd married John.

"You don't have to stay," I said, collapsing into it, though the idea of being left alone scared me more than I would admit.

"It is the way of life. You'll get through it as your mother did."

He said it in such a plain and matter-of-fact tone, as if there were nothing about me that would make him question my ability to do this.

At least Father hadn't compared me to an animal.

The midwife arrived with John a little while later and shooed both men away.

After hours of labor, the babe emerged quiet and still. The midwife rubbed her vigorously with linen strippings until a choking cry came from the small mite. Mewing, like that of a kitten, sounded from within the folds of the cloth.

"She's too early, but she's alive," the woman said gently. "Keep her warm and let her eat as much as she likes, poor lass."

She set her in my arms.

Our babe was a red, wrinkly thing, so quiet and skinny that she resembled the mummified piglet Phil and I had found on the side of the path one day, its skin hanging on its bones. Dread settled in my stomach. I'd mothered my siblings through fevers and scrapes, but this was different. "Will she live?"

The midwife clucked. "Only God can say."

My daughter stared up at me, her eyes trusting and grave.

A fierce feeling came upon me, stronger than any I had known.

"You will live," I whispered to her in defiance to the woman's words. The babe was mine, and I would keep her.

John rushed in and dropped to his knees by our bed. "Are you well?"

I nodded. "You have a daughter."

He looked then to our daughter. "She's so quiet." Tears glimmered in his eyes as he brushed his daughter's hand with tentative fingers.

The baby curled its fingers tight around John's pinky.

"We will do what we can for the girl," he said, looking at me unashamedly through his tears.

I'd never seen John so gentle. Something clicked into place then. Love may not have been what brought John and me together, but perhaps it could grow.

"Forgive me," John whispered. "I'm no good when I don't know what to do."

I touched my forehead to his. "Should we name her?"

John thought for a moment. "Sarah Bordroyne, for your mother's given name."

I smiled a little and studied the quiet babe in my arms. Wouldn't my brother like that? I would just have to pray that my daughter was born more Sarah than Bordroyne.

TWENTY
ROSANNA

1764

"Captain, *Queen Anne's Revenge* is coming behind us!" Johnny yelled, sitting atop our headboard and waving his wooden sword that I'd fashioned for him.

"His cannons are firing!" Sarah said, jumping upon our bed, holding the top of her breeches so they didn't slip down her slim frame.

I'd allowed her to wear her brother's pants after she'd argued that pirates didn't wear dresses. *I am wearing a dress,* I'd responded. *You are the captain—you can do what you like,* she'd said, as if that put an end to it. It was true. I *was* the captain, and I could do what I liked. And what I liked was the way my skirts swirled when I fought at swords with my little beasties.

"We'll show Blackbeard we're just as fierce as he," I called from my post at the foot of my bed. I slashed my arm forward, unfurling a scarlet length of linen. "Bears, attack!"

Samuel and Landon jumped from the bed and scampered on all fours to the boys' tick mattress where Thomas stood—Blackbeard with his own sword, guarding his ship. At only two and five,

Samuel and Landon were the youngest of my lot but wouldn't be kept out of their siblings' rough play.

"You mangy ship-rats!" Thomas hooked both arms around their necks and threw them to the blankets, wrestling them into a shouting muddle.

Pearl, content to watch from her loom, laughed. "Save them, Captain!"

"Unhand them, you murderous pirate!" I leaped off my bed and onto theirs, and Johnny landed just behind me. I fell into the middle of them and tickled every foot and belly I saw.

The front door clicked closed.

I sat up, straightening my hair.

"Papa!" Samuel ran to John and collided with his legs.

"We had to take our games indoors with all the rain." I plucked the feather I'd set in my hair and pulled off my linen sash.

John patted Samuel's back and stepped out of his youngest son's hold. He walked to the mantel and hung his rifle, but instead of turning to us and adding his noise to the clamor, he stayed there, his back turned to us.

The oldest four rushed to him, pulling at his hands, climbing and hanging on him like a passel of opossums.

Landon had made it to his shoulders and hung about John's neck. "Papa! It's my birthday, and I am to have a cake! Sarah made it."

"You're to share it with everyone," Thomas said, as an elder brother would.

"Only me! It's *my* birthday."

"No!" Johnny grabbed the waist of Landon's trousers and yanked. "It's for us too!"

Landon fell in a heap. Johnny jumped on top of him and pounded his brother with his little fists.

"Only me! Only me!" Landon shouted, returning blow for blow.

Little Samuel, the sweetest of my pirate crew, wailed that he wanted cake too. I settled him on my hip and kissed his sweaty cheek. "Don't you worry. You'll have some, sweetling."

John didn't move, not even to wade into the boys' melee and pull them apart as he normally would.

I pulled Johnny off Landon by the scruff of his shirt. With a pointed finger, I directed them both to Freddie's Chair, named after the nemesis of our childhood. The well-worn stool was used to subdue youthful mutinies, reforming agitators and dissenters, of which I had five, excepting sweet Samuel unless he was hungry. Many hours of their lives had been spent sitting there, their little faces glowering until they realized they'd stay there until I believed them sufficiently contrite. They might be stubborn; I was more stubborn still. Skirmish by skirmish I'd wage the battle to preserve them into adulthood.

They should be glad only two of them balanced upon the stool. When Thomas joined them, it was difficult not to laugh at their struggle to look contrite while fighting for every inch of territory for their behinds.

"Thomas, take Samuel to bed, please."

"Yes, Mama." Thomas transferred Samuel to his own hip obediently enough but then smiled smugly walking past his brothers. "I'll get all the cake, and you skunks won't get any," he whispered.

I breathed slowly through a flare of exasperation. My court of justice would deal with him later. "Sarah, go outside and help Pearl."

My daughter walked past us, one hand cinching her brother's breeches around her waist.

John made no comment.

He never let it pass without a remark when I let her dress like the boys.

My heart tapped an extra beat. Something was wrong.

In our ten years of marriage, I'd learned to read John's feelings in the set of the muscles in his back and the angle of his head. "John?"

His hand slipped from the rifle to his side, his face shadowed under the brim of his hat.

"What happened? Is it Father?"

"Peter Blake's parcel was sold off."

My heart dropped into my belly. He'd been saving for years. We'd forgone Christmas, new shoes, tea, all with that parcel of land in mind. Northerners had been coming to Virginia in droves, buying every available scrap of land and driving up prices. Without Blake's land, we couldn't expand our farm, not like John dreamed of. "Then we find another farm close by. One bigger than ours."

"No."

I pressed my lips together. It was a sticking point in our marriage, him discarding my ideas without giving them a moment's consideration. Once his mind was made up, there was no convincing him of anything else. I'd begrudgingly come to admire his determination but only when it wasn't directed against me. "Then we do nothing? You won't be happy."

"Not nothing." He held my gaze, a strange light in his eyes. One that made my heart trip. "They are giving away land in the backcountry of South Carolina. Just for the working of it."

My world shifted. South Carolina was past the boundary of polite society, the very edge of the frontier. Within the space of seconds, my imagination had me cutting new paths through virgin thickets, discovering hidden, black-deep pools of water, diving in and holding my breath as long as it took to touch the slippery bottom with my fingers.

Then reality set in. We couldn't move, not with me pregnant with our sixth child. And not with Pearl, who had been left feeble-hearted after a fever and wouldn't survive the trip. Did they even have doctors in South Carolina's wilderness? John loved her just as much as I did—surely, he wouldn't risk her life by forcing this hardship on her. "You can't be serious."

"Acres upon acres, Rosanna. We can have ten times what we have now. For nothing."

"It won't be for nothing, John. If the land were free, why don't the Northerners bypass us and go straight through to South Carolina?"

"Many of them have."

"But they don't just give land away. Bad land, perhaps. But not the kind of land you dream of."

In two steps, he grasped my hands and drew them to his chest. "They are, and we will have our piece of it."

I took my hands out of his and stepped back.

I was happy here. I'd thought John happy too.

He'd gotten what he'd wanted—children, a farm, a wife to work beside him, and so had I—a home of my own and the freedom to run my life as I saw fit. It wasn't pirating a ship or living with the beavers, but I found I rather enjoyed motherhood. Loved it, really, more than anything else. I still tromped through the forest, but now it was with five very silly children and Pearl at my side, me answering a hundred questions about moss and animal burrows and how to best skip a rock. John said not a word when I took his rifle from the mantel and left the children in Pearl's care so I could hunt. He didn't complain when I filled our stores with meat or when I taught Pearl to shoot his rifle.

"There must be some cost in it, John. Some reason others have not farmed it already. Mayhap the land is too marshy or too rocky or full of disease or hookworms."

"Hookworms?" His incredulous laugh made my hands itch to box his ears.

I was older now, wiser and more mature. A woman. But there were times—oh, how there were times!—I was thankful for the small, white scar puckering the skin on the tip of his ear, the one I had given to him when we were children. At least once he had felt the consequences of being an obstinate mule. "What if we are being swindled?"

"Everything I do, you have an opinion on. Why cannot you be like other wives?" John asked.

"You wish me to say nothing? To care not at all?"

"I wish you more biddable."

"Like Charity would have been, you mean."

"Yes, like Charity."

The words sank into my chest like a poisoned spearhead, along with an unbidden thought. *Callum would've never said anything like that to me.*

All in the work of a moment, my heart throbbed with aching need. Just like that, I was a young girl again.

As soon as I was aware of what was happening, I restrained my imagination. It was a dangerous path to tread, thinking of what might have been. Especially when I'd pledged my life to another.

I forced my mind back to John. "If you would but *listen...*"

He wrapped an arm around my waist and pulled me down into a chair, sitting me on his lap.

"John!" I slid a look to the children. They had quieted to little mice, their ears pointed toward our conversation.

"Never mind them." He dipped his mouth to my neck, nuzzling it. "You always said you wanted an adventure."

How dare he use my words, spoken to him in our tenderest moments, against me? "And *you* always do this when you want to win the argument!" If there was some feeling in his touch, an affectionate light in his eyes instead of a teasing one, I might forgive him, but using my heart against me was too much to be borne.

"You know I am nothing without you, my sweet. But it would be much easier if you would just *go along* with it." He set me back from him and peered into my eyes. "This is my chance. *Our* chance. Don't you want to build something to be proud of?"

A few years before, when I didn't have children who depended on me, I would have been excited for the change, but it was too late for adventure now. "We may not be rich, but we eat well enough and are respectable enough for most people. Why can't you be satisfied?"

This home, *my* home, the one I'd found my freedom in and built with my own two raw, bleeding hands, left him wanting. *I had left him wanting.* I hadn't forgotten that I wasn't his first choice. He'd wanted me only for what I could give him, and I'd given it to him, embarrassingly eager for a place to belong.

Couldn't he love me and the life we'd built enough to stay?

I tried again. "What about Pearl? She isn't well enough to make the journey."

"She will return to your father. Charlotte is gone and married. It will be good for him to have Pearl's company."

Pain stabbed through my heart. "John, you cannot ask this of me!"

He didn't meet my eyes. "I have already sold our land."

I scrambled off his lap, swallowing billows of anger. So this was it, then. There was no choice. What could I do? Stay behind and ask Father to house and feed us? John would leave, and we could do none other than join him.

I lifted my chin. "You'll get me my own rifle. And I won't leave until Pearl is settled at Father's."

Three days later, I stood inside Father's home with Pearl while John and the boys waited in the wagon. I was numb, still half in shock, that what John had planned had actually come to pass.

In a haze, I lined her old collection of rocks by her bed so she would see them first thing when she woke tomorrow. Would she think of our happy times together, walking the trail between my house and Father's and pocketing them along the way? Or would she think herself too grown for them and put them away?

I hugged Pearl to me, this sister who had become like a daughter. I kissed the top of her head, and my tears wetted her hair. I'd poured every ounce of motherly affection into her clean, neat braid this morning, the last time I would plait her hair. "Goodbye, sweet girl."

Her thin arms snaked around me and held me tight. "I don't want to be the only girl. What if I never see Sarah again?"

Her sobs tore at my heart. The two had become more than aunt and niece. More than adopted sisters. They were inseparable, even with Pearl being older than Sarah. I swallowed and swallowed again, trying to rid myself of the lump in my throat. "You aren't well enough to come."

She pushed me away. "I don't care if I die! Let me come. At least I'll die happy, with you and Sarah and the boys."

"You'll be just as happy here. I promise."

"How could you let him do this?" Her voice trembled with unspent rage.

Him. John.

I wouldn't have understood it either at her age. But life had forced me to see just how little I held in my control. First, Mama's accident. Phil's and Callum's leaving, and now, my leaving Pearl. The fear of waking to a dead Sarah for months and months after she was born weak. Pearl's illness and two babies born too still. It was just how it was.

"Pearl, I've no choice."

"Yes, you do!" She tore outside and fled the dreary scene.

I yelled after her. "I wouldn't leave if I—"

Father held me by my shoulders.

"Let her be."

I twisted from his hold, but Pearl was already a dot in the distance.

He went to the fire and busied himself with the ashes.

I took in the rough-hewn boards filled with hardened mud, the plank floor, his sunken-in mattress, dark with dirt and sweat. How long had it been since Father had refreshed the straw and cleaned the ticking? When would he have had the time? He couldn't be expected to remember, especially with a farm to take care of.

Guilt twisted my stomach. I should have noticed.

I took three large steps over to the bed and began to tug it off its frame.

"What are you doing?" Father's strong hands pulled mine from the tick and threw it back on the bedstand.

"Why has Charlotte neglected your ticking?" But that was unfair. It was as much my fault as it was hers. She was distracted with her new husband and little one, and I, with my children. "I'll clean it before I go. Do you have straw in the barn?"

"Leave it."

I dropped my hands to my side. "I could make you and the boys a pottage for supper."

"John is waiting for you."

That was it?

"Goodbye, Father."

He grabbed my arm as I passed him. "Wait." His voice broke on the word.

I stopped. "Yes?"

"I didn't mean... it is only that..." He tucked his gnarled fingers into his waistcoat and carefully pulled out a small bundle wrapped in linen. "I saved these for you."

The uncertainty on his face surprised me. Did he think I would reject his gift? What was in the bundle?

He held it closer to me.

I took a cautious step forward and peeled back the linen wrapping.

There, in the palm of his hand, lay Mama's pearl-dotted hair combs.

The close room tilted. For one glorious moment, she'd come back to me, her apron smelling of fire smoke and bayberry, her shining hair swept back in these combs, dots of white planted in her black strands.

I didn't breathe, didn't move for fear she would be lost to me again.

"I could think of nothing but my grief in those days. I—I fear I ignored you."

His words broke the spell. My mother's ghost faded, leaving only the smell of acrid bed linens and dust floating in the morning's light.

He took the combs and stuck them in my own hair, kissing my temple softly.

"I don't blame you for being angry with me," I said, leaning into the kiss and closing my eyes. "Had I not defied her, had I not—"

"She wouldn't have you blame yourself. Nor would I."

That was fine for him to say, but it would take a long time to untangle the pain of his past silence. "I'm sorry I haven't been around as much, especially with Charlotte married."

He pulled me to his barrel chest. "Tush," he said and then no more. He was never one for speeches.

My tears splotched onto his shirt. This would be the last time I saw him, unless something went terribly wrong in South Carolina. I pulled away and wiped my face.

Father's troubled gaze caught my own. "You're a pretty thing, like she was. Do you remember?"

Of course I did. Though she'd been gone for many years now, her presence lingered in every corner of this house and in every breath of wind that rustled through the trees. The words he spoke were poetry, coming from him, and the closest thing to a benediction I would ever get. "Oh, Father." I squeezed him tight and buried my nose in his shirt, drinking deeply of his scent: pipe smoke and freshly cut tallgrass.

He gave me a swift kiss on my head and pushed me gently away. "Go."

I fled the cabin without looking back.

After saying goodbye to my brothers and failing to find Pearl for one last goodbye, I climbed onto the wagon wheel. I batted John's hand away and hefted myself and my swollen belly through the cloth opening.

John climbed on one of the horses and slapped the reins. The wheels creaked forward, then the wagon quaked over the pitted road, with Henrietta, our milking cow, tied behind.

"Wait!" Pearl's cry sounded in the distance.

My heart leaped into my throat. "Stop the wagon, John!"

But Sarah had already crawled out of the wagon and was running toward Pearl.

The girls collided, sobbing and holding on to one another.

Tears streamed down my face. It took everything in me not to look at John and say, *You did this.*

I carefully made my way to the ground and hugged Pearl again. Whispering words of love, I promised I would write as often as I could.

Finally, Father came and took Pearl away.

A sniffling Sarah and I went back into the wagon with John's help, who rightly kept his mouth shut. I tucked Sarah in my arms and let her grieve. The boys, stuffed inside along with all our worldly goods, were alight with curiosity and excitement. To them, this was an adventure. Would that they felt the same after a month of hard travel.

John stretched out his neck to the side as he did when unsettled. "How did it go?" he called back to me after we moved forward.

"Not now, John." I would tell him later of what I felt. This was the last I'd see of the land I loved.

We passed under a canopy of branches thick with green, dappled spots of shadows gliding over our skin. Suddenly, I was sixteen again, stepping through a shaded thicket, Callum's hand in mine. His head turned, his teeth flashing in a grin. Pain, swift and fierce, stabbed to my quick. I had put him from my mind, as was right, but some part of me, a part I couldn't kill, was kept alive by these forest trails. This would be the end of it, then, as it should be. I wouldn't be reminded of him in South Carolina.

Leaving these trees was leaving who I was.

I'd run with my brother here, as hard and as long as he did. I'd been a beaver, a queen, a pirate. My imagination had been birthed in these wilds. As we drove out, I greedily took in the sight of every climbing tree, each hill rise, each bend of the river, until I could see them no more.

For hours, we followed the two dirt tracks cutting their way through the grass, our bodies swaying to the dips and rocks in our path, with the beating of the sun on my lap. The heat dried my tears, leaving my skin tight and swollen.

John glanced back at me from time to time but said nothing. The boys' laughter filled the space of our silence. After a while, Sarah left the cocoon of my arms and joined them. I closed my eyes and soothed myself by listening to her resilient and cheerful spirit, so like Mama's. Remembering the hope that my little Sarah Bordroyne would be more Sarah than Bordroyne, I smiled. She was more Sarah than I could ever hope to be.

Landon fell quiet, then Samuel and Johnny. Thomas was the last to doze off under the shade of our wagon covering.

In the quiet, the hardness between John and me became a volley of shots.

John shifted in his saddle, barely meeting my eyes. "Please don't be angry with me."

I couldn't bear starting this new life with this distance between us. He would be my only friend on this journey, for better or worse. I sighed, ceding a little of my territory. "I'm sad, mostly."

He faced the path again. "It'll pass."

TWENTY-ONE
ROSANNA

One month later, John emerged from the land office, clutching a map in his hands. "Our land is on the banks of the Enoree River." He took one giant step onto the wagon and, leaning in, pulled me to him. His hungry mouth took mine, and just as quickly, he drew away, grinning.

I put my fingers to my lips and stared.

His eyes held a fever in them.

Well, now. My heart quickened its pace.

"They say it's good land, just as I dreamed. And all at once. Not piecemeal or on condition. Even better than what we see here." He squeezed my shoulders and leaped back to the ground. His eager gaze darted from rolling grass to hill to grove, his eyes as fiery as when he'd looked at me.

My flicker of excitement died. It was the prospect of his land that drove his hunger, nothing else. I rubbed my chin against my shoulder, turning from him and hiding my burning cheeks. How foolish to be jealous of dirt and trees.

After three more days of travel, we crested a hill and were greeted by a silty, pebbled riverbank and rushing water.

"Will you look at that?" he exclaimed.

Ash, hickory, and sycamore trees towered above us, forming a canopy and enveloping us in their shade.

"See? Good trees. The soil must be good for growing after all," John said with a hint of crowing in his voice.

"We can't eat trees," I replied sharply.

"We can build with them though, and that's almost as good."

He pulled the wagon to a stop in front of the river, the only flat place big enough for it to sit.

"This is it," he said, descending from his horse. "This is where we'll build our future."

There was no house, no shelter. Just raw earth and the daunting task ahead of us.

"Do we have neighbors?" I asked.

"Out here, a neighbor can be miles and miles away."

We would be truly alone, then. What if something happened to me when I gave birth? What if one of the children got sick and all my remedies failed? It would take days to find a doctor and bring him to us. When my children struggled to breathe or when I couldn't lower their fever, every second was an agony. I couldn't wait days.

He swooped me down beside him. The children bolted out of the wagon and ran ahead of us, hollering about who would be first to the trees.

Johnny kicked his thin little legs into a run and collided into Thomas, who laughed and tumbled to the ground with him.

"Be careful!" I yelled, even though it wouldn't do any good. They probably thought they *were* being careful, for there wasn't a bloodied nose or torn shirt. Yet.

Sarah, Landon, and Samuel catapulted themselves on top of Thomas and Johnny, and their mingled shouts and laughter echoed around us.

As the tallest of all the children, Thomas wrestled himself to the top and jumped to his feet. The others followed suit. If Thomas was done wrestling, so were they, for not only was he the tallest, he was their self-appointed leader.

"Let's go explorin'," he said.

He high-stepped through the grass, and the others followed close behind, a little gaggle of geese—his brothers looked at him with something akin to worship, and Sarah was just happy to be included in the fun.

They were too close to the thick line of trees. Another second, and they would disappear from my sight.

I took determined strides away from the river and toward the trees.

"Let them be," John said. He came beside me, laughing at their antics.

His laughter set my teeth on edge. How could he be so light-hearted when we didn't even have a roof over our heads? "If I *let them be*, we might never see them again."

"They've been caged for too long," he said, with a hint of a smile still in his voice. Then his voice boomed over the rushing water. "Stay where we can see you."

Satisfied with their *Yes, sirs*, he bent and brought up a fistful of dirt, holding it to his nose and drinking deeply of its scent. "Rich and fertile, just as I told you."

I peeked at it, begrudgingly. In one glance, I could see the harvest from seed to hogshead in the dark soil.

The hard lump I'd carried in my chest softened a little.

God forgive me, but the entire trip, I'd bolstered my spirits by imagining the crestfallen look on his face when he would realize our land was untenable—relished the idea of him understanding he was wrong and dolefully admitting it to my face. I'd rehearsed my words. I would be forgiving, kind, generous to a fault. *You couldn't have known*, I'd say, though he could have if he'd listened. *It's no one's fault*, I'd murmur, sweet as sugar, except he would know it was his.

But my imaginings always came to a sticking place.

We would go home, but he'd be the fool for selling everything he'd had and leading us in a merry dance. As mad as I was, it pained me to think of my single-minded husband without a pursuit. For who was John without his dreams? They drove him, lighting his movements and our lives with a fire I had grown fond of, as infuriating as it could be.

"Come, this isn't the Rosanna I know."

I stared unseeingly at the river, my mouth clamped shut, not quite ready to be cajoled into good humor.

John rigged a makeshift tent with canvas for the children. He and I slept under the wagon, our bodies not touching. If everything were to go back to normal, he might uproot us again. I had to make him truly taste how difficult this was for me. I scooted away another few inches.

The river flowed by swift and deep. Under a sliver of moon, the forest came alive with *cricks* and knockings. A cool mist rose from the ground and crept underneath the wagon, up my legs, and down my arms.

A twig snapped. Some unknown creature gave a startled scream.

I retreated into the safety of my husband's arms.

"It's nothing but a bobcat. He won't bother us if we don't bother him," he said.

Still, I wrapped the edge of the quilt over our bodies and pulled my rifle closer. I would be ready if any creature came against us.

Raindrops pelted the stretched cloth of our wagon's cover. Moonlight glinted off the slanting rain. John's heavy arm, thrown over my middle and cradling our unborn child, held me close.

"John?"

A soft snore rolled in and out from the cave of his open mouth.

"I'm sorry," I whispered.

The rain swelled, pelting the grass lining the riverbank and bending it under its weight. Drops of water bounced off the silt surrounding our wagon. My eyes grew heavy. I unclenched my fingers from my weapon but kept my finger, relaxed, on the trigger.

Distantly, like in a dream, John's voice drifted to me. "Wake up!" Someone pulled at my shoulder.

I shifted away from the voice. My shoulder bumped into something hard, and I couldn't go further. What was this? My eyelids flew open. The rough painted wood of the wagon bed lay above me, much lower than it had been when we'd drifted off to sleep the night before. "John?" The sound of rushing water was close. Closer than it had been in the night. I tried to raise myself on my elbows and hit my forehead.

"Lay back. I'll drag you out."

The quilt beneath me shifted, and in one swift movement, I was lying face up, the sun shining directly into my eyes. I shut them tight, but I still saw a bright red orb and swirling trains of fire. "What happened?"

"The river rose, and the wagon sank in the riverbed. The wheels are stuck."

A large lump fell on my chest, knocking the wind out of me.

Two little sweaty hands clamped onto the sides of my face. "Wake up, Mama! I've been waitin' to tell you—"

The boulder yelped and was lifted off me.

I sucked air into my strained lungs. My hands went to my belly. A fraction lower and who knows what could've happened.

There, hovering above me, was Johnny, the back of his pants gripped in John's hand.

"Thomas kilt a squirrel!" Johnny exclaimed, suspended in the air.

"*I* wanted to tell her!" Thomas pelted his brother with his fists.

John swung Johnny out of reach.

I dragged myself to a seated position, still gulping air, my back soaked from the wet ground. I swallowed and held out my hand to Thomas. "Hand it over."

Thomas hesitated and slid his eyes to his father.

"Do as your mother says."

Thomas reached into the front of his pants and pulled out a slingshot. My slingshot. The one I'd confiscated the last time he'd tried to use it on my bum.

John laughed. "How'd you know he used your slingshot?"

I knew because Thomas was the one most like me. Tucking the slingshot into the back of my skirt, I lurched to all fours and tried to get upright. Thomas and Landon rushed to my side and pulled my arms, launching me to my feet.

"Thank you, boys."

"What's wrong with killin' a squirrel? You do it all the time," Thomas said.

"There's nothing wrong with that. He'll be a part of dinner tonight, and I thank you heartily for it. But you were to keep your hands off the slingshot until you learned to control your aim."

"How am I to learn if you don't let me practice?"

The rascal raised a good point. I fought back a laugh and refused to look at John. My battle to appear stern would be lost if I saw the usual twinkle in John's eyes. He was too proud of their antics. "There must be *some* punishment for flying pebbles into your mother's seat."

"I've just the thing," John said. "Thomas, come help dig out these wheels."

Thomas' face lit as it always did when he felt a part of something important. "Yes, sir!" He ran to John's side and went to work, scooping his hands in the mud and flinging it behind him.

Not to be left out of the fun, the others joined him, even little Samuel.

The horses, grazing nearby, were hitched again.

Even with the horses added to the effort, the wagon stayed put. The wagon's wheels had sunk into the riverbank almost to the running gear.

"Well, I suppose we could use it for our guest quarters," John said, hands on hips and breathing hard.

It would remain empty, then. We would never have guests, with us being too far away for family and friends to visit.

TWENTY-TWO

ROSANNA

The rest of the day was spent clearing the land for a sturdy shelter. John smoothed the dirt, and I picked out rocks or prickles that would hurt our bare feet. John then began felling trees.

With the baby's arrival fast approaching, it would have to be a simple shelter, then a real home later on, with a room for us and one for the children, John promised.

I whistled a birdcall into the trees.

Thomas and Landon answered, their little warbles airy and strained. At least they were close enough for me to hear them. Sarah, Johnny, and Samuel hadn't mastered the art of whistling yet, so they'd have to stay close to their older brothers.

"Stay on the trails!" I yelled. Thin paths cut through crooked ash trees—Indian trails, cut over time by the natives who were here long before any settlers had arrived in South Carolina.

A line of smoke rose from deep within the forest. Perhaps it came from a chimney, a morning fire tended by another wife and mother like me. John had told me that our nearest neighbors were many miles away.

John and I slept that night at the side of our sunken wagon. He'd tacked a piece of canvas from the wagon to the ground and greased it with linseed oil to protect us from the rain. All night, I breathed in the biting scent of the coating. I was nauseous, on edge with the dread of every inhale. It was almost enough to forgo the protection and lay out under the downpour.

The work to make our new land livable claimed every moment of our time.

The shelter was the first and most important consideration, then clearing land to get a crop of indigo. We were already late. Other farmers had their first cuttings after planting in April. It was June. With no indigo to sell, we would have to survive on what we fit in our wagon.

It didn't bear thinking. Five children depended on us, trusted us to provide for their needs. It drove me to join John's side, hacking at the logs. When he accepted my help without a word as to my condition, fear settled deeper in my belly. I attacked every worry with the hit of my hand ax. The sooner our shelter went up, the sooner we could get the indigo planted. Everything else could wait.

I was building the fire for our noonday meal on the third day when Landon and Thomas came hurtling through the trees screaming, their eyes wide with terror.

Fire swept through my limbs. "John!" It came out as a moan. I couldn't move. I couldn't breathe.

My husband bolted toward the two.

"Papa!" Landon yelled.

John swept him into his arms. "Where are the others?"

Landon wept through gulps of air.

Thomas' teeth chattered. He could hardly spit out any words.

John set Landon down and grabbed his gun. He ran toward the woods, veering off the path and leaping over felled logs.

"Go to the wagon," I yelled at Landon and Thomas.

They scrambled inside the wagon without protest. I stood guard outside of it, shaking. Whatever was out there would have to go through me before getting to any more of my children. Johnny, Sarah, my little Samuel! My heartbeat pounded in my ears and in my throat.

A gunshot rang out.

My legs gave way. Landon and Thomas screamed and cried even louder. If John was shooting, something truly did have my children.

A second shot rang out.

I folded in half and laid my face on the ground, breathing so fast and deep my head swirled. With every inhale, I took in a lungful of dirt.

"Rosanna!" John cried. His footsteps pounded through the trees.

I forced myself to drag my gaze upward in the direction of John's voice.

He was running through the trees bearing Samuel, who was screaming as if all his limbs had been torn off. Johnny traipsed behind John, swinging his arms at his side as if he were going for a stroll with his father through the forest to hunt for mushrooms. But there was blood on his face and streaming down his bare little chest. Sarah trailed behind, bewildered.

I rushed to them and grabbed Samuel from John's arms.

"He's fine, Rosanna. Just a cut on his mouth."

I wouldn't let myself be comforted until I saw for myself that he was whole. I ran my hand over his bloodied flesh, his head, his small dirt-caked feet.

"A boar had found them. Devil creatures," John said. He patted Johnny's head. "This boy here got the little one into a tree and threw rocks at the boar so it'd chase him instead."

Johnny grinned at me through bloodied teeth. "Then I climbed a tree, but it was fat and couldn't climb like me." He spit onto the ground, sending a pool of saliva and blood into the grass.

"He took a branch to the lip," John explained. "Thomas hit the boar with his slingshot and then it took off after Samuel."

I spun around quickly toward the wagon. Thomas ducked back inside the covering. That boy! How did he get my slingshot again?

Sarah hadn't said a word during this whole exchange.

"Sarah, are you well?"

She looked up at me with sorrowful eyes. "I wasn't there. I was picking berries."

"Go inside the wagon," John said, his voice serious. "Johnny, Samuel, you too."

I slid Samuel to the ground, who joined Johnny.

When all five met together, their voices collided with exclamations of how the boar fell when Papa shot it and how mad the boar had been when Thomas had hit it with the stone.

I smiled shakily at their antics. "I feared the worst, John."

"If anything had happened…" His throat bobbed on a swallow. "Stay with the children in the wagon while I scout out the land. I need to make sure it's safe before you venture into the woods again."

"I won't have the children caged another hour, John. We'll be fine outside, but we'll stay close to the camp."

He grabbed my rifle, propped against a tree, and thrust it into my hands. "You better be in that wagon when I return."

To be commanded like a child! "John—"

He held up his hand. "*Do not leave the wagon*," he ordered as he pulled himself on top of one of our horses. "I'll be back before sunset," he added. "Thomas, take care of the family while I'm gone."

I crouched near the opening of the wagon's cover, cooling my anger-chapped cheeks in the fresh, clean air. It wasn't good for children to see their parents squabble openly, so I'd put on a smile and climbed into the wagon as if it had been my idea from the first.

My five little pirates had been tested by too much journeying and too little play. Behind me, the boys fought for the right to hold the slingshot. I'd allowed Johnny to hold it since he'd saved his little brother, but the others weren't pleased with that state of affairs.

"*I* get the slingshot the whole night. Mama said." Johnny's voice was filled with pride.

"Papa said *I* am to protect everyone," Thomas countered.

I swiveled around. "Thomas, fetch the bag of beans and hand ten to each of you. You may take turns shooting them at the willow. Samuel, come sit with me."

Samuel came, and he settled in the hollow of my crossed legs in front of my burgeoning belly. The others leaped to the barrel where our goods were stored, tipping the wagon to the side.

"She asked *me*! Let go!"

"You let go!"

The wagon jostled. A clatter of dried beans went off like buckshot. Every clack on the floor, each thud against the canvas and on sacks and barrels, pricked my temper to boiling.

They didn't often feel my disapproval. I'd vowed to love their little spirits in whatever form they came, but I wouldn't let them become pests. Neither would I have any Fredericks for sons.

"Sit! And not another sound until I say so."

They rustled behind me and then settled into silence.

The tension retracted its claws from my shoulders.

Samuel relaxed against me. His little fingers weaved into my curls the way they had ever since he was a babe and I fed him at my breast. His sweaty, golden head drifted to the side. His breathing deepened. I untangled his fingers and kissed his dimpled knuckles, holding them to my chest.

I hugged him tighter and buried my nose in his hair. The scent made my heart swell. How could someone love another creature so much? God had given me five such creatures, six including Pearl. I woke in the mornings with a smile on my face no matter how tired I was, because another day meant another day enjoying the gift of my children.

Even in this wagon, I could choose to be happy with my lot because I was with them.

The day marched on, drowsy and hot.

Where was John? I would kill him if he left me here alone on this earth to finish what he had started.

I rested my head against a support pole.

It was the first moment of rest that I'd had to think, to pause from the frenzy of work.

My heart clenched in sudden pain.

My home.

My Pearl, a daughter of my heart. Taking her in when I married John had knit her to me. Had she adjusted to sleeping in her own bed without Samuel beside her? Would I see her grown? Would I ever receive a missive scripted in those blasted letters I'd despaired of ever teaching her? Oh, but her writing was beautiful now. Through fits and tears, we'd accomplished that together. At least I could take comfort that she was safer staying near doctors in case her heart weakened further.

"Mama?"

Sarah's small voice sounded behind me.

I turned my head to look over my shoulder.

"I'm sorry for leaving the boys. It was wrong of me."

"Come here, sugar." I reached out, and she crumpled into my side, sobbing. "It's not your fault. None of it is your fault."

"All I could do was scream, Mama. I felt so... stuck."

Stuck. The word sank into my chest and spread its ripples.

Fie on John. Why were we here, stuffed in close quarters, when there was blue sky and open space to stand in? Yes, I hadn't wanted the children to see us fight, but surely, if John had been thinking clearly, he would have seen my way of things.

All I knew was that I couldn't stay *stuck* for another moment. And neither would my children.

I grabbed Sarah's hand and gazed into her eyes. "You'll never feel stuck again. I promise." I raised my voice to the boys. "Thomas? Grab the powder horn. Landon, you get the slingshot."

I slipped a few lead balls into my pocket and handed Sarah the rifle. "It's time I teach you to shoot."

I wiggled over the edge of the wagon and onto solid ground, then pulled Samuel out and onto my hip. The children's eager faces stared at me from the opening. "You stick close to me. No running into the forest, like Papa said."

Johnny looked yearningly to the river and then to me. "But Papa said to stay in the wagon."

"Let me deal with Papa."

He needed no more permission than that. He leaped out and landed hard with both feet on the ground. The others followed.

"Johnny, stack some river stones on top of that fallen log."

I showed Sarah how the weapon worked and how to load it, just as Philemon had taught me. I tucked it close in the wall of her chest. "Keep your arm tight to your side. You'll have to stretch to the trigger since your arms are small, but your shoulder will keep it from knocking you back."

She licked her lips and squinted. I held my breath. She pulled the trigger and fired off a clean shot, knocking the rocks to the ground.

I whooped.

"She's just as good a shot as you!" Thomas exclaimed.

"What have we here?"

My breath whooshed out of me. *John.* He stood behind us, his face stoic.

Black dots swam in my vision.

He was at my side in an instant. "Is it the baby?"

"The baby's fine."

"You need to rest more."

No amount of telling him I was strong and healthy would make him believe it. "You know I'm a crack-shot with that rifle. What protection does a wagon add, truly?"

He sighed roughly. "I'll get our home's walls up first thing tomorrow so you can take shelter if there's trouble. But your only job"—he put his fingers on my lips, which were already open and ready to protest—"*your only job* is to cook and rest."

· · ·

John had the four walls built first thing the next morning. He laid bark sheets on top and tacked them in, promising he'd build us a sturdier roof with a flap we could open to the stars.

It stood in a small clearing on a flat rise just above the river in the shadow of the thick, impenetrable forest. The fast-flowing water could be seen from the doorway. Did the river ever get fat enough with rain that it swelled above its banks? I tamped down my unease. At least I wouldn't have to go far lugging water for our daily needs.

John left that morning for the far field, determined to get it ready for planting.

The children played happily along the river.

We had shelter. Our horses and Henrietta—our beloved Henny—were snug in their pens. John would make a table and benches for us on the morrow, and there was plenty of well-drained, sloped land, perfect for growing indigo.

There was much I should be thankful for.

But I would go mad, waiting in this endless sea of trees with nothing more than resting and cooking to occupy me. John was being overzealous. I'd given birth to four sturdy boys. It was true Sarah had been born weak, but that was no fault of mine.

The small patch of land to the side of our cabin called to me.

The sun was high in the sky, and the air was thick with the scent of pine and earth.

A little labor was good for the spirits.

On impulse, I grabbed the shovel, pointed it downward, and shoved it in the earth.

Satisfaction sang through my limbs. Just the same as when I sang about John Barleycorn, a drinking song not meant for ladies.

I flipped the pillowy dirt, dark and laced with earthworms, venting my anger with each shove of my tool in the ground. *I didn't want to leave Pearl. I don't want to give birth in this forsaken place.* Then, bravely, I allowed myself to give voice to another hurt if only to lance it from my soul. *Why did life make me say goodbye to the ones I loved?* Before long, I had a long trench dug.

At the start of the next row, my shovel clanged against something hard. I fell to my knees and scraped at the dirt with my hands until I reached the large stone. When I finally pried it loose, I lifted it high with a laugh of triumph and tossed it to the side.

By thunder, it was good to move my body with such vigor.

I was still useful, still capable.

More stones cropped up, but it was no matter. I promptly dug them out and added them to the pile.

"Can I help?" Landon's gravelly voice sounded from behind me. He stood by the pile of rocks—a pile to his waist.

Perhaps it would be better if John didn't see the full extent of my disobedience today.

"Landon, get your siblings. I've a job for you to do."

They came over, their faces a little downcast, for they had just found a hole and were digging to get to the poor animal hiding inside. But they brightened when they discovered the job involved hauling rocks that their mother couldn't move without their help. I knew my boys worked most eagerly when allowed to display their growing strength. And Sarah always went along with what her brothers did.

I sat to the side, *resting*, so I could say I'd done as John had asked. When the rocks were gone and I released the children from their dutiful toil, I worked on creating another pile for them to carry off later.

A familiar sound of hoofbeats pounded from the woods.

I froze, standing with my hands cradling a large stone I'd just pulled from the soil.

John rode toward me, his face shadowed. He reined in his horse and dismounted in one smooth movement. "What are you doing?" he asked, his voice low and angry. "I thought I told you to rest."

I dropped the stone and brushed my fingers against my apron, already stained with the evidence of my labors. "I'm removing a rock from our garden, as you see."

"Why don't you just... if you could..." He looked off into the trees, shaking his head furiously. He was quiet for a long moment, his face tense.

"I can't just sit around. I need to feel that I'm doing something useful."

"You *are* doing something useful. You're growing our babe." His anger gave way to something else—something softer. "I can't do any of this without you. If you become ill or, heaven forbid—"

My mind went back to the day he'd asked me to marry him, his shameless, almost insulting, honesty... *you work hard without complaint... a fine choice for a farmer's wife.* If he didn't want me to work, he shouldn't have set those expectations long ago. "It seems, husband, we are at a crossroads."

He exhaled a long, overacted sigh. "A compromise then. Let me do the heavy lifting. I'll prepare the plot, and the boys will water it. You can plant and tend to your seedlings."

I tipped my head. "Fine."

He raised an eyebrow. "This means being mindful of the fact that you're carrying our child."

"I was trying to be careful."

He laughed. "Your careful is another man's peril."

I gave his shoulder a light push. He gave way, a teasing light in his eyes. The memory of that aggravating boy was getting hazier and hazier by the minute.

"By the by, I told our neighbors we'd be by on the morrow," he said, gazing into my eyes.

My stomach leaped into my chest—a glimmer of hope, for the first time since leaving home. "John! We have neighbors?"

"As much as people living miles away could be called neighbors, but yes, the smoke belongs to them. Their names are Elias and Hester Brown, and I've promised them a visit on the morrow."

TWENTY-THREE
ROSANNA

The next day, with the dark crescents of dirt cleaned from under the jagged edges of my nails and my dirty dress exchanged for a clean one, we set out on the overgrown Indian trail snaking its way through the tall grass.

In my hands I carried one of my precious raspberry canes, its clotted roots and soil wrapped with linen. An offering of goodwill for the woman. Perhaps it might encourage her to befriend me.

The children whooped and tumbled about us. Samuel fussed that his legs were tired, so I swung him onto my hip and belted out the words of a ballad, bouncing him to the beat. As easy as that, his complaints became belly laughs, and once again all was light and joyful.

It wasn't long before we broke through the ash trees into a clearing with a little cabin. Nearby stood a neat pile of stacked and notched logs. A large-brimmed straw hat with a blue ribbon hung on the wall of the barn. Excitement nipped at my insides. The hat was the first hint that there was a woman around. Threadbare linen coverings fluttered at square openings in the cabin walls, and the door was wide open, giving me a peek into a neat and sunshine-lit interior.

"Hullo! Farrow here," John called.

The children ran to the cut-log pile of planks and climbed atop it.

"Be careful," I warned them.

A hand pushed aside the covering. A woman with a long, neat braid of yellowing white hair peeked outside before disappearing behind the curtain.

My chest pounded. I wiped my sweating palms against my apron.

In an instant she was at the door. Her dress was as neat as her braid. "Welcome," she said, her voice warm and inviting. She glanced at the children and then to John and me.

I tucked my mud-splattered shoes further under my hem.

"This is my wife, Rosanna. And those animals climbing your pile are my children."

"They are welcome to it. The wood was meant for another barn, but it might as well be used for climbing as for anything else." She motioned us inside and called, "Elias! We have visitors."

A man stepped out of the trees, holding a hand out to John. He had a thick shock of silver hair and a beard so long and bushy it looked as if it could be shorn and made into a rug. John and Elias shook hands. My husband's muscular, tall body dwarfed the older man's thin, wiry frame.

"I was hoping you'd bring your family by soon," Elias said.

I held out the raspberry cane, careful to hide my jagged nails. "From our home in Virginia."

Hester eyed it wonderingly. To my surprise, her eyes glittered with tears. "Raspberries! I haven't had any since I was a child in England. I thank you."

"It might be years yet before you get a bountiful crop."

Elias cleared his throat. "Come," he said, directing us inside his home with an outstretched arm. "My pants are too snug, so Hester has asked that I share my pie with you."

John and I exchanged amused glances. Elias could have worn Thomas' breeches if he'd had a mind to do it.

Elias called over to the woodpile. "Have you ever seen a cat with six legs?"

Thomas straightened. "Are you fooling us, Mr. Brown?"

"I see. Ten minutes is not long enough to know my character. I shall prove myself to you, then." Without another word, he walked into the house.

My children descended the wood pile in an instant and chased after the man, with Samuel trailing behind.

"Come, Samuel. I will help you." I picked him up and hastened to join my other four.

Inside, the children hovered over a purring, orange-striped cat, curled upon the kitchen table. Its eyes were closed, its tail swishing slowly. Elias hadn't lied. There, hanging limp behind the cat's haunches, were two extra legs, dangling over the edge of the table.

"Shoo!" Hester swept the cat to the ground.

The extra pair of legs slapping behind the cat as he ran from them was a sight to behold.

"Her name's Three-Tail," Elias said. "Go on. You can hold her if you can catch her."

Samuel struggled from my arms and flew outside with the rest of the children.

Elias and John moved to the mantel. The older man handed John something that resembled a hand ax with strips of beaded leather wrapped around the top of the handle. John took it and weighed it in his hands, running his fingers over the beadwork.

"It's no longer the Indians that are trouble," Elias said. "It's those rum-soaked, thieving land pirates. You better put your animals away, Farrow. Lock them up, good and tight. And anything else that can't be nailed down, put in your home."

John glanced at me, his eyes troubled. "Land pirates?"

"No one told you about the outlaws before you came out here?"

John studiously avoided my gaze and shook his head.

"Started during the Cherokee War. When folks abandoned

their farms and returned home, the criminals moved in. They terrorize the rest of us now."

My body broke out into a cold sweat. How were we going to keep an eye on our boys, our crops, our duties, all while watching for any brigands that might appear?

John didn't say anything for a long moment. "Once the indigo is in the ground, I'll build our barn."

Mr. Brown shook his head. "You've got to get your things secured first. What good's a barn with nothing to store in it?"

John's face hardened a touch. "I'll keep that in mind."

He never liked anyone else telling him what was best, least of all me. The harder someone tried to make him see sense, the more stubborn he became.

Hester finished setting trenchers out and invited me to sit at the table with her.

A breeze from the door blew through their home, carrying the scent of sun-warmed bark and soil. It pulled me to its peace and settled my drumming heart.

"Thank you for having us, Hester."

"How do you find it out here?" she asked.

I opened my mouth to speak of all the hardships we'd faced, of how I didn't want to come to the wilderness at all. But something in her tired eyes and the lines across her forehead told me she'd had twice my share of trouble. "I'm adjusting."

"There are always new things to adjust to out here, it seems." She stared out the door into the yard where the children sat huddled around the cat. Johnny held him in his lap, and the animal rubbed his head against Johnny's hand. "That cat's never let anyone pet him before."

My heart swelled to the point of bursting. That was my Johnny. Hester couldn't have known that even a deer would be at ease in Johnny's lap, drawn as animals were to him. "Perhaps he's fed her a treat." How many times had I comforted Johnny when a butterfly died after all Johnny's effort to save her? "How long have you been here?"

"I—I've forgotten. It's been so long..." The poor woman trailed off. She brought a hand to her throat and tapped a nervous rhythm against her collarbone. "We lost a daughter a few years back, to the war."

My heart dropped. On impulse, I laid a hand on her back. "How long... what I mean to say is, how did..." How did one ask about another's greatest pain? *Should* one? Only days away from civilization, and I'd already forgotten. "Would you like to talk about her, Hester?"

Elias came over and put his hands on his wife's shoulders. "Hester, I'm tired of waiting for my pie."

She reached behind her and patted Elias' cheek. He leaned down and kissed the top of her head with lingering tenderness.

Something about it made me inexpressibly sad, and I looked away.

John's hands clamped on my shoulders. "Shall you go fetch our ruffians, or should I?"

"You stay right there, the both of you," Elias said. "You're our guests."

He stepped outside and gave a sharp whistle. Within moments, our children tumbled into the little cabin.

Hester cut me a generous piece of pie and handed it to me on a scratched and beaten trencher. Elias passed around the rest.

She returned to her seat without any of her own.

"Won't you be having any?"

"I want to make sure the children have their fill before I have a piece."

She must not have sons. There was no filling them with anything, no matter how much there was of it.

I put a bite in my mouth and almost spit it out. These were the tartest gooseberries I had ever eaten.

I swallowed the lump post-haste and forced myself to smile at Hester.

"How is it?" Hester asked, her eyes a little anxious.

Forgive me, Mama. "Why, this is the best gooseberry pie I've eaten."

A smile spread across her face, lighting her features with joy and what resembled relief. For a moment, the cloak of heaviness lifted. How young she looked!

If one little falsehood brought her some happiness, I'd tell her a dozen.

Johnny took a bite. He looked up at me in horror.

The children! A heat of panic swept from my chest to my cheeks. The other four sat in a row on her bench, digging into their portions. They would do it. They'd tell her that her pie was sour and spit their bites back on their plates. They were too honest to do otherwise.

Samuel put a bite in his mouth.

"Come here, Samuel." I couldn't keep the desperation from my voice.

"Why do you look like that, Mama?" Landon asked. "Is it on account of the pie being so foul?"

The table fell into silence.

Samuel chose that moment to retch like a cat gagging on a clump of fur. He scraped the pie off his tongue with his hand and threw the bite onto the floor, his eyes stricken with disgust.

Everyone's attention swiveled to me.

John held a fist to his mouth, his face red and his eyes crinkled at the sides. He was *laughing?*

I slumped and covered my eyes with one hand.

Our only neighbors, and we had just revealed our faults to them.

A strangled sound came from Hester's direction.

Bent over and shaking, she hid her face in her apron.

Elias gave me an apologetic shrug and patted her back awkwardly.

Then a laugh rang out, high-pitched like bells. Another joined it, and another, mountains and valleys of merriment.

Hester pulled down her apron and wiped her eyes.

"I'm so sorry," I began. "Your pie isn't foul. It's only... well, it's that..."

She reached over and patted my hand. "Dear girl, there's no need for that. I'd forgotten how honest the young can be." She pulled my trencher in front of her and took a bite. "Well, you were right, Master Landon. Thank you for being brave enough to tell me the truth. I was almost out of sugar and hoped I might get by with what I had."

He puffed out his chest and looked to me as if for my approval. I gave him a small smile.

Hester reached for my hand and squeezed it. "Your mother was only trying to be kind. Weren't you, dearie?"

I squeezed her hand in return, my heart so full I couldn't answer.

And with that, she stood and began clearing the plates. "Don't let my pie scare you off from visiting again, young Farrows. Three-Tail needs the company."

Elias secured our promise that we would allow him to help John build the barn. Hester promised to bring the cat in a basket for the children and help me make our cabin into a home.

We left with our gaggle of five. I glanced back at Hester and Elias, standing on the porch, alone.

Samuel was perched on John's shoulders, slumped over with his little chin resting on his father's head.

"Mama, why did you lie to Mrs. Brown?" Johnny asked.

"Yes, why *did* you lie?" John asked, laughter in his voice.

I pinched his stomach. "Don't you throw me to these wolves," I whispered.

"This is your comeuppance for teaching them to be honest."

I should've taught them that sometimes it was better to be silent. "I didn't want to hurt Mrs. Brown's feelings," I said.

"Why are feelings more important than truth?" Thomas asked.

I opened my mouth to defend myself, to say that it was justified as a kindness to Mrs. Brown. That my own mother had lied when it came to killing chickens and making babies. But the boy was right.

I squatted before Thomas. "Gather 'round, children."

Johnny perched his chin upon my shoulder, and Thomas stood in front of me, solemn and quiet, next to Sarah. Landon swung his arms from side to side and craned his neck to see a hawk flying overhead. It was as good as could be hoped—he was never still.

"I was wrong to lie. I should've thought of a way to tell her the truth without hurting her feelings. Can you help me think of something to say when the truth is better kept quiet?"

"You could've said that her pie was the most special pie you ever ate. That's what I was gonna say if she asked."

I stared at Thomas. Such a simple solution that would have helped me save face with my sons. "Yes, that would've been better. Thank you."

Landon stopped moving and patted my head. "It's alright. I didn't know what to say either."

In a gush of tenderness, I squeezed Landon to me. Then I opened my arms wide and pulled them all in for a hug.

Thomas was the first to pull away. "Can I lead the way?"

I nodded, even as my heart twinged. He was never much for affection, too much like his father.

John and I followed behind them, quiet.

"What are you thinking?" I asked.

"I'm worried for the Browns," he said. "Did you notice how little they had in the way of provisions?"

"She made a pie. They can't be too bad off."

"A pie without enough sugar. I've never had such terrible pie. Samuel had the right of it, spitting it on the ground."

I wouldn't let my new friend be so slandered. "Come now. It wasn't that terrible," I shot back.

"Elias showed me the cabinet he made where they store their dry goods. He wished for me to see the way he cut the pieces. There was naught more than dried corn and a little flour inside. And did you notice their clothing?"

Their clothes *had* been a little threadbare, but living so isolated, why make new dresses and pants when there were no visitors?

"They had no animals, except their horse. Without a cow, how do they get milk and cheese? Imagine, no butter for your bread. There were no pigs, no chickens. I peeked inside his cellar when he wasn't looking. It was empty, Rosanna."

I thought back to what I had seen. Their horse's lean haunches, no bread waiting on the table for their supper, the spareness of their furnishings. What I'd mistaken for tidiness had perhaps been an absence of plenty. A sickening feeling settled in my middle. "But how do they have so little where there's so much abundance around us? To not even have meat, John... doesn't he own a rifle?"

"He has a rifle, but a rusted one at that. Why, it might explode and kill both him and the animal. But it's not only that. Elias said the outlaws have made special targets of them. Whatever is stored is stolen, and Elias has been shot trying to defend his property. Before that, the Cherokee burned their fields—twice, which is why his land now lies fallow. They're too old to manage starting all over, especially without sons."

A zeal, blistering hot, raged inside of me. Was there any rest in this life? Any respite from the constant sorrows? "I'll share our butter and cheese. When we have chickens, there will be eggs and meat to give them too."

"I'll get them a deer, and when I am done with our fields, I'll see what can be done about theirs. I don't know how to keep the thieves from harassing them, but I'll put my mind to it."

I gave him a quick squeeze. Today, I was thankful for the husband I'd chosen. If not for him, the Browns would've struggled through the upcoming winter. I'd been too distracted by the children.

What would've become of them if we'd not moved here?

For the first time since coming to this place, I could see Providence's hand upon it.

TWENTY-FOUR
ROSANNA

I bent over the row I had just sowed, a deep throbbing ache in my back. Fear nipped at my hands, urging them to plant each furrow faster than the last. The sooner they were done, the sooner I could unpack our provisions, hang my curtains, and feel myself at home.

My little one dragged her heel under my ribs. She was anxious to be settled too. I placed my hand on my rounded stomach, assuring her that I'd received her message. I would meet her within weeks if she didn't arrive early as Sarah had. At least I had a shelter to birth in.

It had been three weeks since our arrival, but the barn had not yet been built. Neither had the stable, storehouse, or smokehouse. Our wagon remained packed and our animals in their pens. All our effort had been directed at the fields and planting the indigo. John had put off Elias' visit, not wanting to turn his attention to anything other than getting the seeds in the ground.

A drop of rain fell on the nape of my neck. For one blessed moment, my sun-flushed skin cooled. As quick as it came, the droplet heated to a vapor and disappeared.

It had rained steadily for a week, and the river had risen but not so much to be of concern. John welcomed the rain. The soil drank its fill and stood ready to grow our crop.

The only trouble was that the rain doused the piles of moss we burned to keep the mosquitos away.

I straightened, an awkward maneuver with my large belly, and arched my back. My skirt peeled away from my legs and hung damp and weighted with dirt.

The children, using sticks to make holes in the soil to place their seeds, laughed and fought and groused. I was too tired to intervene. Samuel, at my feet, patted the soil where I'd placed the seed with loud, exuberant thumps.

The wind kicked up. I closed my eyes, savoring the tickle of loose strands dancing across my skin. It wasn't enough. I unpinned my straw hat and shook my hair free. The breeze combed its fingers through my locks and cooled my sweat-slicked scalp.

I sat on the ground. Just a moment of rest, and I'd go back to planting.

The moment turned into long minutes.

A shadow darkened my eyelids.

Thick gray clouds billowed across the sky, swallowing gaps of light in its path. They towered, dark and heavy.

A gust whipped the hat out of my hand.

"I get it," Samuel said. His feet pounded away.

John gave the sky a passing glance but returned to his furrow, moving twice as fast to sow the indigo.

Crackles of blue light webbed through the churning clouds. The sky roared and shook the ground.

"Samuel!" I screamed and ran to him, catching him up in my arms.

Lightning rent the darkness and struck the lone ash tree in the middle of our field, exploding it and sending pieces of bark flying through the air.

John dumped his seeds and scooped up Landon and Johnny, one in each arm. "Thomas! Sarah! Come!"

Sarah grabbed Thomas' hand and ran toward John.

At the cabin, John swung open the door, and we all piled inside.

Five little white faces stared up at me.

Fear screwed deeper in my belly.

"Goodness." I forced a laugh and swept my heavy curls over my shoulder, wringing a stream of water onto the floor. "That was the adventure! Wasn't it, John?" I begged him with my voice to play along.

He ignored me and stared out the door toward the river.

Our hastily assembled roof kept out some of the water. Soon, rivulets of rain flowed through our cabin and under the walls.

"All will be well," I whispered to the children. "Are you hungry?"

Thomas' arms lingered overlong around my neck. "What of Henny?" he whispered.

"Papa will take care of Henrietta. As soon as the lightning stops, he'll fetch our animals and bring them to higher ground."

A crack of thunder rattled our home. The cups and trenchers clattered on our table.

John turned from the window. "Take them to the top of the hill."

"But the lightning!"

"*Go!*"

"What about you?"

But he was already out the door, riffle in hand.

A tremble rolled deep in my belly. "Come. Quickly." I'd left my rifle in the field, so I grabbed the hand ax and darted out the door behind them.

I clattered to a stop.

The river had broken its banks, rolling, rushing white-capped around trees and stones. Edges of land sheared away into the river.

John was with the animals. He tore down a section of the pen and yelled at the horses, slapping their hind ends, urging them to higher ground. The horses' white eyes flashed bright as the lightning.

I hooked my hands under Samuel's arms and swung him to my back. "Run!" I commanded the others.

We slipped up the hill face, chunks of grass giving way under our steps. At the top, we stood, numb and silent, peering through the sheeting rain to the rushing river.

Where was John?

I frantically searched the scene for a glimpse of his black hair, a speck of his red waistcoat somewhere in the deluge.

Legs trembling, I fell to my knees and the heels of my hands.

In the distance, the water pressed against the wagon. For a moment, it seemed it might hold its ground, but with one horrifying splintering, the wagon gave way and crumpled in rushing, twisting swells. Our barrels and crates floated away, bobbing once or twice and then disappeared from sight. Pearl's doll she carried when she was little, Mama's books, the drawstring linen bag where I kept all the dried flowers the children had picked for me—all gone. I felt into my curls and almost sobbed with relief—I'd worn Mama's pearl combs today.

Another crack of lightning slammed into the ground.

"Lie flat!" I yelled over the din.

Everyone did as I said except Samuel, who screamed and pulled away from my restraining arms.

"Hush, Samuel. Be still!"

Sarah grabbed him from me. Blessed child. It was hard to wrangle him around my stomach.

He wiggled out of Sarah's hold. "Papa! I want Papa!"

I yanked him to the ground, forced him to his back, and covered him with my body, my round belly between us. I wouldn't let go of him, no matter how much he kicked.

The sight of the wagon cracking apart, of it washing away in the muddy river and our things dipping below the surface and disappearing for good rolled through my head like a wave, over and over.

We had nothing except for what was in our cabin. No more indigo seeds, no clothes, no wagon. How could you eke a life out of the wilderness with just an ax and a rifle?

"Rosanna!"

I pushed myself up on my forearms. Relief swept through me. "John!"

He was running in a half crouch and slid to a stop beside me. "Give him to me."

I rolled off Samuel and laid flat on the ground. Fat drops pelted my face, each a stinging pellet. I'd ached with relief from just one that had fallen on my neck a short time ago. How could one continue through life knowing that things could change in an instant?

The booms of thunder sounded further and further apart.

The children wept softly in the storm's weakening fury.

I was too weak to turn to them, to give them what they needed. John comforted them instead, and their crying quieted into sniffles.

The storm rolled in the distance, the clouds still sparking with lightning.

In the absence of sound came an empty roar of nothing.

John leaned over me. "Are you well?"

The will to open my mouth and speak was lost to me.

He shook my shoulder. "*Are you well? Speak!*"

I shoved him off and sat up. "We've lost everything, John." I gasped. "Elias and Hester!"

He twisted his hat, draining a stream of water from it. "I tried to get to them, but the path was blocked. I had to turn back."

Pride and anger warred within me. He had children, a wife. I had been too close to being left here on my own in the backcountry. But the memory of Elias and Hester, standing alone, watching us go the day we met, was a check upon my anger.

He got to his feet. "Come, children. Let's see if we can find our horses and cow. Rosanna, go with Samuel to our cabin and see what can be salvaged."

But when I went to check on our cabin, I discovered that, like our wagon, it was gone, washed away with all our things in it.

There was nothing to be done but sit with Samuel and draw pictures in the mud.

Night fell. John returned with the children. We had no supper and fell asleep on the ground, little caring that it was uneven from pockets of soil that had been swept into the river.

I woke in the morning with my stomach growling and the sun shining in the bright blue sky. John was gone, and so was my ax.

I stood on shaky legs. My wet clothes hung on my frame. I almost stumbled back to the ground with the weight of it.

The damage was even worse in the morning light.

The riverbed had carved a canyon, the place where our wagon had once been a large crevice. Branches were scattered everywhere.

Our shelter, lost.

The money we had left from the sale of our old farm and the purchasing of supplies had been kept in a tin inside.

The landscape swirled. I grabbed a nearby tree and rested my cheek upon the rough bark, my eyes closed. *John is alive. So are my children. My babe kicks within me.*

"Jo—!" My dry and sticky throat locked. Pulling in air was like drawing breath through water. With each wheezing inhale, I hacked and hacked until my throat and my lungs were freed at last.

I almost cried at the irony of it. Too much water, now not enough, and the river too muddy to drink.

A cow's lowing pierced the quiet.

My heart stopped. I shaded my eyes and scanned the horizon.

"Henny?"

In the trees beyond our property, inside a twist of broken branches, was our cow, our darling Henny.

I crawled down the uneven hillside and ran to her.

She stared at me with her glassy, dark eyes as if everything was as it should be.

I wrapped my arms around one of the logs and pulled. My arms shook against the weight. It only needed a hair's breadth to be free of the branches. I put all my strength into it, and the log fell, hitting the ground with a thud.

Henrietta moseyed forward and lowered her head to a patch of grass.

I ran my hands over her flanks. No gashes or bleeding to be mended. I bent and peeked beneath her. Her udder was stretched to its limit.

We were saved!

But where to put the milk?

I had no bucket, no cup—nothing to catch her milk.

She bellowed.

"I know, girl. I know. How much pain you must be in!"

There was nothing to be done but to crouch at her side and pull a teat, directing a stream into my mouth. I would just take a little until the others awoke, enough to relieve Henny of the worst of her discomfort.

Just when I freed a length of vine to tie Henrietta to a tree, a call carried through the newly formed gully.

"Rosanna!"

John!

He climbed the ridge and ran toward me. I crashed into his arms. "Henny's just over there," I said, breathless. "With milk aplenty. I despaired of..." I trailed off at the heavy look on his face. I pulled back. "What? What is it?"

"Elias has invited us to stay with him while we rebuild. You get Henrietta. I'll wake the children. We must hurry if we are to get there before dark."

I stared at him. Six, almost seven of us, living in a home with only room for two? But there was nowhere else for us to go. "At least let the children eat."

"What will they eat, Rosanna?" he snapped, his face flushed where it wasn't streaked with dried mud.

I bit my tongue and waited for his flash of heat to cool. He was at the limits of his endurance. So was I. "Henny's milk."

He nodded without emotion. "Rosanna..." His hand went to the back of his neck. "Hester's gone."

I pushed him away. "What do you mean, she's gone?"

"The flood swept her away. Elias is looking for her now, but..."
He shook his head. "It's a fool's errand. He saw her taken in the
flood."

I couldn't speak. Couldn't even cry. If I did, I would fall to
pieces.

John marched off in the direction of our sleeping sons.

Henny happily chewed her grass.

I rested my head on her neck, staring across the land at
nothing.

The quiet was deafening. How many creatures had been
washed away and were now buried under silt?

How could I face Elias when all of us had survived? I thought
back to the day when we met. Elias had leaned over Hester, and
she'd reached behind and given him a squeeze. They'd lived a lifetime still loving each other. I had wanted to ask Hester how she
had done it—how did she love her husband even when it was hard
to like him? Now I would never get the chance. How much good
her wisdom might have done me.

John came back a short time later with the others and Samuel,
sleeping in his arms.

The children made a game of catching milk in their mouths.
Their laughter rang through the torn landscape.

Once they had their fill, we journeyed over the broken path,
me pulling Henny with Samuel atop her back. John carried the
youngest boys over deep gullies where the path had been washed
away and cleared fallen logs so Henny could move forward. None
of us talked.

After several hours, we broke into the Browns' glen. Miraculously,
their house was spared, though their land was made unrecogniz-
able by the storm.

Elias met us on the porch. He wore a wobbly smile as if it
pained him to give it. "I don't have much, but I share it freely."

I said nothing and went straight to him, putting my arms around his neck.

He started to sob.

Later, I boiled some beans that Elias had, and my boys sat around one trencher, trading turns picking up one bean and eating it.

When they were done, John and I tucked them under one of Elias' blankets. I wrapped them extra tight as if it could keep danger from touching them.

They were asleep before we finished the prayer.

We settled in for the night, but I couldn't sleep. I stepped over the bodies and went outside to check on Henny.

She lay on the ground, sleeping, her side rising and falling with her gentle breaths.

Something stuck out of the broken ground. I fell to the ground and scraped the sludge with my fingers. A brim appeared, then a ribbon covered with mud. Hester's straw hat, the one that once hung on the barn.

Hester was dead, along with all the moments I'd dreamed of living with her. Waiting for their first visit to our home—the one John had put off, my imagination had conjured laughing with her in the kitchen as we baked my tarts. Her teaching me how to love my husband like she loved hers. The path between our homes growing more worn over time with all the visits we would pay each other. I'd never had a woman friend, had never felt I needed one, but with Pearl gone and my mother before her, there was an emptiness I hadn't named until I met her.

I laid my head against the post and let the tears come.

It wasn't only Hester. John said we would only be with Elias while we regained our lives, but how long would that take? We were dependent on a man who had little more than we did.

Our planted fields were destroyed, along with our home and all our earthly possessions. It wasn't just starting over—it was being birthed again, helpless and naked, wholly dependent on each day's mercies and powerless against each day's cruelty. How long would it be before we could survive on our own again?

At the word *survive*, my body began to tremble. The outlaws were fixated on the very home where we had taken refuge. If I had my rifle, they would find themselves at the other end of it if they should try again.

John met me outside. He stood at my side and stared off into the darkness.

Moonlight made ghosts in the mist creeping through Elias' fallow fields. We were enclosed by the deep forest, hemmed in by the deceptively calm river just beyond it.

"Is it too late to go back?" I asked in a small voice.

For a moment, I thought he might not answer, but then he spoke, low and urgent. "I'll make it safe for us, Rosanna. Whatever it takes."

TWENTY-FIVE
ROSANNA

"I'm tellin' you, your woman needs rest," Elias said.

Sitting on the bed, I jiggled my new little daughter, Mary, who screamed in my arms.

I tried to muster guilt for sitting, but I didn't have energy for even that. With as much blood as I lost giving birth shortly after the flood, I hadn't been able to do much more than lie in our bed and feed Mary.

"It's been two weeks since the birth. She's never stayed abed so long," John said.

Elias took little Mary from my arms and cooed into her face. "Your father is the stubbornest man I ever knew."

"You must be ready for us to be gone," John said.

"Who says I want you out of my home? You're welcome to stay, as long as you like."

John had been at our land every day felling trees with my ax and putting up a shelter and a barn. We could survive on trapped animals and forage for mushrooms and berries. With Henny's milk, I could make butter and cheese. But with our indigo crop lost, we were one year behind. There'd be no replacing our horses, our wagon, our clothing, or money for flour and salt. And with only one rifle, we were more vulnerable to the outlaws.

Elias promised us the blankets we slept on and the use of his horse if John needed to go into town. I hadn't the heart to tell him that the poor old girl would drop dead if it so much as went a mile.

Poor, dear, patient Elias, who had already given us so much. I tried to stand and closed my eyes, waiting for the swimming in my head to pass. Our diet of near-starvation hadn't helped my recovery either. "John, he's trying to help."

"I finished the shelter yesterday. I'll gather the children while you collect our things." John turned to Elias and held out his hand. "Thank you. You were the saving of us."

The older man sighed and clasped John's hand. "I'll be by soon to see how you get on. Thank you for mending the spring on my rifle."

"It'll do for now, but once I get settled again, we'll find a better way to protect your property."

It didn't take long for us to eat and collect what little we had.

After the children gave Elias a proper goodbye, I handed over Mary to him.

He took her gently and cradled her on her back so he could look into her eyes. "Don't make me wait too long before I see this angel again."

Did he think of his daughter when he held Mary? Elias loved the children, but with Mary, he was a pile of cotton fuzz.

"Goodbye, sugarplum." He handed her over. "Take care of her."

"Dear Mr. Brown." I kissed his cheek. "Thank you for taking us in. We'll be back soon."

I wrapped Mary to my chest, and off we went.

My stomach knotted the closer we came to our property. I hadn't been back since the flood.

John took my hand and squeezed it. "It'll be alright."

"Am I so obvious?"

"You look like you did after our wagon was lost."

"I don't know how we'll ever get over it."

"We will."

I stumbled over a branch and stopped myself with a hand on a tree's trunk. A wave of dizziness swept over me.

"Are you well?" John appeared in front of me, bending to look in my eyes.

"Let me rest a moment." I steadied my breathing. "I'll catch up."

He led me to a fallen log. "We can wait until you're ready."

I laughed a little at the humor in his voice and sat.

"Let me take the baby."

I was in no position to argue. I unwrapped her from my body and handed her over.

We went on, but this time, John held Mary in his arms.

We wound through the last of the ash trees.

John stopped short and grabbed my forearm. "Look!" he breathed, pointing to our fields in the distance.

"What is it?" Our fields were the same as we had left them—uneven, pock-marked soil with the ash tree in the middle, split by lightning and burnt to the roots. "What is it?"

"Look closer." He put his hands on my shoulders and directed my sight to the upward edge of the slope.

Oh!

Bright green stabbed through the soil, not in furrows, but in swirling pools in the little dips where water must have collected the seeds.

The indigo had sprouted.

A canvas of beauty created by a raging storm, a story of hope painted among the ruin.

It wasn't as we planned, but there would be at least a little harvest, if we were careful.

His boisterous laugh bounded over the budding field. "We are saved!"

Sarah twirled. Thomas, Landon, and Johnny did silly little jigs. Samuel, who knew only that we were happy, raised his hands and laughed too.

They ran their hands over the little sproutlings gently. They didn't need to be told to be careful.

John blew out a breath. "I can't tell you how relieved I am."

I grabbed his hand and squeezed it.

The little ones started a game of Fox in the Henhouse, chasing each other in the trees, weaving in and out with screams of laughter.

John sat at the edge of the field, his knee drawn up to rest a forearm upon it.

I took Mary from him and settled her into the dip of my lap.

"I think you very brave," he said quietly.

I regarded him with narrowed eyes. "Do you now?"

"You are. Much braver than me."

"Enough, John," I said wearily.

"You don't believe me?"

"You've never paid me a compliment before."

His mouth dropped open. "Yes, I have!"

"You've praised the supper I prepared and the number of eggs I've fetched. Now you say I'm braver than you? I fear I might swoon, husband." I fanned myself as if I might faint.

He playfully slapped my hand down, giving me a pointed glare. "Cease your jesting. On my very soul, I mean it. Here I am, laying praise at your feet, and you criticize how often I give it."

I hooked my arm through his and sagged against him. "Why do you call me brave? I'd still return home if we could."

He pulled my arm out of the crook of his elbow and stood, turning his back to me. He laid his palm against a tree trunk and dug his fingers into the bark. His back began to shake.

A prickling uneasiness traveled through me. What was this?

I'd never seen him cry, not even when we'd lost our babes.

I stood and put a tentative hand upon his back.

"I'm sorry," he choked out.

I couldn't say that he had nothing to be sorry for, but neither could I blame him for the flood, for our wagon, not even for bringing us out here. This dream was so woven into who he was, he could do nothing else.

"Hullo, there!" A deep voice carried over the field.

John dashed the tears from his eyes with his forearm.

A tall man rode into the fields on a horse, crushing our little seedlings under its hooves.

I waved frantically toward the small path at the side of our field. "Go around!"

John caught my arm and held it fast.

Little Johnny ran in front of the horse before we could stop him. He put his hands on his hips. "Get off our indigo, mister!"

The man chuckled. "What a brave little man."

My stomach twisted at the sound of the stranger's voice. There was something familiar to it.

"You must be new at farming indigo," he said to us. "One can hardly kill the plants."

"That might be so, but it's a miracle they exist at all," I replied, my voice sharp. "And I'll guard them with my life the next time they're threatened."

John took hold of my shoulder. "Hush," he whispered in my ear.

The man put his heels into his horse's side and cut a straight path toward us. He stopped only feet away. "John. Rosanna. What a happy accident, finding you here."

My heart knocked against my ribs.

"Why, is an old friend from Virginia so changed that you don't know him?"

I studied the chiseled hardness of the man's face, and then the scar on his upper lip. The one given him by Callum in Mr. Edwards' store. "By my very teeth," I breathed.

"Frederick Grenville," John said slowly. "What are you doing out here in the backcountry?"

He was the same Frederick, but different.

His youthful, bloated carcass had stiffened into a body of

action, thick with muscle draped on a towering frame. He'd grown a foot, at least. But the same hardness was there in his eyes.

"I've been here for years. I'm surprised you didn't know it."

Fire kindled my cheeks. *You're here because of what you did to Charity Taylor, you sack of suet!*

John clamped his hand tighter upon my shoulder.

Frederick slid off the horse. "I didn't know that you married." His eyes bored into mine. "I thought you were for Callum."

John stiffened. I gasped in outrage.

Frederick's lips curled. "You haven't heard from him, have you? He stole my horse, and I'd like to get it back."

"I'm sure he's hidden himself so he won't be found," John said.

Sarah burst forth from the forest, laughing with Landon, and stopped short.

"Who's that?" Sarah asked, staring at Frederick.

"Sarah, take your brothers to the blackberry bush and see if any berries are left."

"But—"

"*Go.*" I softened my command and smiled. "I'll join as soon as I'm able."

"Yes, Captain!" Sarah grinned and tugged Samuel's hand. "Race you to the blackberries!"

The boys followed her, laughing and running behind her.

My breathing eased.

"Captain?" Frederick raised a brow. "Are you doing so well as that?" His gaze flicked over my dirty skirts.

All my other clothing had washed away with the wagon, and no amount of scrubbing could remove the dingy brown stains in the skirt that remained.

"What do you do out here?" John asked.

"I have the second-largest plantation in the backcountry." His glance roamed discreetly about our land. "This your farm?"

John stretched the silence until my body began to sweat. "Aye. The flood set us back a touch, but we'll have our harvest this year."

Frederick laughed. "It set you back more than a touch! It'll take years for you to recover. Go home for the sake of your wife and children. I'm looking to expand my holdings, if you're interested in selling."

I gripped John's forearm and dug my fingernails into his skin. John could only be pushed so far until he let his tongue fly.

"Why are you here, Frederick?" I asked. The sooner his business could be done, the sooner we could be done with him.

"I was going to Mr. Brown's to discuss backcountry matters, but seeing as you're determined to stay..." He waited, and when we said nothing, he sighed. "You are aware that we have murderous thieves in the area?"

Murderous?

Frederick didn't give John a chance to respond. "They've become bold—too bold. But if Charles Town won't give us what we need to protect ourselves, we've no choice but to take the matter in hand ourselves. As the owner of one of the largest plantations, it's my duty to protect the weaker. The planters have chosen me to rout the strongmen. We call ourselves the Regulators. Will you join us, Farrow?"

"I've no time to chase after criminals."

"Then they'll be chasing you."

"Why would they come for me? I've nothing for them to take." John's control was slipping.

"So you'll leave it to me to protect your family?"

"No need. I protect my own."

Frederick's horse danced on its hooves, still for too long. "Ignore me at your own peril, Farrow. I won't warn you again." Our old acquaintance dug his heels in his animal's flanks and galloped away.

TWENTY-SIX
ROSANNA

Golden light pushed against my eyelids, threatening my dream. I held tighter to the stag leaping through the rain-soaked ferns and moss. Callum's arms were wrapped around me, holding the reins. Our laughter joined together, creating a song that made me both want to weep and rejoice. The wind pulled through my hair, tickling my scalp, weaving my curls into a tapestry unfurling behind me. The sun's rays stabbed through the canopy of leaves, drying the cool mist dotting my skin.

I startled awake.

My eyes were wet with tears. Callum's laughter still rang in my ears.

Guilt gripped my middle. I loved John. I was glad I married him. I didn't want to think of Callum any longer. But what control did I have over dreams?

I said a prayer for Callum's safety and happiness. I could still be a friend to him, if only in my prayers.

I glanced down at the blanket stitched lovingly by Hester, the sunlight picking up the pretty patterns of flowering vines and willow trees.

Above us, the flap on our roof was firmly shut. I hadn't felt much like looking at stars the night before.

John fished under the covers and settled his hand in the valley above my hip. "Do you feel better?"

I stretched my toes, feeling the crackles of dried mud between them.

It all rushed back—our squabble the night before.

Our fight had started over something petty—his chewing overloud. He slurped his next spoonful, staring straight at me. It was childish, but my tongue had been sharp.

We were both ragged with fatigue. It was winter, and we'd been gaining back what we'd lost, bit by bit, for months. Mary had never been a good sleeper, and with her in our bed, neither were we.

All my hurts had tumbled out of my mouth—of him not replacing my lost rifle and begrudging me his—and John shared all of his. I'd run to the creek, leaving my children open-mouthed behind me at our table. Better to leave than to stay and do something I might regret. It would do John good to see what it was like to be left alone with five wild children and a fussy baby.

He'd brought the stack of dirty trenchers to the riverbank, and we'd scrubbed them with river silt in prickly silence, bumping elbows without any pardons. Our walk back was quieter still. When we were in our bed and the children fast asleep, our argument continued with a swell of harsh whispers and devolved into a childish struggle over our covering. Truly, we'd lost our minds.

"You'll feel better in the morn," he had said.

And I did.

I flipped to face him. His hand stayed in the groove below my ribs. "Forgive me, husband."

He leaned forward and kissed my forehead. "'Tis already done."

He crawled out of the covers and was on his way to the animals by the time I realized he hadn't returned my apology.

The children pounced upon the bed.

Johnny bent over me, peering into my face. "Father told us to keep quiet so you may sleep. I gave Mary my boot to chew upon. Are you happy with me?"

I tickled his middle, and he squealed with delight and jumped off me. "I am *so* happy, my darling. So happy that I'll let you dig your hole before lessons today."

The children cheered and leaped off the bed, running to don their breeches and shoes.

"Wait! You must eat first," I called, but they were out the door, heading to John's far section of land. I relaxed back on our mattress. He'd keep an eye on them.

I fed my sweet, fat Mary, whispering an apology for making her wait. My second apology of the day. I couldn't be sure there wouldn't be a third.

"Up you go, Mary." I swung her upon my hip, bouncing her up and down, and walked out of our cabin. "What say you to pulling the last of our—" I froze.

A group of men and one young woman stood feet away, the butts of their rifles resting on their hips. The men were rough and unwashed, with stringy beards to their chests. The woman wore a stained moss-green silk dress with dingy ruffles and bows, some hanging by only a thread. A feathered bonnet lay upon her head, the fur rubbed bare on the edges. Held in her dirty hands was a rifle pointed at me and Mary.

"We'll take what goods ye have, sugar an' such," she said. Her speech came out spongy and thick, her black and rotted mouth moving with difficulty around the words. She motioned her head toward the others. One man shoved past me into the house with two empty burlap sacks. The other two men loped to our barn.

"Long as you stay still, no one gets killed," the woman said. She tipped her head at Mary. "Pretty little babe. Tempted to take her too."

My body trembled but not with fear. If I hadn't lost my rifle in the flood, she'd think twice about coveting my baby. "If you so much as touch a hair on my child's head—"

She shot her rifle into the air. "Say it again. Go on."

I ground my mouth shut. She didn't know it, but she'd just done me a favor. John would come running back home at the sound of the gunshot.

The outlaws picked us clean, as far as their sacks could be filled, with tools strapped to their backs and trenchers tucked in their pants. One of them had Hester's quilt tied around his neck. It fluttered behind him like a royal robe.

I could have recovered from that, but then they dragged away Henny, who bellowed against her rough treatment. Of course the smart girl would sense the lowliness of her captors. The outlaws hadn't rubbed her chin and her silky neck, and she'd do nothing without a little buttering up first.

John broke through the trees and ran to us, but the outlaws had already left.

He grabbed Mary from my arms without a word and buried his face in her neck. She took a fistful of his hair and stuffed it in her mouth, heedless of the storm clouds swirling around her. He gently pulled the soggy piece of his hair from her mouth. "What happened?"

"A band of outlaws threatened us."

"What did they take?"

"They took Henny. The rest can be replaced."

He plunked Mary back in my arms. "We've started over before. Go inside and lock the door. I'm going back for the children."

The next day, John went back to the fields without the children and placed Elias' borrowed rifle in my hands.

I'd just swept the morning's ashes from around the hearth when a voice boomed across the meadow. "Farrow!"

My heart seized. Frederick.

I waved Thomas over and handed Mary to him. "Take the rifle and the others to our bed," I whispered in his ear.

He nodded once, his eyes serious.

With one hand, I gripped the polished bone handle of John's

hunting knife, hiding it within the folds of my dress, and stepped outside.

Frederick Grenville sat tall in his saddle. A long whip lay across his lap, dangling in the dirt. He had coiled the end of a rope around one hand, pulling the line taut against something behind his horse.

A long and lazy *moo* distracted me.

Henny!

She came around the side of the cabin led by one of Frederick's Regulators.

"Good day, Mrs. Farrow," Frederick said. "This your cow?"

I hurried over to her and took the cord from the Regulator's hand. "Where did you find her?"

"As to that. Do you recognize this man?" Frederick yanked the line roughly.

A man stumbled into view, tied by the wrists at the end of the rope. His face was bloodied, swollen, his clothes ripped and caked with dirt as if he'd been dragged. From his shoulder, flesh hung in ribbons.

"How can I tell if I know this man? How can you tell, for that matter? You've bloodied him so badly not even his wife would recognize him."

"The cow was sold to me. I swear it!" the man cried.

Frederick jerked the rope. The man stumbled and fell flat. "We're on our way to hang him, whether you say it's so or not, Mrs. Farrow. If it wasn't your cow, it'll be someone else's tomorrow." He pulled the rope again. "Stand tall, man!"

The man clawed his way back to his feet. He swayed. His eyes rolled back as if he fought for consciousness. Then he locked himself upright.

Tears ran down his cheeks, mingling with the blood.

This wasn't justice.

Not when the man deciding this was a criminal himself.

Unsheathing my knife, I strode forward, heart pounding in my ears.

Frederick turned toward me, the leather of his saddle creaking. "Stay away from him!"

"A cow isn't worth a man's life." *Even Henny.*

I bent and gently grasped the man by the elbow.

The other henchman stepped in my direction.

"Stay where you are!" Frederick commanded. "She's for me to deal with."

The bleeding man fell against me. There were two choices open to him—he could try to escape, or I could hide him inside the barn. Either way his chances weren't good.

The man stumbled to his knees again and then dropped to all fours.

I leaned close to his ear. "Can you run?"

The man gave a jerky nod.

"What are you saying to him?" Frederick yelled.

"Run to my barn," I whispered. "I'll do what I can to keep you safe." I sawed at the rope with my knife.

Frederick tied the rope to his saddle and leaped to the ground.

The rope held together by one frayed strand. With one last slash of the knife, it snapped in two. The man collapsed to the ground. Frederick grabbed me by the neck and pried the knife from my hand.

"Run!" I screamed.

I caught a glimpse of the man running toward the barn and the other man giving chase when Frederick lifted me, his hand like a vise around my neck.

My hands clawed at his wrists.

He pulled me so his mouth was at my ear. "Most would take the cow and be grateful for it."

I scraped at his hands with my fingernails, kicking and twisting my legs. My heel swung backward and landed in his groin.

He groaned and loosened his hold just enough that I could suck in a lungful of air.

I screamed. "John! *John!*"

But he was already there.

Frederick's hand was torn from my throat. I fell to the ground in a heap. Seeing the knife where Frederick had dropped it, I crawled forward and grasped the handle in my palm.

John pointed his rifle at Frederick. "Get off my land. And you!" He shouted at the henchman about to enter the barn. "Get over here, or your boss gets a mouthful of lead."

Frederick stood, wiping the blood at the side of his mouth. "Your land. It won't be yours for much longer."

"Do you threaten a man on his own property?"

"Not at all. I can't help that you'll sell it when it's become unbearable to live here."

"Rosanna, get inside the house." John kept his weapon trained on Frederick.

Frederick climbed atop his horse. "No need. Tell your wife to keep away from her outlaw friends. I'd hate if she were hurt in the middle of Regulator business."

He and the other man rode away, leaving the cow thief behind.

John turned to me. "I told you to get inside the house."

Still coughing and trying to fill my lungs with air, I struggled to one knee.

He cupped my elbow and pulled me to my feet.

"John, I couldn't let him kill an innocent man."

The man in question stumbled from the barn and into the trees. How would he survive in his condition? Perhaps he really was an outlaw and was running to a camp where his fellow thieves would tend to him.

John brushed his thumb over my cheek.

I sucked in a breath. He'd never looked at me that way before.

"Are you hurt?"

I shook my head.

His hand fell away, and his face turned hard. "Don't you ever do something like that again. I don't care about his life. You're worth more than a thief." He shook me by the shoulders. "I don't want us in the middle of it, do you understand?"

"If Frederick thinks he can get away with this, he'll only be emboldened to do more."

Without another word, John turned around and strode toward the barn, the muscles in his back set in that stubborn way I hated.

"You said I could do what I liked once we were married!" I yelled at his back.

"I've changed my mind. From now on, you're an obedient wife."

He didn't speak to me for three whole days after that.

But I didn't speak to him for a week.

TWENTY-SEVEN
CALLUM

1764

Almost ten years had passed since I'd enlisted.

In that time, Phil moved on to Charles Town to petition for his land grant, but I, with nowhere to go, continued with the British to Canada. In battles I shuddered to recall, I became a skilled fighter and stayed to keep peace until the Treaty of Paris, where France conceded its claim on the continent.

My years of warring had come to an end. There was no more need of Jack Drummond, the soldier.

The road ahead was free. Tileman Cruger had written, urging me to join him in the West Indies. Likewise, Philemon invited me to Charles Town, but he was struggling to form his own prospects, and I wouldn't strain him with mine.

I could sail or trap or survey, but there was only one thing on my mind—assuring myself that Bembe was well.

I hadn't written to him but the once, not wanting to implicate him in a runaway's escape, and with all my movements, perhaps his replies had been lost. I'd asked Philemon to find out what he could when he sent his letters. Charlotte only reported that they'd seen him in town several times over the years.

Then the mentions of him trickled off.

The silence regarding Bembe grew from a nagging worry to a battle drum beating in my head.

I would not rest until I saw him again.

I traveled to Virginia and stabled Obsidian in a village a day's walk away to keep him far from Mr. Grenville. No matter the hazards I chose for myself, I wouldn't endanger Obsidian.

I went by foot on an overgrown trail to my old home, where Mr. Grenville had kept Bembe on to manage things after Smythe's death.

The trees stretched their bare, tangled branches across the path, and brambles grew up to block it. Even in setting darkness, a flit of color flickered between the trees.

I squeezed my eyes shut then opened them again.

There was nothing there. It was only the memory of a lass with shining black hair weaving through the trees.

Rosanna.

A twisting pain came, reminding me what it was to be eighteen again. Full of young hot blood and desire.

I pushed away thoughts of her and broke into a large clearing illuminated by a large moon.

There stood the big house. Imposing, shuttered, dark.

Memories of another sort assailed me. Through that shadowy window there—sitting long hours at my books with Smythe standing guard over me. The stables, where I first encountered him, unaware that he was my master. The day and night I spent in grief, and Bembe's hand, heavy upon my shoulder, when he finally found me.

There, past the main house, Bembe's home—ghost-quiet, the cold chimney void of even a trickle of smoke from a dying fire. It was too cold to be without a fire. Cobwebs filled the crevices in the wooden slats. A bank of leaves was pushed against the doorstep. The last leaf had fallen months ago—how long had it been since the door was opened?

I used my sleeve to wipe the dust from the windowpane. Inside were all his things as I'd remembered them, even his painting of Jamaica.

My heartbeat quickened.

Bembe wasn't here.

He wouldn't have left without taking his painting.

Movement shifted in the window's surface. Light floated in the wavy glass, swinging, as if held by a ghostly hand.

I turned my head slightly so as not to attract movement.

Behind me, someone wearing a dark cloak traveled the same path I'd taken, holding a lantern.

I crouched in the tall, dead grass beneath the window.

The person soon passed by me and made their way to the stable, disappearing inside but leaving the door cracked open.

I took out my knife and stepped softly until I reached the door and put my eye to the opening.

The person threw back their hood.

Fire and thunder, it was Charity Taylor.

Her long golden hair and pale skin shimmered in the moonlight as if she were a faerie on her way to join the Seelie Court.

She opened a simple burlap bag and dumped a bloody mess of what resembled chicken innards.

What witchcraft was this?

I'd have never suspected a gentle thing like her to be involved in the dark arts.

Before I left, her father had given her a cottage on their property when he realized she'd refuse every last man he put before her to wed. Her youngest brother, whom everyone knew to be her child, lived in her father's house and was being raised apart from her as her father's heir. I had only seen her once with him. She had been sitting with him by the creek that ran through their property, singing him the loveliest lullaby. Her voice was of the angels in its purest joy. It must've pained her greatly to not be a part of her son's life as a mother.

Something brushed against my leg and squeezed past the door.

Out of the shadows, cats.

They rushed to the pile of organs and swallowed pieces whole. She wasn't a witch. She was a saint.

"Charity?"

She pushed to her feet. "Who goes there?"

If anyone could be trusted to not report me to Grenville, it would be she. Charity wouldn't do him a favor even if her life depended upon it. I pushed into the light of her lamp.

"Callum!"

I was surprised she remembered me. She'd always been kind, but we'd never been more than acquaintances. "Aye."

She raised her lantern and stepped closer. "Why are you here?"

"I'm looking for Smythe's overseer. Bembe."

Her eyes became troubled. "You haven't heard."

The air in my lungs turned to mud. "What happened?"

"Mr. Grenville has died. Frederick came to dispose of the property, selling the slaves and horses, then returned to South Carolina."

"And Bembe?"

"Apoplexy. Mr. Grenville had no patience and cast him aside. One of the slaves took pity on Bembe and cared for him until a few weeks ago, when Frederick sold her. I didn't find out until yesterday."

To be this close and too late! "Where's Bembe?"

"There's no finding him unless it is in the graveyard, Callum. He wouldn't have survived without her."

I ground my fist against my mouth so I wouldn't cry out. I shouldn't have left him. Fie on myself! Fie on Mr. Grenville and everyone who left Bembe to rot. Why hadn't I tried harder to convince Bembe to leave with me after Smythe died?

"There's no chance you're wrong? Speak! Tell me if there's a chance I might save him."

Her face convulsed. "He's better off, I say."

"How can you say such a thing?"

She knotted her hands in her shawl. "You think I don't grieve

Bembe's sad end? That I couldn't help him? He saved me... when Frederick was... when he had..." She lifted her chin. "I wish Bembe free from the troubles of this life."

I was a brute, a devil, to be pressing her after all she'd been through. When I'd been forgotten in that dank, moldering prison, with my flesh melting from my bones and my spirit roused only by hunger, I, too, had wished to die.

"It doesn't matter if you know. Everyone does." She lowered her shoulders. Her wrap pooled in the crooks of her elbows. "Bembe was too late, but I have my Gabriel. Though I'm more a distant aunt than mother, he still knows me."

The cats disappeared, one by one, leaving only the darkened mark of blood in the dirt.

"So you feed them, do you?"

"The place has been abandoned, yet they stay. It's winter, so the mice are snug in their burrows."

She couldn't mother her son, so she would mother abandoned cats. The poor heart. "Charity, where do you suggest I go to find Bembe's grave?"

"The servants' burial ground behind Mr. Grenville's home."

I nodded once. "Goodbye, Charity. And thank you. Will you be safe going home?"

She smiled a little at that. "I've since learned to protect myself. Go."

I left her and set out for the long trek to Grenville's property.

When I arrived and found the burial ground, there were no fresh-dug graves and no wooden markers bearing his name.

I scanned the property and the outlying structures. Did he lie dead in one of them? I went from building to building but had no luck.

Then a shadow appeared far beyond the servants' homes, a small outbuilding with the roof half caved in. I'd looked everywhere but there.

I strode to the hut and opened the door.

I gagged and hid my nose in my elbow.

It smelled like death.

There were shelves lining the wall straight ahead, and empty glass bottles strewn on the floor.

A shaft of moonlight fell on a pile of rags to the right.

A figure lay there, covered in a thin blanket.

I dropped my arm and stared.

The small figure was as still as the biting winter air.

I stepped into the room and was hit by an even greater stench. Unclean linens and sick, a putrid sourness no man deserved to lie in.

"Bembe? It's your boy. Callum."

A movement. Just barely, but it was there.

I fell on my knees at his side.

His large eyes moved, searching. His mouth worked to make some reply, stretching his sunken cheeks over his bones. A strangled, breathy sound caught in his throat.

"You're thirsty." I went to the bottles. They were all uncorked and dry. I remembered my waterskin looped on my belt and untied it. Lifting his head, I dribbled a few drops into his mouth. His throat bobbed. I tilted it higher to give him a few more.

He coughed. His bony hand wrapped around my wrist and pulled the drink away.

He would need much more than this if he were to survive. "You must drink. Just a wee more."

His grip, already loose, weakened. I gave him a little more water and gently laid his head on the pillow. "That's enough for now."

One of his hands was drawn to his chest, unnatural-like, clutching a dirty, crumbled piece of paper. "Boy," he said. The word was raspy, like the creaking of metal.

Tears stung my eyes. I wouldn't let him stay in this hovel for another second.

I swept him up in my arms. He weighed no more than a child, and a sob caught in my chest.

Snow fell silently from the black sky. I walked as gently as I could for what seemed like hours over the winding path to town, praying the entire way that Bembe would survive the journey.

I reached the inn and shifted him in my arms to pound on the back door.

It swung open. A thin woman in a shift and wrapper peered at us, holding a candle to our faces. She shrank back, holding the shawl to her nose. "What's this? I'll have no trouble here."

"I need a fire and a clean bed."

I pushed my way forward, but she angled herself in front of me. "We've no room, not for his sort. I can allow you a place by the fire, but him, you leave out here."

I shifted Bembe again and pulled from my pocket two coins from my meager savings. "Please, miss. His life depends upon it."

She eyed the coins greedily. "Be quick about it, then." She stepped back from the door and led me to a room with a small bed and little else. "He sleeps on the floor, mind?"

"I'll have hot water, rags, a clean shirt, and gruel for my friend," I said, drawing myself to my full height.

She put her hands to her hips. "Coo! I didn't know we'd be housing the King of England!"

I softened my tone. "I'd be grateful, my lady."

She curtseyed low, her skirt pinched between two fingers and held out to the side. "Yer grace." Her cackle trailed behind her as she left the room.

She returned a short time later holding a large, steaming bowl and strips of cloth draped over one arm. A maid carrying a kettle of water followed behind her.

After stripping him of his rags and throwing them into the fire, I uncurled Bembe's fingers and pulled the dirty paper from his fist.

I carefully unfolded it. The words were smeared and faded, but there was no mistaking *Jack* and *safety*. He'd kept the letter I'd written to him years ago, assuring him of my arrival with the regiment.

With the greatest of care, I bathed him and settled him into the bed.

His skin was covered in sweat.

"Are you in pain?"

He shook his head.

I dipped a rag in the hot water and directed all my fury into twisting it dry. How could Mr. Grenville abandon Bembe? Heartless, cruel man.

Think. What was to be done?

Bembe had the use of his voice and one hand, weak as it was. He could eat and drink a little, if one was patient enough for the time it took to help him do it.

I couldn't stay here and look after him. Though Grenville was dead, Frederick could still assert his rights over Obsidian if word were to reach him of my whereabouts.

A plan came to mind. It wouldn't be easy, and it couldn't be done without help.

Bembe's leathery, cold hand brushed over mine. "Leave... me."

I brought a spoon to his lips and tipped the thin gruel into his mouth. "I'll never leave you again. But I must find a way to support us." I lowered his head and wiped his mouth with a clean rag. "The *both* of us."

What little money I had wouldn't aid us forever, but there was a door open to me, one that would give Bembe his comfort and Charity a way to get her son back if she would only hear me out.

I scribbled a note and asked the inn's boy to deliver it for me.

Bembe slept peacefully, at times so still I feared him dead. I woke him often through the night to take water and sips of gruel, if only to reassure myself.

Just as morning's gray light crept through our one window, a small knock sounded at our door.

I jerked to my feet, knife gripped in my hand. "Who's there?"

"It's Charity," came the soft reply.

I opened the door. "Come in."

"I received your note." She slipped in and removed her cloak. "I never thought to see you again," she whispered.

I nodded toward the bed. "I have found him."

She gasped, and in three steps, she was kneeling at his side. "Oh, Bembe, Bembe! Look at what Grenville's done to you." Taking his frail hand between hers, she cupped it to her cheek.

Bembe awoke and settled his eyes on Charity.

Charity turned and glared at me. "How can this be? How could another man leave him like this?"

"Charity, we need your help."

She laid Bembe's hand gently on his chest and stood. "Anything. You've only to ask."

"You know I'm an outlaw. If I'm to care for Bembe, I must make a home for us away from here. A friend from the regiment has offered to hire me. It'll keep me away for many months at a time, but at least it would provide for you, Bembe, and your son."

She drew back. "*What?*"

"All I ask in return for my provision is that you care for Bembe when I'm gone."

"Father loves Gabriel and promises him a future."

I resisted the urge to laugh. If her father truly loved Gabriel, he wouldn't have taken him from his mother. My own mother died when I was his age, and I would've given everything to see her again—to hear her disappointed clucks when I forgot to clean my nails, to have her laugh and sing and feel her fingers on my brow as I drifted off to sleep. I would give that to Gabriel if Charity would let me.

"If you could support him, would you have him with you?"

Hope flickered in her eyes. But just as quickly as it came, it faded. "I won't live with an unmarried man. I know what it is to lose a reputation."

"I'll marry you." The words came out before I had time to think, but once said, I could see there was no other way. "For your protection and Gabriel's. I would see you as my sister. I'd be a brother to you and nothing more."

In a small voice, she said, "What if Gabriel doesn't want to come?"

"Does he know his story?"

"He can hardly escape it."

My heart twisted for the boy, eleven years old and powerless. I knew something of what it was like to be considered unworthy in the eyes of others. "Then he will want to come."

"How can you be sure?"

"This is your chance to find out."

A fiery hunger leaped into her eyes. "Then I will take it."

TWENTY-EIGHT
CALLUM

1769

A thin trail of smoke rose from the forest. On the other end of it, a hearth in a cabin where happiness dwelled.

Home.

Gabriel and I spurred our horses into a canter.

He would be especially anxious to return, this being his first trip from home.

The clearing where our cabin sat, swathed in sunshine and encircled by dried pine needles, came into view. My breathing eased. In the peace and comfort of this sanctuary, perhaps I could untie the knot in my gut that had been there since the incident on the docks.

We had been absent for months to do business for Tileman Cruger, collecting goods in the West Indies and then selling them to trading posts, armies, and merchants in the Carolinas. We'd gone first to Charles Town, where we boarded Tileman's ship, then to St. Croix. There we met with Alexander Hamilton, the Cruger family's agent, who at fourteen was two years younger than Gabriel. I could hardly credit so young a man being entrusted with so great an operation, but the lad's talents could hardly be denied.

He was with us when the slave ship came in. It was the first time I'd witnessed such a thing, but Hamilton said he'd seen it before, and worse. The only thing I could comfort myself with was the decision I'd made because of it.

We gave Hamilton our cargo of Philadelphia flour and apples, and then went on to Curaçao, a jewel dropped in a setting of brilliant blue, an island of steep, rocky cliffs and hidden coves. We had loaded our ship with sugar, rum, and cotton, and returned to the colonies.

In the distance, Charity stood in the doorway, smiling widely and waving her arm. Bembe sat beside her in a chair, a bowl on his lap.

Gabriel whooped and urged his horse into a full gallop, coming to a sliding stop feet away from the house. "Mother!" He leaped to the ground and nearly knocked her over with the force of his embrace.

The knot untied a little looser at the sight of them together, free to be mother and son.

"I'm so relieved to be home," Gabriel said, his voice thick.

I slowed my horse into a walk and dismounted. Sidestepping Charity and Gabriel, I came before Bembe and kneeled.

He put one hand on my head and grinned his half-smile, showing off his whalebone-white teeth. "Boy."

Tears rushed to my eyes. It never failed to overwhelm me, seeing him happy and well, his cheeks plump and his eyes sparkling with life once again. "How are you, my friend?"

"It is good you are home." He still spoke slowly around his sleeping muscles, but to me, there was no finer sound in all the world. "But where is my favorite boy?" he asked, peering around me.

I laughed. So easily I had been replaced.

Gabriel left Charity and bestowed a hug upon Bembe. I hadn't yet been so lucky as to receive one of those from the boy, but at least Gabriel had found our old friend worthy. "I've missed you!"

Bembe handed him the bowl that sat upon his lap, full of peas. "Help me with these."

I turned to Charity. "Did you enjoy your break?"

She came over to me, rosy-cheeked and golden in the midday sun. "Hush. I'm very happy to have you both home."

The moment called for a greeting beyond words. She was my wife, though not in every sense. I was happy in our life together and glad to return to her. I would have her know it.

I lowered my lips to her cheek.

She started and pulled back. Not so much that others might have seen it, but it was enough for me to know her feelings.

I swallowed my disappointment and immediately pulled away, forcing a smile. "The wood pile is low. I'll set that to rights after I put the horses away. Gabriel?"

He looked up from where he crouched by Bembe. "Yes?"

"Help me with the horses."

Without another word, I went to Obsidian and Gabriel's horse and led them to the barn.

After I chopped the wood and we ate supper as a family of four, I sat on a fallen log, wrapped in the heavy solitude of night. The frogs trilled and chirped. The crickets sang the same note, again and again, loud and insistent.

Their vexing song matched the inescapable thoughts circling in my head.

The memory of what happened on the dock.

The way my stomach twisted at the sight of human suffering and Gabriel's horror. Knowing it was an innocence he would never get back.

It was Charity, and the worry that I would spend the rest of my life knowing her but never really belonging to her after all these years. Not in body, not in spirit.

It was as I had said all those years ago—she was my sister, and I, her brother. But I never imagined feeling so alone, even surrounded by the ones I loved.

Behind me, the cabin's door opened then closed.

Charity joined me, her thin body wrapped tight in a quilt. "Thank you for cleaning the trenchers." Her voice was soft, apologetic.

"I was happy to do it."

"Why was Gabriel upset?"

I sighed, deep and heavy. On another night, perhaps when time had passed and my feelings weren't so strong, I might've been able to give a polite recounting of our time in the West Indies.

"What happened?"

"We were asked to take on African slaves when we were in St. Croix. The poor souls had been left there by a sea captain who refused to go any further with them. They were... they were sick. I enlisted the help of the young Mr. Hamilton. By the time we found a doctor willing to treat them, it was too late. The captain had drowned most of them in the bay."

Charity gasped. "How can anyone be so cruel?"

"Hamilton is Cruger's agent, Charity. Even he has had to take part in slaving at the firm's direction, though Hamilton is troubled by it. I'm no fool. I knew some ships carried human cargo, but I thought I could, well... " I rubbed my hands over my thighs. "If Hamilton can't refuse Tileman's father, how can I? I won't do it. I can't."

"How did Gabriel take it?"

"He was furious." I wouldn't tell her that some of his ire had been directed at me. In a rare moment of openness, he told me that when he had a ship of his own, he would do more than find a doctor for them.

I knew there was nothing more I could have done, but Gabriel's unspoken criticism cut like a shard of glass. He might think himself adept at hiding the depth of his sentiments, but he didn't know I was once as he was, a boy with feelings so strong that to give voice to them might have unleashed a ruinous fire. Mr. Smythe had listened without judgment, and I would do the same for Gabriel.

When he asked how I could align myself with such a business, all that would matter was the action I took.

"I've decided to go out on my own, Charity. I haven't had to take on any slaves yet, but the day will come when I have no choice. I've saved enough for my own ship, and Tileman says he will partner with me, so there is little risk. The important thing is that I will have the freedom to choose what I carry and the ability to intervene in the injustice where I can."

Charity nodded distractedly. "That is good." She pulled her blanket tighter around her shoulders.

"Do you agree, then?"

"Of course." She settled into silence again.

"Are you well?"

"Callum, I... I'm sorry for not being a good wife to you."

"How can you say such a thing? You've done nothing wrong." And she hadn't. The wrong was done to her and by another hand than mine. "It's only... don't you want a little more?" At the stricken look on her face, I suppressed a groan. "Not *that*."

Why couldn't I explain that I had known what it meant to be seen and loved by another and how grievous it was to realize I would never have it again? And perhaps that was the truth of it—I missed another, even after all this time, and had hoped Charity would put her out of my mind for good.

But that wasn't fair to her. It wasn't fair to me.

"It isn't what you promised me," she said.

"I know."

We continued in silence for a while longer.

"I thank you for all you have done for me and Gabriel," she said, not looking me in the eyes. "I am happy here. I have a home and my son and freedom to do what I like. I can never repay your kindness. I will care for you and take care of your home, but I cannot be more to you than what I am right now. Can you accept that?"

I nodded. "Aye. You have no need to worry. I will never speak of this again." It was not her fault, nor was it mine. She had been broken by another, and I would never be enough to repair those parts of her.

TWENTY-NINE
ROSANNA

1776

Dear Rosanna,

I received a <u>most alarming letter</u> from Phil. He reports a clash between the loyalists and the rebels in the town of Ninety Six and that some are dead, with more wounded. That is but miles away from you, Rosanna! He expects hostilities to <u>boil over at any moment</u>. He says neighbor has set himself against neighbor in your district and especially against John—loyalists are angry he doesn't stand with them, and the rebels are angry he doesn't fight for their cause. What's worse, he says the glass windows I gifted you were broken by a band of loyalists.

I'm filled with the <u>most tremendous concern</u> for the children's well-being. If you but send me Sarah, I would be a little comforted. There's peace in Virginia still, and Sarah will have opportunities not afforded to her in the backcountry, namely <u>the safety of her person</u> and perhaps a husband.

I love you, Rosanna, but don't let your obstinance come between Sarah and a better life.

Your most devoted sister,

Pearl

I folded the letter with trembling hands.

She was right to be worried.

In the twelve years since the flood, we'd coaxed our farm back to life. The river stayed contentedly within its confines. We rested a new wagon on the hill and built a home beside it.

Bit by bit, crop by crop, we replaced horses and oxen, acquired two milking cows, and expanded our house—another room and a loft for the boys. I even had enough from my garden that I could share with Mr. Brown and any Indians who cut through our land, and a little to sell in town.

When the last tool, bucket, and saddle was replaced, I took some of the money I'd made and bought a pistol, a genuine Virginian flintlock long rifle, and a pocketful of scrap lead.

John's command that I be a proper wife was lost in the fullness of running our farm and raising our eight children—adding Jane two years after the flood, and William, three years later.

Our life appeared idyllic. It *was* idyllic, except for the tensions deepening around us, just as Pearl wrote about.

There were murmurs. A shifting in the air. British soldiers roamed the Ninety Six. Neighbors plotted against neighbors.

I tucked a cloth over the pottage I'd prepared for Mr. Brown and stepped into the sunshine. "I'll be back!" I called to the girls and William, who were pulling a piece of wood into their tree fort with a rope.

Sarah climbed down and joined my side.

It would do Elias good to see her. He'd been forgetful of late. Confused. But he always remembered the children.

Sarah plucked some white, pink, and purple coneflowers—Elias' favorite—as she walked along with me.

I smiled at her. "How's your lookout coming?"

Her face fell. "You think I'm too old for playing with the others."

I wrapped an arm around her and tugged her to my side. "I think you a good sister and young at heart." She'd always be my freckle-faced little girl who healed my heart after I left Pearl in Virginia.

It was what made the contents of the letter I'd just received so wholly disturbing to me. I couldn't lose her, but Pearl was right—the situation out here was getting more dangerous by the day.

It started with a tax to recoup what had been lost in the war, then grumbles of taxation without being granted a voice in Parliament. One restrictive act layered upon another due to the colonists' refusal to submit, until we were on an inevitable march to war against our own government.

A war the Farrow boys were determined to join, thanks to Philemon.

My brother's letters were fiery, passionate, recounting battles in the most vivid terms. The boys soaked up every word. I tried to hide Phil's letters when they came, for I recognized the same light in my boys' eyes that had been in my brother's when he'd left home for soldiering. It was a foolish enterprise when the missives were delivered by a postrider who came flying in on a cloud of dust. But it was too late. Overcome with zeal for the patriot cause, they joined our militia and would soon be gone.

We came to Elias' house and entered.

He was asleep in his rocking chair, hands folded on his stomach. "Elias?"

He snorted and opened his eyes. "Hester?"

My heart skipped a beat. "No, Elias. It's Rosanna. I've brought Sarah to visit you."

He sat up. "You've brought me Elizabeth?"

Sarah and I exchanged glances. "No, not Elizabeth."

But Elias didn't seem to hear. "Oh, my Lizzie. My dear sweet one!" He reached for her hands. "I missed you, my girl." Tears spilled into his cottony beard. "Why have you stayed away so long?"

He'd never been this confused before. I couldn't bear it, watching him grow worse.

"Let me hear you call me *Papa* again. Go on."

Sarah glanced at me uncertainly.

"What's this?" John's voice carried into the little house. "I've come to build the fence. Is everything well?" He looked at me, a question in his eyes.

I gave him a sad little shake of my head.

"John, welcome." Elias' voice was clear and strong as if the past moment had never happened. He pushed himself to his feet. "What's this about a fence?"

"It's to keep the foxes away from your chickens."

And Elias from tumbling down cliffs. John's plan was to build a fence without an exit so Elias wouldn't wander off.

"That's fine, that's fine. Don't want anything to hurt our chickens, do we, Three-Tail?"

On cue, the cat weaved in and out of Elias' legs, rubbing his chin against the man's breeches.

"Elias, come. I've brought you food." I pulled out his chair at the table.

"Now, this is the way to treat a friend. A fence and food, all in one day!"

I smiled. "Yes, Elias."

John took my hand and guided me toward the door. "Sarah, take over for your mother."

"Yes, Papa."

I followed John outside. "What is it?"

His throat bobbed. "I have news."

"What is it?"

"My mother's died of smallpox, and my father's soon to follow."

"Oh, John!" I grabbed his hand and squeezed it. "I'm so very sorry."

He grasped the porch railing and stared into the trees lining Elias' land. It was some time before he could speak again. "There are affairs to attend to. The farm to sell. Their belongings. The timing isn't good, but you have the boys to look after things when I'm gone."

"But they're leaving."

"They'll be here when the militia isn't drilling, and I shouldn't be gone for more than a month."

"What about Elias? John, he's getting worse."

"I don't have a choice." His voice held a bite I seldom heard anymore. "Is there anything you wish me to bring to your family?"

"I have nothing to—" I remembered Pearl's letter and her offer to take Sarah away from this madness. My heart thudded with what I'd decided to do. "Pearl invited Sarah for a visit. I'd rejected the idea out of hand, but with the war, and you going there anyway, perhaps it's for the best."

"Go and tell her to ready herself." He stepped off the porch.

"Wait!"

"I'm already getting a late start."

I ran out to him and pulled him around to face me. "Your parents had smallpox."

"I'll be careful."

Years of marriage had given him the ability to read my thoughts. Which made it strange that he couldn't read the ones I was having now.

"When did you start thinking of me for a wife?"

He gave me a strange look. "Why do you ask this now?"

I shrugged. "I've always wondered."

He blew out a puff of air and looked to the sky. "I suppose it was after the accident. You seemed different. Less wild. More like a girl, I suppose, with your hair done up in your cap. Really, Rosanna, you used to look like a forest witch." He brushed a piece of hair from my forehead and tucked it behind my ear. "But even then, you were..." His gaze roamed over my forehead, my eyes, then down to my lips. "Interesting."

Interesting. "But did I mean something to you?"

He hooked his arm around my waist, pulling me to him in a way as familiar as breathing. "Us not getting along, that's how we started, but it's not where we ended up."

If he wouldn't say it, I would. "I love you, John."

"I'm not staying, Rosanna."

"I know."

His eyes softened, and he lowered his head to mine.

Just before our lips touched, I tried one more time. "Where have we ended up, John?"

He didn't answer but crushed his mouth to mine. In his fervor, I could imagine that he said he loved me too.

THIRTY
CALLUM

1780

I strode the docks in Charles Town with Gabriel at my side, a man full-grown in his own right and almost as tall as me.

My heart was wooden, my steps mechanical, when before the sight of the barnacle-rimmed harbor of home would have filled me with anticipation.

What was home without Charity and Bembe to return to?

It had been four years since they'd been taken by a lung fever and almost as long since Gabriel and I last stepped foot in the colonies. We'd purposefully taken on cargo destined for other places, losing ourselves in the unfamiliar. Whether that was the right thing or not, I had no other answers to his mourning, having found no answers for mine. There'd never been any other way through my losses but to move forward, one plodding step at a time.

I turned my attention back to our purpose. "Do you have the bill of sale for the sugar?"

"With the others in the pouch."

"Signed?"

"All is in order."

I stopped him with a hand on his shoulder. "You have done well."

"All the more reason to leave the *Zephyr* to my care so you can enjoy the fruit of your labors."

"Gabriel..."

"You know I don't wish you to leave. But it's time I make something of myself."

"Being a purser of a ship is a fine, respectable job. Why, anybody should be glad to know you."

"Of course *you* feel that way." He softened his words with an apologetic smile. "You are my father."

Warmth filled my chest so I could hardly speak. I would never tire of hearing him refer to me as such. Buying my own ship had eased things between Gabriel and me. He saw that I meant what I said, just as I did when I promised to care for him as my son.

Before me, Gabriel had endured years of being called a child of sin. A bastard. Even his grandfather had taken part in it. But even all my love and attention hadn't been enough to heal it. He only allowed Charity to speak to that part of him, perhaps because she'd faced the same mockery he had. Without her, he was lost. A man without his mooring.

"It's not the right time, Gabriel."

"When, then?"

When, indeed? I had built it all for him, after all. And hadn't I been preparing him for this very thing? I'd been handing more and more of my responsibilities over to him with an eye to the future. I hadn't been able to help myself. He was smart, quick, eager to learn, and I had proudly cultivated his gifts.

Why *not* hand it off now?

I had enough money to last a lifetime. Gabriel could go, with my blessing, and I'd be comfortable the rest of my days in whatever place I pleased.

Panic beat beneath my ribs like a bird caught in its cage.

Without this, without Gabriel, I had no place in this world. "I should like things to stay as they are."

"Jack!" The voice boomed far behind me. "Jack Drummond!"

I trailed off mid-sentence and turned around.

Philemon strode toward me, a hand raised in greeting. "You make it devilish hard to find you. Why haven't you responded to my letters?"

I shook his hand heartily. "I haven't received any letters."

"Where have you been?"

"I've had business in the West Indies."

He raised an eyebrow. "Four years' worth? I came as soon as the *Zephyr* came into port. I have something to discuss with you." He nodded at Gabriel. "My, but what has my friend been feeding you? You've turned into a man since the last I saw you."

A look of amusement crossed Gabriel's face. "I should hope so."

I grabbed Philemon's shoulder. "Come aboard, then. We'll have tea there."

We walked the docks, and soon we were settled in my cabin. It was richly furnished, with thick carpet and shining mahogany and Bembe's painting of the Jamaican bay hanging on the wall opposite my desk.

Philemon snapped the silver snuff box closed and looked around the cabin, eyebrows raised. "Never thought I'd see you in a room like this."

"You saw me at Mr. Smythe's, and it was no less fine than this."

I held out a hand to two armchairs, and we both sat.

"May I go?" Gabriel stood by the door, impatience in every line of his face. "I still have business at Weatherby's."

I gave him a tight nod.

The boy was out the door before I could say goodbye.

"How goes it with him?" Philemon asked.

"We rely on one another, but he is... restless."

Philemon rubbed his hands along his thighs. "Well..."

I raised an eyebrow at him while I poured our tea. "Well?"

"I was sorry to hear of your loss."

My throat tightened. I turned my face away so he wouldn't

bear witness to my pain. The time away hadn't been long enough to soften the edges of sorrow. "What news of you?"

"I joined the Continentals a while ago." He had a sparkle in his eyes.

"Of course you have." He'd hardly stopped complaining about the injustice of being controlled by a parliament that hadn't given colonists a voice. Colonists believed themselves to be full British citizens and were only asking to be considered as such. *If I'm to be taxed as a British citizen, I will be treated as one*, Phil had said. Did he understand that the choice urged a fire that could raze his way of life to the ground?

"Did you hear they made Washington a general?" Phil asked.

"He'll have to watch his back, unless you've decided to stop aiming at commanders."

Philemon rolled his eyes. "He's forgotten, surely."

"That you almost shot him from two feet away?"

He settled deeper into his chair, his posture of a defiant brat. "It was more like six."

"All of six? Well, then. I don't see why he should still be angry."

"If it weren't for you making such a to-do of holding me back from shooting him, he might never have noticed it from the corner of his eye."

"He commanded me to tell him the story. What else could I do but tell it?"

Phil barely held back his grin. "I beg you to stop repeating the story. I will be thrown out of every tavern and town once it becomes known far and wide that I almost killed the leader of our cause."

I laughed. "Then you take away one of my few joys in life."

Philemon shook his head. "But what of you? Will you go back to being a soldier?"

"Why do I keep getting dragged into other people's battles? My warring days are over."

"Then you have no sympathies with either side." He watched me carefully.

"If I do, they aren't strong enough to induce me to kill another man for them."

Philemon stared out the port window. "What a fine ship you have. Rosanna would be jealous of your adventures, you know."

Rosanna. A bittersweet ache settled in my chest. As much as I'd tried to forget her, she stubbornly kept to her post inside me, as was her way. It was one thing not to be able to forget her, but another to hear her being spoken of so easily in the open. "Is she and her family well?"

"Ninety Six is crawling with redcoats. General Greene tried to retake the Carolinas once Cornwallis moved into Virginia but couldn't dislodge them. If the armies fighting weren't enough, loyalists pit themselves against rebels, rebels against the loyalists. Nowhere is safe, Callum, not even the wilderness."

"And which side does Rosanna take?"

He blew out a breath and shook his head as if to say, *What can you do with such a sister?* "She thinks by not choosing a side, both the British and the rebels will leave her alone. Her oldest sons have joined the militia and are in my unit, though Landon is further north." His brow darkened. "I'm worried for her, Callum. She's quite alone."

"Has John joined too?"

He blinked. "I'd forgotten you hadn't received my letters."

"What is it? What happened?"

He glanced away, his mouth tight. When he looked at me again, his eyes were shadowed with grief. "Callum, I'm sorry to tell you that our friend is dead."

I sucked in a breath. "Dead!" John was supposed to protect her, not leave her on the frontier with a farm and children to manage on her own. "*How?*"

"Smallpox."

A terrible way to die. My poor friend. He hadn't planned on his dying either.

It was some time before Philemon spoke again. "He left their oldest daughter in the care of Pearl. Because of the war, Sarah's been unable to return. It would do Rosanna good to have her daughter with her again, but I have my militia duties. If *you* were to go... " He let the suggestion hang in the air.

My heart beat a wild rhythm. "I couldn't possibly."

"Why not? You said yourself the boy is restless. Give the ship over to him and help my sister. You're the only one I trust to bring Sarah home safely."

What could I say? He couldn't know that the last time I'd seen her had been the night I'd left her standing cold by their mother's grave. It haunted me still that I'd abandoned her when she needed me most.

Would I deny her again for the sake of my discomfort?

The contents of my stomach tossed and turned. "How long is the journey from here to Virginia?"

Philemon clapped his hand on my shoulder. "Good man. Oh, and I suppose I must tell you that Frederick Grenville is her neighbor."

He said the last so quickly it took me a moment to catch it. "You tell me after I already agreed to the scheme?"

"I wouldn't worry. Frederick's father is dead. Your indenture-ship is all but forgotten, I'm sure."

Somehow I doubted Frederick would let go so easily of what was due him.

"Now, on to other business. I have a letter for you from the general himself."

I didn't reach out to take it. "Come, Phil. I'm not in the mood for another of your jokes."

"I am all seriousness. He gave it to me hoping I could find you." He tossed it on the table. "You'd be proud of my self-restraint. I have had it in my pocket for months."

"What could be so important that he enlisted you to bring it to me?"

Philemon looked behind him though we were the only two in

the room. "I imagine he might mention something of a... sensitive nature." But instead of telling me what it was, he stood and poured himself a drink then drained it to its dregs. "There is some talk of raising those who might be of, well, of *service* to the cause." He studied me for a moment. "We are at a disadvantage and need to know what they will do before they do it."

"He wants me to *spy*?"

"Quiet, man!" He put a finger to his lips.

"I haven't talked to Washington in years. Why would he think of me?" A darker thought came then. Perhaps Washington had discovered who I was and was using it to force me into working for him. "The British won't take Callum Stewart, runaway horse thief, into their confidence."

"No, but Jack Drummond they might, for all the years you spent making a name for him among the British. They still talk of your feats in Canada."

I steeled myself against an intrusion of memories. Tales of my exploits followed me long after I left the regiment. Exaggerated stories, to my mind, but what I went through to survive those battles were hardships best left forgotten. "I've already told you—I'm through with soldiering."

"I don't see as you have much of a choice. You say you are tired of war, but war is already at your doorstep. Bring my niece to Rosanna, then see what that Colonel Cruger is about. You already know Cruger's brother—he can't be suspicious if you introduce yourself based on that connection. It's that close association to the Cruger family that gave Washington cause to consider my suggestion."

Was this why he asked me to bring Sarah to Rosanna? To set the trap for this request? It would land me neatly on Cruger's doorstep. "No."

"No?" He spat out an outraged laugh. "I never thought I'd live to hear you say no to one of my schemes. I told Washington you'd be game for anything."

"Then make your apologies for telling him wrongly."

When another hour of needling me over the advantages of helping the rebels got him no further, he left after jotting down directions to his lodgings should I change my mind.

I stared at the fat envelope he'd left behind.

There'd be no going back once I read it. I either denied the offer, earning Washington's ire, or I accepted and returned to war. But at the very least, a man didn't refuse to read what a general penned directly to him. I picked up the letter and tore the seal.

Dear Mr. Stewart,

I imagine the surprise you must feel at receiving a letter from me and addressed to your given name.

You must wonder at how I came to this information or why it matters at all. To put it simply, I could not get out of my mind the beads you wore, even in the years since I left the regiment.

These two sheets, taken from my brother's daily accountings, were unknown to me until a month ago. If not for them, I would never have found my answer.

I lowered the pages. There was nothing here about spying at all. What could his brother have written related to me, and what had it to do with Bembe's beads? My stomach tightened as if preparing for a blow.

3 March 1752

I visited my old friend today. He is hearty well, just as he ever was. We recalled the day we met, and I determined to write it down here with some details he reminded me of.

I had been commissioned as an officer for a Virginia company sent to fight for Britain against the Spanish in the West Indies. Our ship came to Jamaica with sickness aboard, and the island's inhabitants would not let us disembark. Food and water dwindled, and soon, the harbor was filled with floating bodies. Our state was such that I, desperate, rowed ashore with several strings of beads for trading raised in my fist, calling for pity from the natives.

One man stood apart from the angry mob and spoke what sounded like a rebuke to his people before he walked into the surf. He took the beads and filled the skiff with skins of water, freshly picked fruit, Old Man's Beard leaf, and chaney root for our fevers.

The villagers did not allow Bembe to return to their shore, so I rowed him back to the ship. He showed nothing on his face as to whether it pained him to leave his village.

With Bembe's help, we recovered. Bembe asked if he could buy passage with his servitude. I can barely think on it now without great emotion, but I told him the only payment I required of him were the same Italian glass beads I had given him. From these, Bembe fashioned two strings for our wrists. He said he would wear it to remember the man who had saved his life, as I should to remember the man who saved mine.

I found a place for him with my friend, Mr. Smythe, and Bembe has prospered in his new country. He has gained Smythe's trust and has taken a young Scotsman, a servant, under his care. One would think this boy were Bembe's son by how my friend boasts of him. It is of great comfort that I leave my friend in such a happy state.

Lawrence W.

I traced my fingers over the last sentence.

I was glad that Mr. Washington noted Bembe's happiness. How strange that the vagaries of life had tossed me to Mr. Smythe, when I just as easily might've been put with Grenville. Without

Smythe's and Bembe's steady influence, what would I have become? Resentful of life. Adrift, undoubtedly.

Washington continued the letter in his own hand.

I am sure you are the young man my brother writes of—Bembe's boy.

I visited Mr. Smythe's so I might meet Bembe, but the plantation is shuttered, the new master is dead, and Bembe is nowhere to be found. In my investigation, I discovered something I had not anticipated—your name, and why you go by a new one. Imagine my shock in discovering you were a horse thief after all. Knowing what I know now of Grenville (for no one in the area had anything good to say of the man), I am inclined to think you justified.

To understand my feelings, you must know that Lawrence was a father to me. I owe him a debt for everything my life has become. He gave me what I needed to make something of myself and trusted me to do it. His faith in me gave me confidence to find my own way.

I cannot help but think it a wondrous turn of Providence that you and I met shortly after my brother's note was written and that you and I both had occasion to be of good to one another. The night you came, I had half a mind to eject you from the camp, but it was seeing the bracelet that stayed my hand. You may thank your Bembe for what I suspect was me saving your life, as I thank him for you saving mine—no thanks to Philemon and his hot head at the surrender.

Please, if you know what has happened to Bembe, I ask that you tell me. If there is still some good I can do for the man, I wish to do it. I ask nothing in return but hope you will consider what Philemon has undoubtedly mentioned to you. You may trust that I won't reveal your origins, whether you choose to aid me or not.

With sincerest regard,

G. Washington

I sat back, letter in hand. A turn of Providence indeed.

Returning to the lines Washington wrote about his brother, I read them again. *He gave me what I needed to make something of myself and trusted me to do it. His faith in me gave me confidence to find my own way.*

The path ahead wouldn't become any clearer.

I penned a response, assuring Washington of Bembe's happiness in his last years and thanking him for allowing me a place in the world when I had no other. But I wouldn't join his cause and told him so.

Sanding then sealing the letter, I tucked it in my waistcoat pocket. But there was something else to do before handing it to Philemon.

Forcing down my pain at the coming change, I left my cabin and descended the gangway to the docks, where Gabriel was sure to be found.

THIRTY-ONE
ROSANNA

I plodded over the worn path to Elias' house, a basket of food hooked on one arm. Mary, Jane, and William trailed behind me, their steps subdued and reluctant.

A pitiful party indeed.

"Did you know, I had the strangest dream last night," I said, loud enough for them to hear. "I dreamed we were a family of cranes. We made a nest so big we all slept in it, nestled together and warm."

"And Papa?" William asked.

I winced. The question scraped a wound my heart had almost healed. "Yes, and Papa."

The news of John's death had come in a letter four years ago, cruel and cold as winter's chill. The smallpox outbreak in Virginia had been worse than anticipated. John perished on his route back to South Carolina and was buried in an unmarked grave. The ache like a splinter lodged itself deep and had yet to work its way out.

The one comfort I had was that before John had left, Pearl had convinced Sarah to stay with her a little longer—Sarah hadn't been stuck in a strange place on their journey back with her father dead. It was a comfort that came at a price, for I had no hope of seeing her again, not with the dangers of war preventing her from coming home.

The thought of returning to Virginia crossed my mind, especially with the boys joining the militia. But the farm was the only way to keep my family together, the only inheritance I could offer my children. I thanked John for providing me with the means to do it with every pasture I cleared and every barrel of indigo I harvested.

But even the farm was a fickle friend. With the British no longer paying the bounty for indigo and our rice plagued by blight, I would have to be doubly careful to conserve what we had. Without that bounty, we were ruined.

I broke into the clearing surrounding Elias' house. "Elias, we've come with—"

My lungs constricted.

Elias sat on his porch, dazed, holding a hand to his head, rivulets of blood dripping through his fingers and down his forearm.

I dropped my basket and ran to his side. "Oh, my friend. What happened?"

He looked at me blankly.

I ran into his home and grabbed a strip of linen and a bottle of rum, and, at his side once again, dabbed the dried blood crusted to his forehead and cheek. The gash had already sealed itself with bits of dried leaves and dirt in its gore.

He hissed and jerked away.

"I know it's painful, but it must be done."

The late sun cast long shadows, lighting his face in a healthy pink—the color of life, though his mind slipped further from me by the day.

I knelt before him and grabbed his hands. "Come home with me. Please."

His eyes met mine, troubled and cloudy. "Where?"

"With me."

It could have been a fall, but I would give a pound if it wasn't the butt of a rifle that had done it. The more wits he lost, the freer he spoke about his objection to the Crown's rule.

Had it been Frederick that had done this? The British controlled the Ninety Six and were best positioned to favor him in his quest for more land.

Elias pulled his head away from my ministrations. "Leave me be."

"I don't like the idea of you being alone."

He patted my cheek. "John doesn't need another man around, telling him how to run things."

"Elias, don't you remember? John is..." I hesitated. The last time I'd reminded him of his worsening confusion, it had frightened him so badly that I stayed that night until he woke in the morning, clear-eyed and unaware of what had passed the day before. "John won't mind."

We returned from our visit as quiet as we came. I made a quick meal of porridge with bits of fried pork and was just setting it on the table when a commotion of hooves broke through the afternoon's silence.

I stepped outside, quickly joined by my children.

Men in red coats brought their horses to a stop in front of us. Some of them held scythes aloft.

A man with powdered hair brought his horse to their front, sitting tall in his saddle.

"Who is it?" Mary asked in a harsh whisper.

"I don't know," I whispered back.

The man at the head slid off his horse and bowed. "Mrs. Farrow?" he asked, his tone formal but warm.

I gave him a tight nod.

"I am Colonel Cruger, commander at Star Fort. I heard of your situation and have brought my soldiers to bring in your harvest."

"My... situation?"

"Your indigo. I know the Crown's removal of the bounty has made selling difficult, but at least it won't be left to rot in the ground. Would that be acceptable?"

His offer stunned me into silence. Did he know my sons fought for the rebels? Was this some trick to gain knowledge of the militia's movements? My mind raced to possible answers I could give that wouldn't endanger us.

He gave me a kindly smile. "Your sons are with the Continentals, and you think I mean you some harm."

"I'd rather be left alone. By both sides."

"I cannot abide a widow in distress. My own mother, God rest her soul, lived many years alone, though not in such a wilderness as this. If you will accept it, my men can relieve at least one of your burdens."

I would be a fool to hesitate a second longer. I bobbed my head. "God bless you, sir."

With one flick of his hand, his men spread to my fields like locusts to sweetgrass. My children watched with wary eyes.

I pretended nonchalance. What did this Cruger play at?

The colonel left for the day and brought his men back the next morning. He stayed to check on the progress, trading brief, polite conversation with me. He asked about the farm, the children, and our way of life here.

"Your brother fought with our General Braddock at the Battle of Monongahela," he mentioned casually, watching my children cut down the indigo alongside his soldiers. "And now, your boys fight with their uncle. Excepting your youngest, of course."

"You didn't offer your men's help in hopes of drafting him, did you?"

He laughed out loud. Several of his soldiers turned in our direction. Doubtless, the colonel didn't have much occasion to laugh while wrestling for control of Ninety Six.

"Well put, madam. But not to worry—the rebellion will be quashed long before your youngest is of age."

Though he didn't press me further about Philemon's service, I would be a fool to think it the last time my loyalties came under scrutiny.

"Would you take some advice?" he asked.

I ignored the children's stares. If they were smart like I'd raised them to be, they would know we tread on dangerous ground. "I listen to anyone with sense."

"King George wishes that all his subjects prosper, as do I. I'm afraid the fight will come to you, whether you wish it or not. I am here to bring order, but I won't always be able to—"

A cry rent the air.

A young man with red hair held one of his hands in the other.

Without excusing myself, I rushed over to the boy. "What's happened?"

His face was drained of color, leaving behind a bridge of freckles pooled in his pale cheeks. He appeared no older than fifteen. "Muncie's scythe got my thumb," he said, his voice shaking. "Will I lose it?"

The men behind him looked at each other and snickered. One mocked the boy's question, repeating it in a baby's voice.

I gave the men the most sour look I knew to give and knelt before the boy. "Let me look at it," I soothed. I pulled his hand toward me and studied his gash, schooling my features so as not to reveal it as one of the most gruesome ones I'd seen. "A man collects a host of injuries such as these over his lifetime. Why, it's said you measure a man's age by the number of scars he has. This gash will make a good one."

"Return to work," the colonel commanded to the onlookers, then eyed the boy. "Will you be alright, Baker?"

He nodded.

"Good lad." The colonel gave him a good-natured thump on his back. "It is as Mrs. Farrow said. Look at this." He pushed his shirtsleeve above his wrist and held it in front of the boy. A thick, puffy line ran from along his forearm and disappeared under the sleeve. "This was my first scar big enough to boast about."

The boy squinted up at his commander. "Will mine make a mark so large, do you think?"

"You might even get a touch of gangrene. What a scar that will make!"

I bit back a smile.

"Come," I told the boy. "Baker, is it?" I pulled him up by the shoulders and led him to my cabin. "Do you have a first name?"

"William."

"Why, that's my youngest son's name!"

By the time I had him bandaged, I also had him smiling.

When the men rode off that second evening, my fields shorn and indigo piled by my boiling vats, I let out a deep sigh.

It was a frightening thing, being beholden to the men my sons were obliged to come against in battle.

"What would the boys say to you accepting his help?" Mary's eyes flashed hot.

"You think I can refuse? I keep a fine balance, daughter." Didn't she understand how little it would take to have all we worked for taken away? "I'll do what I can to keep my family alive, and I won't be judged for it, Mary Waters Farrow."

THIRTY-TWO

ROSANNA

Ice-cold fingers covered my eyes. I yelped and whipped around. There stood Johnny, or what looked like Johnny. He was all bone, cheeks sunken and lips dry. A breeze would blow him away.

My legs almost gave way.

Another voice came from outside the door. "Hello, Mother."

There stood Thomas, the very image of his father, and Samuel.

I let out a cry of joy and gathered them in my arms. "I can hardly believe it! All three of you. All we need is Landon."

"He couldn't get away from his unit."

Johnny slumped and fell sideways to the floor.

I fell to my knees beside him. The boys joined me, their faces lined with worry.

Johnny patted my arm as if I were the one needing succor, not him. "It'll pass. I think I'll go lie down, if that's fine with you?"

Thomas' and Samuel's faces were grave, anxious when they had never given a moment's worry to anything in their whole life, even when they should have.

I settled Johnny in my bed. I brushed my fingers over his forehead like I used to. "Can I get you something to eat? Drink?"

"I need sleep. And don't you think of staying and watching over me either."

A slight snore already came from his parted lips before I could agree to that.

I returned to the boys. "Tell me straight what happened."

Thomas' mouth tightened into a grim line. "He was captured and locked away on a prison ship."

"I don't know how he survived," Samuel said. "You only have to look at him to know how bad it was."

"And you, Thomas?" His face was thinner, his jawline more pronounced. There was a hollowness to his eyes that hadn't been there before.

"I was imprisoned but not in a ship. I was caught in an ambush and taken prisoner, but Cruger released me on the condition that I not fight against the British again. Same as the conditions of Johnny's parole."

"Tell me you'll keep to it," I demanded.

He stayed silent.

"You won't get that lucky again."

"I know," he answered.

"Thomas, you'll be hung if they catch you again."

"I have to finish what I started."

I held back the flood of chastisement building on my tongue. I should be proud of a son with such conviction.

Samuel covered my hand with his own. "How are things with Father gone?"

I turned my hand over and grasped his. My sweet boy who saw everything. "I am managing."

"Don't you worry about us adding to your work burden while we're here. We hope to get Skunk broken."

"Do you, now?" The colt, named by William for the white stripe on its nose, had never once let me near him. What we'd needed was a dependable plow horse, but William had taken pity on a wild colt with ribs showing and a coat caked with mud.

"William introduced us to him this morning. I can see he's a handful."

"When do you return to the militia?"

They exchanged glances. "A few days," Samuel answered. "Captain Williams wants us all back to fortify our position at Musgrove Mill."

"Except for Johnny, you mean."

The boys refused to look at me.

I stepped outside into the sticky heat and laid my back against the door. The children had been hard to settle after their brothers' arrival. I'd tucked them under their blankets and gave them a thousand kisses. As happened every night, Mary asked for something to imagine. I told her there existed a burrow, and at the other end, a doorway to any place she could think herself—in a palace, exploring the sea floor, on a powerful horse, riding the woolly clouds.

It wasn't lost on me that I imagined her ways out of this place.

Like a sea-tossed ship, my stomach churned with bile.

I would never forget in all my life the shock of seeing Johnny in his condition.

The sun dipped into the trees, softening them in a hushed, warm glow. It was the saddest part of the day when light melted into darkness. After seeing Johnny, I needed the light to stay a little longer.

Frog song swelled and beat the cooling night air. The river was wide, carrying the day's last rays in its glossy, undulant water.

I stepped out of my shoes and trod the grass to the smooth silt of the riverbed. Stripping my cap and my clothes down to my shift, I strode into the water.

Icy cold water sluiced through my toes, encircled my calves, swallowed my knees.

I cupped my hands around the last bit of light in the water. By the time it trickled through my fingers, the sun disappeared below the horizon.

The moon began its age-old trek, rising from the mist and tangle of scrub and fern to hang above the trees.

I wrapped a trailing root around my palm. Moored against the current, I floated under a blanket of stars and dark bombazine—a widow's mourning cloth draped across the sky.

I tried out the words that had been building in my heart since John died.

You have made life harder than I should like.

My rebellion was only met with silence. No fireballs from heaven, no trumpet blasts, no sign at all that anyone listened. Perhaps I should be more plain.

Will I always have to worry what horror you might hurl at us next? You took John. Will you take Johnny too?

I cinched my cheek to the side. I probably shouldn't have gone so far, but I hadn't talked to him much since Mama's fall, not like this. Over the years, the Book of Common Prayer had supplied my words when times required praying, but it was something altogether different to say it from the heart.

I won't mind if you give us a rest from sorrow. For a little while, at least.

That was better and more likely to be listened to.

A fiery light swung above me.

I sucked in a breath and let go of the vine, sinking below the surface.

Had my prayers called down brimstone?

A hand grasped my arm and pulled me from the water.

I came out in a great, sucking pull, my shift clinging to me like a second skin.

A lantern, tossed to the ground, made a halo upon the grass.

The man who pulled me out of the water took off his coat and held it toward me, his face averted.

A man who meant me harm wouldn't give a thought to my modesty. Still, how could I have been so foolish as to leave my pistol behind? My mind had been too distracted by Johnny's condition. I whipped the coat out of his hand and draped it over my shoulders. It smelled of fire smoke and leather and brushed against my calves.

I pulled it tighter across my chest. "State your business, and be quick about it."

"Is that any way to greet an old friend?"

My heart leaped in a painful throb.

He stepped out of the shadows.

It couldn't be. Could it?

Before me stood a man in every sense of the word, broad and hard with uncharted depth, his deep-red beard threaded with silver. A tale of griefs written in the set of his mouth and the creases at his eyes.

"Callum?"

He held my gaze, his eyes inscrutable. "Aye. Though I go by another name now."

There was not one word I could pluck from my brain that could make sense of this. I'd think him a ghost if his coat didn't smell of him. "I thought I'd never see you again."

"I knew a lass who once wished to be a pirate. Are you she?"

"I play at ship battles with my children, if that's to be counted."

His mouth lifted in a secret smile. "Of course you do. I brought you a gift from Phil."

"You traveled all the way here to give me a present?"

"Are you not worthy of a little trouble?"

I could weep at the kindness in his voice. *A little trouble?* He had likely traveled days, perhaps weeks, to get here, depending on where he started. But it would've been more shocking had he done anything less.

He picked up his lantern and ascended the riverbank. "Your present is in the house."

Just as I was about to ask him where he was going, someone called behind me. "Mother!"

My heart leaped.

Sarah—could it really be she?—stood in our doorway, wreathed in light, waving her arm above her head. She left the porch and ran toward me.

I collided into her with a cry of joy. "Sarah!" I pulled back and studied her. Time had done its work. She was beautiful—a woman, with a graceful brow and high cheekbones, her eyes sparkling with secrets she'd collected in her time away from me. Splotches of river water were the only thing marring the thin pleats and embroidered sweet pea vining her silk dress. "Look at you! Why, you're almost as tall as Landon."

Sarah gave a wobbly laugh. "Aunt Pearl says I'm not to wear hats or heels if I want to catch a husband, even out here."

I hugged her to me again. *Please, let me have a little time with her before she marries and leaves again.*

I turned to invite Callum into our home, but he was already gone.

THIRTY-THREE

ROSANNA

We whispered late into the night, Sarah cuddled beside me in bed, mingling laughter with tears as we talked about our time apart. I told her about Colonel Cruger and explained what had happened to Johnny. She told me what her father had said when she'd last seen him.

"How are you faring with Father gone?" Sarah asked.

I picked at the loose threads of our quilt. "It's like learning to walk again."

She turned on her side and put her hand on mine. "The farm isn't the same without him."

"I miss him. He seemed too strong and full of life to—" My voice caught. I swallowed the tightness away. "I'm well enough. It takes me unaware sometimes, the sadness."

"I know he was anxious to get back to you."

I smiled sadly and tucked my hands under my cheek. "Sarah, how is it you came with Callum?"

"Uncle Phil asked him to bring me here. And he is called Jack Drummond to others."

Of course. He'd have to hide his true name if he were to be safe from Frederick. "You know him as Callum?"

"Uncle slipped and called him that once. They both swore me to secrecy."

"What do you think of him?"

"I like him very much." She elbowed me. "He's a well-favored man. Were you never sweet on him?"

"Sarah!"

"What?" She snuggled deeper into the covers. "I think he must've been sweet on you."

What did it matter now if he'd been sweet on me? There'd been no promises between us. We could never go back to being friends again, not like we were. In the midst of my excitement over Sarah, he'd slipped away without saying goodbye.

My heart gave a sad little thump.

Callum had stood on the riverbank—had seen me float, with my tangle of hair swirling around me. When I went under, he'd grasped my upper arm and plucked me from the river as if I were no weightier than a leaf.

I'd think it a dream, if not for the coat he'd left behind. Would he come back for it?

My skin still prickled from where he'd touched me.

I laid my hand over my heart and drummed my agitation on my breastbone.

I didn't sleep through the night, my thoughts returning again and again to Callum.

Finally, boisterous chatter drifted to me through my closed bedroom door. Mary's laugh, like a meadowlark's song, crested above the din.

I lowered my feet to the floor, threw on my dress, and came out to a merry party of four Farrow children sitting at my table, eating, talking, and swinging their hands in dramatics as they told their stories.

Johnny was there, with a blanket wrapped around his shoulders and a steaming tin cup held by his thin fingers.

I bit back a grin. His hair was mussed like a clutter of twigs assembled by a wren. How many times had I come out to the table and seen him sitting there as a boy with his hair sticking out in all directions?

"Where are Thomas and Samuel?" I kept my voice calm and snipped the thread of worry before it could sew a quilt. They were grown men now. Thomas could defy Cruger's conditions for parole and return to the fight without any thought to what I would say about it. Same for Johnny. Samuel, though he didn't have the same mark on his life, would be just as quickly strung up for abetting Thomas.

"They're outside with Mr. Drummond," William said, spooning corncake soaked in honey and cream into his mouth.

My breath caught in my chest. He hadn't left.

"They've been catchin' us up on chores," said Mary. "Thomas is breakin' Skunk and havin' a hellish time of it."

"Mary! Where did you hear that word?"

Johnny hid a smile behind his cup. "Don't look at me. She pestered Samuel and Thomas to tell war stories. It might've slipped in a time or two, along with a *da*—"

I clapped my hand over his mouth, though my heart bubbled in delight at the bit of healthy pink in his cheeks.

They had just begun to make plans to add to their tree fort when I slipped away and headed to the paddock. There, running in the enclosed space, was Skunk.

Thomas approached the horse carefully with John's saddle in hand. The whites of Skunk's eyes flashed, and he backed into the far reaches of the circle. As soon as Thomas threw the saddle on Skunk's back, the horse kicked its legs and ran the circle, knocking Thomas to his seat.

"You've got it!" shouted Callum from where he stood at the paddock's railing. "Now, let him run it out."

Thomas clapped the dirt off his hands and got to his feet again. He stayed like that in the center, watching Skunk gallop.

I came to Callum's side and set my arms on the railing, propping my chin on the heel of my hand. "I thought you left."

He kept his face forward. "I camped in the forest. You've a full house and don't need me intruding."

"You wouldn't have intruded."

He said nothing to that.

I turned my head and peeked at him.

He was freshly clean-shaven and more like the friend I'd known. Before I could stop myself, I remembered my fingers running along the side of his face, our bodies so close it could only be understood as the first stirrings of passion. I covered my cheek with my fingers, hiding its heat.

"Callum, you can't imagine what it was like, seeing you again after so long."

He pushed up his sleeves and fiddled with a strand of sweetgrass, stripping it in two pieces. His bare forearms revealed several white scars, wide, slashing marks that couldn't have come from brambles.

He smiled a little. "I thought you were a selkie in that river."

"A selkie?"

"No offense meant. Seals aren't so different than beavers, and you like those, if I recall."

I laughed. He remembered that day by the river.

Skunk slowed to a trot and stopped at the outer edge of the paddock, nostrils flaring and sides heaving. Thomas came close to the horse with careful steps and lifted the saddle.

"Well done," Callum said.

Thomas threw the saddle on top of the fence and came over to us. "I'll give him a rest." He took off his hat and wiped his brow. "Thank you for the advice, Mr. Drummond. How do you know so much of breaking horses?"

"My master was a horse breeder."

Thomas quickly masked his surprise. "So you're a freeman now?"

Callum's smile faltered. "In every sense of the word."

"Hope you stay on a while." Thomas hoisted the saddle into his arms. "I need to return to the fields. There's work to be done."

Callum took the saddle. "Go on. I'll take care of Skunk."

Thomas set off, and I followed Callum toward the barn. "Sarah told me you go by Mr. Drummond now."

"When it's just the two of us, you can call me anything you like." He winked.

My mouth went dry. It was all I could do not to roll my eyes at myself. I'd lived too many experiences to be blushing every time he teased me. "It's good to have the boys home."

"Do you side with the rebels since your boys fight with them?"

"Did you see Johnny?"

"Aye."

"Then you can guess where my loyalties lie. And you?"

Callum shrugged. "I sympathize with the patriots, but I understand why England can't let the rebellion stand. I don't think the Crown knows just how far these rebels are willing to take this, though."

"Anyone against my sons, *I'm* against."

"Don't you be joining any militias, Rosanna."

"I'm a little more restrained than when you last knew me." As soon as the words were said, I wished them back again. The last time we'd seen each other, I'd clung to him and begged him to take me away.

"Still, you must be careful."

"So must you. Did you know Frederick lives in Ninety Six?"

He nodded and opened the barn door. I ducked under his arm and went inside.

A weathered horse, black and sleek, greeted us from a stall with a nicker. "Obsidian!"

"The old boy's been with me through it all, though I don't know for how much longer."

He hung the saddle on the wall to the side of the stall and reached over the gate to give Obsidian a long, slow rub along his cheek and down his neck.

My throat tightened, seeing him with his beloved horse.

Obsidian's hide was nicked by one thin scar across his belly, along with a few smaller marks on his legs. The scars on both him and his master told a tale of troubles I would never truly understand.

I stepped closer and ran the back of my fingers over the horse's nose. "What you must have suffered."

A moment of silence stretched into two. "Aye."

My heartbeat quickened. Had it been so bad for him he couldn't bear to speak of it? "But you survived."

He forced a wooden smile. "It wasn't so bad. If I hadn't run away, if I hadn't joined the regiment, I'd never have married Charity and taken on Gabriel as my own."

I drew in a sharp breath. "You married Charity? *Our* Charity?"

His eyebrow raised a mite. "Yes."

My stomach sank. It was irrational, I knew. But he'd married someone my husband considered the model by which all women should be measured. "How did it come to be?"

"She needed a way to take back her son, and I needed someone to care for Bembe. We were happy together until a fever took her and Bembe four years ago."

The news doused my selfish concern in an instant. I would be glad for him that he'd not been alone. "I'm sorry, Callum. Truly, I am."

"As am I for the loss of John."

Callum turned toward the oats box, smacking his face into a long rope hanging from a rafter and looped over a support beam. A humorous light danced in his eyes. "What's this?"

"A swing. See?" I set my foot in the loop and stepped backward as far as I could. Then I let go and swung forward. "I hung it for William when he said he wished he could fly." I dragged my shoe across the floor and skittered to a stop. "Will you head back to Charles Town soon?"

"Gabriel left with our ship to the West Indies and won't be back for months. Now that I've delivered Sarah to you, I'm thinking of returning to provisioning settlements and armies with what Gabriel sends back. It's what I did for Tileman, and I still know the land well."

Panic fluttered in my chest. I wasn't ready for him to go. Not yet. I braced my shoulders and faced him fully. "I've need of someone to sell my indigo."

"Oh?"

"The bounty is gone, and my indigo sits without a market," I continued. "Do you know that the Continentals have decided to dye their uniforms blue?"

He studied me carefully. "I had heard something of that nature."

"So you can sell my dye to them. You'll be selling other goods. Why not mine?"

"Well, I suppose—"

"Then it's settled. You will sell my indigo, and I'll give you a portion of whatever price you fetch for your troubles."

He grabbed the rope above my head and locked his gaze with mine.

I grew heady with his nearness.

"That kind of business might keep me here for a long while." Heat burned in his eyes. "A very long while. Will you mind?"

"N-no, I won't mind."

"Then I'll agree to your scheme on one condition."

"Which is?"

"I'll need a place to stay if I'm to do this right. Thomas told me of Mr. Brown's troubles and how you divide your time to care for him. Perhaps I can help. I can stay and watch over Mr. Brown, leaving you free to tend to your farm."

I nearly sagged with relief until I remembered Frederick. I couldn't let Callum risk his freedom for the sake of my deliverance. "But what of Frederick?"

His eyes glinted. "I am tired of running."

THIRTY-FOUR

CALLUM

The moment I pulled Rosanna from the water, nature fell to a whisper.

She didn't touch me. She wouldn't look into my eyes.

I dared not breathe, lest she vanish.

For a moment, only just, my fingers tightened on her arm. Her flesh was warm and solid and dripping in river water.

The realization roused me to action. I'd slipped off my coat and handed it to her.

Had she thought of me in our time apart? Did she feel anything seeing me again?

Then she said my name, and our eyes met.

In that moment I knew.

I had never stopped loving Rosanna Waters.

The knowledge had fastened itself to every waking hour since that night. Even weeks later and tending to Elias' needs, I could think of little else.

"Three-Tail!" Elias called.

I froze, my shovel suspended midair.

"Three-Tail, come!"

Elias' steps plodded the dirt path.

I quickly swiped the mound of dirt into the hole with my foot. I winced at how it thudded on poor Three-Tail.

Elias rounded the corner of the barn. "Have you seen my cat?"

I had, in fact. I'd found her dead that morning, still curled in a ball in front of the hearth. As lost as Elias' mind was, it hadn't dislodged Three-Tail from his memory.

Three-Tail was the anchor, tethering him in the bay of reality. Elias' days centered around his cat—feeding her, petting her, holding her on her back and in his arms like a baby. Three-Tail had been content to lay there, kneading Elias' downy beard.

As long as he held her, he was calm and content. What would he do without her? I'd scooped Three-Tail in my arms and carried her to the patch of late summer goldenrod, where she liked to hide and watch the butterflies flitting from bloom to bloom.

I stepped out of the patch and set the shovel on my shoulder. "Good day, Elias. You're up early. I'm on the lookout for raspberries."

His eyes brightened. "I'll make us a pie."

I forced my smile wider past the twinge of guilt. "Will you help me?"

"Oh, aye!" He took a step toward me, then swayed and sat hard on the ground.

"Elias!" I rushed to his side and propped him up with a hand gripping his shoulder. He wouldn't have eaten yet, not without me there to remind him. "Let us get you some bread and butter, friend."

He looked at me, dazed. "Where's Hester?"

"She is in her garden. Come." I helped him to his feet. I hadn't told so many lies in all my life as I had these few weeks with Elias. "She will join us later."

A horse's whinny penetrated the quiet. A commotion, a muddle of scarlet and horseflesh weaving through the trees. Men in uniform on horses.

Thomas had told me about Elias' rantings against the Crown, his threats against Cruger himself.

"Elias, go inside the house. Now."

The man's eyes darkened with fear. "Where's Three-Tail?"

Heat flared in my chest—frustration, not at him, but at the confounded illness that kept this man locked in its grip. I picked him up by the arm and was just about to hide him in the barn when the horses broke into the clearing.

At the front of the group of six soldiers was none other than Frederick Grenville in a British uniform.

I shoved Elias behind me. "What business have you here?" By my own estimation, I hardly resembled the boy Frederick had known. I had grown thick with muscles, and my hair had turned dark as oxblood. Unless Frederick was smarter than I remembered, I would escape detection.

His lips curled in a smile. "As I live and breathe! Callum Stewart."

So he had grown cleverer with the years. "Frederick."

"Just the man I've come to see." He swung a leg over his horse and jumped to the ground. He stalked closer to me. "I didn't believe it when I heard a horse named Obsidian mentioned by the youngest Farrow boy in town." He slapped my shoulder in a gesture that would have been friendly if it weren't for the way his face was set in flint. "Don't blame the boy. He was bragging about his new friend and his fast horse. He couldn't have known our history. And here you are! Now, where is that horse young Master Farrow was talking about?" He pushed closer to the barn door.

I lifted my shovel, blocking the doorway, and lowered my voice. "Leave now, and I won't make a fool of you as I did at Mr. Edwards' shop."

Frederick lowered his voice to match my own. "I will take my horse back, with or without your leave."

It was the work of an impulse.

Nay, I couldn't even blame it on that.

It was the pain Charity had carried because of his appalling violation—the pain that had come between her and me—that lifted my shovel and smacked it under his jaw.

Chaos erupted: Frederick's call for my arrest; soldiers running to my side, pulling my hands behind me, shoving me to my knees.

Elias picked the shovel off the ground and ran toward Frederick.

"Elias, no!" I shouted, but it was too late.

A rifle shot went off.

Elias dropped to the ground in front of me.

A strangled cry escaped my lips. "Let me go to him, I beg you!"

Frederick swung open the barn doors and stalked inside.

Elias strained his head to face me. "Where's Three-Tail?"

A lump formed in my throat. "Three-Tail is hunting raspberries. He will have them set out for us on our return."

The man's eyes slowly closed, and his head fell to the side.

Frederick led Obsidian out by his reins. "Leave the old man. We set out for Star Fort at once."

I spent the better part of the hour's journey setting aside my grief and rage to formulate a plan. Frederick might've killed Elias, but he wasn't going to take Obsidian, and as long as I still stood, he wasn't going to imprison me.

Frederick shoved me past sentry guards into a room where a man bent over a desk studying a map with two other soldiers and a Catawba guide. At our entrance, the man straightened. Colonel Cruger, if I guessed correctly. "What is the meaning of this?"

I didn't give Frederick a chance to speak. "Colonel Cruger! What a pleasure to finally make your acquaintance. Jack Drummond, at your disposal." I gave a crisp bow.

"Drummond?" Cruger straightened. "Jack Drummond? Tileman's partner?" He was in front of us in three strides. "I cannot believe it!" He held out his hand, and when I didn't shake it, he looked down at my manacled wrists. "Oh. I see." He turned to Frederick with a grin. "You mean to play a joke."

Frederick's face turned a mottled red. "It is no joke. This man hit an officer with a—"

Cruger seemed not to hear him. "You know, I wondered if I should ever meet the man who saved my brother's life. Every time Tileman tells the story, you are fighting an additional five men."

I returned his grin. "How like him."

"Quite. He makes us all proud." He paused and looked between Frederick and me with a displeased frown. "Grenville, why is this man still in chains?"

"He assaulted an officer of His Majesty's army!"

Cruger put one hand behind his back and squinted one eye at me. "Well? Was the officer annoying you?"

"Very gravely indeed. He rode my horse without asking." I had thought of mentioning Elias, but Frederick's soldiers had witnessed the old man raise the shovel.

"There you have it. Release him, Grenville, and see to it that you have this man's horse returned to him."

Frederick's face twisted in outrage. "But, sir!"

Cruger paused. He eyed Frederick's bruised and swollen jaw. "Oh. Oh, yes, I see. You are the man who was hit, and you are the man who took his horse. I could make you both apologize and that would be an end to it, but there must be some punishment, or everyone will think they can come against my officers."

The side of Frederick's mouth ticked a notch higher. "Very wise, sir."

Cruger sat at his desk. "From what I hear from my brother, Mr. Drummond has been quite adept at navigating these forests provisioning our troops with his goods. We are in need of a scout. What say you to that, Mr. Drummond? Unless you've already sided with the rebels and that is why you have attacked my officer... Answer carefully. I won't be so inclined to return your horse to you if that is the case."

He assessed me with a piercing gaze I felt all the way to my innards.

I could see why Tileman was terrified of displeasing his brother.

Washington's request echoed in my mind. If I were forced to

fight, it would be on my own terms. I bowed my head. "Nothing would delight me more."

"Very good. Grenville, my hands are tied. We cannot put our best scout in jail." Cruger gave me a crisp nod. "Outfit him at once. We mean to go against the rebels soon."

THIRTY-FIVE
ROSANNA

I discovered Elias, shot through the heart, and Callum, nowhere to be found.

My boys had already returned to the militia, so I dug the grave on my own, covering my dear friend with earth.

My head pounded with grief and worry. Where was Callum? Something terrible must have happened. He would've never left Elias alone to die.

Something held me back from going into town and inquiring after Callum. Instinct, perhaps. Strange currents swirled in Ninety Six, with both armies vying for control of the area. I couldn't risk getting caught in it, not with young children still at home.

One day bled into another. I went about my work, numb. Haunted by visions of Elias being shot in the heart and Callum being dragged off and hanged by Frederick.

Eight days after Callum's disappearance, Sarah took Mary, Jane, and William to fish in the river.

The air was hot and swollen with yesterday's rain. Tendrils of hair stuck to the back of my neck. I'd long since removed my stockings and shoes and tied my skirts above my knees. Who cared for propriety when no one here would judge me?

I hung parsley and dill from nails I'd hammered into the wall.

As soon as I was finished with this task, I'd wade through the river's ice-cold shallows, cooling my legs to prickling numbness and letting my heart be soothed by the children's shouts of laughter.

Pounding hooves cut the silence.

"Rosanna!"

My heart stopped. *Philemon?* He was supposed to be north with his unit. The boys' unit, excepting Landon. Had something terrible befallen one of them?

I dropped my last bundle of herbs and ran outside.

Philemon galloped to a stop on Obsidian. My brother's face was streaked with sweat, his hair loose on his shoulders. A British soldier lay draped in his arms, the man's scarlet coat open, revealing a chest wound.

He slid off the horse and pulled the man into his arms carefully. "There's been a battle at Musgrove Mill."

My hearing blunted. Musgrove Mill. My boys had headed there after leaving home. I stepped aside, and Philemon pushed past me.

"Here," I said, clearing our table with a sweep of my arm. Cups and trenchers clattered to the dirt floor.

Philemon laid the man down with a grunt. "Good thing John built a sturdy table."

"Are my boys safe?"

Philemon's curt voice cut me off. "Bring me hot water."

The man upon the table groaned, snaring my attention.

I froze. "Callum!"

My friend, bleeding and pale as death, wore the uniform of a British soldier.

This was what had caused him to leave Elias? To join the redcoats in battle?

Then another thought came, even worse. *Had he killed Elias?*

My heart rebelled at the very thought. It wasn't true. He would never have hurt so much as a hair on Elias' head. But he'd left him defenseless, and perhaps that was worse.

Callum's mouth was slack, his face tinged with gray. He'd answer no questions now.

Philemon ripped Callum's waistcoat open, sending buttons clattering to the floor. "Bring the water!" he repeated.

I pushed past him and filled the kettle from a pail, sloshing water on the ground. "How can you help him? He joined forces against you!"

"Would you have a man dead to hold a grudge?"

Dead?

Callum's skin, ghostly white, draped a body all too still. "We'll tend his wounds, but he cannot stay here."

"Rosanna..."

"This is *my* home. I won't have my children at risk. What if another rebel discovers me aiding the enemy?"

"I'll do my best to hide him somewhere else, but I have to return to the battle straight away."

Not once did Callum stir when I extracted the bullet, nor when I sewed his wound closed.

Blood seeped between the stitches, even after a few minutes passed.

"The wound must be burned shut," I said.

"Do what you must."

I stuck the poker into the fire, and when the end glowed a bright orange, I sank it into Callum's wound.

He didn't move, not even to flinch.

Philemon's hands covered mine. "It is over now."

I dropped the rod and ran outside to the grass, heaving air into my lungs.

How could Callum have become this stranger?

Philemon came beside me. "He is resting."

I steadied my breathing. He was still alive. No matter what he'd done, I couldn't be happy if he was dead.

"How did it happen?" I asked.

"He was shot by one of our own as he rode fast toward our entrenchments. One of our sentries saw him and fired."

My last bit of rebellious hope died. It was true, then. Callum had been fighting against the rebels. "Why did you come here?"

"I had nowhere else to bring him."

I nodded. I wouldn't deny him aid. "Help me hide him before you go."

Philemon carried Callum to the barn, placed him in an empty stall, and galloped away on Obsidian's back.

I went back inside the house and scrubbed our table with scalding water and sand, then the floor beneath where Callum's blood had pooled.

The food at dinner was dust in my mouth. The children didn't notice my quiet, as loud as they were.

My gaze went to the window and the barn beyond. Callum was lying in a pile of hay, in pain, if he was sensible to it by now. Dying, more than likely. But when I pictured him lying there, I didn't see the British soldier Philemon brought to my house. I saw the skinny boy with a ragged head of bright red hair, holding the orange I'd given him as a reward for defending me.

I slipped on my shoes. Swinging my lantern aloft, I trudged through the dew-damp grass and entered the barn.

Moonlight streamed through the cracks in the slatted walls and fell upon his stone-still figure.

I held my breath. Even wounded and disheveled, he sent my heart racing.

He groaned.

I dipped behind the wooden fence, my heart hammering so loudly I was sure he could hear it.

"Rosanna?" There was the rustling of hay, then a hiss of pain.

I rushed to him and pushed him gently to his back. "Be still."

"How did I come here? Where's Obsidian?"

"With Phil."

He groaned and brought a hand to the bandages covering his wound.

I slapped his hand away lightly. "Here." I lifted his head and tipped a cup to his mouth. He grabbed it and greedily drank the cider. Within seconds, the cup was drained, and he fell back, panting.

I gave him a dose of laudanum and sat back on my heels. "Were you forced?"

He gritted his teeth. "Leave it be."

"How can I when my sons might die at your hands?"

His silence was confirmation enough that the Callum I knew was gone. "And Elias? Did you kill him?"

His hand caught my wrist. "What you must believe of me to ask such a question."

"The British will come searching for you."

"And they'll be thankful for your care of me."

"What if rebels find out I harbor the enemy?"

"You worry overmuch."

I ripped my wrist from his grasp. "Worry overmuch?" My voice trembled with barely suppressed rage. "Do you know what I've had to do to keep my family alive? To make sure we *survive*? You'll forgive my being concerned for how this might harm my children."

"Rosanna—"

"When you're well enough, you'll go and never come back, do you understand?"

I fled the barn before he could respond.

THIRTY-SIX
ROSANNA

The sun had set.

All was quiet.

The chickens were squeezed together on their roost. The children on their mattress, fast sleep. Callum, in the barn.

My prisoner had languished in the barn for over a week now, with Philemon not returning to retrieve him.

I peeled away my garments to my shift and opened one of the shutters. Sarah was on my bed, murmuring in her sleep. A breeze lifted my shift and tickled the hairs at my neck. John had advised covering the open spaces with greased paper, but I couldn't abide the dull light it cast in our home. I'd cut boards and nailed together shutters, but now that John was gone, I rarely closed them. The mosquitos, the rain, the occasional bird were all welcome, as long as sunshine and fresh air had their turn.

I sagged against the windowsill and gazed at the sky. A star stabbed through the black, a pinprick of light journeying through the darkness. It had come from as far away as John and Mama were to me. As far as I felt from Callum.

Far off in the distance, Star Fort teemed with soldiers, men who had fought against my sons, had wounded them, imprisoned them. Though Colonel Cruger had been kind, he was mandated by the king to keep control of Ninety Six. There would be a limit to his generosity once he discovered I sided with the patriots. Perhaps he already suspected.

A cry rose from deep within the forest.

An owl's cry?

It came again, closer, clearer. "Mrs. Farrow!"

Pounding hooves and the cry again: "Mrs. Farrow!"

Sarah lifted her head from the pillow. "Mother, what is it?"

"Stay here." I threw on my dress without my stays, grabbed my rifle, and ran into the yard with bare feet.

A man rode to a sliding stop. A young man with bright red hair.

I lowered my rifle. "William Baker?" The boy whose thumb I'd bandaged a few years ago sat on horseback, his eyebrows knitted tightly over his serious eyes. We'd been friendly since I'd bandaged him. He'd returned a time or two to help with chores, and I'd always sent him off with a full belly. But he'd never had cause to ride in at night unannounced.

He stayed atop his dancing horse, his coat open and shirt untied. "Thomas, Samuel, and Johnny were captured and are in the jail at Ninety Six."

I reeled back. Once Cruger found out Thomas and Johnny had broken their parole and that Samuel helped them, my boys were as good as dead. *You won't get that lucky again,* I'd told Thomas. And still, they'd gone.

"There's to be a hanging—"

"When?"

"Day after next if we don't hear from the captain at Fair Forest that he'll trade our soldiers for your boys. But the rebels have denied such a request from Cruger before."

It was worse than I could have imagined. All three of my boys were dead if I couldn't convince Cruger to give them back to me. "Tell your colonel he'll get his men."

His jaw grew slack. "*You* will do it?"

"There's no one else."

"He'll know I spoke to you. I—I'm sorry, but if I tell him, it'll be me on those gallows."

I forced a kindly smile to my face. "Of course, William. Thank you for riding all the way out here to tell me. I know it was a risk."

He nodded and pulled on the reins, kicked his horse into a gallop, and disappeared back down the road.

It was three hours to Fair Forest—two if I pushed hard. Then, if I convinced Captain Williams of the trade, it would be at least a day's ride to the British fort. More, if the prisoners I'd have to bring with me were on foot. I would have to make it to the fort by sunrise and could, just, if there was no trouble with my prisoners, or storms.

Or animals. With no other horses, I would have to take Skunk.

Sarah stood on our porch, holding a blanket tight around her shoulders.

I swept by her into the house and pulled open the curtain around the girls' bed. "Mary? Jane?" I shook their shoulders. "Awake!"

Mary shot up. "Mama? What's wrong?"

"They have the boys."

Jane joined Mary, their two pale faces lit by the moon.

"You must be brave. Can you do that?"

They nodded, wide-eyed.

"Sarah, take the pistol." When she didn't move, I placed the gun in her hands.

William's mussed head lifted from the covers of his pallet. "What's happened?"

"Get dressed, William."

He hurriedly did my bidding and squeezed between the girls on the bed.

They all stared at me, their chins trembling.

I took two steps to them and gathered them in my arms. "All will be well. But I must see if I can save your brothers."

I kissed the top of their sweet heads. "Don't open the door to anyone."

I filled my waterskin and placed dried meat and bread in my haversack, then grabbed my rifle and went into the yard.

The door creaked open behind me.

"Get back inside the house!"

I waited for the sound of the crossbar being lowered into place and strode to the barn, laying some of the meat and water by Callum's side. Thank heavens for the heavy dose of laudanum I'd given him hours before. He wouldn't wake for quite some time.

I shifted the rifle to my back. Slipping a coil of rope off its hook, I looped it over my shoulder and stepped carefully toward the colt. "Come, boy."

He skittered to the back of the stall.

I held out a shriveled apple. "I won't hurt you," I said softly.

It was an agony, forcing myself to wait for Skunk to come to me when my boys waited for rescue.

At last, the horse stepped cautiously, one hoof in front of the other, until he stood before the fruit. He lipped the apple, then with one bite, crunched it between his teeth. I quickly threw the rope around his belly and climbed atop, then tied it across my legs. He startled, but I had already fastened myself and kicked my heels into his side.

He shot like a cannonball out of the barn.

With my hands digging into his mane, I held on with all my might.

My children watched from the window, their faces blurring as Skunk whipped past them.

"It's not the most comfortable way of riding!" I shouted, comforting myself that they would hear the humor in my voice and be soothed.

Hours passed. In the distance, firelight glimmered, and shadows danced amongst the trees.

"Hyah!" I led Skunk to the edge of the camp just outside the fire where a handful of soldiers gathered.

They scrambled for their weapons and pointed them at me.

The largest of them, tall and sinewy, stepped forward. "Who goes there?"

"Tell Captain Williams I've news of his captured soldiers."

"Who are you to come by such information?"

"I'm mother to the Farrow boys."

The man laughed. "Are you, now?"

I kicked my horse forward, pointing my rifle at him. "Quick, now. They'll be hanged if you don't do as I ask."

Another man stepped from the darkness. He held a razor in his hand, his face half-shaven. "What's this?"

"She says she's the Farrows' mother," the lanky man answered. "What do we do with her, Captain?"

I turned my rifle on Williams. "Do you still have the British soldiers you captured at Musgrove Mill?"

Captain Williams tilted his head to the side. "By whose authority do you ask?"

"My own. I need six redcoats to exchange for my sons."

He only stared.

The temptation to rattle his brains into action was almost beyond my ability to control. "Thomas, Johnny, and Samuel Farrow. They've been captured by Cruger. I mean to trade for them."

"Do you intend to take six British soldiers, on a colt such as that, all the way to Star Fort on your own?"

"As you say."

He spoke in a low voice to the man next to him, who spun on his heel and walked away.

He turned back and faced me. "Done."

A smattering of disbelieving scoffs came from the men.

I almost joined them. "I didn't think it would be so easy."

"A woman who rides into an army camp and gains the respect of its captain, well, I should like to see if she can do the same with a colonel. Now, put your rifle down, Mrs. Farrow."

"I'd rather wait until I have my prisoners, if you don't mind."

His eyes danced. "Of course. You'll go with a guard, but I can't spare more than that. The prisoners shouldn't give you trouble since freedom will be at the other end of the ride."

"Let's hope it's as you say."

"You may leave your... *horse*," Williams said, signaling to another man. "Bring Cleo. And you there," he said to the man who'd first approached me. "Help her down."

I untied myself, tossing the rope to the man, and leaped off Skunk.

As I expected, the colt jumped away from the man and yanked his restraints. A few other men grabbed onto the rope and coaxed Skunk away.

The most beautiful horse I'd ever seen was led in front of me. She was much taller than Skunk and shining white.

"Cruger will take you more seriously on a horse like this," Williams said. "Her name is Cleo. Short for Cleopatra. A name fit for a queen, and she should be treated as such. Understood?"

I was tempted to ask what made him think I'd treat a horse poorly, but he'd seen me tied with a rope to an unbroken colt. "You have my word."

"You can retrieve your colt when you return her to me."

A single guard led out six manacled men dressed in British uniforms.

I stepped into the stirrup and straddled Cleo. A few murmurs rippled through the crowd. I looked down. I could hear Mama's sharp intake of breath from across the heavenly distance. My dress was cinched to my knees. Firelight flickered off my legs, displaying their shining strength. Not bad for a mother of eight.

I wouldn't ride side-saddle on such a long journey just to appease the gods of decorum. Still, I yanked my skirts lower and walked Cleo to the front of the prisoners. "Be good, and I'll get you back to Cruger. Cause trouble, and you'll find out how good a shot I am. There'll be no rest until we get there."

THIRTY-SEVEN
ROSANNA

The guard led the way, while I followed behind with my rifle pointed at the prisoners' backs. We picked our way through thickets and rocky trails winding through the forest, stopping only to feed and water our horses and fill our waterskins.

My head buzzed with fatigue, and my limbs hung thick and heavy. Hours passed, then a full day and night. I dared not sleep and bit my cheeks to bleeding, keeping my weapon pointed at the men.

Morning broke. Tendrils of pink stretched across the grassy horizon with Star Fort in the distance.

The guard helped me tie the men around a large tree.

"You're close to your freedom," I told the prisoners. "I promise to release you to your colonel, even if he shouldn't let my sons go, but if you make so much as one move, the guard has leave to shoot you."

With shaking fingers, I tied my apron to the top of a long stick, climbed Cleo, and clenched my legs together to ride side-saddle. I wouldn't have Cruger think me uncivilized. Holding my white flag aloft, I exited the forest and rode toward the fort.

I was within sight of the gate when the sentry guards caught sight of me and blocked the entrance. "Back away!" one commanded.

I lifted my chin. "A word with Colonel Cruger, if you please."

The soldiers eyed me from the top of my head down to my muddy shoes.

I had no need of a mirror to tell me what they saw—my hair, an even more tangled mess than when I'd arrived at Fair Forest camp, my skirts, more brown than blue, mud-spattered and torn. Me, upright only by gripping the edge of my saddle. Exhausted, desperate. Alone and without protection.

"Wait here," one of the sentries said. The others stayed, pointing their bayoneted rifles at me.

My apron snapped in the wind. Cleo danced upon her feet. I leaned down and murmured encouragement in her ear.

At long last, the man returned. "Please, if you will follow me."

I hesitated. Was this how one normally conducted prisoner negotiations? If I went inside, I might lose what little bargaining power I had. "I'll wait here."

"The colonel's requested that you—"

"I'm not moving until he comes out and speaks to me himself."

The guard bowed a little, his eyebrows raised. "As you wish."

A few minutes passed. Two soldiers came out, bearing a small table. Two more followed, one with a chair hooked in each arm and the other with a covered tray.

Once the linen was laid and the dishes set, they faded into the background.

From one of the doors strode the colonel, dressed in his uniform, immaculate in every respect. "Mrs. Farrow, I wished to give you refreshment, but it appears the refreshment must come to you." His mouth held a hint of a smile, but as soon as his gaze roved over me, he sobered. "Are you well?"

"Are my sons still alive?"

He pulled out a chair at the table. "My dear Mrs. Farrow, please, have a seat."

"I won't get off this horse until you tell me if my sons have been hanged."

His mouth tightened. "I'm not used to conducting business with someone seated upon a horse. But no, we have not hanged anyone. *Yet.*"

My vision darkened. I gripped my saddle tighter.

Cruger snapped his fingers.

One of his men put his hands on my waist and pulled me from my horse.

I twisted away from him as soon as my feet were on the ground.

"Please. Sit." The congeniality in the colonel's voice had hardened into double-edged sharpness.

I sat.

Cruger held out a cup. "Drinking chocolate. It is medicinal, they say."

I took the drink and tipped it to my lips. My stomach convulsed the moment the bitter, grainy liquid hit my tongue. I held it in the hollow of my mouth before forcing myself to swallow.

"My thoughts exactly. Tastes like poison when it's supposed to be the cure." He took a sip and sucked air through his teeth. "As to your sons..."

I clattered my cup back on the saucer. "Yes. You have three of them."

"Three?" He turned and glanced at his aide. "*Three?*"

The aide bent and whispered in the colonel's ear.

Cruger's eyebrows lowered a tick with every second of the aide's whispering.

The aide straightened and stepped back.

Cruger lowered his cup and wiped his mouth with a cloth. "Sad business, Mrs. Farrow. Sad business. But it can hardly be helped. Two of your sons have been paroled on the condition that they not return to their units. On the threat of death, you understand, and yet... and *yet.* Even your third son deserves the gallows for aiding their crime." He drummed his fingers on the table in an unsteady beat. "You see my difficulty."

"I can't deny the position you're in and, as their mother, I promise I'll talk with them about making promises they don't intend to keep. But tell me, wouldn't you wish your own men so brave?"

He blinked. "You're very bold, madam, to say such a thing."

"I honor you too much to speak lies."

"Then I'll do the same for you. Even if your sons aren't men of their word, *I* am. There are ropes at the gallows ready for their necks, and it would be in my power to hang them. One might say I was too generous to let one of them go the first time. All three of your sons are in rebellion against a good king. What we all want is this war at an end, but not at the cost of justice. Think of a world in which the throwing off of order is rewarded."

I leaned forward. "I'm just as interested in the cause of justice as you. That is why I've come with a trade. Six of yours for my three."

Cruger stared for a long moment. "I knew it would come to this —us at odds with one another. I regret, Mrs. Farrow, that we must be enemies now. What I could have done with your talents of persuasion." He took his napkin and wiped his mouth slowly again. "Where are my men?"

"They are under guard somewhere close."

He laughed incredulously. "I would think you a liar if I hadn't already seen what you are capable of." He signaled to his aide. "Let it be done."

My breath caught in my chest.

"Retrieve the Farrow boys and a wagon with horses. I do expect them returned, Mrs. Farrow. When convenient."

White light—the purest joy—filled my heart near to bursting. How did one act when one's children were restored from death to life again? "I thank you, sir."

He folded his napkin and placed it upon his plate. "How did you not drown the troublesome whelps before now? They are too obstinate for their own good."

"I'm afraid I can't punish them for something they inherited from me."

He gave me a tight smile. "Quite."

"Mother?"

I bolted from my chair, toppling it to the ground.

Thomas and Samuel exited the fort, with Johnny propped in the middle.

I ran to them, laughing, my voice wet with tears, and gathered them to me. "This is a merry party, isn't it?"

As the boys exclaimed over my being there, Cruger stood and straightened his coat. "I'd suggest you keep them under lock and key, but I suspect it will do no good. Tell your sons I won't be so kind again."

I was tired. I was dirty. I had been tied to an unruly colt for two days straight. I could be forgiven, then, for saying exactly what I felt. "I have given you two for one, Colonel Cruger, but I consider it the best trade I ever made, for now on the Farrow boys will whip you four to one."

THIRTY-EIGHT

ROSANNA

Voices drifted to me as if through a veil. A pan clanged against the hearth. The light through my window was a subdued yellow. Was it morning or night?

In a rush, the events of the past few days came back to me. The cold dread that swept through my limbs when learning of my sons' capture. The relief when Captain Williams handed over the British soldiers. The sight of my sons, alive and well. Were they truly here, or did I imagine it?

I listened closer.

They were discussing next year's planting, of all things.

"I'll go check on Colonel Williams' horse," Thomas said.

I leaped out of bed and pushed open my door. I hadn't yet told them a British soldier hid in our barn.

The boys looked up from the table, their hair ruffled and sticking up. Johnny grinned at me, more full of life than the last time I saw him.

Tears rushed to my eyes. It was just like years before, when my scrawny boys gathered at the table like hungry chicks waiting for a mama bird to feed them.

Thomas pulled out a chair. "Sit, Mother."

The setting sun slanted over a table filled with a pitcher of wildflowers, a stack of corncakes, salted pork, a large slice of cheese, and a bowl of blackberries.

"You did all this?"

Samuel held up his fingers and wiggled them. They were stained a dark purple.

"We've been cooking our own corncakes for ages," Johnny said.

The image of the little boys vanished. In their place were rugged men with a week's growth of beard on their faces.

I squeezed Thomas' cheeks with one hand and scratched at his stubble. "Papa's razor is near the bucket," I whispered with a wink.

He covered my hand with his own. "Thank you, Captain," he said, his voice thick with emotion. "It's not every boy whose mother has saved his life."

"Hear, hear!" Johnny and Samuel held their cups aloft. "To the captain!"

Their eyes were filled with such shining admiration, I couldn't speak.

Oh, John. Look at what your dreams have come to. How had a marriage that had started without love created such an abundance as this?

I slipped into my seat. "Are the others still asleep?"

"They didn't wake even with all our commotion," Samuel said.

Poor dears. They'd taken turns guarding the house, and when I brought the boys home, they nearly collapsed with relief. We'd all been brave, every one of us.

"I'm curious—how did we end up with Williams' horse?" Thomas asked.

"He let me borrow her."

"But how did you get to *him*? He is hours away."

I popped a blackberry into my mouth and avoided their gazes. "I'd rather not say."

A tousle-headed William poked his head into the kitchen. "She took Skunk."

"Come here, you brat!" Samuel opened his arms, and William ran into them, laughing. Samuel squeezed him tight.

Mary and Jane entered next and flew to Johnny and Thomas, throwing their arms around their brothers' necks.

"We thought you were killed dead for certain!" Jane exclaimed.

The brothers burst out laughing.

Thomas gave Jane a kiss on the cheek. "You will have to put up with me for at least another forty years, I should think."

She took his cheeks and brought him close so they were nose to nose. "A hundred," she said in a deep, scolding voice.

"I'll see what I can do." He set her back from him and put her on his knee. "Dearest Mother, I see by the look on your face that you are dying to ask me a question."

"Will you return to the militia?" The rescue had probably emboldened them to think they were invincible. Now I would never be able to keep them from trouble.

Johnny answered for Thomas. "Thomas and Samuel will go back to their units in a few days. I think I'll stay on awhile and get my strength back. Now, about you riding Skunk—"

I swatted his knee. "How could I let you hang when I had a perfectly good horse to use for your rescue?"

"Good? You could've died."

"Better risk one dead than you three." My stomach growled. In a twinge of conscience, I remembered my hideaway soldier lying in the barn. I pushed away my trencher. "There's something I must tell you."

They stopped eating and looked at me.

"Callum—the man you know as Jack Drummond—is here. In the barn. He was wounded, and I'm caring for him." I summoned courage for the worst of it. "And he has sided with the British against you."

The cabin filled with weighted silence.

The boys sat back in their chairs and eyed one another.

Then Thomas leaned toward the younger children in a conspiratorial manner. "Mary, Jane, William—I have something in my saddlebags you'll like. But only if you are very brave."

They whooped and jumped from their seats.

"I wish Sarah were awake to see it!" Mary exclaimed as they ran out the door.

The boys laughed.

"What is it?" I looked between them. "What do you not want them to hear?"

An impish spark lit Thomas' eyes.

Johnny leaned close, sliding his crossed forearms forward. "Callum is a spy for the rebels, Mother."

I opened and closed my mouth again. "You're not serious." But as soon as they'd said it, I knew it was true.

The signs had all been there.

Phil hadn't seemed bothered by Callum's betrayal because he had known it was nothing of the sort. Callum had been brought to me, not as a traitor, but wounded in our cause.

Why hadn't Callum said anything when I'd chastised him?

All the awful words I said to him mocked me for my folly.

Oh, Mama.

Your daughter is still a flick weed, even after all our efforts.

"Philemon made us swear to keep it from you. He didn't want you to be dragged into this if Cruger should find out. He only told us so we could help Callum if he came to us."

I bit back an angry retort. Still, after all this time, Philemon thought he knew better than me. I would have to tell him exactly what I thought of that.

My younger three returned to the cabin in high spirits. Sure enough, Mary held a paper-flat frog in the palm of her hand. The others fought over who would get to hold it next.

I surged to my feet. "I have something I need to do."

"*Again?*" William whined. "I want to go."

"Another adventure, Mother?" Sarah said, awake now and at the doorway.

This was no adventure. It was a harrowing mission to put to rights what I'd risked by not trusting my dearest friend.

I picked up my skirts and ran to the barn, swinging open the door. Doves in the rafters flapped their wings and sent whirls of dust floating in the waning light.

"Callum?"

The silence stretched thin.

There was nothing but a mouse's patter down a wooden beam. A beast grinding its teeth. The soft fall of dried grass from the feed-trough to the floor.

"If you are alive, speak!"

With trepidation, I approached the stall and peeked over its side.

Callum lay on his back, one hand tucked behind his head and one folded on his stomach. His skin was luminous in the golden dusk. His face, so much like home it made my heart ache.

Handsome as ever. More than ever. A man carved by a lifetime of experience.

No one would know by looking at the strength of his body how much gentleness and kindness he carried in his heart.

I knew, because he had given it to me, over and over, until I felt my worth.

All he'd asked was for me to trust him. It was so little a thing when he had given me so much.

I pulled open the gate and knelt beside him.

"Please wake." I leaned over him, my hair spilling onto his bare chest. I placed my hand on his shoulder then pulled away from his heat. It was too intimate a touch for a friend.

Callum's eyes drifted open.

He studied me for so long without a word, the quiet became a beating drum.

"Magpie."

Tears pricked my eyes. He hadn't forgotten.

He touched my curls, reverently. "Are ye selkie, or are ye sprite?"

I took his hand and cupped it to my face. "I am your magpie or nothing else." I swallowed all I felt and made myself speak. "Go back to Colonel Cruger. The longer you're away, the more danger there is of your loyalties being questioned."

Thomas' voice carried to us from the door. "What if he went instead to Captain Williams at Fair Forest?"

I sat up quickly, pulling away. Callum dropped his hand back to his stomach.

Thomas poked his head above the stall door. "Or we could continue to hide you here."

Callum sat up with a wince, guarding his wound with his forearm. "Your mother's right. Every day I stay is a risk to your family. I go back to Cruger. Today."

I ran to the house and retrieved a clean shirt and a haversack filled with food. When I returned, I found Cruger's wagon in the yard with Callum atop one of the horses, and my boys, getting him settled.

I came to Callum's side. "What will Cruger think when you ride in with horses he lent to me?"

"That you found me and tended to my wounds, nothing more. We've no other horses besides Captain Williams', and I can hardly arrive on the enemy's horse."

"But *I* am the enemy." I had left no doubt of that with my parting words to Cruger.

"*You* are a good woman, and if he doubts it, I will do my best to change his mind."

"It is not me I am worried about."

"There's greater risk if I don't return at all."

I climbed the stool at the horse's side. "Let me help you with your shirt."

He hissed through his teeth when I slid his arm nearest the injury through the sleeve.

"I wish this didn't hurt you."

He put his mouth close to my ear. "If this is what it takes to have you touch me, I'll gladly give my other shoulder to be shot."

Every inch of my body heated with the promise in his words. "You don't need to go so far as that."

His answering grin made my stomach flip.

"Come, Mother," Samuel called from the ground. "This is no time for courting."

I gasped. "Hold your tongue, Samuel Farrow, or I will hold it for you."

Callum's laughing eyes met mine. "You are just as I imagined you would be as a mother."

I jumped down and held the haversack toward him. He grabbed my hand along with the food, and leaning down, he whispered, "I'll be returning so you can finish making your apologies."

And with that, he straightened, slapped the reins with one hand, and guided the wagon to Star Fort.

THIRTY-NINE

ROSANNA

But he didn't return, not for months.

Winter came, quiet and dim.

The boys returned to their units. Landon came home for a visit, astonished by all that had taken place in his absence. But within a week, he was off again to fight.

Days flowed from one to the next with no word from Callum.

It wasn't that I expected it. He would have to be careful not to arouse suspicion, especially after returning to Star Fort in the wagon Cruger lent to me. He must have succeeded in proving his allegiance, for there'd been no reports of a traitor's hanging. Even so, I kept one ear tuned to the road, my eyes to the hills between our farm and Ninety Six.

On Christmas morning, I found Skunk tied to my railing and an orange on my doorstep. Tucked underneath was a slip of paper with these words: *Surely, ye know*.

My breath hitched.

The same words he'd spoken when we stood together in the sourwood trees near Mama's grave.

The memory of it burned, both fire and ice. I'd been impatient to belong to him. Too full of passion, embarrassing us both, and then he left.

I locked my feelings away. I married John. I gave myself over to my husband, my family, our farm. The days were so full, I had no time to think about what might've been.

But with Callum's note, it all came back like a sleeping seed awakened by spring.

That was the thing about hope. It was stubborn, like me.

I waited for another message, but none came.

The rhythms of farm life were a blessed distraction. Summer came, and our indigo bloomed. On a hot day in June, Mary, Jane, and William cut the stalks and tied them into bundles. Sarah and I then threw the piles into vats, boiling and beating the leaves.

I dragged another bundle in each hand toward the tubs. "Sarah, will you—" The words died on my tongue.

A rider in the distance, coming fast.

My heart stopped. It was all too reminiscent of when that Baker boy had raced up the road, bearing news of my sons' imprisonment.

I dropped the cuttings and clasped Sarah's hand in mine.

The horse slid to a stop. A young man jumped to the ground. William Baker. I gripped Sarah's hand harder. "I don't think I could take it if you were to tell me my boys have been taken again."

"I've come to say farewell, Mrs. Farrow."

"Farewell?" I hadn't expected that. "But why do you leave?"

"There's been a siege at the fort—a battle between your General Greene and Colonel Cruger."

Callum. My heart pounded against my ribs. "And?"

"Greene has retreated. Cruger has abandoned the fort and is burning the town, leaving it to the patriots. I didn't want to leave before thanking you for your kindness toward me."

Sarah let go of my hand and put her arm around my waist, holding me upright. "What of Mr. Drummond?"

I squeezed her side. Good girl.

"Jack? He must've gone forward to Lord Rawdon with the rest of the reinforcements, but I don't know if I should be saying so."

I sagged against Sarah. Callum hadn't died in the siege. As long as he lived, there was hope. "I wish you well, William. And thank you."

He nodded. "Goodbye, Mrs. Farrow." And with that, he turned his horse and traveled the road to the fort.

Sarah rubbed my back. "Breathe, Mother. He will come back to you."

That night, I went to the river and sat on its bank, stretching my toes into the coolness.

I dipped my hand in the current and trickled water on the back of my neck and down my spine.

I couldn't sleep after William's visit. All I could think of was the last time I had seen Callum.

If this is what it takes to have you touch me.

Thoughts of him besieged me even here, sitting on a bed of damp silt and knife-sharp rocks.

I had waited years. Decades. Why was every second without him an agony? All the love I'd locked away when he left me standing at Mama's grave begging to be freed.

I'd be consumed by it—me, a grown woman, sick with love.

Movement sounded in the grass behind me. An animal, stepping through the leaves.

My fingers inched toward my rifle. I turned my head a little. There was nothing except suffocating darkness and the glint of silver moonlight on the leaves.

Then a man in a faded blue coat stepped from the shadows. He led a knob-kneed horse with a black hide.

Obsidian.

I surged to my feet. "Callum!"

He came no nearer but studied me as if he saw my heart and knew it all. "I'll tell you a story, and you'll tell me if it's true."

I dared not speak or move, should he disappear like a dream at the breaking of dawn.

"A woman came to Cruger with six enemy soldiers to trade for her sons. With only a horse and her rifle, she led them through a dangerous wilderness for a full day and night without stopping for rest."

I could barely breathe. "You haven't got it right. There was also a guard."

"A woman and one guard," he amended. "Did you truly tell Cruger that your boys would whip his men four to one?"

"Did I?"

He took another step closer. "The men said it was a pretty good speech for so dainty a lady."

"Pretty good! I should like to see them do better."

He laughed.

"Why aren't you with them now?" I asked.

"Cruger let me go."

"But why?"

"I told him that I'd had enough of scouting and that it was time I returned to Tileman. Cruger must have suspected the truth. In the end, I think he didn't have the heart to disappoint his brother by revealing me as a traitor."

"You're free, then."

Callum tied Obsidian's reins to a low-hanging branch. "Aye. Though Frederick is dead, and I plan to fight for Gabriel to be named his heir."

"Dead!"

"In the battle at the fort."

"He has plagued us so long I assumed he always would."

"An empty life. Wasted, if not for Gabriel." He now stood so close it would be nothing to close the distance between us. "Now, I've come for my apology."

The reminder hit like the blow of an ax. I'd been faithless, a fool, a blackhearted villain, and to the most selfless of friends. "I've barely had a moment of peace since you left. I can't bear to think on how I treated you. I was cruel and—"

"Hush." He pulled me close and tucked my head under his chin. "I can't think with you so near."

"Why do you bring me nearer, then?"

"Because I love ye, Rosanna. I always have. Ever since you told me to give that puffguts Freddie a knocking."

I pulled back. "*That* is what made you love me?"

"A lass with that much mettle is an uncommon treasure."

Light flickered in the shadowed places of my heart. To be called a treasure, and a rare one at that! "But I am older."

"So am I."

"I'm not the girl I once was."

He touched my cheek tenderly. "The years have been kind to you." He ran his fingers down my neck. "Very, very kind."

I ached to lean into him, to take what he offered. But there'd been too many years between us, too many times I'd been found ill-fitting to risk it again. "I haven't learned to be less wild."

His lips curved. "I should hope not." His face turned serious. "Look at what you've done, Rosanna. Your children, the farm. Even after John died, you kept it going. You didn't give up. I'd have wagered all my fortune on you doing just that. You call it wildness. I call it heart." He lifted my hand, kissed my palm, and clasped it against my chest. "And what a beautiful heart it is."

His words seeped into every broken part of me like honey.

My spirit might be contrary to what a woman's should be, but perhaps it wasn't *wrong*. I, who felt too much and listened too little, was loved for the very thing I had tried all my life to change—me.

Mama's words returned through the ether: *There'll be good from this yet.*

And there had been good, though perhaps not in the way Mama had imagined.

The satisfaction in scratching life from the wreckage. Married affection, forged from nothing. Delighting in my children in defiance of life's perils. And a ride strapped to an unbroken horse, proving how far I'd go for the ones I love.

And now Callum, believing my worth since the beginning.

"All this time..." I couldn't keep the regret from my voice.

"The years have shaped me too," he said. "I've gone hungry and lain near frozen in the ice and cold. I've been imprisoned and rejected and just when I felt I belonged in a place, I was forced to leave it. I was alone for many years, marching miles upon miles in the mud and enduring battles from here to Canada. But my greatest suffering..." He threaded his fingers through the hair on the nape of my neck and brushed his thumb against my jaw. "My greatest suffering, love, was in leaving you."

Joy burst through my heart. After a speech like that, all there was left to do was to kiss him and kiss him well.

But this time, I would wait.

It was his turn to embarrass me with the strength of his affection.

He slipped a familiar golden band from the chain around his neck.

The ring from the day we met—the one I'd saved from Freddie.

He took my hand again.

"*Come live with me and be my love...*"

The lines Phil had recited at the river, the poem Callum had liked. Realization washed over me. The panic on his face then had been fear that I'd discover his feelings. Callum had meant that poetry for me from the beginning.

He placed the ring upon my finger and kissed my fingertips.

"*... and we will all the pleasures prove...*"

My skin turned to gooseflesh at his emphasis of *pleasures*.

"*... that valleys, groves, hills, and fields, woods, or steepy mountain yields.*"

He tipped my chin and looked directly in my eyes.

"*And we will sit upon the rocks, seeing the shepherds feed their flocks, by shallow rivers to whose falls melodious birds sing madrigals.*"

Anticipation turned to impatience. Why did he not kiss me? "And then what will we do?"

"*I will make thee beds of roses and a thousand fragrant—*" He crushed his mouth to mine as if he couldn't bear another moment without me. Then his kiss turned achingly tender, as if I were the most precious thing in the world to him. As if he had held me close through all the time and distance and we stood at the other end of it.

Free.

And in our place of belonging.

A LETTER FROM THE AUTHOR

Thank you for reading *Every Bend in the River*. If you would like to join other readers in keeping in touch, sign up for my newsletter here:

www.stormpublishing.co/emerson-ford

If you enjoyed it and could spare a few moments to leave a review, that would be hugely appreciated. Even a short review can make all the difference in encouraging a reader to discover my books for the first time.

I first heard of Rosanna, my sixth great-grandmother, when I was a young girl and was inspired by her bravery. I'd been born with a fire to do *great things*, and I wondered how much of that had trickled down the family line from her to me?

But I see her story a little differently, now that I'm older and a tad wiser.

Rosanna's greatness wasn't in her ride—it was in her *why*.

When revisiting this story as an adult, her perilous ride by herself on an unbroken colt to save her sons resonated with me deeply. How far would a parent be willing to go to save their child? That far, surely, though few of us see our love come to bear so powerfully. It requires great courage to parent—to open your heart to something that has the power to take you to your knees with the unknown. The consequences of not parenting well are heavy and deep. We feel this keenly—we know our weaknesses, that we're human and won't always get it right. But we love anyway, like

Rosanna did. We risk ourselves to it because the joy of loving is the richest and best part of life.

Her courage didn't stop there.

What kind of strength did it take to leave her family and move to the frontier? To stay after her husband died and her sons joined the militia? To keep her farm going with her four remaining children? There wasn't space in the story for detailing the war between the Regulators and the Moderators, but between that, the outlaws, and America's War of Independence, Rosanna kept her farm and family together through it all. The backcountry of South Carolina was no place for a civilized woman, and perhaps that's why she survived—too stubborn to quit and too determined to fail.

History grows murkier the further you descend in time. Fiction based on history must walk a fine line between truth and imagination, putting flesh and bone to what are only whispers. Writing about someone who was born almost three hundred years ago can be daunting as what documentation does exist can't always be trusted.

To tell Rosanna's story, some holes had to be filled. Callum is solely of my imagination, though informed by several true accounts (one being that of a Scottish indentured servant who was given an inheritance from his master, along with the man's best horse). It would've been highly unusual for a widow with the burden of a working farm to remain unmarried for the rest of her life. Perhaps that was the case for Rosanna, but it can't be known for certain. I did find a tantalizing hint that she might have remarried, and I chose to chase that shadow. Callum flowed easily from my "pen," inspired by the men in my life who are just like him, strong yet gentle, a husband, a father, sons who would go to the ends of the earth for the ones they love.

Bembe and Mr. Smythe are also fictional. I wanted to gift Callum with two men of character who would shape him into the man he becomes. It could've turned out very differently for Callum had Bembe not taken Callum under his wing then convince Mr. Smythe to keep him. Frederick is technically fictitious but based on the very real "Bloody Bill" Cunningham, a Regulator who terrorized the backcountry. If the timelines had matched up a little better, Frederick would have been a Cunningham. Apologies to any Grenvilles for the use of your name for such a dastardly character.

Of small note, there are a few names I changed for the sake of clarity. I can't tell you how many more Johns, Thomases, and Sarahs you would've had to wade through if I hadn't. In addition, a few dates were tweaked, but only when necessary for the story, namely Rosanna and Philemon's date of birth, which was moved forward two years. I also wanted readers to have an understanding of the horrific conditions of prison ships, but because of the tight structure of the story, that experience had to be given to Johnny when in reality that fate belonged to Landon.

We have quite a bit more recorded about Rosanna's brother. The account of Philemon as the sentinel at Fort Necessity comes from George Washington himself, as recounted in his diary. He records that Philemon shot three men in one blow; another account records that with "three hails in one, [he] fired and killed two Indians and three Frenchmen." I could hardly expect my readers to believe Philemon killed five men with firing his weapon only once, so I thought it better to stick to Washington's account.

I recognize that I've presented a more human side of the much-revered president. There are different accounts of the skirmish at Jumonville Glen, each blaming the other for what happened. I do believe Tanacharison wanted to assert himself as someone to be reckoned with and that Washington didn't fully understand what he had set in motion by joining him. No one can know for sure who fired first on that fateful day, but one thing is clear: The battles at Jumonville and Fort Necessity shaped Washington as a commander for the better.

Some might pin the entire war's beginning on Jumonville. Others would say it was the shot fired by Philemon (killing the hogskin-wearing spies) that sparked a world war fought across continents—the French and Indian War in the New World and the

Seven Years' War in Europe, South Asia, and Africa. Though the inevitable march to war started long before Philemon got involved, it isn't hard for me to imagine his fiery spirit being the circumstantial spark that blew the powder keg.

The story of Colonel Villiers asking for the sentinel at the surrender and Washington lying and saying the man had already been killed is true, according to at least one account. So is Philemon's response that he would've shot Washington had he given Philemon up to the French.

Two years into his presidency, Washington toured the South and met with Philemon. Their last day together was spent engaged in a shooting contest, as detailed in the following: "It was a meeting of brother soldiers who together had faced many dangers and shared many difficulties. Both had been great shots with a rifle, and on a challenge from the general, their last meeting on earth was signalized by a trial of their skill off-hands at a target one hundred yards distant, with the same unerring weapon. Who was conqueror in the trial of skill is not remembered." The winner might be lost to time, but if Philemon had won, I like to think he wisely chose not to crow about besting the sitting president, a man he had almost killed years before. After all, our nation was still deciding its laws, and treason could be made retroactive.

As to the heroine of this story and why I felt compelled to write about her, she gave me a gift. The *great things* I wanted to do? She showed me it doesn't always look like what you think it will. It's facing head-on what tests your endurance and mettle. It's going even beyond that when you think the last of your strength is gone. Like she did.

Until next time,

Emerson

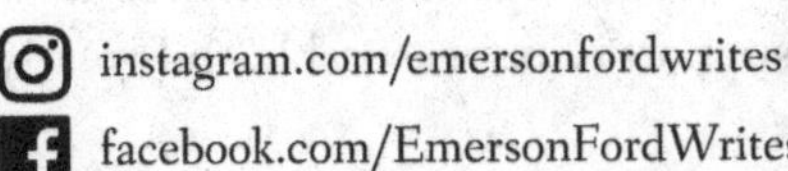

ACKNOWLEDGMENTS

Thank you to:

Keith, who brings me breakfast in my office and encourages me to stay on this path.

Wyatt, Hudson, Emmalyn, Arianna, and my beautiful new daughter-in-law, Jill. I hope you read this and feel a little of just how much I love you.

My dad, who was by my side through it all. Discovering the story with you is my favorite part of writing. Here's to our next research trip!

My mom, who brings my books to her friends and cheers me on along the way.

The team at Storm Publishing, with Oliver Rhodes doing incredible work at the helm. I continue to sing Storm's praises to readers and authors alike.

Claire Bord, my editor. Your kindness and support are unparalleled. My stories are always stronger because of you.

April Barcalow. A wise advisor, a well of encouragement, and a friend for life.

My writing group—Bekah, Gina, Emily, Katie, and Stevie. I read things I've written and see you reflected in them. Rosannas, all, in your fierce love for friends and family.

John and Connie Kallerson, who bolstered and loved me long before my first book was a twinkle in my eye. Everyone needs a John and Connie in their lives.

My readers, who champion my stories to family, friends, and followers. Your support is immeasurable and greatly humbling.

Challenges arose during the writing of this book that make me especially thankful to God, who saw me through to the end of it.

www.ingramcontent.com/pod-product-compliance
Lightning Source LLC
Chambersburg PA
CBHW010429170726
48283CB00011B/3124